STRAW MEN

continued . . .

SHADOW IMAGE

"Martin J. Smith writes a damn good whodunit."

—Michael Connelly,
New York Times bestselling author of
Angels Flight and *Void Moon*

"Powerful figures tread a dangerous path through demen-
tia, pity, and murder in Martin J. Smith's compelling new
novel . . . No reader will walk away untouched."

—Taylor Smith,
author of *Random Acts*

"Martin J. Smith is a master of suspense . . . *Shadow Image*
is a great mixing of elements from the legal thriller with
that from medical novels (a la Cook), a blend that makes
this work one of the best books of the year. The characters
are all top rate . . . However, it is the premise of the story
line—that our legal system is built around the faulty memories of the victims—that is brilliantly portrayed."

—Harriet Klausner

TIME RELEASE

"*Time Release* sizzles, cooks, and singes! It's a whipcord thriller full of deftly drawn characters, intrigue and taut action . . . This is a spellbindingly accomplished first novel. Martin J. Smith may well become a thriller force to be reckoned with."   —James Ellroy,
author of *American Tabloid* and *My Dark Places*

"A good creepy debut thriller."   —*Publishers Weekly*

"[Proves] that fear isn't a tamper-resistant emotion."
—*Los Angeles Times*

"Unexpected plot twists and breathless tension combine for a suspenseful ride that doesn't let up."
—*The Kansas City Star*

"*Time Release* is a fast, smart read and one fine thriller."
—Robert Ferrigno,
author of *Heartbreaker*

"*Time Release* delivers a powerful dose of suspense as memory expert Jim Christensen confronts the guarded secrets of the mind and darkest corners of the soul . . ."
—Pulitzer Prize winner Mary Pat Flaherty,
The Washington Post

Straw Men

MARTIN J. SMITH

JOVE BOOKS, NEW YORK

This is a work of fiction. Names, characters, places, and incidents are either the product of the author's imagination or are used fictitiously, and any resemblance to actual persons, living or dead, business establishments, events, or locales is entirely coincidental.

STRAW MEN

A Jove Book / published by arrangement with
the author

PRINTING HISTORY
Jove edition / January 2001

All rights reserved.
Copyright © 2001 by Martin J. Smith.
Cover design by Robert Santora.
This book, or parts thereof, may not be reproduced in any form
without permission.
For information address: The Berkley Publishing Group,
a division of Penguin Putnam Inc.,
375 Hudson Street, New York, New York 10014.

The Penguin Putnam Inc. World Wide Web site address is
http://www.penguinputnam.com

ISBN: 0-515-12950-X

A JOVE BOOK®
Jove Books are published by The Berkley Publishing Group,
a division of Penguin Putnam Inc.,
375 Hudson Street, New York, New York 10014.
JOVE and the "J" design
are trademarks belonging to Penguin Putnam Inc.

PRINTED IN THE UNITED STATES OF AMERICA

10 9 8 7 6 5 4 3 2 1

For Lanie, the exuberant one

Acknowledgments

Straw Men is a complicated story conceived and written by an uncomplicated mind. Because of that, I relied on various people who were unfailingly generous with their time, insights, and expertise.

Former Los Angeles Police Lt. William T. Dumbauld of Los Alamitos, California, put me in touch with Capt. Bradley Merritt, chief investigator of the Internal Affairs Group of the LAPD. Both Dumbauld and Merritt helped me understand the role that internal affairs investigators play in a large metropolitan police department.

Criminal-defense attorney James Brott of Bailey & Brott of Orange, California, patiently explained the legal circumstances that in this book lead to the early release of the Scarecrow, Carmen DellaVecchio. Brott also helped me understand the possibilities and limits of court-ordered electronic monitoring. I bent reality a little to fit the needs of my fiction, but I hope Brott, as a fellow writer, will forgive me that indulgence.

I also want to acknowledge Dr. Elizabeth Loftus, whose research has for years raised fundamental and persistent questions about the reliability of eyewitness testimony. Her conclusions and opinions make many people involved in the criminal-justice system uncomfortable. And they should.

Susan Ginsburg, my literary agent, helped shape *Straw Men* from the beginning, and her insights helped this book and its predecessors reach their potential. She is a writer's dream. Hillary Cige, my first editor at Berkley, believed in me when Jim Christensen was still just an idea on paper. I'll always be grateful to her for that, as well as her contributions during the early stages of this book. The late-stage suggestions of Berkley Senior Editor Christine Zika greatly improved the final product. As usual, copy-editor Amy J. Schneider did an extraordinary job.

The members of my two writing groups have acted as midwives to all of my books, and their ideas and sugges-tions always improve my best efforts. Carroll Lachnit, in particular, offered helpful insights into the character of Teresa Harnett. While I was writing this book, Philip Reed, my "Dads Tour" road buddy, became a friend and much-needed sounding board. He once thanked me "for making this solitary pursuit a lot less lonely," and I wish I could be as eloquent in thanking him.

The success of my previous two books, *Time Release* and *Shadow Image*, was due in large part to enthusiastic booksellers who recommended them to their customers. I hope *Straw Men* reaffirms their faith in my stories.

Ultimately, there'd be no joy in any of this without the love of my wife, Judy; our son, Parker; and our daughter, Lanie, to whom this book is dedicated.

—*Martin J. Smith*
Palos Verdes Estates, California

Prologue

Teresa heard the voice again, deep and familiar, a menacing whisper jolting her from a restless sleep. *You never rose...*

The words shot through her, surfacing from somewhere dark and deep. She was shaking, her knees pulled up against the T-shirt clinging to her chest and back. *You never rose.* Whose voice? Not his. Goddamn. Not his. The thought triggered a sudden sob, and she covered her mouth with her hand so she wouldn't wake David again.

His face was turned away. She listened for his breathing, held her own breath as she did.

"You're dreamin' again, Terese," David said.

She found her voice. "I know. I'm sorry."

"Need a pill?"

"No. I'm OK."

"You sure? I'll get you a pill."

"I don't want a pill."

She threw back the damp sheets and dangled her legs off the bed, listening to her blood pulse. She closed her eyes, but the face, that unforgettable face, was still there. Always there. But something was different. The mouth still moved behind the ski mask, but the voice was different, deeper. Whose?

In the dark bathroom, she lifted handfuls of hot water to her reconstructed face. It soaked the dark hair that hid the surgical scars along her scalp, pasting a few strands to a forehead cross-hatched by the fading lines of long-ago incisions. Her face steamed from the water, but she still couldn't stop shivering. She pulled her terry robe off the back of the bathroom door and put it on, drawing the belt tight around her narrow waist. When that didn't stop the chill, she wrapped herself in bath towels, one around her shoulders and one around her legs. One of the towels swept across the countertop as she lurched toward the light switch, knocking a plastic jar of aloe gel into the sink. It bounced and clattered and finally rolled to a stop against the drain as she shut the door. She closed her eyes against the harsh light and groped back to the toilet, where she sat quaking, trying to make sense of the voice. Not his. But whose?

"You OK?" David called.

"Fine," she said. "I'll be fine."

When she opened her eyes the walls began to expand and contract, as if the bathroom itself were breathing. Its corners disappeared. Shapes shifted. Colors transformed. Everything started to move. She gagged once, then leaned over and vomited into the bathtub. She retched as the smell rose, then vomited again as she reached for the tap. A rush of cold water washed the worst of it away.

He knocked lightly. "Terese?"

She couldn't answer, just heaved again.

"Need some help?"

She clutched the sides of the tub, wiping her mouth on the towel around her shoulders. The worst was over, so she turned off the water. "No. Just . . . I'll be OK. Don't come in."

"You sick? Or dreamin' again?"

"Must be sick," she lied.

"Want me to get you something?"

Privacy, she thought. "Just go back to bed, OK? I can handle it."

"You let me know if you need anything. Pepto?"

She retched again, but nothing came up.

"Some toast?" he asked.

She turned on the water again, letting it drown out David's good intentions. It spilled into the tub, then began its search for a way out. She knew the feeling. So easy for water in a tub. Only one place to go. But what about her? What to do with these doubts after eight dead-certain years?

She turned off the tap, gathered the towel regally around her shoulders, and stood swaying before the mirror, a prom queen from hell. The face was familiar, but a storm raged behind her eyes. She felt the ground beneath her shifting, eroding everything she knew, everything she swore had happened that night. These memories didn't fit a version of reality that now seemed as carefully rebuilt as the face in the mirror. Something unthinkable was pulling her down, and she was whirling closer and closer to some dark truth. For her, there was no easy way out.

1

"Freakshow start yet?"

Christensen refused to look up, just stared harder at the borrowed black-and-white TV on the corner of his desk. He knew who was standing in his office door. No one else in the University of Pittsburgh's Department of Psychiatry and Human Behavior spoke with the rolling cadence of a West Virginia native. No one else had Burke Padgett's flair for the ill-timed interruption.

"Not now, Burke, please. They just went live—"

"Crazy, ain't it? All three local channels down there covering this thang. Bumped the soaps, even. Mercy, man, you'd think they were unleashing Lucifer himself."

Christensen finally turned. "No argument from you, right?"

Padgett shrugged. "I understand fear."

Christensen pointed at the grainy screen, where a news anchor was about to toss to a field reporter at the Allegheny County Courthouse. Behind the anchor, a stylized graphic of Blind Justice.

"Then surely you understand fearmongering," Christensen said.

Padgett smiled and stepped fully into Christensen's office. He was dressed, as always, in a three-piece suit fitted to his sprightly frame, a dapper elf. Perfectly proportioned but startlingly short, he was nonetheless an imposing figure in the country's elite circle of forensic psychiatrists. Padgett still hung around the department offices—some long-tenured professors still pretend they enjoy teaching—but he'd long ago grown bored with the more mundane aspects of scholarship. He now spent most of his time preparing psychological profiles of the nation's most complicated killers for prosecutors who adored his folksiness on the witness stand, if not his astounding fee as an expert witness.

Padgett's full beard and thick hair were as white as his skin was pink, and his penetrating green eyes made his face seem almost ethereal. It was a face once featured on the cover of *The New York Times Magazine*, where it appeared beside the bloodred cover line "Killers on the Couch." Christensen was sure the profile pleased the little showman with its accounts of his dramatic psychological showdowns with various stars of death row. A book contract followed, and Padgett's heroic *Waltzing with Demons* spent several weeks on national bestseller lists.

"Still don't believe in the bogeyman, eh?" Padgett stepped forward, set his leather briefcase on Christensen's desk, and stood up straight. He looked like a man about to make a speech. "Well I do. He's real. I've met him. He's Dahmer and Bundy and Berkowitz. He's Speck and Ramirez and John Wayne Gacy. We maybe can figure the bogeyman out, but that doesn't make him any less dangerous."

Straight from the book's cover copy, Christensen thought. He sighed as Padgett perched on the armrest of the wooden chair facing the desk.

"But you're not here to talk about Dahmer and the rest, are you, Burke?"

Padgett gestured toward the screen, which was filled now with the bulging face of Channel 2's Myron Levin, the dean of Pittsburgh's courthouse reporters. Levin's toupee looked like a shag toilet-seat cover.

Today, of all days, Levin and the other reporters in Pittsburgh's Allegheny County Courthouse should have been hanging their heads. For eight years they'd played the mob role in a media-age lynching, unable to contain their contempt for the freak in question, Carmen DellaVecchio—the Scarecrow, to use the media's cruel nickname. Now, thanks to Brenna, a judge had turned eight years of assumptions about DellaVecchio's guilt inside out, tossing out key evidence that linked him to the city's most notorious case of sexual savagery and attempted murder. But Christensen saw no trace of remorse in Levin's face, only the fleeting thrill of breaking news. The word *Live* blinked on and off in the corner of the screen.

Christensen reached for the volume knob and cranked it high enough to discourage conversation.

"—looks like the Scarecrow is headed home, at least for now," the reporter said. "What I'm seeing around the courthouse here, as far as reaction to the judge's ruling, is a sort of stunned disbelief. I think a lot of court watchers thought the new DNA evidence was strong enough to get Mr. DellaVecchio a new trial, but no one—least of all the district attorney—could have predicted the judge would release him after nearly eight years behind bars. In all my years covering the courthouse beat, I've never seen J. D. Dagnolo so angry."

Levin set his mouth in a grim, aggressive nonsmile, then lifted a small notebook and riffled the pages.

"District Attorney Dagnolo argued his point rather emphatically, I thought, during this morning's hearing, but Judge Reinhardt disagreed. What the judge said was, 'In light of this compelling new DNA evidence, this court is inclined to grant the defense request for supervised release of Mr. DellaVecchio until the district attorney can prepare an appropriate answer.' Which means, basically, that the Scarecrow will be free until a hearing three weeks from today."

" 'Supervised release,' " the off-camera news anchor asked. "What exactly does that mean, Myron?"

"Short term, Marci, DellaVecchio will wear an electronic monitor around his ankle to enforce an overnight curfew, but he'll most definitely be out of prison. And if this new evidence holds up, the conviction will be set aside. At that point it'll be up to the D.A. to decide whether to try him all over again. We expect a statement from DellaVecchio's defense attorney, Brenna Kennedy, anytime now."

Padgett grinned. "Your lady friend bring an umbrella?"

Christensen stared.

"Helluva shitstorm she's about to walk into. She ready for that?"

Christensen turned back to the screen. "You obviously don't know Brenna."

On the screen, Levin pressed his earphone deeper into the side of his head.

"What about Teresa Harnett?" Marci asked. "Any reaction from the victim in this case?"

Levin cocked a brushy eyebrow. "She wasn't in court today, but her husband, David, was. I'll try to get a word with him shortly. But I think we can all imagine how the Harnetts are reacting to the Scarecrow's unexpected release."

Cut to Marci's frowny face. "We'll keep them in our thoughts," she said.

Christensen blew a disgusted breath. "For God's sake, can you believe this?"

"Face it, Jim. Your guy scares the hell outta people."

Cut to Levin. The camera jostled, then pulled back to a wider shot. Behind the reporter, the doors of Allegheny County Courtroom 29 swung open. A small herd of large men slipped past the media pack before it could react. The tallest of them, District Attorney J. D. Dagnolo, tossed a brusque "No comment" over his shoulder as his group moved down the hall. The pack wouldn't be fooled twice. The moment Brenna and her client stepped through the door, they found themselves at the center of a harsh, klieg-lit pool—a replay of a scene Christensen had watched once before.

The first time he ever saw Brenna was on TV, the day

of DellaVecchio's preliminary hearing eight years before. The cops and the D.A. were blitzing the media, proclaiming the case solved, sharing credit, trying their damnedest to ease public outrage about the Harnett attack. Even before the prelim, DellaVecchio's court-appointed public defender was practically waving a white flag. Then Brenna had stepped into the breach. She agreed to take up DellaVecchio's defense *pro bono*, and Christensen had listened with profound respect that day as she explained her reasons to the reporters swarming around her new client.

Carmen DellaVecchio clearly was an individual of diminished capacity, she'd said, unable to control his impulses because of his damaged brain. The charges against him did not reflect his condition, leaving him open to the law's harshest penalties. "An attempted-murder charge is the only choice available under state law as written, and that's wrong," she'd said. "I think this case can change that."

The case had changed so much more. The closer Brenna looked, the more holes she'd found in the prosecution's case. During discovery, the question of diminished capacity blurred into a question of innocence. Even after a jury convicted DellaVecchio in record time, Brenna never let up. It took her eight years, but science had finally affirmed her early faith in the damaged young man beside her.

Christensen leaned forward. Would she now blast the reporters for twisting her own "straw man" theory that someone had framed DellaVecchio into the impossibly cruel nickname "Scarecrow," and for the gleeful way they chronicled the most humiliating courtroom defeat of her career? He hoped not, but then he noticed something only a lover might: Brenna was trying hard not to smile.

Beside her, DellaVecchio was grinning like a cadaver, showing rows of teeth ruined by chain-smoking and twenty-eight years of neglect. His wild, hollow eyes moved constantly beneath a brow that jutted like a mantelpiece. His ears looked like tiny fists. Somehow, they fit someone whose head was so misshapen. His cheeks seemed shrink-wrapped to cheekbones as sharp and angular as an unfinished marble carving—the unmistakable face of fetal alcohol syndrome. The sports coat and tie Brenna had bought for him earlier that week had an unintentionally comic effect, as if one of Satan's shock troops had dressed for church.

"She wanted this one bad, huh?" Padgett said, poking at the screen. "Needed a win after all these years in the Scarecrow's corner."

"Use his name," Christensen snapped.

Padgett blinked. "DellaVecchio."

"Don't be like the rest." Christensen stood up. "Burke, maybe you should leave. We've been colleagues a long time. We respect one another's work. But I don't see any benefit to having this conversation. I may say something I'll regret."

Padgett rose to his full 5-foot-1 and clasped his hands behind his back. His suit jacket bowed open, revealing a delicate gold watch fob trailing into a vest pocket. He didn't so much look like Freud as someone trying hard to look like Freud. The man wasn't handling celebrity well.

"DellaVecchio's like a downed power line, Jim," Padgett said. "Doesn't think about consequences. Doesn't make moral choices. He's a constant threat."

"Yes, Burke, he is. But that's not the point here, is it? This isn't some legal technicality. Brenna didn't help him wriggle off the hook. If DellaVecchio's conviction is overturned, blame it on one annoying little detail: he didn't do it. I can understand the media losing sight of that. It makes the story so much more complicated. But you should know better."

Padgett held up both hands, pink palms out. "Got no

quibble with the science, Jim. This new evidence, the DNA, it's troubling, isn't it? Your girlfriend found the flaw in Dagnolo's case and just nailed it. And the evidence you developed during the original trial, that business about how the victim's memories evolved, it's groundbreaking stuff. I believe that. I really do."

Christensen spread his arms wide. "The issues are so much bigger than this case, Burke. It's about how a shattered victim can go into a mug-shot session with investigators and come out with more and better memories than she went in with. It's about how a cop's phrasing can set a sketchy memory in stone. Look at all the research grants that rolled in after I started asking questions."

"Envy of the department," Padgett said.

"Because the more questions I ask, the more I find. About the malleability of post-traumatic memories. About factors that influence them most." Christensen nodded at the TV. "Ever wonder if cops sometimes shape a victim's memories to fit existing evidence? To fit the description of a suspect? It happens, Burke. It happened here."

Both of Padgett's hands took flight, a man waving away gnats. "So, what? You're gonna throw out all the basic assumptions about the value of eyewitness testimony?"

"Damn right I am."

They both looked back at the screen, at a tight, devastating shot of DellaVecchio's face.

Padgett shook his head and hoisted his briefcase. "So now he's loose," he said, turning for the door. "Sure hope y'all know what you're doing."

2

The sharp report of Christensen's slamming door echoed along the Cathedral of Learning corridor. He imagined a chastened Padgett slinking off down the hall, but knew better. The man was a walking ego. Christensen twisted the TV's volume knob down to a more reasonable level as he crossed back to his desk. Brenna's voice blared from the tinny speaker.

"—until the hearing, he'll have to be in his father's house between 11 P.M. and 7 A.M. But the judge went that far because the new DNA evidence we presented today undercuts the prosecution's entire theory. In other words, if this whole thing happened the way the district attorney insists it did, then someone other than Mr. DellaVecchio stalked and attacked Teresa Harnett. Which is what we've said from the start."

"So this is a final ruling?" a Channel 11 reporter asked.

Brenna shook her head. "The district attorney has three weeks to make a case against the new DNA evidence, and I'm sure Mr. Dagnolo will do everything within his power to convince the judge that our evidence proves nothing. That's his job. But Judge Reinhardt released my client pending that hearing, and that speaks, I think, to the credibility of the new evidence. Frankly, this case has confounded me since the beginning, so I won't try to predict what'll happen three weeks from now. We're not looking beyond that."

Someone off-camera cleared his throat, and the scene widened to include Myron Levin's bloated face. The reporter smiled. He always did just before lobbing some journalistic grenade. Brenna actually liked the guy, even respected his skills. But her left eye stress-twitched as she offered a pleasant, "Another question?"

"Ms. Kennedy, considering the brutality of the crime for which your client remains convicted, do you think it wise for Judge Reinhardt to release him, even on a provisional basis, before making a final decision on the case?"

"I'm the one who *asked* the judge to release Mr. DellaVecchio, Myron. Are you asking me if I agree with his decision to do so?"

Levin shook his head, showing the folks at home he could laugh at himself. "Good point. I'll rephrase the question then." He paused until he was sure everyone was listening. "A jury convicted your client of one of the most savage attacks this city has seen in decades. He's accused of stalking a woman, a police officer no less, then bludgeoning her nearly to death with a wine bottle. He then, the jury agreed, stabbed her with that bottle's shattered remains and sexually assaulted her with the broken neck of that bottle as she lay bleeding and semiconscious. Then he left her to die."

Levin took a breath, and Brenna took advantage. "Or so the theory went until today."

"All things considered," Levin pressed on, "do you feel this ruling is fair to the public, including the jurors who saw the evidence eight years ago and found Mr. DellaVecchio guilty?"

The wait was forever, the camera unflinching. Christensen hoped Brenna was calming herself before opening her mouth. He'd taught her the technique himself. Finally, she said: "You mean the jurors who bought the prosecution's cockeyed version of the crime based on wishful thinking and the D.A.'s few shreds of circumstantial evidence? The jurors who never saw the DNA evidence we presented today that proves he didn't do it?"

Levin tightened his grip on his microphone. "Hyperbole notwithstanding, Ms. Kennedy, your client was—and is—convicted of this crime. Do you think it's fair that he's now going free before the court rules on *all* the evidence?"

"If the court can put him in prison for eight years based on partial evidence, why shouldn't it be allowed to free him on the same basis?"

Levin edged closer. "If your client wasn't at the scene of the Harnett attack, then how did his shoe end up tracking blood all over the crime scene? How do you explain the threatening letter to Teresa Harnett that was written on a typewriter found outside DellaVecchio's home in Lawrenceville?"

Brenna's delicate jaw tightened, but she managed a calm smile. "I won't retry this case in the courthouse hall, Myron. But for your information, we conceded long ago that Mr. DellaVecchio's shoe made those tracks. The tread wear pattern was an exact match and very distinctive due to my client's unusual gait. But we've argued since the beginning that Carmen wasn't wearing those shoes at the time, and that he did not write that letter."

"Then who did?"

Brenna took her time answering, letting the moment ripen. She reached into her briefcase and pulled out three 8½-by-11 photocopies of the foamboard displays she'd presented to the judge that morning. She held them up high so the reporters in the back could see. One was labeled 00-65921/A, DELLAVECCHIO; the others were 00-65921/B, SALIVA/ENVELOPE, and 00-65921/C, STAMP. The details were lost in the TV's electronic snow, but Christensen knew each display showed a spotty trail of DNA markers running vertically down the page. Anyone could see the difference between DellaVecchio's DNA pattern and the DNA sample lifted from the letter Harnett received just days before she was attacked.

"Remember," Brenna said, "the letter was the cornerstone of the prosecution's theory that my client stalked Officer Harnett, and that stalking theory is the foundation of the argument that he later attacked her. But if it's not Mr. DellaVecchio's DNA on the letter—and we know now that it's not—the whole case comes tumbling down. It's that simple."

Beside her, DellaVecchio thrust a defiant fist into the air. His voice, raspy and strained as always, rose above the din: "Fuck-an-A!"

Brenna, unflustered, whispered in one of Della-Vecchio's shrunken ears. He stepped back, still grinning, and she picked up where she left off.

"Who wrote that letter, then wiped that typewriter clean and dumped it near my client's home? Who licked that envelope, not knowing we someday could extract genetic material from saliva just like we can from blood and se-men? Who set Mr. DellaVecchio up from the very begin-ning? All good questions, and we might have had answers years ago if the original investigation hadn't been so nar-rowly focused."

"But you're forgetting Officer's Harnett's testimony," Levin said. "She identified—"

"Memories can be wrong, Myron. Memories can be manipulated. This . . ." Brenna held up the unmatched DNA strands again. "This can't. Carmen DellaVecchio has lost almost eight years from his life because someone set him up, and because the district attorney built a con-vincing case from unfair assumptions and flawed logic. Eight years of injustice is enough. It's long past time—"

Christensen flinched at the soft knock on his office door. He turned the volume all the way down and listened.

"Go away, Burke," he said.

The heat kicked on, its hum the only sound in the small office. Another knock, a little harder, insistent.

"No apologies necessary. Just come back some other time, OK?"

"Hello?"

Woman's voice. Christensen poked the power button

and the set blinked off. One of his grad students? He checked his planner. No appointments. He smoothed his hair and stood. "Be right there." He crossed the room and pulled the door open. "Sorry, I—"

The face registered immediately, still pretty but with hints of ruin that showed when she offered a hesitant smile. One of her eyes seemed lower than the other, just slightly, and the skin at her jaw line was tight as a drum head. A subtle ridge ran from beneath her hairline down to the bridge of her nose. He'd never noticed it before, but he'd never looked her straight into her face from this close up.

"I'm Teresa Harnett," she said, extending her hand.

Christensen leaned forward to take it, pure reflex. He felt a powerful pulse in her fingers. She looked him in the eye, actually stared long and hard enough to make him uncomfortable. He felt suddenly out of phase. He looked back at the silent TV, then at the woman before him.

"I don't understand," he said.

Teresa surveyed the hall with a tormented look, like someone being pursued. "I'd like to talk to you. Privately."

The best he could manage was, "Do you think that's appropriate?"

"No," she said.

"Neither do I."

She nodded. "So, can I come in?" Another glance down the hall. "Please?"

Christensen stood aside, knowing he was opening the door into an ethical minefield. He raised another weak objection, but Teresa sat down in the chair across from his desk with no apparent intention of leaving.

"Close the door," she said.

He stood dumbstruck. Finally: "Ms. Harnett, I—"

"Lock it if you can."

3

Christensen's utter confusion felt like vertigo. The woman sitting across from him shouldn't be here. He felt that as deeply as he'd felt anything during his professional life. He couldn't imagine the tortured road that had led Teresa Harnett to the door of his obscure academic office at virtually the same moment the man she had accused was being processed out of prison. He took off his glasses and adjusted the wire frame, stalling, plucking nervously at the short hairs of his salt-and-pepper beard. What could he say?

"Does anyone know you're here?" he asked.

She shook her head.

Christensen hooked the fragile gold stems around his ears. Teresa's features sharpened again as his eyes adjusted, but they still seemed skewed in the same way the image in a jigsaw puzzle never looks quite right. He imagined her head the way it must have been after the attack, a shattered sack of crushed bone and damaged brain tissue. The top of a velvety pink scar peeked from the open collar of her yellow oxford shirt just above her right breast, the place where her attacker stabbed her with the broken neck of the wine bottle he then used to rape her. Christensen felt absolutely certain, at that moment, that whoever had attacked her wanted her dead.

But here she was, eight years later, walking, talking, a miracle of trauma medicine, neurosurgery, bone grafts, and intensive physical and mental rehabilitation. She was thin but not frail, obviously fit enough to have been one of the first women to crack the clubby, all-male ranks of the Pittsburgh Police Department. Her dignity and confidence apparently survived the brutality and degradation she'd endured.

"David's Downtown," she said.

The husband, also a cop. Christensen remembered him as a block of granite with a head, one of the men he'd seen with Dagnolo as they slipped past reporters just a few minutes ago. Teresa offered nothing else, just crossed one denim leg over the other with considerable effort.

"And you didn't tell him you were coming here?"

"Not to see you, no. Told him I had a rehab appointment. I'm putting you in an awkward position. I realize that."

Christensen nodded, glad for the acknowledgment. "You understand I have no official role in this case. I testified during the original trial as an expert witness on memory, but other than my relationship with Brenna I'm in no way—"

"There was a time I would have killed Brenna Kennedy if I ever got the chance. I want you to know that up front."

Christensen studied her eyes for the hatred behind those words, but saw none. Was she just trying to provoke him? He wished they were in his private counseling office five blocks away, rather than this cramped and comfortless working space.

"In a therapy situation, this is where I'd say, 'Now we're getting somewhere!' " he said. "But we're not, and I guess I'm trying to understand where that came from."

"You're a smart man, Dr. Christensen. I'm sure you'll figure it out eventually."

"Because she defended DellaVecchio?" he said.

Teresa leaned forward and looked him in the eye. "You'll never understand what it took for me to get up on that witness stand during the trial. Looking and talking like I did back then, like Frankenstein's bride with a mouthful of marbles. Having to face down that smirking little shit at the defense table, having to sit twenty feet away from the face in my nightmares for two full days, smelling his BO, reliving that night. Pray to God you'll never know what that was like."

"You're—"

"She tried her best to make me look like a liar," Teresa said. "Then she put you on the stand to make it worse. You with your little theory about 'evolving memories,' telling the jurors that what I'd said, what I'd turned myself inside out about for two fucking days, was basically a crock—"

"No, I never—"

"—that what I remembered was unreliable, 'polluted' was your word. That I wasn't really remembering what happened, just parroting back a convenient story concocted for me by investigators who just wanted a collar. I wanted you both to die when I heard that, Dr. Christensen, and I wanted to watch. DellaVecchio, Brenna Kennedy, and you. Those were the names on my list back then, in that order."

Christensen knew better than to react, so he waited. She'd delivered her rage in a reasoned narrative, passionate but without obvious emotion. Just as when she testified, her voice never once wavered. She might have been telling him about picking up her laundry, or locking her keys in the car. It was one of the most remarkable moments of self-control he'd ever seen.

"I just wanted you to know that," she said.

He nodded. "I understand."

She offered no apologies or absolution, but the room seemed to depressurize as she leaned back in her chair. "But that's not why I came."

"It gets worse?" he asked.

She didn't smile, but instead looked down and cleared her throat. "I came to tell you . . . you might have been right."

Christensen opened his mouth, but nothing came out. He looked away, then back into those penetrating eyes.

He'd imagined this moment, wondered if it might some-day come for her, but he never once imagined that he'd see it firsthand. But here she was, openly questioning a narrative that for eight years had grown from damaged and sketchy memories of a vicious assault into a vivid and horrifying tale of Carmen DellaVecchio's brutality.

She was no longer sure. That's what she was saying. But why was she saying it to him?

"It started after the DNA story broke a couple weeks ago," she said. "It rattled me, understand? Hell, I was a cop. We use DNA to convict people all the time. Brenna Kennedy's right. You can't ignore it. So that started work-ing on my head."

"In a psychological sense, you couldn't reconcile the conflict between what Brenna found and what you be-lieved," he said.

Her brow furrowed.

"You finally gave yourself permission to question," he said.

"Maybe."

There was something else. Christensen hoped his si-lence would bring it out.

"Then I got a phone call," she said.

"From?"

"Him."

Christensen sat up straight. "Who?"

Teresa turned her back. She stayed that way, looking toward his office window. Her shoulders suddenly heaved with a series of quick breaths and she started to tremble. "I don't know," she said. "I've heard DellaVecchio talk in court. He sounds like he swallowed gravel, and this guy who called sounded like that, too."

"But you're not sure?"

"This guy . . . It's what he said that made me—"

Remember, Christensen thought. "What did he say?"

She took a long time to answer. "You never rose," she said at last.

"You never rose?"

She winced. "It's what he said that night. In my ear, he whispered it after . . . everything. I was fading out, and he bent down and whispered it."

"So you think it *was* DellaVecchio on the phone? I'm confused."

"No. Maybe." She waved away his words. "Goddamn it. *Goddamn* it. It could have been him. It sounded like him. What I'm saying—oh Jesus Christ! It's *what* he said."

Christensen sat back. She needed no more prompting.

"He whispered it in my ear that night, but I didn't remember it until now, when the caller said that phrase on the phone. 'You never rose.' So I know this caller has to be the one who attacked me. Thing is, the voice I remember is different from the guy who called, the guy who sounds like DellaVecchio." She leaned forward. "The voice I heard that night . . . it was someone else."

There. The truth lay between them like a land mine. Teresa had pulled the cornerstone from the reality to which she'd sworn.

"You're remembering the real attacker's voice," he said. "And it's not DellaVecchio's voice."

She stood suddenly and walked to the office window, which overlooked the gothic roof of the Stephen Foster Memorial sixteen floors below. "I've had this nightmare. For years, since it happened. The attack. But before it was like a silent movie. Now, I can hear his voice. 'You never rose.' Like that. 'You never rose.' He thought I was dead and he kissed my cheek and whispered it in this voice, this—"

"A different voice."

"Somebody else's voice." Teresa turned to him suddenly. She yanked the sleeve of her jacket up to her el-

bow. The hair on her arms was standing on end. "*Look*
at this. Goddamn it. Something's wrong."

Three quick steps brought her back to the front of his
desk. She grasped its edges, held on like a woman afraid
of falling. Her desperate eyes brimming. "*Help me.*"

"Coke OK?"

Teresa nodded, took the cold can, and held it to her
forehead. She'd composed herself in the minute it took
Christensen to get her a drink from the machine one floor
below. But in the uncontrolled moment just before, with
her pleas coming in choked sobs, Christensen knew their
lives had suddenly knotted. No one in the city, maybe no
one in the country, understood the uncertain terrain of
human memory the way he did. He was uniquely qualified
to work with her, to guide her safely back, to explore her
contaminated memories for the truth of what happened
that night.

Still, he couldn't. "I can recommend someone," he said.

She shook her head. "I came to you for a reason. These
things I'm remembering, they feel real to me. And maybe
they are. But I don't need a shrink."

"Ms. Harnett—"

"Teresa."

"Teresa, what is it you want me to do?"

"I need somebody who can help me sift what's real
from what's not. Otherwise, it's all just smoke. And if
what I'm remembering *is* real, I need somebody who can
help me corroborate it. You know the details of this case
as well as anybody. You know the players. You have
access to everybody. We've got three weeks before this
hearing. Dagnolo's already told me he's putting me back
on the witness stand to tell my story again. I want to be
sure this time, one way or the other."

She offered a weak smile. "Kind of an impossible situation, isn't it?"

"Absolutely. Teresa, what you're talking about goes way beyond traditional therapy. I'm bound by laws and ethical standards. Whatever you told me would have to stay between us. I breach the doctor-patient relationship—"

"I won't sue you, damn it. This is my idea."

"But it's more than that, Teresa. The conflicts of interest here . . . I mean, where to start? I know how much nerve it took for you to come this far, to tell your doubts to me of all people. But if you're willing to go through with what you're talking about, you need to start with Dagnolo. Tell him. Then I could put you in touch with someone who—"

"You think Dagnolo wants to hear this? My testimony . . . that's all he has left now. Last thing he wants to hear is that I'm not sure."

She popped the top on her Coke and took a long drink, then stared into the middle distance between the desk and the window. "I know I'm letting people down. The D.A. The investigators. David. People who believed me from the beginning, who busted hump to find the guy I was sure did it. And I'm not saying DellaVecchio wasn't involved, understand? There's the other evidence. And I can still see him, smell him. But what I hear . . ."

"You're not sure anymore."

She nodded. "I either let everybody down, or I pretend nothing's changed. Rough choice, know what I mean?"

That she'd even acknowledged that choice was remarkable enough. Her willingness to confront it was astounding.

"I'm not doing this for DellaVecchio," she said. "Don't misunderstand that."

"Why then?"

Teresa took her time framing the answer. "People on the outside think cops are all the same. That all we're about is putting people away. A lot are like that. Face it,

DellaVecchio's a time bomb. Is it so bad he's been off the streets for eight years?"

No way he was answering that.

"We're not all the same, Dr. Christensen."

"Jim."

She nodded. "I was a cop for four years, Jim, but I'll be a human being a lot longer than that. I've got to live with myself, and the right thing to do is tell them I'm not sure. That's my piece to this puzzle. If that piece doesn't fit like it used to, I won't force it. I can't."

Christensen wanted to touch her, to somehow acknowledge her courage. Still, he struggled against his impulse to help, knowing the situation was impossible. "Teresa, what you're asking me to do, to take these emerging memories, if that's what they are, and try to fit them into existing evidence from the investigation, I'd need help from police, prosecutors, practically everyone involved. I'm not sure that's something—"

"Isn't there some sort of waiver I could sign?"

"Yes, but—"

"I'll sign it." She moved to the edge of her seat. "You can help me."

Christensen studied her face, struck by the intensity in her eyes. After a long moment, he sighed. "I can't."

Another tear crawled from the corner of her eye, and she made no attempt to stop it. It scored the heavy makeup she used to hide the surgical scars, turning milky by the time it reached her chin.

"You could, but you won't," she said. "It's a choice."

"I can't argue that, Teresa. It is a choice. A rough one. But I'm making it for the right reasons, just like you."

She finally wiped the tear from her chin.

Christensen turned to his address book, looking for Chaytor Perriman's phone number. "I'll give you the name of a guy. I've worked with him since—"

Teresa shoved herself away from his desk, chair legs

screeching. She scorched him with a sarcastic smile. "Don't off-load me to somebody who won't get his hands dirty. And don't you dare talk to me about what's right."

"I'm sorry, Teresa. Maybe if you talked to Dagnolo—"

"Who thinks regression therapy is horseshit, by the way," she said.

Christensen conceded the point with a nod. "There's a right way, and a wrong way."

Teresa turned toward the door, and Christensen noticed for the first time the awkwardness of her stride. In the mechanical operation of her feet, he could tell she struggled with motor control. When he looked up, she was facing him from the door frame.

"This conversation never happened," she said. "Not a goddamned word. To anybody. I want your promise."

He nodded.

She stared until her lower lip began to quiver, then slowly closed the door through which she'd come.

4

Chain link dipped near the porta-shitter, almost to the ground. Two quick steps and he was over. Good thing, too. Streetlight as bright as it was, couldn't be dicking around down here looking for a way onto the roof of some vacant Shadyside apartment. Get in, get an answer, get out. That's all he was here for.

He stepped on a Burger King cup, *goddamn!*, then crunched through ice in what looked like the track of a backhoe's tire. Ducked behind a construction Dumpster, waited till he was sure nobody'd heard. Took a long look up and down Howe Street. This cold, not an open window anywhere. Some band in one of the Walnut Street bars making more noise than him, so no worries. Around a pile of shattered plywood and Sheetrock, up six concrete steps, into the building. Piece of cake. Got to do something about that streetlight, though.

He'd seen her house before, earlier in the day, and noticed this building across the street, gutted for renovation. Three stories high, twenty yards away from what he figured was her bedroom window. Suddenly, he had a plan, at least the start of one. The devil's in the details, and tonight he was doing detail work. Distance. Sight line. Trajectory. Looked fine from street level, but he couldn't know for sure unless he made the climb.

Up the stairs. Scrap wood and nails all over, but he was careful. Nose burning—somebody'd been pissing here. Contractors probably, the lazy fucks; maybe just bums. Each step up, the song in his head a little louder. The Boss's voice, always, a cross between a Jersey punk and a heavy-equipment breakdown, Bruce from his dude period. *Got to learn to live with what you can't rise above . . .*

One more flight. Hand running along the rough wall, feeling the way, moving by touch, ears, instinct. Then stopped dead. He'd figured on a door, planned on it. Even a locked one. Go figure these contractors. Too lazy to piss where they're supposed to, but they lock the roof door of a gutted building? Life's just too weird.

He wedged his pry bar into the crack and gave it the old *snap-crackle-pop* for the easy walk-through.

Roof gravel now, crunching underfoot like crusted snow. But no worries. He dropped from his toes, walking regular toward the redbrick wall that rimmed the roof. Plenty high, maybe five feet. Nothing behind him but the tops of trees; no nosy neighbors would see. He checked up and down the row of perfect Victorians, so goddamned quaint. He was standing on the block's highest building, invisible to anybody below, to the right or left. Free to operate. Even better than he expected.

He moved across the roof toward the front of the building, the side nearest her house. Crouching low, just to be sure. At the wall, he checked his watch—10:24, later than he thought—then stood up halfway, peeked over. A low lamp on somewhere in the room, maybe even a candle the way the shadows danced on the walls. Let his eyes adjust and squinted through the wide-open miniblind.

Whoa.

She was kneeling on top, riding Christensen at a slow canter. Couldn't see his face, just his hands on her bare back, but who else would it be? They moved together, the carved oak headboard pulsing as they rocked, her head down except for one wild toss of red hair that got him hard. Guy's hands moving back and forth across her skin, easy, no hurry, tracing little circles at the base of her spine while she ran the show.

Mr. Sensitive.

She'd hate that. Women like her always do. Get all the civilized stuff they can stand during the day, with their power meetings and conferences and lunches. In bed they want it dangerous, from a guy who knows fuck from fruit cocktail. Want somebody medieval on their ass, real primitive, jungle stuff. She definitely had it in her. He could tell.

He unzipped, knowing he should go. Already answered the only question he had—couldn't be a better spot than this when the time came. But he wanted her to feel what he had in his hand. Do her right. She'd scream and squirm and shudder and beg for more and finally understand what it means to taste God's great glory. He spit into his palm and ran it along the soft underside, felt his cock jump in his hand. He squeezed it hard once, then fell into their rhythm. When that got old, he closed his eyes and pushed her down on it, felt her soft hair on his thighs. *If you want to ride on down in through this tunnel of love . . .*

When she started to gag, he grabbed her hair and held her down until he couldn't stand it anymore. He opened his eyes and she was still over there, bent to him and ready. He shoved it all the way across the street, through those miniblinds, put it right up there where she needed it most. And right then, swear to God, she bucked and grabbed that mannequin underneath her and kissed him deep. He swore he heard a scream.

And laughing. Somewhere down below.

The fuck *was* that? He checked his breath, tucked in, crouched, and leaned into the bricks, right next to where he was still dribbling down. He kicked some gravel over the tiny dark pool at the base of the wall, then looked over and listened.

Jesus H . . . Some drunk hanging from the chain link, jacket snagged at the back, just hanging there laughing maybe a foot off the ground, some other guy laughing too, trying to unhitch him. Dumb queer tried to climb over the high part, right around the corner from where the fence was down. Probably trying to get to the toilet. Probably both trying to get in there. Fags can't think when they're hard.

The one hoisted the other down and followed him over the fence, singing, *Let's go up to the roof*... Big hug. Other one answering, ... *where we can see heaven much better.* Laughing again like chicks.

Now what?

The pry bar inside his leather jacket tingled against his ribs. Maybe whack them both? Doable, long as the one he took last didn't have time to squeal. But he'd lose the perfect spot if he did. Be too hot to use when the time came.

He scanned the dark roof for the fire escape's metal railing, found it in the back corner just behind the air conditioner. Looked down again, saw the giggle boys disappear into the ruined front entrance three stories down. How long for them to climb six flights of stairs? Up on his toes, he stepped like a cat across the roof gravel and pulled himself up and over. Quiet as he could, he started down the metal grate. The alley below was deserted, so he stopped below roof level to zip up. Up top, the shattered roof door creaked open. Come looking for heaven, they did. Them boys'd never know how close they got to hell.

5

Allegheny County District Attorney J. D. Dagnolo glanced up at the two men who'd just stepped onto the thick Persian rug fringing his walnut desk. "Sit," he said.

He'd summoned them both; he trusted one. Capt. Brian Milsevic was a pro. Early fifties. Smart. Level-headed. The man to watch in a police department gaining national attention as a model of law-enforcement professionalism. Kiger had confided during a recent lunch that he was recommending Milsevic to succeed him when he retired as chief next year. Dagnolo liked that idea. Milsevic's department record was rock-solid, and Dagnolo especially liked the way he'd led the DellaVecchio case. A real pro.

David Harnett was another story. Good cop, no question, and one of Milsevic's best friends. But Dagnolo couldn't trust Harnett's judgment on anything having to do with DellaVecchio. He was just too close to it. Hotheaded. It was his wife who got savaged, for Chrissakes. But Dagnolo needed him here. Nobody was closer to Teresa Harnett, and right now Teresa was his trump card.

"First things first," the D.A. said. "Where's our boy now?"

"Lawrenceville," Milsevic said. "Least he was as of twenty minutes ago."

"Sleeping in?"

"Probably."

Milsevic smiled. His teeth were the color of refined sugar, no doubt bleached, and his hair was just messy enough to look styled. Except for his thick wad of chewing gum, he could have stepped out of a Calvin Klein ad. "Looks like the Scarecrow stayed out late his first night back home, J. D."

Dagnolo raised his eyebrows. "Late enough?"

Milsevic shook his head. "But late. Definitely pushed his curfew. Bracelet showed him back at his old man's house at 10:58."

"Figures. Partying?"

Milsevic shrugged.

"Let's get somebody on the house," Harnett said. "Nail the little retard some night at 11:01, then ask the judge to haul his puny ass back inside. Least keep him off the streets till the hearing."

Dagnolo turned back to Milsevic. "Can you spare someone, Brian?"

"If that's what you want."

"I want him back inside," Dagnolo said. "We know he'll fuck up sooner or later. Be a shame to miss it."

Milsevic made a note. "Will do. He litters, you get a report."

"Exactly."

They both smiled, but not Harnett. The guy was simmering rage coming to a boil, a scary thing in somebody that big.

Dagnolo smiled at him. "How's Teresa handling all this, David?"

Harnett shrugged. "Up all night. When she does sleep, she's having nightmares again, like she was right after the attack. She was pretty much over all that till Kennedy and company . . . Those fuckers. They should be there when she starts jumping at shadows, see what this is doing to her. Or take her down to rehab some day and see the hell she goes through just so she can live halfway normal. Get a little taste of reality for a change."

Dagnolo picked up his Waterman pen and jotted himself a note. The caregiver angle might play on the judge's sympathies, and he'd need whatever breaks he could get. But could he trust a hothead like David Harnett on the stand?

"Hold that thought," Dagnolo said. "What's important

now is how Teresa will do if we call her again. Testifying was brutal for her last time, I know. You think she's up to this?"

"She'll be fine," Harnett said.

No hesitation. Dagnolo felt better. "Then let's talk strategy, gentlemen," he said. "Do we go after the DNA results or not? We can raise the usual stink about lab reliability, chain of custody, all that. Even if the results are accurate, they only suggest that someone other than DellaVecchio licked the stamp and the envelope. It proves nothing at all about who attacked Teresa."

"Absolutely," Harnett said.

Milsevic was less sure. "Reinhardt made it pretty clear how he feels about the DNA results yesterday. I think we should concede it. They're vulnerable in other areas."

"The memory stuff," Harnett said. "That's way out there."

Dagnolo studied the pair over his steepled fingers. "Christensen's good. Credible. That's the problem. He's—"

"But it's bullshit," Harnett said. "That crap about us tweaking Teresa's memories so we could railroad the little creep . . . What planet are these people from?"

Milsevic put a hand on Harnett's beefy forearm. "Smoke screen, Dave, pure and simple. You know anybody in prison who thinks the cops did a fair and thorough job of investigating their case? DellaVecchio's no different, but that's not what this hearing's about. This is strictly a hard-evidence situation."

Dagnolo nodded. "The memory thing . . . maybe cast that as the sad fantasy of Brenna Kennedy's biggest fan?" He sat forward. "There's nothing there, right?"

"The investigation was clean," Milsevic said. "But if you have concerns, J. D., put 'em on the table now. Better here than in court. We don't want to get suckered into playing their game."

"No concerns, Brian. None at all." Dagnolo said.

Milsevic nodded his appreciation, then leaned forward. "The DNA is all Kennedy's got, remember. I think what you have to do is keep that in perspective. Make it seem irrelevant."

"Like she's trying to blame a Steelers' loss on warm Gatorade," Dagnolo said, and the two cops smiled. He savored his analogy before pressing on.

"Maybe you're right, Captain. She's arguing this whole thing comes down to the question of who sealed and posted that letter, that if DellaVecchio didn't lick it then he must be innocent. But they know goddamn well my prosecution wasn't based solely on that letter. We can't let the judge forget it was written on a typewriter to which her client had access, or about DellaVecchio's shoe print at the scene. And we're sure as hell not going to let Reinhardt forget about Teresa. We'll put her right in his face, front and center. Let her tell her story again, let her ID DellaVecchio just like last time."

Dagnolo glanced at his watch. Shit. The Democratic Committee luncheon. He stood suddenly, and Milsevic and Harnett did the same.

"I'm late," Dagnolo said. "We're agreed, though. We let the DNA thing pass. I think if we belabor it, it works against us. Makes it look like a bigger deal than it is."

"Focus on our strengths," Milsevic said.

Dagnolo slid one long arm into tailored Italian wool and tugged the suit jacket across his broad shoulders. "We've still got Teresa. She'll balance that scale real quick."

He turned to Harnett. "You watch her the next couple weeks. Keep me posted on how she's approaching all this. Any problems or concerns, I want to know. That clear?"

"Will do," Harnett said.

"Brian, you'll get somebody on the house in Lawrenceville?"

Milsevic nodded. "First screw-up, J. D., we bust his balls."

Dagnolo smoothed the handkerchief in his breast pocket and adjusted the matching silk knot at his throat as he moved past the two cops. "The bad guys won this battle, gentlemen. Let's make damned sure they don't win the war."

6

The gateway into Lawrenceville is a fork in the road. To the right, up the hill, Penn Avenue runs along the southern edge of sprawling Allegheny Cemetery toward East Liberty. To the left, Butler Street parallels the Allegheny River, past the cemetery's black-iron front gate, through a sturdy, redbrick hodgepodge of decrepit urbania—remnants of a time when Pittsburgh's immigrant workers created their own worlds apart.

Brenna steered into the neighborhood where Carmen DellaVecchio grew up and for the past twenty hours had lived relatively free. She entered his world beneath the watchful gaze of the weathered doughboy statue that had stood for generations at the point where Penn and Butler split. She sipped her Starbucks latte, but what she tasted at the back of her throat was infinitely less savory, the taste of fear.

Silly, she thought. Stopping by DellaVecchio's house was just a spur-of-the-moment detour from her regular morning commute, a chance to get some face time with her client the morning after his conditional release. But that was bullshit and she knew it. Something else was bugging her. The cops told her this morning that DellaVecchio had barely made curfew the night before. She'd called his house at about eight-ten as she drove into town, but there was no answer. By the time she had exited the Parkway onto Grant Street, two blocks from her Oxford Centre office, she was running through worst-case scenarios, one of which included a torch-toting mob of irate citizens. She kept driving, past the City-County Building and the courthouse, past the rusted Cor-Ten hulk of the old U.S. Steel Building, past the bus and train stations, and onto Penn Avenue. She tried calling again as she moved toward Lawrenceville, but again the phone rang and rang.

Brenna checked her watch—not quite eight-thirty. He could still be asleep, right? But what were the chances of that after eight years of 7 A.M. prison breakfast calls? Antonio DellaVecchio, Carmen's father, had probably left already for his job at a small scrap-metal reclamation yard along the river. By her reckoning, Carmen should have been home alone.

Where was he?

Brenna absently tilted too much hot coffee into her mouth, snapping her attention back to the moment. Scenes from another time slipped past the Legend's windows. Almost every shop sign needed paint. Migliorino's Barber Shop. Gruppo's Family Restaurant. Lipinski's Roll-O-Mat—a 22-lane "Automatic!" bowling alley—occupied the second floor of a building that someone had apparently tried to pretty up with leftovers from an aluminum-siding sample case. As weird as the building looked outside, Brenna figured it was even weirder inside. Fusaro's Funeral Home was on the ground floor.

At a stoplight, she slid a file folder from her briefcase and checked the 44th Street address again. She'd visited only once, and that was eight years ago. She'd been looking for character witnesses for Carmen who might do more good than harm if she put them on the stand. In the end, Antonio DellaVecchio was the only person she dared call on Carmen's behalf, and that was just so his father could describe the mental and physical scars left by the young man's mother, Rose. She'd died in a Dumpster when Carmen was five. When Brenna asked Antonio to describe the cocktail that eventually killed her, he told the jury in broken English all it needed to know about the mother of his only child: "Halfaquarta antifreeze."

Brenna turned left onto 44th, suddenly self-conscious driving a Japanese luxury car in a neighborhood filled with salt-rusted GMC Jimmys, Ford Broncos, and ancient bad-ass Lincolns. She pulled to the curb three blocks from the river and parked, scanning the street for a house she was sure she'd recognize. She spotted it on the opposite side four doors away, a three-story bunker of illogical design, half-finished construction, and peeling paint—a house only a remodeler could love.

Brenna could see Antonio DellaVecchio's humble dreams etched on the building's face. The house had been bright red once, but the painted wood had long ago faded to the color of dried blood. He'd tried to remedy that the year Carmen was born by covering the house in champagne-colored siding. That effort ended in a jagged tear just above the halfway point, as if the installer had held tight to that panel as he fell to his death. Antonio had planned decks for each floor, and he got as far as installing the structural supports and doors for each. The first-floor deck door opened onto the building's concrete stoop, but the second- and third-floor doors opened to sheer drops of fifteen and thirty feet, respectively. The unfinished supports were black and rotted after years of exposure.

Shortly after his son's arrest, Brenna asked Antonio if he would ever finish the project. He'd shrugged and waved the idea away with one of his rough hands. All he said was, "Life's too crazy," and she'd understood him perfectly.

Brenna spotted Carmen as she crossed the street. His image appeared as an alarming flash between parked cars, and her stomach clenched. She wasn't sure why, but she better understood the reaction as she stepped up onto the curb. DellaVecchio was holding an open quart bottle of King Cobra, high-test malt liquor. Despite the cold, he was still wearing the thin prison slippers he'd worn the day he was released after the jail's property officer couldn't find his sneakers.

Slumped beside him on the cracked concrete stoop was a disheveled young man in a sweatshirt and greasy coveralls. She recognized him from her visit long ago, one of the neighborhood pals she dared not call to endorse DellaVecchio's character. They both noticed her at the same time.

Brenna raised her Starbucks cup, as if toasting this lovely scene. DellaVecchio raised his bottle with a sloppy grin, oblivious to her sarcasm. She tried to make her disappointment clearer.

"Little early for that, don't you think?"

"Breakfast of champions," DellaVecchio rasped, raising the bottle again. He reached for a crumpled plastic bag at his feet. "Dorito?"

He smiled, displaying rich deposits of orange residue between his scattered yellow teeth. Brenna thought of the periodontal-disease photos in her dentist's office. How could someone actually look worse in morning's soft light than in a prison's cold fluorescence?

"Thanks, but no," she said. She stuck her hand out to DellaVecchio's miscreant friend, and he reached up and shook it. His hand was cold and damp from his own bottle. She thought, *Carmen's a fuck-up because he can't help it. What's your excuse?*

"I'm Brenna Kennedy," she said. "I'm sorry, I've forgotten your name."

"Frank."

"Popko," Brenna said, remembering him after all.

"Popcorn!" DellaVecchio said in a spray of Dorito mulch. This cracked them up. Brenna waited as the pair howled and clinked bottles to toast DellaVecchio's sparkling show of wit.

"Carmen, I need to talk to you," Brenna said.

DellaVecchio took another long draw from the King Cobra, then clawed another handful of chips from the bag.

"Frankie Popcorn!" he said, and the two men dissolved into laughter again.

"Inside," Brenna said, nodding toward the front door behind him.

The two men looked at each other, raising their eyebrows at the same instant. "Ooh la la," Popko said.

Without taking his eyes off hers, DellaVecchio held his free hand up to his face, spread his index and middle fingers into a V and flicked his tongue between the two fingers. The gesture was so blatant, so crude, that Brenna could only turn away. She was used to DellaVecchio's tastelessness, but her first impulse was to smack him. Instead, she turned back around and glared until he retracted his tongue and lowered his hand. The man wasn't stupid.

"Apologize," she said.

Popko snickered. DellaVecchio laughed too, but it was a nervous thing that faded fast. Brenna waited. DellaVecchio sipped his beer, looking to his friend for reassurance. Popko studied the King Cobra label, suppressing a smile.

"Give m'self a boner," DellaVecchio said finally.

Popko was in midswig, and DellaVecchio's confession convulsed him. Malt liquor foamed from his mouth and nose as he laughed, and the fallout sprinkled the toes of Brenna's Joan & Davids.

Enough.

Brenna stepped closer, got right in DellaVecchio's face, close enough to smell the Doritos and beer. His smile disappeared. "Listen, you little shit," she said. "You're never gonna get closer to heaven than where you're sitting right now."

DellaVecchio laughed, but he was clearly uncomfortable. Brenna leaned even closer.

"Keep this up, Carmen, and you'll be looking for somebody else to save your sorry ass, as if anybody else would bother. I've got limits, and you're damned close. Am I being clear enough?"

DellaVecchio set his bottle on the stoop and wiped his damp hand on the front of his faded green sweatshirt—more startled than contrite.

"Clear enough?" Brenna repeated.

DellaVecchio nodded.

She stepped back and shook her head, swept an arm across the scene. "What the hell are you thinking? Out drinking on your stoop first thing in the morning? You've got every cop in this city looking for an excuse to haul you back inside. You've got neighbors who'd rather have a child molester on their street than you. And what are you doing? You're out here confirming their worst fears."

She jabbed her index finger at his temple, just above his misshapen left ear. She did it hard enough to hurt. "Carmen, think! I know you can."

Brenna knew she'd connected, but immediately regretted her tone. Sometimes it was hard to remember his history, that he was born with a brain marinated in alcohol. Brenna could see that his eyes registered real pain. DellaVecchio glanced at his friend, but found no solace there. Popko was getting unsteadily to his feet, and as he rose he slid his beer bottle into a pocket of his coveralls.

"Call you later, C. D.," Popko said, and walked down the shattered sidewalk toward the river.

DellaVecchio watched him go. "He's my friend," he said after a while.

"I know that, Carmen."

"You pissed him off."

"I'm sorry about that. Really. He's the only one besides your dad who came to see you in jail, I know. But he needs to understand what's happening. You can do yourself a lot of harm pulling shit like this. He needs to know that."

Popko turned a corner, but DellaVecchio kept watching the spot where he'd been.

"You've got a chance at a new life, Carmen."

DellaVecchio's head swiveled back to her, an almost mechanical movement that betrayed nothing, not anger, not fear, not even comprehension.

Brenna seized the moment, hoping she had his full attention. "Don't screw it up, is all I'm saying, for you or me. We've got a chance to change the diminished-capacity laws of this state, to give people like you a fairer shot. We've got a chance to clear you completely, to show everyone how shoddy this investigation really was and maybe make some meaningful changes on that level, too. Don't screw that up. I've got just as much at stake as you do."

He stood. They were about the same height, but DellaVecchio was standing on the house's stoop. He looked down on her, and for the first time Brenna felt the same dread menace that others saw in him. This was not the damaged young man to whose side she rallied eight years ago; here was the Scarecrow, unpredictable, capable of anything.

He turned and pushed his way inside. The house's dim interior was lit blue by a chattering television. Brenna could hear the bright banter of Channel 2's regular morning news team as DellaVecchio turned toward her.

"Carmen?" she said, but his toxic smile disappeared behind the slowly closing door.

7

Christensen stared down at the roof of the Stephen Foster Memorial, his thoughts shifting between Teresa Harnett's startling disclosure the day before and Brenna's unbridled passion last night.

"There's just something about a girl with a death wish, eh?"

Burke Padgett held a copy of the morning *Press* as he stood in the door frame of Christensen's university office. A three-column photo of Brenna and DellaVecchio ran across the top of the front page. The photographer had caught DellaVecchio at his most demented, both arms upthrust in triumph, mouth curled into a sneer. Christensen could almost hear the blustery "Fuck-an-A!" that had briefly derailed Brenna's courthouse news conference.

"I was going to apologize for being rude yesterday," Christensen said, "but never mind."

"This a good time?"

"I'm busy."

The pompous little gremlin stepped forward and laid the newspaper on the desk, covering the galley copy of the *Journal of American Psychology* article Christensen was proofing.

"Got the feeling yesterday wasn't the best time to talk," he said.

Christensen moved the newspaper aside and continued making final changes to the article he'd been researching for more than two years. "What was the tip-off, Burke?"

Padgett cleared his throat. "I'm gonna say my piece here, Jim, and you can listen or not. But I'm gonna say it anyway. I'd appreciate you hearing me out."

Christensen looked up, pulled by something unfamiliar

in Padgett's voice—sincerity. The two men glared across the desk. Padgett spoke first.

"You already know my concerns about DellaVecchio. Well, I thought of one more."

"Why am I not surprised?"

"It's your friend, this Kennedy woman. Did you ever wonder if maybe DellaVecchio might go after her?"

Padgett's green eyes didn't waver. His concern seemed genuine, a startling departure for a man usually focused on his own macabre celebrity.

"Sit down," Christensen said.

They sat stiffly, silent except for the scuffing of Padgett's chair across the linoleum. Christensen studied him as Padgett eased himself onto the seat, then sat down in his department-issued desk chair and waited.

"Got your attention, eh?" Padgett said, raising one white eyebrow.

"Don't play games."

Padgett sat forward to rest a forearm on Christensen's desk, but couldn't quite reach. He slid to the edge of his seat and tried again, trying to appear casual. "I've made no secret of this; you know I believe he attacked this Harnett woman, DNA or no DNA. But I never much agreed with Dagnolo's theory about why."

Common ground, Christensen thought. "So we can stipulate that Dagnolo's stalking scenario is fantasy?"

Padgett shrugged. "Miss Kennedy raised some valid points. The mayhem at the crime scene in some ways obscured the fact that this was an extremely organized attack."

"Which, from a psychological perspective, rules out DellaVecchio."

"Not necessarily," Padgett said. "He's not as dumb as he looks—bright enough, I think, to understand the idea of revenge. I think that's the story here."

Christensen stared. "You've got another book contract, don't you, Burke?"

Padgett cackled. "Haven't pitched it to my agent, but now that you mention it . . ." The little man stroked his beard as if contemplating the possibilities, then laughed out loud. "Kidding! Really!"

Christensen shook his head. "Tell me your revenge theory."

"OK, it's like this." The man actually rubbed his little hands together. "I didn't see it at first, but I started thinking about it as the case went along. The one thing no one ever questioned here was DellaVecchio's capacity for sexual infatuation. You know the history there."

Christensen nodded. "The harassment cases. A possible attempted rape."

"Exactly. But nothing on the order of this, violence-wise. Those were basically gropings, right? Your boy acting like a dog in heat, humping-on-the-bus stuff. True, it was escalating, and that's not unusual. But this attack was a leap. Damned vicious stuff. So I'm saying there was some other component here that pushed him further. *Something* that made this woman different than the others."

Christensen was lost. "Burke, they'd never even met. Why would he want revenge on someone he'd never met?"

Padgett smiled, having arrived finally at the crux of it. "Not her," he said. "Her husband."

"David?"

"Yes, David. David Harnett. He got little mention at the trial, but I've done a little homework. Did you know that all three times DellaVecchio was arrested before this, David Harnett was involved?"

Christensen feigned a yawn. "Old news. Brenna looked into it and didn't even think it was worth bringing up. Didn't fly then or now. Yes, David Harnett was involved in those arrests, either directly or peripherally. So what? He worked sex crimes at the time. The idea that DellaVecchio attacked Harnett's wife as a payback is a big stretch. Ludicrous, even."

Padgett wouldn't be denied. "Explains a lot, Jim. This was more than just a sex fantasy. The violence was just too over-the-top. The crime scene, the wine bottle rape, that reads like punishment, pure and simple. Trying to kill her wasn't enough. This guy wanted to humiliate her."

Padgett sat back, inviting a response.

"Excellent work, inspector," Christensen said. "But you're forgetting one annoying little detail."

"The DNA."

"Right. DellaVecchio didn't do it. Somebody else did and then set him up."

Padgett dismissed the idea with an elfin wave. "You could argue that, Jim, but whether he did or didn't almost doesn't matter. What I'm saying is DellaVecchio is *capable* of that kind of violence. I think he's capable of worse. That's all I'm saying. This guy's a constant threat to anybody who gets too close."

"So, it's OK to lock away somebody who's *capable* of a crime? Isn't prison supposed to be for people who make bad moral choices? You said yourself DellaVecchio's not capable of that. You said—"

"Look, I'll just say this flat-out: Somebody else is gonna get hurt. That's my concern."

Christensen studied Padgett's face, wondering where this was going.

"Based on what I know—" Padgett weighed his words for a moment. "Based on what I think really happened eight years ago, and what's happened since, I'd say the person at risk right now is your friend, Miss Kennedy. She's been closer to him than anyone else for eight years."

Christensen shook his head. "Why would he hurt someone who's worked her ass off to set him free, someone who hasn't charged him a penny since this whole thing started?"

"You're thinking logically, that's your problem; DellaVecchio thinks like a runaway truck. The guy's got no brakes on his impulses. For one thing, your girlfriend's probably the only woman he's had any contact with since he went in. I'm guessing she's got more than a cameo role in his fantasies at this point."

There was no need for Padgett to elaborate. Anyone with a basic understanding of DellaVecchio's psychological makeup would come to the same conclusion.

"Consider his take on this whole thing," Padgett said. "You can bet he remembers all the talk afterwards about Miss Kennedy's 'tactical mistake' during his trial. That's code and he knows it. If she'd pleaded him down to aggravated assault instead of trying to prove Dagnolo wrong, he'd have been out in three years. But she didn't. For him that translates: It's her fault he was in prison five years longer than he had to be. Plus, he knows the whole Scarecrow nickname started with her 'straw man' theory during trial. He's smart enough to understand all that, and resent it."

"It's not like we've ignored the possibilities, Burke. We know what we're dealing with here. And I think you're underestimating Brenna. Defense attorneys aren't exactly delicate."

"Can she defend herself?"

"Burke, why are you doing this?"

"Because DellaVecchio's different."

"Because of fetal alcohol syndrome, Burke. Diminished capacity. That's been Brenna's point from the start. The law shouldn't ignore the truth, and she's trying to make sure it doesn't. Especially since, as it turns out, DellaVecchio's not guilty."

"You're still dealing with a malevolent force here."

"Oh Christ, Burke." Christensen stood up. "Thank you

for your concern. Really. But what about the other psychological aspect of this case? It's not just a sideshow here. Let's not let the bigger issue get lost in all the Scarecrow hysterics."

"The memory stuff?"

Christensen picked up the galley proof of his *Journal* article and shook it. "None of this would've happened if the investigators hadn't led Teresa on. I examined every stage of the identification process in this case to show how it skewed everything, *everything*, from that point forward. This was a classic case of memory manipulation, and here we are eight years later cleaning up the mess."

Christensen sat down again. "They walked Teresa Harnett through a couple dozen photo six-packs, and when she finally pointed to DellaVecchio's mug shot and said there was something familiar about him, do you know what Milsevic said? 'We *thought* that might be the guy.'"

Padgett nodded. "Reinforcement."

"And the next stage, the lineup. Brenna dug out the videotape of that session, and I'm telling you, it's an indictment. They walk DellaVecchio in with five others. Before she says a word, Milsevic points to DellaVecchio and says 'Guy's got a record a mile long.'"

"All of a sudden, she's pretty sure DellaVecchio's the one," Padgett said, nodding.

"So by the time Harnett gets to court, she remembers every disgusting thing that bastard did to her, in living color, with full orchestration. Her original statement had none of that. I mean, where are all the people demanding to know how we got here from there?"

Padgett picked up his briefcase. "You're right, Jim. Absolutely right. And none of that changes anything I've said. Guilty or not, the young man Miss Kennedy's just put back into this community is dangerous. There's no other word for it. And based on what I know about him—. one man's opinion, mind you—I believe he's a young man with a score to settle. That's all I'm saying. You want to be real careful of that."

If Padgett had turned and left, if he'd tried to infuse the moment with the drama of an exit, Christensen would have had the excuse he needed to dismiss the whole conversation as a staged moment in an increasingly public career. But the psychiatrist remained, fixing his eyes on Christensen, not smiling, like a man delivering a message he considered urgent. That was utterly disconcerting.

"You're serious."

"As a heart attack," Padgett said. "One man's opinion, for whatever it's worth."

"So noted, Burke."

Padgett turned finally to go.

"Burke?" he said.

Padgett looked over his shoulder. Christensen scanned his face for signs of smug satisfaction, but found none.

"Thanks."

8

Brenna bounced the Legend's back tire against the curb, then wheeled the front end neatly into a spot in front of their house. She turned the key and sat, watching her breath fog the windshield, summoning the energy to move.

She'd finally hit the wall about three and left her office in a daze. She needed rest, but also some distance from it all. In the days since the hearing, media interest in DellaVecchio's release and her role in it had remained at fever pitch. Dagnolo kept busy demonizing them both. He'd leaked everything from decade-old police reports filed by women DellaVecchio had harassed to an excerpt from her closing argument eight years earlier in which she acknowledged the "unpredictable incubus" that DellaVecchio's alcoholic mother had "unleashed upon the world." Quack calls were coming in at a dozen a day, including a psychic who saw "a handsome man" attack Harnett "in an unfolding vision, like a slo-mo replay" in a reflection on the lid of her nonstick frypan. Would Brenna like her to testify?

The house was dark except for the front-hall lamp, which was on a timer that clicked on at dusk. Jim wouldn't be home from Pitt until five-thirty. Annie and Taylor were still at the sitter's down the street, where they went every day after school. Should she summon them home early, or take advantage of an hour of silence in the house? A hot bath sounded like heaven.

The Legend's door scraped the curb as it opened. She reminded herself to redistribute the two boxes of hate mail in her trunk. Their combined weight had the car riding low on the left side. She was a long way from having time to read it all, if she ever decided to do that, but for now she'd vowed to keep the letters from outraged citizens from cluttering up her office, distracting her from the work at hand.

"Claire64," she reminded herself as she turned the brass deadbolt and pushed through the front door.

The new alarm system's red eye winked at her in the front hall's dim light. On the panel's alphabetical keypad, she punched in C-L-A-I-R-E—her mother's name. She shifted to the numeric keypad to add the 6-4—Claire Kennedy's age when ovarian cancer finally took her. The red light turned green.

Jim and the kids must have left in a hurry. A pile of Taylor's clothes lay in the middle of the foyer. Her son was a fussy dresser, and Jim was accustomed to his last-minute changes, but they usually got the discards back into the right drawer before leaving. Annie's lunchbox sat forgotten at the base of the banister. Nothing unusual. She was nine and preoccupied with her overwhelming need for pierced ears. Little else mattered.

Brenna suppressed a tingle of guilt, wishing she could be more help in the morning, wishing sometimes she could be the doting mother and loving wife other people expected her to be. But she wasn't, couldn't be no matter how hard she tried. Thank God Jim understood; thank God he brought to the relationship the patience her eight-year-old son needed so badly. She couldn't imagine a better man for the job. So why couldn't she commit? Why had she twice postponed the civil marriage ceremony Jim planned, both times using the DellaVecchio case as her excuse?

She picked up Taylor's clothes, folded them, and set them on the bottom step. She unloaded the Tupperware sandwich container from Annie's lunchbox into the refrigerator. The PBJ would keep for tomorrow's lunch. She kept the one filled with grapes. It would keep Annie from starving while they fixed dinner. Brenna put the ice pack back in the freezer and started toward the stairs when she heard a chirp from the far side of the kitchen, over near the microwave. The answering machine. She poked the Play button and turned back toward the stairs, then stopped to hear which of Annie's many friends had called.

Long pause. The low hiss of an open line, but nothing. Then something indecipherable, mechanical, followed by another hiss, this one pitched higher. An electronic solicitation? Brenna was about to hit the Erase button when the music began:

> Got to learn to live with what you can't rise above
> If you want to ride on down in through this tunnel
> of love.

Husky voice. Springsteen. Chillingly familiar. The message ended with a *click!* as abrupt and startling as a gunshot. The answering machine's digital voice followed: "End of messages."

Brenna's hand shook as she reached again for the Play button. She thought of the mail in her car's trunk, of the obvious anger this case was generating. Somebody's idea of a joke? Maybe, she thought, but it would have to be somebody who remembered DellaVecchio's trial in remarkable detail.

Brenna flashed on the letter Teresa Harnett had received two days before she was attacked. She remembered its odd weight the first time she held it during pretrial motions. The chunky letters of the manual typewriter. The distinctive, truncated letter *y* throughout that tied it to the battered Olivetti found in the Dumpster near DellaVecchio's house. The Lawrenceville postmark on the envelope. She remembered Harnett on the witness stand, holding the note in her rock-steady hands, reading aloud the lyric for a jury transfixed by her courage:

Got to learn to live with what you can't rise above
If you want to ride on down in through this tunnel
of love.

Harnett's voice was just as strong when she finished
reading as when she'd started. If she'd broken down, the
moment would have been less powerful. But she'd set the
note on the table in front of her, looked straight at
DellaVecchio at the defense table and said, "I used to
think 'Tunnel of Love' was a beautiful song." Her un-
derstatement back then became one of the most devastating moments of DellaVecchio's trial.

Brenna looked around. The house never seemed bigger.
She willed away the phantom prickle that suddenly made
her hair stand on end. She'd expected the hate mail, hadn't
she? Even anticipated the threats. So why the pounding
in her chest? Why the trembling hands as she reached for
the answering machine's Save button?

Who would do this?

Brenna knew the answer, couldn't will that away. Only
one person would lose if she proved Carmen Della-
Vecchio innocent—the animal who really did attack Teresa Harnett. After eight years free and clear, he was
watching the slow absolution of the man convicted of his
crimes. Was this his pathetic attempt to reverse that process? Did he really think he could intimidate her?

"Dumb bastard," Brenna said, and laughed out loud.

Even as her words filled the empty house, she considered another possibility. Her bravado turned to anger as
she paced the kitchen floor. The straw man was back on
the street. The Scarecrow was unchained, a menace
loosed. Any hint of trouble and Dagnolo would be all over
the judge, arguing to put DellaVecchio back behind bars.
Maybe someone was setting him up again.

The kitchen wall clock read 4:23. What now? She
played the message again, its creepy power diminishing

each time. She could ignore it, but Jim had a right to know if this ugliness was seeping into their home. She thought suddenly of Alton Staggers, the Underhill family's security goon who a year earlier had snatched her son and Jim's younger daughter from school after she and Jim had unearthed the Underhills' sordid family secret. In situations this volatile, there are no boundaries.

No, she decided, this had to be done by the book. It was risky, but she saw no other way. She picked up the phone and dialed.

"Public Safety Building," the operator answered.

"Chief Kiger, please."

"Who's calling?"

Brenna gave her name and waited. Would he remember her? No matter. Patrick Kiger was the one man in the Pittsburgh Police Department she felt she could trust. In the years since he arrived from Memphis, he'd turned the department from a swamp of institutionalized vice and debilitating internal politics into one of the most effective and best-managed forces in the country. His low tolerance for misconduct among his officers earned him loyalty and loathing in equal measure. The police union filed regular grievances against him, but few ever questioned his personal integrity. Even Dagnolo knew better than to cross him.

"I'm sorry, Chief Kiger's out this week."

Brenna swore under her breath. "Is there any way—"

"Hold on, I'll transfer you."

She considered hanging up, but didn't. What choice did she have? She wanted this on record, just in case it happened again. Just in case whatever.

"So, what?" came a familiar voice. "You take it all back?"

Milsevic. Damn.

"Uh, Captain," she stammered, "I was looking for the chief."

Milsevic laughed. "Surprise!" he said. "He's in San Diego. Had to speak at a DEA seminar. Left me holding the fort. What can I do for you?"

As Kiger's second-in-command, Milsevic more than made up for the chief's lack of personal charm. It worked on most people. She had always felt that if his police career didn't work out, he showed promise as a hot-tub salesman, or maybe a motivational speaker. Her friends in the department's rank-and-file considered Milsevic ruthlessly ambitious, but cops have better bullshit detectors than the general public. Kiger, on the other hand, understood Milsevic's value as the department's unblemished public face.

"Nothing," she said after an awkward pause. "Just . . . nothing."

"Look," Milsevic said, "let's not play games here, OK? If there's something we need to know—"

"Nothing personal, Captain. I do need to talk to somebody there. I'm just not sure you're the right guy. You're too involved in my case, and with the Harnetts. I'm just not comfortable—"

"If this is about your boy DellaVecchio, no worries. Unless he's slipped his collar, he's at his dad's house in Lawrenceville right now. The wonders of electronics."

"I know," Brenna said. "Talked to him an hour and a half ago, just before I left the office."

"What then? The lynch mob's torches keeping you awake at night? Swear to God, they didn't get your address from me."

Asshole, Brenna thought. "I'd take a mob any day over some spineless little prick who just phones in his threat," she snapped.

The line went quiet. The bluster was gone from Milsevic's voice when he finally asked, "What are you saying?"

"I'll just talk to Kiger."

"Look . . . sorry. If there's a problem, we need to know."

He was right. The message was too scary to ignore. Brenna thought again of the kids, of Jim. This was her battle, but they were in the crossfire. She thought, too, of Teresa Harnett. If it was the same guy, she could be a target again.

"I got a phone message, a threat, I think," she said. "Nothing overt, just implied. I'm no Chicken Little. I think you know that. We've had plenty of this bullshit since the release. But this one was different. I just got a feeling about it. Plus, it was on my home machine."

"You saved the answering-machine tape?"

"It's digital. Not sure how that works."

"But it's still on the machine, right?"

"Right."

"You recognize the voice?"

"There's no talking. Just a recording. The verse from 'Tunnel of Love.' "

Brenna didn't elaborate; the police captain was intimately familiar with the details of the Harnett attack. He knew what it meant.

"I'll get someone over there," he said.

"No hurry."

"Look for a patrol officer in the next fifteen minutes. You're in Shadyside?"

She gave him the house number on Howe Street. "Brian?" she said, regretting the uncertainty she betrayed by using his first name. "It's probably nothing."

"Or it could be a lot of things."

"Just make sure to keep the Harnetts in the loop," she said. "They should know. But don't screw me on this."

"You did the right thing, calling. Let us do our job. I know what you're probably thinking. You probably know what I'm thinking. But either way, we need to be involved. Fifteen minutes. If it takes longer, call me back."

As reassuring as she found Milsevic's words, they suddenly struck her as overly concerned. "I'd almost rather you didn't take this so seriously," she said. "What exactly are you thinking, anyway?"

"You don't really want to know," he said.

"Humor me."

Milsevic waited. "It is kind of funny, sort of a coincidence. You spring DellaVecchio, and suddenly we've got a Springsteen fan with an attitude running around out there."

Bastard. "He wouldn't threaten me. Just forget it, OK. I should have known better."

"You asked my opinion."

"Your opinion is so goddamned predictable," she said. "You want to know what I think, Captain? I think whoever savaged your friend Teresa is still out there. I think he's worried Carmen's off the hook. This misguided soul may actually think someone there would take a new investigation seriously. He may not know any better. So he's going after me, because I'm the one all over TV and the papers talking about how somebody other than Carmen DellaVecchio nearly killed Teresa. That's what I think, Captain, and you can bet your ass I'm going to track down your boss in San Diego and let him know what I think."

She was breathing hard and covered the phone's mouthpiece so Milsevic wouldn't hear. After a long pause, he said "Touché. Fifteen minutes, OK?"

Brenna hung up without another word.

9

Fifteen minutes, on the nose. The young patrol officer knocked, politely introduced himself, and stepped into the foyer. He looked like somebody's kid. Over his shoulder, Brenna could see a panting German shepherd pacing in his cruiser's back seat. She showed the cop to the living room, briefly told him her story of coming home and finding the phone message, then waited while he scribbled some notes.

"And you think it's somehow connected to a court case you're working on?" he asked.

"Long story, but yes." She told him the shortest possible version; he nodded as though he'd never heard of Teresa Harnett or Carmen DellaVecchio. As they talked, she memorized the name above his badge and the badge number itself.

"May I hear the message?" Officer Plantes asked when she was done.

Brenna led him into the kitchen, to the corner where the answering machine continued its red-eyed wink. He listened to the recording, scribbled a few more notes, then tried to find the machine's cassette-tape bay. "Go figure," he said. "I'm way out of date. Mine still uses tapes. Guess I'll take the whole thing."

"I'd like a receipt for it, though," Brenna said as she unplugged it. "And if you wouldn't mind, officer, I'd like you to note the time and date on the receipt. Oh, and just note on there the reason why you're taking it."

Brenna smiled. He actually blushed. If her paranoia bothered him, it didn't show. The young patrol officer complied with all her wishes and apologized for the trouble.

"So you'll file a report when?" Brenna asked.

"Before I'm off tonight," he said. "Not supposed to send out copies, since they're available in the records room. But I could send you a copy if you'd like. This address OK?"

Brenna touched his hand lightly and nodded her appreciation. "ZIP code's 15232," she said. "Thank you so much. Is that all you need from me?"

She opened the front door just as Jim was herding Annie and Taylor away from the police cruiser and the huffing beast inside. "Bren?" he said from the sidewalk, shifting two plastic bags of groceries from one hand to the other. He picked up the briefcase he'd set down during the switch. "What's up?"

"Your dog smells," Annie interrupted as the smiling cop approached his car. "You shouldn't feed him beans or else you should keep the car windows closed or something."

"Does he bite?" asked Taylor, her eight-year-old bundle of anxiety.

The cop ignored Annie's commentary. "He only bites bad guys," he said to Taylor. "You're not a bad guy, are you?"

Her boy's eyes strayed to the cop's holster and the weapon inside. Taylor shook his head, speechless.

"Then you wanna pet him?"

Taylor shook his head again. The cop turned to Annie. "How about you?"

"What's his name?" Annie demanded.

"Carmack."

Brenna blanched, then shot a look at Jim. He seemed just as astounded as she was. Did Kiger know his cops had named a K-9 dog after the victim in one of Pittsburgh's most notorious police brutality cases? Brenna filed that delicious little tidbit away for the next time one of the city's finest got too rough with one of her clients.

"But we call him Ace. You know, like Ace Ventura?" He paused. "Get it?"

Annie rolled her eyes. "Pet detective. Duh."

The officer bent low so he could look Jim's younger daughter in the eye. He tried again to win Annie over. "Ace loves kids. Wanna pet him?"

"No way."

"You sure?"

"He smells and probably has fleas and I saw a show once where this guy was wearing one of those big padded suits and a police dog chewed on his arm."

"Ace only does that with bad guys."

"Yeah, well," Annie said. "Why are you here, anyway? Somebody gettin' busted?"

Officer Plantes stood up and turned toward the porch, apparently convinced that nothing he could do would impress her. "I'm gonna let your mom explain that, OK? Time for me and Ace to hit the road."

"She's not my mom," Annie said. She pressed her nose against the car's rear window and sang, "Beans, beans, are good for your heart—" until the dog's low growl backed her off.

"Annie," Christensen said. "Inside. Now."

Taylor was already clinging to the jacket hem of Brenna's Jil Sander suit as Jim and Annie climbed the stairs.

"I'd like both kids upstairs," Jim said, his eyes fixed on Brenna's. "Let's get the homework started. Dinner'll be maybe forty minutes, and the grown-ups need to talk."

"What are we having?" Annie asked.

Jim held up the plastic bags. "Tacos!" he said.

"Ooh, there's a new one," Annie said.

"First time this week," he protested. "You guys love tacos."

"I like tacos," Taylor agreed.

Annie withered the boy with a glare, then trained it on her father. "Remember, no cheese."

They watched the kids haul their backpacks up the stairs. Jim sighed. "When did Patty Hearst move in?"

"She's pretty angry these days."

"Is it me? Her dominatrix-in-pigtails thing used to be charming, right? Now it's, I don't know, bitter."

"She misses her mom," Brenna said.

Jim's face fell. "Why? She said something?"

Brenna shook her head. "I found Silkie two nights ago, under her pillow."

"Molly's old nightgown? She hasn't asked about it for, what? Almost a year?"

Brenna shrugged. "You know, for somebody who's supposed to understand people, you can be pretty dense. Maybe it's a guy thing. Think what time of year it is."

She knew as soon as she said it that she'd connected.

"Oh God," he said. "The sixth anniversary of Molly's accident. First time I forgot."

"That's not a bad thing, you know," Brenna said. "You're healing."

"But Annie remembered?"

"Melissa mentioned it when she called from Penn State last weekend. Annie must have dug Silkie out of her closet after talking to her big sister."

Jim stood there, a tightening knot of guilt. "I'll talk to her tonight." He leaned forward and tried an awkward hug. His briefcase and the grocery bags bounced against Brenna's back and shoulders. "Thanks."

The cop started his cruiser, and they both turned. Officer Plantes waved brightly, then eased the black-and-white out onto Howe Street. They watched the car turn the corner onto South Aiken and disappear. Jim turned back to her.

"Mind filling me in?"

10

The streetlight outside their second-floor bedroom was broken, its lens and bulb shattered. Glass shards sparkled like diamonds on the street below each time an oncoming car's headlights swept across the debris. Christensen stared down at the glimmering pool of glass, then at the cars lining both sides of the street. He was a man on the edge of darkness.

"Close that, would you?" Brenna said as she stepped from the bathroom.

He watched her reflection in the window. She wore only a towel, which she unfastened as she crossed the room. It fell to the floor in midstride, and he hesitated before twirling the miniblind rod. When he turned around she was naked, but he found no joy in it.

"You don't usually care, open or closed," he said.

"Not usually."

He studied her face for implication. "The call, you mean?"

Brenna shrugged. "It's probably nothing. I told you that."

"Crank caller, you said." Christensen thought about the similar call that had so rattled Teresa. He wanted desperately to tell Brenna, but couldn't.

"Right," she said.

"And you wanted the cops to know about it."

"I wanted it noted. Why take chances? Plus, I wanted to make sure Milsevic let Teresa Harnett know what had happened."

Teresa knows. Christensen choked back the words, remembering his promise, struggling with a silent surge of fear. He was struggling, too, against an impulse to confront the most explosive issue between them: Could he trust Brenna to make unselfish choices? She enjoyed the spotlight's glare—and the glare had never been more intense than during DellaVecchio's original trial—but at times it had blinded her to danger, both to herself and to their blended family. Once, during the Underhill case a year before, she'd put the kids in harm's way. Christensen wasn't sure their relationship could survive something like that again. Lately, he wasn't sure it could survive, period.

For nearly six years, he had loved her intelligence, her powerful sense of right and wrong, and her extraordinary passion as both a lawyer and a lover. He knew Brenna loved him to the best of her ability in ways that only someone who knew her well could appreciate. She loved him as much as she would ever love any man, and that he never questioned. But he'd known for some time that he ranked third behind Taylor and her role as one of the city's most sought-after criminal-defense attorneys. Was it enough?

"So, you think Milsevic will follow through? I mean, crank call or not, do you think he's taking it seriously? We're all exposed here, you know."

She slid some panties on and turned away from him as she tugged on a well-worn T-shirt. Her movements grew sharp as she stood before their dresser's mirror and pulled a brush through her hair. Suddenly, she wheeled on him.

"If you've got something to say, just say it," Brenna said. "Don't give me twenty questions."

He stared. "The only dumb question is the one you don't ask."

"But why don't you just say what you're thinking?"

He crossed the room and tried to hug her, but she pushed him away.

"Bren, it's just weird, is all. I mean, whoever left that message is smart. No spoken words, just a recording. Nothing that could identify who it came from."

"You think I haven't thought of that?" she said.

"So what if it wasn't just some crank? What if it was somebody worried about you recognizing their voice?"

"You think it's DellaVecchio, don't you?" she asked.

"Not necessarily."

"But you think it could be. Just like Milsevic."

Christensen paused. "What did Milsevic say?"

Brenna circled him, out of range, stopping at the head of their bed to strip back the covers.

"You're not convinced the police are going to investigate this, are you?" he said.

She didn't look up, busied herself setting her alarm. Her hands were a blur as she moved from task to task, a study in agitation.

"Please talk to me," he said.

Brenna took a long, deep breath. Her hands slowed, and she ran one through her hair, pulling it back from her face. A single tear had rolled down her cheek. It fell onto her shirt, leaving a translucent mark in the cotton above her heart. He approached again, and this time she stood still as he took her in. He waited for a sob that never came.

After a while, she said, "Don't you see how this plays perfectly into their theory about DellaVecchio? He's dangerous, and now he's out. I just handed them something they can use against us at the hearing, or before the hearing if they decide to push it."

"But you called the police anyway," Christensen said.

"I wouldn't take a chance with the kids, with you. Never again. Even if it's just some idiot getting his giggles."

Christensen hesitated, thinking again about Teresa. "And if it's not?"

She tried to pull away, but he held her. She tried again, feebly, then put her arms around his neck and looked him in the eye.

"Whoever did this to Teresa Harnett, he's still out there," she said. "But we don't know how he's reacting.

In a couple weeks, this becomes an open case. *We* know the cops probably won't reinvestigate the attack. They're afraid of proving themselves wrong. But *he* doesn't know that. The real attacker just knows it's all coming undone. What he thought was over isn't really over."

"And it's your fault," Christensen said.

Brenna nodded.

"Why can't Milsevic see that then? Tunnel vision?"

"Exactly. Nailing DellaVecchio's the goal here. Nothing else matters."

"But what if—"

"I've made a liar out of Teresa Harnett. I've made liars of the cops. How can I expect them to get excited about somebody making phony phone calls?"

"Because you're a private citizen, just like anyone else. Because you have a right to police protection."

Brenna pushed away with an impatient-teacher look. "What planet did you say you're from?"

"Other options, then? State police? The FBI? Don't they get involved whenever someone uses the phone to commit a crime?"

Brenna walked to the window. She absently twirled the dangling plastic rod, opening and closing the miniblinds once, twice, three times. Beyond the window, only darkness instead of the streetlight's soft glow.

Christensen snapped off the bedside lamp. "Somebody broke the streetlight," he said.

Brenna turned to him. "I'll call Milsevic again tomorrow," she said, her voice calmer in the darkened room. "By then he'll have heard the message. Then I'll get a better feel for where he's coming from."

"And if he's blowing you off?"

"I'll figure something out. I left a voice-mail message for Kiger. Maybe he'll call. If nothing else, at least we've alerted the Harnetts. Teresa's the linchpin here. If this guy's scared enough to be watching me, I'd bet he's watching her."

Christensen stopped Brenna's hand as she reached for the miniblind rod again. He rolled the blind shut tight, then laid his hand on her left cheek. "I love you, Bren."

She kissed him, her lips lingering on his as she spoke: "I know."

11

Flasher coat. That's what the hump-backed greaseball at Army-Navy called it, like, twelve years ago, when he laid out twenty dollars and took it home. Heavy as hell. Hung way down past his knees. Air Force blue. Looked fine. Main thing was the collar, man, big as a pair of wings. Turn it up at the back, button it at the neck, pull a Pirates cap down over your eyes. Shit, you practically disappeared. No worries, especially in this neighborhood. People just think it's a new look. Come back in a week, see this getup all over Shadyside, cap and all. Fucking sheep.

How long she been in there? Guess if you pay three bucks for a cup of coffee, it better take some time to make.

Junkies were easy. Didn't matter—crack, booze, caffeine. They all had their routines. Practically set your watch by 'em. Every morning he'd followed, three times now, she got here the same time, 8 A.M. on the nose. Left her house and drove a couple blocks, straight here, parked in the alley behind the coffeehouse. Got a takeout coffee and something to eat. Only thing he didn't know was whether she took cream and sugar, and he wasn't about to get that close. Wasn't *that* invisible. From half a block away, she'd never know.

Same thing Downtown, depending on traffic. Two mornings now he'd watched her there. She wheeled that nice ride of hers into the Oxford Centre parking garage, both times between eight-twenty and eight-thirty.

Beautiful.

What was taking her so long? Couldn't see a thing through the glare on the front window. But she was in there somewhere; he could still see her car's back bumper sticking out of the alley. She'd be out in a minute with a cup of whatever, then down Fifth through Oakland. Onto the Parkway, off at Grant, into the garage and the deserted corner near the stairwell where she parked every day. Knew her routines as well as he knew his own. Anytime he wanted, she was his.

But the best place? No question. Right there in her bedroom, one clean shot from the empty roof across the street. One shot to end this bullshit and put everything right. He could almost see the red LaserShot beam dance across her skull, feel the SIG jump in his hands. Just thinking about it made him hard. Better adjust. Don't want people thinking there's a tent pole under this peacoat.

Well, finally. Out the front door and headed for the car, juggling her keys and her cup and a little bag with her muffin. Even so, even with that Columbo coat, she moved nice, like chicks who really know how to strip, the ones who know what drives guys nuts. It's not bumping and grinding like a paint shaker at the hardware store. It's those little jukes from side to side, like she's mixing a martini, makes you see stars. You watch a woman like that move, can't help but picture her working that magic with you inside.

Around the corner, into the alley. The alarm chirps. The car door slams. Take her a few seconds to get everything set—cup in the cupholder, key in the hole, maybe a quick bite of muffin before she rolled. Every morning the same. Then, ignition and blast off. The rear bumper disappeared and she was gone, headed for town. Watch said 8:07. Two minutes later than the last time he followed her, but close enough to know she'd be where he wanted when he wanted, if he wanted.

Bitch might as well wear her schedule on a sandwich board.

12

"No calls for a few minutes, Liis. I'll be tied up on something, maybe half an hour. I'll get back to people this afternoon."

Liisa Wyatt looked up from her keyboard. "Good morning to you, too," she said.

Brenna tossed her Starbucks cup and a crumpled muffin bag into her secretary's trash can. "I'm sorry. Good morning. Just take messages for a while, OK?"

"What's wrong?"

Life had seemed so right just after DellaVecchio's release. Now, a week later, everything seemed wrong. Brenna thought again about the odd phone call she got last night, the third. Just menacing silence on the line. She thought about the lie she had told Jim when he came home from the kids' basketball practice and caught her pacing like a caged cat. She wanted to tell Liisa what was happening, that someone was scaring holy hell out of her. But when she opened her mouth, "Nothing" came out. She forced a smile as she said it.

"You sure?"

"Just some stuff I need to take care of, and I need a chunk of time to do it. I'll let you know when I'm done."

She closed her office door and leaned back against it. Already, a dozen pink message slips were wedged beneath a corner of her desk phone. They'd have to wait. She couldn't, wouldn't, put up with this. She wasn't easily intimidated. Hell, she could intimidate with the best of them. But this guy was calling her at home, three times now if you counted the song recording he'd left on their machine that first time. He always seemed to know when she was alone, when she was the one who'd pick up the phone. As if he'd been watching the house, figuring out their schedules.

The cops still had her answering machine, so all she got the second time was the weighted hum of an open line. She'd slammed the phone down on instinct, but wised up fast. She'd called the phone company to order Caller ID. It was activated just hours before last night's call, and it worked like a charm.

She hung her coat and scarf on the burnished-steel rack in the corner of her office and sat down. She fished the yellow Post-it note from her briefcase and read her scribble—412-358-4491. The number that had flashed onto the LCD readout when last night's call came in. She'd tell Jim about it eventually, let him know what was going on. But first she wanted some information.

She reached for the Greater Pittsburgh White Pages. She opened it to the pages marked "Prefix Locations/Area Code 412" and traced her finger down the page. She stopped when her finger hit 358. She ran her finger across the page. It came to rest on a word she never expected— Lawrenceville.

Her hand shook as she dialed the number. On the fourth ring, a woman answered. "Depth Charge."

"I'm sorry?" Brenna said.

"Depth Charge. Who ya lookin' for?"

"Is this 358-4491?"

"Yeah."

"Somebody asked me to call them at this number," Brenna said. "This is the Depth Charge? What's that?"

"I'm busy as hell," the woman said, and hung up.

The bar was flanked on one side by a showroom full of granite headstones, and on the other by a narrow, car-choked side street. On the side of a building facing south on Butler, a billboard offered "Caskets Unlimited" to passing motorists.

Brenna had driven past the Depth Charge four times as she eased the Legend up and down Butler. She'd even circled this block twice before she spotted it. Maybe the odd billboard distracted her, or maybe she hadn't seen it because the front door was nearly hidden by an ancient refrigerated display case, which someone had left out on the pitted sidewalk for scavengers to haul away.

She eased the car to the curb and set the parking brake. Even at 10 A.M., even in the day's bright sun, Lawrenceville had a gloomy, claustrophobic feel. She'd gotten over the initial shock of finding that the latest call came from somewhere in DellaVecchio's neighborhood. But by the time she canceled her morning appointments and drove out of the Oxford Centre parking garage, her heart was pounding.

Brenna hesitated before opening the car door, trying to calculate the odds. Even if this *was* the phone the caller used, wouldn't that make sense? Whoever set Della-Vecchio up the first time was smart. He made sure back then that the most obvious clues pointed to his straw man. If he was setting DellaVecchio up again, why wouldn't he use a phone from somewhere down here?

She opened the car door and stepped out. The only noise came from the steady hum of traffic along Butler. The sidewalks were deserted except for a stoop sitter, an old woman dressed in black, more than a block away. Brenna thought the *click-click-click* of her low heels on the concrete seemed obnoxiously loud as she walked toward the front door. She stepped into the dim tavern, ignoring the half-dozen regulars who turned to look at her as they sipped beer for breakfast. The pay phone was on the wall just inside the front door, so she picked up the sticky handset, pretending to make a call. Leaning back, she read the numbers on the tiny white stripe underneath the touch-tone keypad: 358-4491.

Brenna checked the Post-it note again, swallowed hard,

and hung up the phone. Back in bright daylight, she noticed a sign for 44th Street at the nearest intersection. She realized then she was less than a block from Della-Vecchio's house.

13

The morning calamities were worse than usual. Christensen had the stains to prove it, and he reviewed them as he pushed through the front entrance of the Harmony Brain Research Center. A falling glob of boysenberry jam had left a tear-shaped indigo spot just beneath the pocket of his white cotton shirt, the result of a PBJ catastrophe while making the kids' lunches. He'd noticed it only after dropping them at school, when it was too late to change. Wouldn't have mattered anyway. Only moments before, he discovered his commuter mug was dripping French roast onto his chest every time he took a sip. When would he learn to get the lid on right? His shirt looked like a Jackson Pollock masterpiece, and the work day had just started.

"Big explosion at Denny's?"

Christensen looked up. Harmony's acerbic lobby receptionist, Petra Smanko, was shaking her head, one of the few body parts her bullet-scarred brain could still control. She was sitting behind her futuristic telephone control panel, strapped in her wheelchair, wearing a cordless headset. She looked like a space shuttle pilot. More remarkably, her easy smile was undimmed by the wreckage of her life and the devastation in her head. Christensen found endless inspiration in Smanko's unshakable good humor.

"It's really bad today, isn't it?" he said.

"Worse than usual. Putting your dry cleaner's kid through college?"

He laughed. "Oh, you know, I let the kids sleep in and—"

"You were late getting out. I know the story. Hold it a sec." She poked at her console with the eraser end of a pencil clamped in her left hand, which still had some function. "Harmony Brain Research Center. Good morning." Then, "I'll transfer you." She poked at the console again and looked back at him, nodding at the purple stain. "Grape jam?"

"Something like that."

At the brown streaks down his chest. "Coffee?"

"Yep." He started down the hall, toward the small research office he kept at the center. "Thanks for the damage report."

"Add some eggs and bacon, make a nice Grand Slam," she said.

Twice a week for the past three years, Christensen had come to this futuristic facility in the hills of O'Hara township, just northeast of the city, to work on one memory project or another. He'd spent two years in the Alzheimer's wing trying to understand how art therapy helps patients in the later stages of the disease reconnect with memories that once seemed lost forever. Colleagues had hailed the resulting paper as a breakthrough when he'd delivered it a year earlier at a conference in Houston, but by then he'd shifted his attention to the malleability of post-traumatic memories—a project inspired by Teresa Harnett's evolving account of the night she was attacked.

Harmony was not only a state-of-the-art neurological treatment facility, but a deep well of potential study subjects in various stages of neural disrepair. Some of their brains were reshaped by disease; others struggled with coordination, function, memory, and psychological scars in the aftermath of an accident or assault. Sometimes their stories hinted at the worst in human nature, sometimes the best. And sometimes the stories were a bit of both, as in the remarkable journey of Petra Smanko, whose ex-boyfriend had left a 9mm slug in her cerebral cortex four years ago. When Christensen first met her, she was just learning how to talk again. Now she was the center's full-time chatterbox, talking as if, any second, she might go mute.

He moved down the smooth concrete hallway, navigating past a young man in a motorized wheelchair. Christensen recognized him from the elaborate gang tattoo on his left forearm.

"How's your game, DeeCee?" Christensen slowed to the chair's pace and looked down. "I'll whip your butt whenever you're ready."

DeeCee laughed. "I'm hittin' the board now at least. Gimme another week, but man, I hate those Velcro darts. Pussy darts. Want the spiky ones, man."

"You bounced one of the soft ones off my forehead last week. Your therapist gives you real darts, I'm not even coming in the room with you."

"Gimme a week, home. Be kickin' your ass."

Christensen shot him a thumbs-up and moved on, turning right into a corridor marked "Skills Testing." In small rooms on both sides of the hall, patients were struggling with tasks they once took for granted. A petite blond woman to Christensen's left was pouring water from a pitcher, soaking the table beneath the cup for which she'd been aiming. In a room to the right, Christensen recognized the back of an old man's bald head as that of former Mellon Bank executive Dwayne Laughlin. He was in his mid-80s but looked older; less charitable staff members called him the White Raisin. He was staring hard at a flash card of a horse, which his therapist across the table was holding up for him to see. "Spoon?" Laughlin asked.

Christensen turned the key on his office door, shoved it open with his foot, and flipped on the overheads. Everything was as he left it, a wreck. At times the place more resembled a landfill than an office, but his papers were deceptively organized. His filing system was drawn from the principle of geologic layering—the oldest stuff on the bottom, the more recent deposits on top. He understood the system and it served him well, though few shared his confidence in it.

He shrugged off his coat and sat down, then looked up when he heard footsteps in the hall outside, slow and measured. A moment later, the incredible hulk of David Harnett moved slowly past the office door. Harnett walked toward the vending area, apparently lost in thought, sipping from one of the small foam cups dispensed by the testing unit's coin-operated coffee vending machine at the end of the hall. The cup nearly disappeared in his huge hand.

Christensen froze, trying to make sense of what he'd just seen. Had that really happened?

On one hand, a chance encounter at Harmony was probably overdue. Teresa had been a physical rehab patient here since shortly after the attack. By the time Christensen began his work at Harmony, Teresa already was a role model for other rehab patients who faced a long and difficult road after their traumatic head injuries. Her skull had been smashed into four pieces by an attacker who swung a thick glass wine bottle against it no fewer than thirteen times. The assault had sent her brain crashing around the inside of her cranium with the same force as if she'd driven a car into a bridge abutment at seventy miles per hour.

But in all those years, her one-day-a-week therapy schedule and Christensen's irregular Harmony research schedule had seldom coincided. Now, a week after DellaVecchio's release and Teresa's troubling visit to his Pitt office, her husband strolled casually past an office hardly anyone knew Christensen kept.

This was weird. Teresa was years past having to be driven in for therapy; Christensen knew he'd seen her alone with car keys in the Harmony parking lot. So why was her husband here, pacing the halls?

Christensen closed his door, peeking down the hall before he did. He felt a tightness in his chest and a buzz in his head as he watched David Harnett feed coins into a candy machine. What the hell was going on? At his desk, Christensen opened a drawer, then closed it. He moved his stapler from one side of his desk to the other. He spun his chair toward the window, wondering how Teresa had reacted to the news that Brenna, too, had received a threatening phone call. Suddenly he was in the hall, pretending to mosey down to the vending area for a midmorning snack.

From the back, Harnett was roughly the size and shape of the vending machine in front of him. He was older than his wife, maybe by twenty years, and it showed mostly in the thinning hair at the crown of his head and the fleshy strain on his belt, which separated his khaki slacks from a polo shirt stretched over his broad shoulders.

Christensen acted surprised and appropriately uncomfortable as Harnett turned his head. For an instant, the man seemed happy to see a familiar face. But with recognition came contempt, and it registered both in Harnett's eyes and in the sudden and wordless *whack!* he delivered to the side of the vending machine.

"Sorry," Christensen said. "I was just, ah, sorry. Didn't know you were here."

Harnett focused on the machine, saying nothing.

"I'll come back later," Christensen said.

Whack! Harnett grumbled, then gently bumped the machine with his shoulder. Behind the window, a Three Musketeers bar in space G3 shifted but didn't fall from its uncertain perch. Harnett pressed the coin return button, but got nothing. Christensen seized the opening.

"Does that all the time," he said. "Pushes it out to the very edge, but the thing doesn't fall."

Harnett shook his head, but he seemed just as relieved as Christensen that they'd found safe ground. "Then you're supposed to write off to Buttsniff, Ohio, or some-place," he said. "Spend 33 cents postage to get your 75 cents back."

"There's a trick," Christensen said, then waited. "Mind?"

Harnett stepped back and waved one of his giant hands toward the machine. He wasn't smiling, but he didn't seem as hostile as Christensen expected. Christensen thought twice about turning his back on Harnett, but he held his breath and stepped forward. He reached up and put his hands on the top front edges of the machine and pushed, rocking it back on its hind legs, then let it drop. The front legs were maybe an inch off the ground when he let go. The hulk shuddered as it hit, and the Three Musketeers bar dropped into the delivery well with a sat-isfying *thud*. Christensen turned, triumphant, and took a modest bow. Harnett nodded his appreciation, but all he said was, "Nice fucking shirt."

Christensen stepped aside as Harnett reached in for the candy bar.

"Rough morning, is all. I should just get a bib."

Harnett pulled the chocolate bar out in a fist the size of a boxing glove, then opened his hand to show the treasure in his palm. "Thanks," he said.

"No problem."

The two men faced each other in awkward silence, alone together in a room no larger than a walk-in closet.

"Were you here looking for me?" Christensen asked.

Harnett shook his head. His eyes shifted briefly to the corridor behind them. "My wife's here," he said. "Regular rehab day."

Christensen nodded, but the answer explained nothing. "You usually come along, then?"

Harnett narrowed his eyes. "Rough goddamn week. Thought I'd better."

"Physical rehab wing's at the other end," Christensen

said. "What brings you down to the testing unit?"

Harnett said nothing. Not even a nod.

Christensen tried to fill the silence. "I keep a little research office, just down the hall." Still nothing. How much had Teresa told him? "Hope the message about the phone call Brenna got didn't upset Teresa too much."

Harnett's face clouded. Christensen imagined him withering a suspect in an interrogation room with the same hostile glare. After what seemed like a minute, Harnett said, "What message?"

"The weird phone message? Brenna talked to Captain Milsevic a week ago, right after it happened."

Harnett's face was as unreadable as a shark's.

"The weird one, with the song lyric in it?" Christensen prompted.

"First I've heard of it," Harnett said.

Christensen felt himself flush. Milsevic hadn't told the Harnetts. "I'm pretty sure Brenna asked Milsevic to let you know about it. She wanted to make sure you and your wife knew what had happened."

"A weird phone message," Harnett said.

"Right. Who knows what it might be, but it gave us the creeps and we thought you should know."

"So, I'm supposed to thank you?"

"No. No," Christensen said. "Look, we were just trying to make sure you knew, and I'm a little concerned you weren't told. It may be nothing. God knows there's cranks out there. Everything else aside, we thought you guys should know. Brenna just assumed, with you and Milsevic being so tight, that he'd keep you in the loop. Just in case."

"Haven't talked to him in a few days," Harnett said.

"And he didn't mention we got this call?"

"Already told you that. What song?"

Christensen felt for footing. The conversation's unexpected turn had taken him down a slippery slope. He was scrambling for an appropriate answer when Harnett repeated the question. This time his voice had an edge.

"The Springsteen lyric," Christensen said. " 'Tunnel of Love.' Somebody called us and played it from a tape."

"That's it? They say anything?"

Christensen shook his head. "That's why it was so, you know . . . Just the recording, the same verse as in that letter to Teresa. So Brenna called it in and turned the whole thing over to Milsevic. There's a report on file somewhere."

Christensen heard soft footsteps in the hallway behind him. Harnett noticed them, too. They turned and saw Teresa walking toward them, uncertain eyes focused on the startling scene in the vending area. She was moving awkwardly, trying to hurry.

"She got this call when?" Harnett said.

Christensen told him the date. Harnett smiled, but it wasn't friendly. "A day or so after the hearing, is what you're telling me?"

Christensen knew where this was going, felt himself sliding into a conversation that should never occur.

"So let's get this straight," Harnett said, his voice rising. "Eight years your little retard's inside, no problem. No threats. No stalking. Nobody gets hurt."

Behind him, Christensen heard the rustle of Teresa's clothes as she approached. He'd let curiosity lure him down the hall, and now he was trapped. "Whoa—"

"Then a few days after you people spring him—"

"I should go, because—"

"Tell me something, buddy. You a rocket scientist?"

"—this is something we shouldn't try to—"

"Don't matter. 'Cause you really don't gotta be a goddamn rocket scientist to figure this one. But I'm gonna connect the dots for you anyway. We've got some bitch lawyer who took it in the teeth eight years ago who'll do anything to win this thing. We got a judge lets her spring her little cretin because of some fucking technicality. We got—"

"Technicality?" Christensen felt his anger rise. "Since when are we discounting DNA?"

Teresa was beside them now, refusing to look into Christensen's eyes. Her husband loomed over them both. Teresa touched David's arm, but he shook off the gesture.

"We got a freak with a hard-on for anything with tits, and he worms his way out of prison through some bullshit loophole. And suddenly, go figure, we got a psychostalker who likes Springsteen. Hmm." Harnett's eyes bulged as he tapped a finger on the side of his head. "Let me think. Who could have made that phone call?"

Christensen took a step back, hoping to defuse the situation.

Harnett stepped forward. "Any guesses?" he said, practically shouting now.

"David, don't," Teresa said. Her voice was sharp as she pushed herself between them. "Just back off, OK?"

David Harnett's eyes never left Christensen's. He moved his wife out of the way with a slow sweep of his arm, his size and strength making the move seem almost gentle. "What is it about this situation you people don't understand?"

Christensen took another step back, almost out of the vending area. Harnett clenched and unclenched his fists, which seemed to pump him even larger.

Christensen looked directly at Teresa, trying to reconnect. "I'm sorry this happened," he said. "Really."

Teresa glared, then stepped between the two men again, facing her husband. In her stance Christensen saw proof of her police training. She barked, "David, back off," and her voice left no room for discussion. It worked.

Harnett blinked, then looked his wife in the eyes.

"Let's just go," she said. "It's not worth it."

Christensen took advantage of the moment and stepped into the hall, finally out of the small room. He was halfway to his office door when he heard Teresa's question echo down the corridor: "What phone call?"

14

Christensen aimed the remote and hit the Mute button.
Myron Levin's mouth continued to move, but Channel 2's
courthouse reporter went suddenly, blessedly silent. Brenna elbowed him from her side of the bed, hard enough to
make him wheeze.

"Don't!" she said, grabbing for the control. She'd been
brushing her teeth when Levin's segment came on. She
left the sink in midstroke, and her lips were rimmed with
Crest.

"Bren, I can feel you getting tense. Or, more tense. You
don't need the aggravation."

Brenna gave Levin back his voice.

"—trouble finding even a single resident of Teresa Harnett's Morningside neighborhood who hasn't taken extra
precautions in the wake of the controversial ruling in the
DellaVecchio case. They definitely have strong opinions
about what should happen at the final hearing and—"

"Myron's such an ass," Brenna said, wiping her mouth
on a hand towel. "He's just hysterical."

"You think this is funny?"

"I didn't say funny. I said hysterical."

True enough, Christensen thought. For nearly two
weeks now, Levin had been working himself into a righ-
teous froth in a series of grave reports for the evening
news. Working every conceivable angle of the story, he'd
revisited the crime scene and replayed key testimony from
the original trial. He'd interviewed the fearful residents of
Lawrenceville about the unleashed monster in their midst,
and now was doing the same with people who lived in
Morningside, where Teresa Harnett was attacked and still
lived. Night after night, Levin had treated viewers to a
somber parade of legal scholars, judicial analysts, skep-

tical forensic experts, and carefully orchestrated leaks from the district attorney's office. Boiled down to its essence, his central message seemed clear: Run for your lives!

"Hysterical," Christensen repeated. "Perfect."

Brenna's face suddenly filled the screen. It was a grab shot from an old videotape. Her eyes were half closed, and her mouth was frozen in a sneer.

"You look like you're about to spit," Christensen said.

"Shh."

"Curiously, Brenna Kennedy, Mr. DellaVecchio's defense attorney, did not return phone calls earlier today," Levin droned from off screen.

"Like I've got nothing better to do, you pompous son-of-a—"

"So it's hard to say how the Scarecrow camp is reacting to the almost vigilante atmosphere building among fearful residents such as these. But as you know, Kennedy makes no apologies for springing the man she claims was unjustly convicted of the brutal attack on the former Pittsburgh police officer. She's still pushing hard to permanently overturn the conviction."

Brenna's face blinked off and Levin was back, looking like a toupeed bulldog. He was standing in the obscene glow of klieg lights along a darkened street, pumping up for a big finish. The word *Morningside* was superimposed across the bottom of the screen. The TV blinked again and Levin was suddenly inside a frame, talking to a square-jawed ten o'clock news anchor.

"Sounds like prison might be the safest place for Mr. DellaVecchio," the anchor said.

Levin heaved a synthetic laugh, then arranged his features into his best but-seriously-folks face. "I can tell you this, Buck: I spoke to a longtime resident of this working-class community this afternoon. He asked not to be identified, but he said he remembers watching his neighbor,

Teresa Harnett, wheeled into a waiting ambulance eight years ago, her skull shattered, clinging to life. This gentleman said if the Scarecrow ever visits Morningside, he'd be waiting with a group of like-minded citizens. And let me assure you he's not with the Welcome Wagon."

"For Chrissakes," Brenna said. "This is fucking *absurd.*"

Christensen cocked his head toward the kids' bedrooms down the hall. "Shh. They were still awake fifteen minutes ago."

Anchor Buck nodded his head, then turned to face the camera. "Thanks, Myron. The stadium-site traffic controversy is back in the news—"

This time, Brenna zapped the TV. Anchor Buck disappeared in a flash, silenced, reduced to a bright blue dot at the center of the screen. Christensen watched it fade, dimming the room. The only light came from the open bathroom door, since the streetlight beyond the open miniblind was still broken.

"Why doesn't Levin just organize the mob himself?" Brenna said. "Pass out torches with the station's logo. Be a great promotion."

Christensen reached over and tried to massage the tight muscles at the base of her neck. If his hands had been electrified, she couldn't have recoiled any more violently.

"They're getting to you," he said.

"Damn right they are."

"You never get rattled, Bren. Why now?"

"The world's full of creeps, you know that?" She threw back the comforter and stood up. "I just get tired of dealing with them sometimes. I feel like I'm surrounded."

"Define creep," he said.

She wrapped her arms around herself, suddenly cold in the loose T-shirt she wore to bed. "Idiots like Levin. Dagnolo. Milsevic. David Harnett. Oily bastards, every one of them. Not a person in this whole fucking mess who isn't a creep."

"Thank heavens DellaVecchio's so lovable," he said.

Brenna stomped toward the bathroom to finish brushing her teeth, slamming the door behind her.

"That was a joke, Bren," he shouted.

She opened the door again, leaned against the frame. "I know he's a shit. God, this case, my life, would be so much easier if he was the least bit sympathetic. It's like defending Hitler."

Christensen shook his head. "Hitler had better PR, and a loyal following. DellaVecchio just has you. But you knew all that from the start, and you took it on anyway."

"Because it was right," she said.

"Don't lose sight of that, Bren. I haven't. It's one of the reasons I love you."

She turned back to the sink. Still agitated.

"Did something happen today?" he asked.

Her answer was lost in a rush of water and furious oral hygiene. Christensen snapped on the reading lamp beside his bed. He angled it to keep Brenna's side of the bed dark. The alarm clock read 10:22, late, because he knew she'd be up earlier than usual as DellaVecchio's hearing date approached.

Brenna stepped out. Her silhouette showed through the thin T-shirt, her body's Nautilized lines defined by the bathroom light. She was forty-seven, but at times she looked fifteen years younger. This was one of those times.

She snapped off the bathroom light. "Something did happen," she said, crossing the room and sliding back under the comforter. "Couple things, actually, going back maybe a week or so. You know that phone message we got?"

Christensen's face flushed. "You got another one," he said. Not a question. He knew from the way she avoided his eyes.

She held up two fingers.

They were back, suddenly, at the precipice, staring down at an issue that nearly destroyed their blended family once before.

"When did you plan to tell me?" he said.

A tiny red dot suddenly wavered across the bed's headboard. What was that?

"I just wasn't sure if it was anything to wor—"

Feathers leapt from the pillow near Brenna's left ear. Her mouth was open, the words still hanging between them, but the moment's soundtrack seemed suddenly, slightly off. There'd been a tiny, distant *pop!*, and a nearby *whuff!* At the same time, the headboard shuddered.

"—ry about," Brenna said. In an instant, her face transformed, a mixture of confusion and indistinct pain.

"Bren?"

She lifted her hand to her left ear. Blood. It was seeping from a three-inch cut that scored the side of her head, just above the ear, matting her hair to her scalp. Brenna pulled her hand away and looked at her red fingertips.

"I'm—" she said. "Jim?"

Nothing made sense. They looked at each other, then at the bedroom window. A tiny, crystalline hole had blossomed in one of the panes. "The floor!" was all Christensen could manage as he shoved Brenna off her side of the bed. He rolled off his own side just as the window popped again, saw the headboard's golden oak splinter where Brenna's head had been a split second before. Christensen checked the window again before he crawled underneath the bed. A second hole punctuated the pane, right next to the first.

Brenna was on her knees on the floor, staring down at nothing, reaching again to the left side of her head.

Christensen belly-crawled under the bed and grabbed her elbow. "Under here!"

She turned and looked at him. Fear had replaced the

confusion on her face. Not panic, but then she couldn't see what Christensen saw as she turned her head. Her left ear and the left side of her face were cross-hatched with blood, which was coming faster now. It ran down the forearm she was using to prop up her head.

"It burns," she said. "What's happening?"

Still talking, Christensen thought. A good sign. He pulled hard on her arm and she wriggled under the bed frame. Then, over the sound of their breathing, a fragile voice from the hall.

"Mom?"

"Taylor, don't open the door!" Christensen shouted. "Stay where you are!"

"What's going on?" he asked.

"Just stay where you are!"

In the confusion, the portable phone had fallen from the night table on Christensen's side of the bed. He reached for it and pulled it underneath along with a corner of the down comforter that lay crumpled beside it. Brenna was crying now, saying "It burns" over and over. He wiped her face with the comforter, told her to press it hard against the wound. "You're OK, Bren," he said. "Press hard, though."

He dialed 911, counting the rings.

Again, from the hall: "Mom? Jim?"

Her son's voice seemed to bring Brenna back from the edge of shock. "Taylor, just wait, OK?" she said. "Don't move, honey. Don't open the door."

"Pittsburgh Police," a dispatcher answered. "Is this an emergency?"

"Shooting," Christensen said.

"Mom?"

"732 Howe. Shadyside." Christensen heard the dispatcher's fingers flying over a keyboard.

"Are you hurt, sir?"

"No, but—"

"Anyone else?"

"One person. She's hurt. Please hurry."

"Mom?"

"We're on the way, sir. What's your name?"

"Jim Christensen."

"House or apartment?"

"Our house."

"Is there still shooting going on?"

"No. No. I don't think so. Two shots right together, from outside."

"So the gun isn't in the house?"

"No."

More typing. Then, to her rolling unit, the dispatcher barked, "Negative on the gun. Repeat. No gun in the house." To Christensen, she said, "How many people in the house? This is important, sir. How many people?"

"Four. Two adults, two kids. Everybody's in the up- stairs bedrooms."

"A two-story house?"

"Three. We're on the second floor."

"Can you get downstairs?"

"Yes." To Brenna, Christensen said, "Press harder."

"Is the front door locked, sir?"

"Yes."

"If you can get safely downstairs, then, I want you to unlock that door. We're probably about two minutes away. Got that?"

"Unlock the door," he repeated.

"But not if you're still in any danger. Do you feel like you're still in danger, sir?"

"I'll meet them downstairs," Christensen said as he backed out from under the bed. "We need a paramedic."

"On the way. Just hang tight."

Christensen laid the phone next to Brenna, leaving the line open, and crawled across the floor to the window. He pressed himself against the inside wall and stood up, twisting the miniblind rod until the louvers pinched shut. He crossed the room and opened the bedroom door.

Taylor stood alone in the dark second-floor hallway, his face reflecting his terror. Christensen picked the boy up before he could look into the bedroom. He carried him past the room where Annie still slept, down the creaking wooden stairs, saying "Everything's OK, buddy, everything's OK," and wishing it were true.

15

"There."

Christensen pointed to the splintered oak headboard about a foot above the mattress on Brenna's side. Milsevic moved closer, and at the same time popped something into his mouth. He noticed Christensen watching him and held out a foil-backed tray of plastic bubbles.

"Nicorette?" he said.

Christensen shook his head. Milsevic knelt down near the bullet hole and chewed his gum. A female detective named Heffentreyer already had excavated the lead-gray blob for the crime lab, leaving behind only a pulpy scar.

"Jesus," Milsevic said. "We got bad juju here. Definitely not a stray bullet. What time did you say this was?"

"Just before ten-thirty," Christensen said. "The detective already took our statements, you know. The paramedics are done with Brenna. It's after midnight and I'd like to get things calmed down around here."

"Right. Sorry," Milsevic said, glancing at the punctured window across the room. His eyes traced the bullet's path to the headboard, then he added another piece of nicotine gum to the wad in his mouth.

"That's not exactly a therapeutic dose," Christensen said. "You're chain chewing."

"We've all got vices," Milsevic said. "What's yours?"

Christensen ignored the question and glanced at his watch. The police captain offered a sympathetic smile.

"I'm not crazy about being out this late either. My cell phone went off and I thought, 'What the hell?' But with everything going on lately, the chief just wanted some administrative oversight on this one. So here I am. I'll be out of your way ASAP."

For the first time Christensen could recall, Milsevic

wasn't impeccably dressed. Dark-blue turtleneck under a distressed leather jacket. Black pants. No socks. Soft leather moccasins that looked more like bedroom slippers. He'd arrived fifteen minutes earlier looking like a man who'd been rousted from bed and dressed in the dark.

"Real quick, I need you to go over something again." Milsevic crossed the room to the window and twirled the miniblind rod until the louvers were fully open. "Detective Heffentreyer told me this blind was closed when she arrived, but she said you told her it was open when the shots were fired. Is that correct?"

"Correct."

"Who closed it?"

"I did."

"When?"

"After I called 911."

"But before you ran downstairs to let the patrol officers in?"

"Right."

"Why?"

Over Milsevic's shoulder, Christensen could see the crime scene photographer on the roof of the apartment building across the street. His camera's blue flash lit Heffentreyer and a uniformed officer as they stood behind a brick façade that rose several feet above the building's roof line. Milsevic twisted the rod and the blind closed, obliterating Christensen's view of what was happening.

"What's the big mystery?" Christensen said. "It was the only way to see into the room, and I wanted to shut it. As long as that blind was open, we were sitting ducks."

"Pretty smart. So you just walked over and closed it?"

"We were under the bed at that point. I'd called 911 and needed to get downstairs to let the patrol officers in. I crawled over to the wall and stood up next to the window and closed the blind. That's all. I don't get what you're after."

Milsevic shifted his cud into one cheek and smiled. "Just trying to tie up some loose ends, is all. Detective training 101."

"Well, look, can we do the rest of that tomorrow? I've got two kids here that are confused as hell, and Brenna's pretty rattled. I need to spend some time with them."

"Of course," Milsevic said, "but try to understand our position." He pointed to the window. "There's somebody out there with a gun, looks like a nine-millimeter from the size of the hole. They've obviously got bad intentions. Anybody dies, 'specially somebody high-profile, we look bad."

"Even if it's the woman who unleashed the Scarecrow?" Christensen said. "That might get you elected mayor in this town."

Milsevic smiled. "I don't care if it's Perry Damn Mason, know what I'm saying? So just bear with us while we make sure everything's kosher."

"Just keep an open mind about it," Christensen said. "That's all I ask."

Milsevic stood up. "What's that supposed to mean?"

"Don't even pretend DellaVecchio's not on your short list on this, OK. He's out. He's a notorious loose cannon. I've even had people tell me they think he's got a grudge against Brenna. I'm guessing nothing would make you people happier than to prove he was involved, and if he is, I hope you nail his hide to the wall. But if he isn't— and be honest, shooting's not his style—this whole thing's even scarier."

The bedroom door creaked slowly open. Brenna stepped into the room, a heavy patch of gauze covering her left ear and much of the left side of her head. Taylor was clinging to her hand, as he had been for the last ninety minutes. The paramedics were still stitching her scalp when Milsevic showed up, so Brenna hadn't yet seen him.

"What's he doing here?" she asked.

Christensen shrugged. "We were just talking about that. He wanted to see the bedroom."

"I'm here because I was asked to be here," Milsevic said. "I don't like it any more than you. But let us do our job. This *is* freaky shit—pardon my French, young man—and we take that very seriously, OK?"

"Really?" Brenna said.

"Really."

Brenna's left eye twitched, a stress reaction. "Then let me ask you something, Captain. Didn't you promise me you'd tell the Harnetts about that phone message I got two weeks ago?"

The color flowed from Milsevic's face, but he recovered quickly. "I don't follow you," he said, moving his gum from one cheek to the other.

"Jim talked to David Harnett. You never told them." Brenna nodded toward the window. "I get a threatening phone call from somebody who knows a fairly obscure detail about the attack on Harnett's wife, and you don't think that's important enough to tell them?"

"Since when do we broadcast details of an ongoing investigation?" Milsevic said.

Brenna crossed the room, closing the gap between her and Milsevic. Taylor trailed behind his mother, holding tight to the belt of her robe. "Not even to a potential victim? Not even to personal friends who might be in danger?"

Milsevic didn't back down. "So I guess this all becomes part of your conspiracy theory, right? All these sleazy cops trying to railroad your client again. Well I got news for you, lady. My ass is on the line here, too."

"And you're just here to make sure it's covered, aren't you?"

Milsevic stepped away, actually turned around to compose himself. When he turned back, he looked straight at Brenna. "I won't be baited, but I will tell you this: Our minds are very open at this point. Mine is, at least. You've come up with this DNA evidence, and that's a tough thing to get around. We'll see if it holds up. But you've been bitching for years that the original investigation was too narrow. Well, OK. Maybe it was. Maybe you're not the only one who could've done better on the first go-round."

Milsevic and Brenna glared at one another.

"What are you saying, Captain?" she said at last.

"You got a second chance to do your job right, Ms. Kennedy. Just give me the same chance."

Brenna's eyes softened. "But why didn't you mention the phone call to the Harnetts?"

"I have my reasons."

The comment seemed weighted, and it brought the conversation to a dead stop. Milsevic looked suddenly self-conscious, as if he'd said more than he intended. "I'm gonna get out of your way now," he said. "I know you've had a long night. Try to get some sleep."

He cocked a thumb over his shoulder, toward the bedroom window. Beyond the closed blinds, another blue flash tore the darkness across the street. "We'll make sure you're informed of any significant developments. I'll let myself out."

Brenna sat on the bed as soon as Milsevic left the room. She reached for her favorite goose-down pillow, but came up empty. It was on its way to the crime lab, along with the headboard slug and the one that had creased her skull, pierced the pillow, and ended up on the floor under the bed like a dropped M&M. Taylor sat beside her, looking to Christensen for reassurance. Christensen looked to Brenna for the same, but she looked away.

"Bren, you can walk away from all this," he said.

She shook her head. "Like it or not, I'm in the middle of it."

He knelt at the edge of the bed. "No, Bren, *we're* in the middle of it. Again."

"I know," she said.

Christensen waited for a sign, some expression or words that suggested remorse at having brought her family to the edge of tragedy. What Brenna said, though, was, "What do you think Milsevic's up to?"

Annie burst through the bedroom door, energized after pestering the cops and paramedics downstairs for the past ninety minutes. The alarm clock distracted her. "12:48! Wait till I tell Julie. This is the coolest night ever."

Then Annie's eyes found the headboard of the bed. Her unshakable bravado crumbled, if only for a moment, as she stared open-mouthed at the shattered wood. Tonight, reassurances wouldn't be enough. He needed to focus on both kids during the next twenty-four hours, to give them the tools they needed to understand and deal with the trauma.

"This was a pretty scary night, huh, guys?"

Taylor nodded. Annie shrugged.

"What say we go downstairs to make some hot chocolate before we all go back to bed? I'm buying."

"Marshmallows?" Annie said.

Christensen nodded. "Taylor? You in?"

The boy shook his head.

"It's OK if you want to stay here with your mom. I'll bring it up to you."

"Then marshmallows for me, too," Taylor said.

"Check. Back in a jiffy," Christensen said. "Want one, Bren? You should be part of this."

She offered a distracted nod.

"Four HoChos," Christensen said, pretending to scribble on an order pad. "I'll bring them up and we can all sit here in bed and talk."

Annie bolted through the bedroom door and down the stairs. Christensen heard her drop to the landing with a thud, then jump the remaining six steps to the first floor. She was already rattling pans downstairs before he was even through the door. Behind him, he heard Taylor's melancholy voice.

"Mom?"

He turned and saw the boy lay his head in Brenna's lap, facing up into his mother's eyes. She stroked his hair, tucking a curled red strand behind his ear. Christensen moved on down the hall, but stopped at the top of the stairs to listen for Taylor's follow-up. It came in a voice wavering with uncertainty and need: "If anything happens to you, and you guys aren't married, can I still live with Jim?"

16

Sleep? Not a chance. Christensen felt like a man on a knife's edge. He'd paced until dawn, thinking, rethinking, wondering if he'd done the right thing by keeping Teresa's secret. He was certain at times that he'd had no choice, and just as certain at times that he'd risked everything, professionally and personally, by keeping his mouth shut.

At one point he dozed and dreamed. He was running toward a thin blue line, chasing a disappearing horizon as darkness overtook him. His lungs burned. His legs ached. But he pushed on, miles to go, exhausted by both the distance and the sudden, aching pressure of responsibility. He looked back for Molly, for Brenna. Gone. Both gone. He dared not stop. No one left to carry on. Just him, and so he ran.

Finally, at 8 A.M., he woke Brenna with a kiss. "I haven't told you everything either," he said.

He explained how Teresa had come to him for help two weeks before, and why he'd kept that from her until now. "I did the right thing, Bren, or what I thought was the right thing, for everybody involved. I couldn't put any of us in that situation, or put myself between her and you." He touched the gauze bandage taped to the side of her head. "Now I'm starting to wonder if maybe we're all on the same side, if there's a common enemy none of us understand."

When he was done, Brenna touched his face, then pulled him into a long and resolute hug. For a moment, he sensed her genuine appreciation for his dilemma. Then she said, "If Teresa's backing off her story, then Dagnolo better not try—"

He pulled away, startled that her tactical mind already

was in overdrive. "Bren, please. Don't push it. There's too much at stake. This has to stay between us."

"But—"

He walked to their bedroom door. "Just leave it alone, OK? I told you so you'd know, because of what happened last night. But what happens next isn't up to me, or you, or Dagnolo. It's up to Teresa. The next move is hers. Understood?"

Breakfast was a frosty affair. He persuaded Brenna to keep the still-sleeping kids home from school so they could all spend the day together. She also agreed to follow his lead in helping Taylor and Annie cope with last night's trauma. They took the phone off the hook after the third reporter's call, and by midmorning all four lay on their bellies on the floor of their living room, chins propped on their elbows. It was boys against girls in a therapeutic game of Pictionary, which Christensen saw as a way to give the kids an avenue for subconscious expression about the shooting without making them feel like lab rats.

Christensen rolled what could be his final roll of the die. A four.

"Showdown," Taylor said. "We get this one, we tie. We don't, we lose."

Annie menaced Taylor with the one-minute sand timer. "Ready, shrimpo?"

Christensen would interpret Taylor's drawing, guessing what the boy was trying to express. Taylor gripped his pencil, his face a study in concentration. He was to draw something from the least abstract of the categories, Person/Place/Animal, but he'd frowned deeply when he pulled his card. Whatever he was supposed to draw, the idea obviously confounded him. But now he was ready. He nodded at Christensen, his teammate, then looked at Annie.

"Flip it," he said.

The sand flowed. Taylor drew a dot not much bigger

than a pencil point, then turned the paper toward Christensen.

"That's it?" Christensen asked.

Taylor nodded.

"A period?" he tried.

Taylor shook his head, motioning with his hands to keep the guesses coming. "A flea? An atom? A grain of sand?"

Taylor checked the sand timer, then drew a large X over the dot. He set to work again, drawing a circle. Inside it, he added two dots for eyes, one for a nose, a line for a mouth.

"A face? Smiley face? Charlie Brown?"

Taylor waved him off, held up one finger for him to wait. With his pencil point, he began making tiny dots beneath the face's eyes. He left a tiny spray of them on both cheeks, then pushed the paper toward Christensen.

"Whiskers? Pimples? Zits?"

Taylor pulled the paper back to him and added a few more dots. These dots were darker, bridging the nose. The boy checked the timer again, then tapped the paper impatiently with his eraser.

"Eyes? Creature with fifty eyes? Alien?"

Taylor's face twisted in panic. He repeated his last clue, this time jabbing the face with his pencil point and leaving a few heavy dots and a couple of slight punctures. He added a crown of curly hair on top of the head as an afterthought, then checked the timer again. Ten seconds, tops.

"Acne? Skin disease? Chicken pox?"

Annie rolled her eyes at Brenna, who immediately stopped fingering her bandage. "Total losers," his daughter said.

Taylor's own face was a frustrated mess. He held up the paper and pointed his pencil at the angry dots across the face. Five seconds. Christensen tried once more.

"Warts?"

That put Taylor over the edge. He stabbed the face, obliterating it with holes the width of his pencil. Then, as the last of the sand drained into the bottom of the timer, he slashed the paper into confetti. Christensen glanced at Brenna, who shouted "Time!" with a bit too much satisfaction. She and Annie exchanged a high five.

"Ahhhh!" Taylor screamed. "Freckles!"

Christensen slapped his forehead. "Freckles! Oh, geez. Taylor, I'm sorry."

The boy rolled onto his back and covered his face with his hands. "Unbelievable! Jiii-im? Little dots on a face?"

"My fault," Christensen said, feigning deep remorse. "Should have gotten that. Really."

Annie stood up, did a victory dance. "Chicken pox!" she howled. "Skin disease!"

"All right already," Christensen said, folding up the board. "I'm a nincompoop."

"Warts!" Annie howled, high-fiving Brenna again. She held an index finger aloft, an unabashed in-your-face we're-number-one signal.

"What happened to your sportsmanship, Annie? You don't want us to feel bad, do you?"

"Girls rule, boys drool!" Annie shouted, swaggering up the stairs. The vanquished Taylor trailed her with his head down, muttering. Brenna picked up the lid to the Pictionary box.

"Warts?" She shook her head. "Oh, man."

Christensen watched the kids march up to the second floor, the ancient wooden stairs creaking with their weight.

"That worry you at all?" he asked. "How quickly and violently Taylor reacted? That's not like him at all."

Brenna leaned closer, punched him on the shoulder. "Baby," she said, "lighten up. I mean, skin disease? If you were on my team, I'd have strangled you. I appreciate your concern, but that little mental-health test cost you the game. You know how competitive Taylor is."

"So it doesn't worry you?"

"He's doing fine for the morning after his mom got hit by a bullet," she said.

"You told him what, exactly?"

"That it was a fluke. Somebody shot a gun outside, and the bullet went through our window. That's it. That's something he can understand. Give him some credit, Jim. Kids are resilient."

"He's still upset, though."

"He wasn't upset, then you could worry," she said, pointing to the bandage. "I mean, I look like a war casualty."

Christensen shrugged and stood up. "What you told him was great. Keeps it real low-key. But I want to keep an eye on him. He was right outside the door last night, listening to it all. That's probably just as traumatic as seeing, maybe more."

Brenna grabbed him from behind as he picked up the game board. He stood with the Pictionary board in one hand and turned toward her, maneuvering the game into an awkward one-handed hug. She kissed him softly. Twice.

"You're in a good mood," he said.

"I just . . . you know. I—I love the way you love my son."

Her phrasing told Christensen a lot.

"I'm sorry about this morning, too," she added. "Teresa Harnett put you in a tough spot, I know, and—"

The doorbell short-circuited the moment. Christensen held her as she tried to pull away, but she slipped from his arms and headed for the front door. The moment faded into a surge of alarm. The window miniblinds were all shut, but had he remembered the long window in the front door? Christensen charged after her.

"Don't go near the door! Let me get it, Bren. Please."

"There's still a patrol car out front," she called from the hall. "We've probably never been safer."

The doorbell rang again. Brenna had stopped short of the door. She waved him forward, and he scissored open the blind to peer out. A pair of ice-blue eyes peered back at him. He swallowed hard and mouthed "Dagnolo" to Brenna. "Somebody else, too," he said. "Can't see who."

She smiled. "Interesting twist."

Christensen slid the deadbolt and turned the knob, ushering in a blast of cold air. Brenna stepped into the doorway with him, wrapping her arms around herself as she did. Their visitors stood side by side. Dagnolo was on the right—tall, lean, more than six feet of prime cut in a somber navy-blue overcoat. The man beside him topped out at Dagnolo's shoulder, all chest and belly, a gritty, 5-foot-8 mound of hamburger wrapped in a standard-issue Pittsburgh Police Department topcoat. The Beelzebub beard along his boxy jaw made his face instantly familiar.

"Chief Kiger," Brenna said, ignoring the district attorney.

The chief nodded. "Heard there was a little excitement last night."

Kiger's eyes strayed to the side of Brenna's head. In the chilly silence that followed, Christensen imagined the reasons they were here. The four of them faced off in the doorway, adversaries separated now by only a few feet.

Finally, Dagnolo forced a smile. "We need to talk."

17

Dagnolo clearly intended to run the show. Christensen knew from the way the two men entered the house, the way they arranged themselves in the living room. The D.A. took the mission chair, the largest and most imperial seat in the room, and feigned civility with a tight-lipped and patronizing smile. Brenna settled on the left side of the couch and waited for Christensen to join her. Kiger sat on the only remaining seat, the brick hearth.

Christensen's mind reeled. Could he stand another odd chapter in the complicated history between himself and Dagnolo? When they first met, the district attorney wanted to prosecute him for disconnecting Molly's respirator. Christensen had decided to end his wife's life—or what was left of it following her car accident and months of what her doctors called a "persistent vegetative state"— to spare their daughters the prolonged agony promised by advanced medical science. He'd barred the intensive care unit door to frantic nurses and let Molly die quietly in his arms at a time when Dagnolo had decided to make mercy killing a noisy election-year issue.

They'd crossed paths again a year ago when, during art therapy research with second-stage Alzheimer's patient Floss Underhill, Christensen unraveled a cover-up involving the death of her three-year-old grandchild. The case had confounded Dagnolo for years, and its violent resolution exploded into national headlines because of the Underhill family's vast wealth and political prominence. Publicly, Dagnolo had acknowledged Christensen's key role in discovering the tragic truth of Chip Underhill's death. Privately, Dagnolo had called him a meddling asshole.

Now this.

"So," Christensen said, "I'm guessing you've spoken with Teresa."

Dagnolo and Kiger traded a quick look.

"She came to my office this morning, yes," Dagnolo said. He looked around the room, a vague, leisurely survey, never letting his eyes rest on anything or anyone. "So *everyone* here knows?"

Something electric passed from Brenna to Christensen. She then fixed Dagnolo with a glare that could melt steel. "Everyone," she said.

Had hearing about Brenna's phone calls convinced Teresa to confess her doubts to the D.A.? Word of last night's shooting? What had she told Dagnolo? And why was Kiger involved? Christensen wanted Dagnolo to fill in the gaps, so he waited.

"This matter obviously is of deep concern to me, to all of us, I think, in law enforcement in this city," Dagnolo said. "As you might expect, Mr. Christensen—or do you ivory-tower types still prefer Doctor?"

Christensen could smell Dagnolo's smug satisfaction. "Four years of college, four years of postgraduate work to get my Ph.D. in clinical psychology, a two-year internship . . ." He smiled. "Doctor's fine."

Dagnolo's arrogance faded, but not much. "As you might expect," he continued, "I have certain questions about how your little get-together with *my* witness came about. I'd like to hear your version, *Doctor* Christensen, before we advise Judge Reinhardt about this complica—"

"Look, J. D., you're in *my* house," Brenna said. "You came to talk, let's talk. But check your bullshit attitude at the door. And don't you fucking *dare* talk to Reinhardt without me there."

Christensen stood up. He met all three sets of eyes in turn. "Let's get a handle on this right now." He had their attention. "Let's just concede this is awkward as hell. Put yourselves in my shoes, opening that office door two weeks ago and finding her there, wanting to talk. I knew the implications. I knew she was putting this whole thing in jeopardy. But what was I supposed to do? I did what I thought was best for everybody."

Brenna turned away from Dagnolo, who shifted so that he faced Kiger. Only the police chief was watching him now, so Christensen appealed to him. He knew from personal experience that Kiger was an honorable man. His reputation for plain-spoken fairness wasn't just a public image.

"I agree," Kiger said in his sticky Memphis drawl. The words, so understated and soft, seemed to shift the balance of power in the room. "I think we should all just talk straight here. We all got questions about where this is headed now. Quicker we answer 'em the better." He nodded to Brenna. "We got a situation here. People gettin' phone calls, both you and Teresa. People gettin' hurt. Nobody wants that."

"Agreed," Dagnolo said.

Brenna hesitated, then said, "Fine, but no bullshit."

Nodding heads all around. And a giggle. Christensen spotted Annie and Taylor on the stair landing and motioned them back upstairs.

"Y'all go on then, sir," Kiger said when the kids were gone. "Tell us what happened."

Christensen took the seat beside Brenna again. Kiger and Dagnolo knew about Teresa's phone calls, so she'd probably confessed her doubts. So he told them everything he could remember about the day she approached him looking for help. He explained, too, how he'd seen Teresa and her husband in the Harmony testing unit, how he'd initiated a conversation then, how David Harnett reacted when he told him about the odd phone message left on their home answering machine.

When he was done, Kiger nodded. "Same thing Miz

Harnett told us. That's fine. Good to know we're all wor-kin' from the same page. Now, you're saying the Harnetts didn't know about that phone call you got?"

"Milsevic never told them," Christensen said. "That was the impression I got from the husband."

"David told you that?" Dagnolo said. "Or that's the impression you got?"

Christensen closed his eyes, trying to recall their tense hallway conversation. "He said it was the first he'd heard of it. Now, what happened, why they didn't get the message, I don't know."

Brenna sat forward, leaning toward Kiger. "You were in San Diego when I got the 'Tunnel of Love' call. Your secretary transferred me to Milsevic because he was han-dling that stuff while you were gone. Believe me, talking to him wasn't my idea. But we wanted to make sure the Harnetts knew about it."

Kiger waved her words away. "Captain Milsevic's a pro, Ms. Kennedy. He got somebody on it, right? Sent a patrol officer by? I saw the report. Same thing I'da done."

Brenna nodded. "The officer took a report. And the answering machine."

Kiger made a face, as if he'd smelled something rank. "That was pretty much worthless, far as information. Sounds like he uses pay phones, but that's no help. So we know there's a head case out there. We already knew that."

"We know of one, for sure," Dagnolo said. He was looking at his shoes, but everyone knew where the barb was aimed.

"Oh, eat shit, J. D.," Brenna said.

Kiger held up his hands, palms out, the plump fingers like pink baby dills. To Dagnolo: "Yep, sir, Della-Vecchio's loose. We got him on a short leash, but he's loose." To Brenna: "The guy you think set your boy up the last time? He's loose too, if he exists." To no one in particular: "Some people just like to mess with us, so we could be talkin' about some piece of dog doo none of us ever heard of. Somebody been readin' the papers and wanted to get in on the act. But nobody knows who it is just yet, so spare me the insinuatin'. Y'all clear on that?"

Kiger waited for affirmation, and got it from all three. He turned back to Christensen. "So, Miz Harnett told you she'd had some calls, too?"

Christensen nodded. "Two at that point, I think she said. I don't know about since then. We didn't talk dates." He repeated what Teresa had told him about the calls she'd received, about the caller once saying, "You never rose."

"She tell you what she remembered at that point?" Kiger asked.

"That the attacker's voice was different than the voice on the phone. Different than DellaVecchio's voice."

Kiger's face betrayed nothing.

"She said the caller *sounded* like DellaVecchio," Dagnolo said.

Christensen slid forward to the edge of the sofa. "But you're missing the point. For argument's sake let's say it *was* DellaVecchio's voice on the phone. That's not what's got her rattled. What she can't reconcile is that the voice on the phone, DellaVecchio's voice—whether it's him or not—isn't the same voice she remembers from the attack. It wasn't DellaVecchio's voice whispering in her ear that night. That's what's significant here. They're different voices."

"Different," Kiger said.

"Yes," Christensen said. "Different enough to raise doubts about her memories."

"Here we go," Dagnolo said. "Now we're leaving solid ground."

Christensen smiled. Here was his opening. "You're dealing with memories here, J. D., traumatic memories.

You were *never* on solid ground." He looked at each one in turn, including Brenna. "That's the dirty little secret about what you people do, isn't it? You all know memories are fragile things. They exist up here"—he pointed to his head—"in this gray blob of chemicals and electrical impulses. They're like wisps of smoke, but you still treat them like absolute truth. When it suits your needs, you all pretend people don't shape and reshape memories to make sense of traumas like this. But they do. Everyone does. Acknowledge the reality of it, you've got a big problem. The minute you stop treating memories like solid ground, you suspend the law of gravity."

Christensen sat back, struck by the uncomfortable silence. Brenna patted him on the thigh. Kiger recrossed his legs. Finally, Dagnolo cleared his throat.

"Mind if we stick to the issue here?" the D.A. said.

"Back to Teresa," Brenna said.

So much for changing the world. "Fine," Christensen said. "Forget the bigger issue. We'll just keep putting out fires."

Dagnolo granted absolution with a sovereign nod. "So, what you're saying is, after all this time, Teresa suddenly heard this guy's voice? Remember, she's lying there, her head caved in, probably unconscious. She could have been hearing the voice of God, for all we know. And she, what? Forgets that for eight years?"

"It does happen."

Dagnolo couldn't stifle his rising exasperation. "And then she remembers it, just like that? It pops right back into her head like a cork and suddenly she's in your office rethinking the whole story she's told from the beginning?" The district attorney shook his head. "I'm sorry. I've got serious questions about what's happened here."

"I can't help that. She came to me, remember?"

Dagnolo shook his head. "This changes nothing."

"Maybe," Christensen said. "Or it changes everything.

What's happened is that Teresa's got a puzzle piece that suddenly doesn't fit. It has her confused, she's trying to figure it out. Listen to her. You owe her that."

Brenna stood up suddenly and walked into the kitchen, returning a moment later with a kettle dangling from her index finger. "This may take a while, so I'm putting water on for tea," she said. "How many?"

"Thank you, ma'am," Kiger said. "Please."

"Two," Dagnolo said.

"Me too," Christensen said.

The three men sat in silence, listening to the water spill into the kettle and the *snik-snik-snik* of the starter on their gas stove. Brenna was back a moment later with an empty cup in her hand.

"Enough with the inquisition," she said. "How about you guys give a little?"

18

Dagnolo looked at the cup in Brenna's hand. His face couldn't have registered any more contempt if she'd asked for a urine sample. "Meaning what?" he asked.

"Meaning you're pumping Jim about what happened with Teresa, like he somehow needs to apologize for the fact that she came to him. He's been honest. He did the right thing. Now you give *us* something."

"Let's get something straight," the D.A. said. "We don't owe—"

"Fair enough," Kiger interrupted. "Tell me what you wanna know, Miz Kennedy. I'll answer you if I can."

Dagnolo's mouth hung open until he slowly winched it shut. But he recovered quickly. "I would remind you, Chief, that these investigations regarding the phone calls and the shooting incident are ongoing. We need to be very careful."

Kiger offered a patient, condescending smile. "Well, I'll just be real careful then." To Brenna: "Miz Kennedy?"

"I want to know if you're investigating DellaVecchio as a suspect in either the calls or the shooting."

Kiger laced the fingers of his hands together. "We are," he said.

Dagnolo shook his head in disgust. Kiger ignored him.

"If we didn't take a look at him, we'd be a few bricks shy of a load," the police chief said.

"You have reason to suspect him, or you haven't ruled him out?"

The police chief squinted at Brenna. "We got some questions we want answered. Until we get those sorted out, it's wide open."

"So you're not investigating DellaVecchio exclusively?"

"No."

"But you're not actively investigating anyone else," Brenna said.

"Didn't say that, ma'am."

"Who then?"

"Nice try." Kiger smiled, but there was no hostility in it. "We're tryin' to keep an open mind, is all. That's a promise."

Christensen sensed Brenna's agitation level rising. "Why is he a suspect, though?" she challenged. "You've got no idea where those calls are coming from."

She turned to Dagnolo, who was studying his perfectly manicured fingernails. "You're watching that bracelet like a hawk to make sure he's tucked in at night, and you've probably got someone watching him during the day. My guess is if Carmen was pulling any of this, you'd have him back inside already."

She turned back to Kiger. "So why is he a suspect? What questions need to be answered? Maybe I can help."

Kiger rubbed the end of his nose, watching her, evaluating the risk of talking more. "All right, here's why we got questions. Maybe a half dozen times since he's been out, your boy's got out of his daddy's house without anybody noticing. Early evening, usually. Manpower being what it is, we got somebody on the front door, but nobody on the back. He disappears off the radar scope for hours at a time. Next time we see him, he's walking in the front door right about curfew."

"So what?" Brenna snapped. "He can come and go as he pleases between seven and eleven. You've read the judge's order. As long as he's back home by eleven, it's nobody's business."

Kiger spread his hands. "No question. And we're allowed to keep an eye on him if we want. We're just kinda curious where he's going is all, why he feels like he needs to sneak off."

He nodded to the bandage on Brenna's head. She seemed suddenly self-conscious.

"I'd think you'd wanna ask him about it too," Kiger said. "Been pushing that curfew every time he's done it. Rolls in right about eleven, slick as spit. He's smarter'n he looks."

Brenna reached over and took Christensen's hand. The obvious question was hers to ask, but would she?

"Was he out last night?" she said.

"Yes."

"And no one knew where he was."

"Nuh-uh."

Christensen watched Kiger's eyes. The police chief seemed to understand the power of what he'd said, so he let the possibility settle like a weight.

"That's just pathetic," Brenna said. "That's it? You can't find him, therefore he's a stalker? He must be out taking a shot at his own attorney? Gimme a break. The guy's been in jail for eight years. I'd go out, too."

"If that was all we—"

"Tell me, Chief, where's DellaVecchio going to get a gun in this town without somebody ratting him out?" Brenna asked. "He's still got a record, so he couldn't buy legally. His picture's on TV every day. He's the *Scarecrow*, for God's sake. The real-life bogeyman!"

"That's not all—"

"Besides," Brenna said, "those shots were fired about 10:30. How's he gonna get from Shadyside to Lawrenceville by eleven?"

"The 911 call came in at 10:22," Dagnolo corrected. "Not 10:30."

Kiger nodded. "Nine minutes from Shadyside to Lawrenceville that time of night if he makes the lights at Liberty and Penn. Eleven if he doesn't. We ran the route twice."

"He doesn't even have a car!" Brenna said.

"That's true," Kiger conceded.

"What then? The only way you'd be pushing this ridiculous idea—"

Brenna stopped herself as suddenly as if she'd been interrupted. Christensen sensed, too, that there was a card not yet played. Brenna studied the faces of Dagnolo and Kiger for clues, but Christensen knew she couldn't turn back.

"What else do you have?" she said. "Please don't play games."

Kiger pointed out the living-room window. "Shots were fired from the roof of that empty building," he said. "Crime lab folks guess it was a SIG-Sauer nine-millimeter, probably with some kinda sightin' scope."

"That's a $3,500 handgun even without the sight," Brenna said. "Where would Carmen get that kind of money?"

"Good question," Kiger said.

Christensen sat forward. There had to be some other reason they were focusing on DellaVecchio.

"Whoever did it was up there quite a while, maybe a couple different times before last night," Dagnolo said. "We found other evidence we need to check out. Some footprints, probably useless. No tread at all. Chewing gum. Main thing is he's a smoker. Camels. Unfiltered. The perch looked like an ashtray, maybe a half a dozen butts."

"Your boy DellaVecchio smokes like a refinery fire," Kiger added.

"Camels," Dagnolo said. "Unfiltered."

Christensen heard Brenna swallow, a harsh, dry sound. He watched her eyes, knowing how resilient she was in situations like this. He'd seen her recover from worse. "Him and a million teenagers," she said. "Ask any high-school kid. Joe Camel rules."

"Know any high-school kids who might take a shot at you?" Kiger asked.

"Besides, if they're Carmen's, how hard would it be to steal his ashtray and drop the butts in the right spot?"

Kiger smiled. "It's just something made us want some answers. So we're gonna take a look, have the lab run some tests, see if maybe our sniper left his DNA in the spit on those things."

"Or on the wall," Dagnolo added.

Christensen and Brenna turned at the same time. "The wall?" Brenna asked.

"The low wall around the roof," Dagnolo said, gesturing through the living-room window. "We figure he was there at least once before he took those shots, maybe more than that, watching . . . whatever. The perch is directly across from your bedroom window, as you know."

The D.A. looked suddenly uneasy. Brenna flushed. With her complexion, it was something she couldn't hide. *The miniblinds*, Christensen thought. The goddamn miniblinds.

"Looks like he liked what he saw, 'cause there's a stain," Kiger said. "If it's semen, we might have something solid. So we got the lab on hurry-up. This works out, we'll know for sure one way or the other if your boy was up there."

Brenna closed her eyes. "When?"

Kiger shrugged. "The lab folks push this to the front of the line, should only take a few days. We let 'em know the story. They know sooner's better'n later."

"We'd obviously like answers before the hearing," Dagnolo said. "I'm sure you understand. I might be willing to petition Reinhardt for a postponement if you're—"

"Worried?" Brenna said. "Not a chance."

From the kitchen, the low, steady rumble of boiling water erased Dagnolo's smug smile. He looked around, apparently confused by the sound. Brenna seized the moment.

"Tell you what, J. D.," she said. "If your evidence doesn't put DellaVecchio on that roof, if it's somebody else's DNA up there, I want a public statement from you clearing DellaVecchio of suspicion. And I want it before the hearing. You talk to Myron Levin pretty regularly. How about leaking something besides hysterical bullshit for a change? Agreed?"

The whistle rose in pitch. No one moved. How much of a gambler was Dagnolo?

"Agreed," the district attorney said. "It's not his DNA, I've got no problem with that." He winked at Kiger. "Now I've got a deal for you, Ms. Kennedy. Ready?"

Brenna nodded.

"If the genetic evidence we found up there puts DellaVecchio on that roof, you call it off, the whole thing," Dagnolo said. "You withdraw your motion to overturn his conviction in the Harnett attack and we leave things just as they are, with DellaVecchio in jail to finish whatever is left on his sentence. I'm sure Judge Reinhardt would understand your change of heart, all things considered. Plus, I file a second charge of attempted murder."

"Moot point," Brenna said. "You place Carmen on that roof, you'll file no matter what. So why should I withdraw—"

"Just hold on," Christensen said. "You're all forgetting somebody here: Teresa. She's the one who put all this in motion, but you're writing her completely out of the equation."

The four of them sat frozen to their seats as the pressure in the kettle rose. The whistle lost its softness, building into a harsh squeal. Christensen jumped up just as Kiger said, "I got an idea."

In the kitchen, Christensen twisted the stove dial and the squeal trailed off. He poured the hot water into the four mugs Brenna had left on the serving tray. He opened tea bags and dropped them into each mug, then filled a cream pitcher with milk. He pulled the bear-shaped squeeze bottle of honey from the cupboard and set it on the tray, then picked the whole thing up and headed back into the living room.

Everyone was watching him as he entered.

"What?" he said.

"The chief had an interesting idea," Brenna said.

Kiger took his time. He squeezed so much honey into his cup that Christensen thought it might overflow, then stirred it like a man in no hurry to speak. The police chief set his spoon in the saucer with a delicate *clink!* and took a wary sip, his pinkie extended like a cotillion chaperone. "Thanks," he said at last, then smiled at Christensen.

"What am I missing?" Christensen asked.

"Here's my idea," Kiger said. "Miz Harnett came to you. That tells me two things: one, something's got her pretty rattled, and two, for some reason she trusts you. God knows there's little enough of that with this bunch. She wants to talk to you, that's fine. Fact is, sir, we need her to remember this thing right. Nobody wins if she's got doubts. Nobody."

"No agenda?" Christensen asked. "Because I won't push her one way or the other."

"No agenda," Kiger replied. "We know you're plenty qualified to work with her, assuming you wanna do it."

Dagnolo didn't flinch—a grudging concession. Christensen watched the D.A. carefully before he committed. "Work with her toward what end?" he said.

Kiger looked first at Dagnolo, then at Brenna. "Wherever it leads," he said. "Miz Harnett started this ball rollin', let's see where she takes it. Let her work this out. We all stay out of it, 'less of course she comes up with something we need to know to bury this thing once and for all. She does that, then you and her tell us. All of us.

Whatever it is. No secrets. We'll help you with your corroboratin' if we can."

Christensen felt a hollowness in his stomach as he studied the three faces of this uneasy alliance. He could imagine any one of them pressuring him to reveal Teresa's confidences as she struggled to rebuild her most traumatic memories. Especially Brenna.

"Let's clarify one thing," he said. "I don't want any misunderstandings. Nobody here is going to put me in the position of betraying her trust, is that right?"

"You got my word," Kiger said. "We all agreed on that?"

"Fine," Dagnolo said.

Brenna nodded.

"Nobody here wants to be in this spot, but here we are," Kiger said. "So let's make this work."

Christensen looked at each one in turn, reassured by their nodding assent. His resistance evaporated.

"I have a counseling office in Oakland." He heard the uncertainty in his voice, and was sure the others heard it, too. "Have her call me there tomorrow."

"I'll do that," Kiger said.

Brenna squeezed his hand. "Baby, we're on your turf now."

19

Slushy rain was falling from a steel sky over Oakland. Christensen watched it puddling in the parking lot beneath the second-floor window of his private counseling office. Pitt students trudging between classes dodged the pools, leaping from one high spot in the uneven pavement to the next like frogs among lily pads. On days like this, he could think of no colder place than Pittsburgh.

"I'm starving."

He turned toward his desk, where his secretary's voice pleaded from the phone's speaker. His watch read 12:18, nearly twenty minutes after Dagnolo had told him to expect Teresa Harnett. He picked up the handset.

"Thought you were gone to lunch already, Lynn. Sorry."

"I wasn't sure how to read the schedule for today. What's with the big X through the next two hours? Somebody coming in or what? There's no name, just the X."

"Didn't mean to confuse things. I do have someone coming in, but not a regular client. Don't wait. Please. Take a couple hours if you want. Just set the machine to pick up before you go."

"Lunch until two-thirty? Really?"

"For today, anyway."

"What's the catch?"

"Just bring me back a salad or something. Oil and vinegar. And a Perrier. I can get that down before . . ."

"Colleen Donegan at three."

"Plenty of time. That's it."

"You know, you keep eating like that, you're gonna die. How about a foot-long from Dirty O's?"

He thought about it—the crisp snap of the first all-beef bite, the pungent brown mustard, the sweet onions. If running five miles every other day had an upside, it was moments like this. "You little temptress. Go with an O's, mustard and onions. And a Coke. Got any Altoids out there?"

"Fresh box. All you want. You can give me the money when I get back."

Christensen stepped back to the window and watched as the white blob of Lynn's overstuffed ski jacket moved out the building's front entrance. She'd pulled her white knit cap low over her ears, and from where Christensen stood she looked like the Michelin Man. At the opposite end of the parking lot, a high-end black sport-utility splashed into a spot against the far wall. Christensen could see the distinctive three-pointed Mercedes-Benz star on the front grille.

The Mercedes's driver opened the door as Lynn passed, and Christensen was surprised to see Teresa Harnett step out in a long, elegant dark-wool coat. He'd pegged her as a Ford Taurus, maybe some midline Mercury. Lynn seemed surprised, too, to find herself face-to-face with the city's most recognizable crime victim. His secretary raised her hand in greeting, then seemed to reconsider. She hurried off without a follow-through.

Christensen heard the *chirp!* of an alarm as Teresa locked the car with her remote key. Two minutes later, the elevator door slid open. Christensen met her in the hall, and she offered him a wary smile. He extended his hand, and she took it in her strong grip.

"The stairs are a little quicker," he said. "Trees go up faster than this thing."

She stepped forward with her uneven gait. "Elevator's easier for me."

"Of course," he said. "I'm sorry."

"Don't be. About that, anyway."

He hung her jacket on the coat rack, then followed her through the waiting area and into his office. The first time, they'd talked in his utilitarian university office five blocks away. It was like hearing confession at the Department of Motor Vehicles. Now that she was here, he wondered how Teresa might react to a space he'd designed specifically to dilute tension and encourage trust. With some difficulty, she eased into the wing chair at the center of the office's sitting area and studied the room—the ficus tree near the window, the inflatable Wham-It stress-relief toy on the coffee table, the gentle pastel walls, the impressionistic landscape lithographs.

"Design by Prozac," she said.

Christensen laughed. "We'll be a little more comfortable than last time, anyway."

"If we can stay awake."

This was a formidable woman, probably with some psychological training of her own. She'd initiated this, but he still expected her to be skeptical about working with a psychologist. It was a cop thing. Christensen had counseled a few of them, mostly in the aftermath of officer-involved shootings. Teresa probably would rather have her teeth drilled without Novocain than talk to him about the things that scared her most. To do that was to lose control. To a cop, control was everything. And yet, here she was. This was her choice. There was a storm raging behind those uneven eyes, Christensen knew, and Teresa wouldn't be here if there were any way she could ride it out alone. Something had her scared.

"We can go somewhere else. Your call," Christensen said, ceding control where he could. "Wherever you'd like."

"Fiji's nice."

Christensen assessed her answer, then clapped his hands together. "Fiji it is, then!" He followed an idea across the room to the stereo cabinet and ran his finger along a shelf of compact discs. "Check this out," he said, pulling one. "*Ocean Moods.*"

He slid the CD into the machine, hit the Play button, and began to read from the liner notes. " 'Experience the wonderful stereo effects of long, rolling waves breaking on great stretches of sandy beach. Sixty minutes of pleasurable listening to the dynamic sounds of the sea.' " The low rumble of a breaking wave began in the speakers on the left side of the office, then rolled across the room to the speakers on the right.

Teresa laughed, and her facial features seemed to fall out of order. Rebuilding them into a natural expression took conscious effort and an uncomfortably long time, or so it seemed to Christensen.

"That what you're looking for?" he asked.

She smiled, a more cautious reaction. "Fiji would be better."

Christensen grabbed two bottles of Avalon water from the small refrigerator and set them on the coffee table between them, then sat in the chair across from her. He folded his hands in his lap. "Tell me why."

Teresa's face turned serious. Or was she pretending to look serious?

"OK, you got me," she said. "I hate my father. Wow, you're fast."

Christensen twisted the cap from his bottle. She leaned forward and did the same, struggling a bit, taking a delicate sip when the cap was finally loose. Swallowing for her seemed a deliberate process.

"Let's try this, then," Christensen said. "Tell me what changed your mind about going to Dagnolo."

She ran a finger around the bottle's plastic rim, avoiding his eyes. "What we talked about before, the doubts . . . I've tried everything I can to sort this out on my own. I can't. And I couldn't get back up on that stand next week and tell the same story when I know . . . when I'm not sure. I had no choice but to tell him and Kiger what was going on. Plus, the calls, then the shooting . . ."

"And here you are," Christensen said. "Dagnolo's more reasonable than I gave him credit for."

"Oh no, he went berserk," she added. "You should understand that. But he knew at that point his case was already in the toilet. He still wants me to testify, but cooperating with you was his only chance, his only choice. Or at least the only choice I gave him."

Teresa smoothed her dark hair down over her lower jaw, obscuring the subtle scars there. "I'll tell you this much right now. If David finds out I'm talking to you, he's gonna shit major bricks."

"Your husband?" Christensen conjured an image of bulk muscle. "He doesn't know about this?"

"Chief Kiger asked me not to tell him, to keep a tight lid on the whole thing. I told David I was going to my sister's in Clairton this afternoon. Had to get her to cover for me. It feels a little weird, to tell the truth."

Too weird, Christensen thought. "Any idea why? I mean, we're here with everybody's consent. There's nothing to hide. I'd think the chief would want him on board, as supportive as he's been all these years."

Teresa nodded. Christensen thought he saw a tear pooling in the corner of her right eye, but she blinked and it was gone. "He's been right there with me, you know, since the beginning. Even when I didn't know who I was, who he was. He was just some total stranger hanging around the ICU when I came to. For weeks, months. Holding my hand. Talking to me. Always there, talking me back."

Christensen nodded his encouragement, but said nothing. She was leading now.

"Not that I could talk to him with the feeding tube. Couldn't even move well enough to scribble notes to anybody. But he was there. All the time. So yeah, it feels a little strange going behind his back."

"Would it be all right with you if I talked to Kiger

about this?" Christensen asked. "I'm not sure I see his logic either, and it makes me a little uncomfortable."

"Would you?"

"I'll call this afternoon," he said. "I'd like to clear it up before we meet again. Deal?"

"Deal."

Christensen sipped his water. "Can I ask you about those first few weeks and months after the attack? What you said about not recognizing your husband. I remember that from your testimony, about how hard you worked on some long-term memory problems. Can you tell me more about those, specifically? You didn't recognize him. What else was affected?"

"Some things I remembered fine," she said. "Like my senior prom in 1983. I could tell you every stitch on the dress I wore, the shade of blue of my date's ruffled tux. But my wedding to David eleven years ago? Zilch. I remembered my first car, but not the one I drove the day before this happened. First Holy Communion? Got it. But I didn't remember squat about the police academy. It's like my past was written on a chalkboard, and somebody took an eraser and went over whole big chunks of it. There was no pattern to it, from what we could tell."

"But you eventually remembered some of those things, right?"

"Quite a few. David calls it a million-piece jigsaw puzzle with about half the pieces missing, and it's true. No matter how much I put together, the picture won't ever be finished."

"You remembered David is your husband. You eventually remembered you attended the police academy, right? And skills. You remembered how to drive, things like that."

She nodded. "Lot of that's because of David. He got me back to where I am now."

"How?"

"With his goddamn photo albums," she said, smiling. "With those goofy newspaper clippings about me in high school that I'd saved. Wedding pictures. All that. Sometimes all it took was a picture, and everything would come rushing back. Other times it might be something he said, or even the way he said it. A whole memory would just blip back on, like somebody turned on a TV. Other times I just had to listen. And trust. The man knew me better than myself at that point. I had no choice."

"Of course not."

"He really came through, you know, considering."

Christensen checked his impulse to follow up. That final word was a signal. She was opening a door, but he wasn't about to push her through it. She'd go when she was ready. The silence weighed on them both, but Christensen just nodded.

"We were splitting," she said.

"When?"

"When it happened. He'd already moved out, him and Buster, a couple weeks before. That's why the dog wasn't there that night, why there was no warning. I was the only one home."

Christensen remembered their separation as an inconsequential part of Teresa's testimony during the Della-Vecchio trial. David Harnett had a rock-solid alibi for the night Teresa was attacked: He was with his friend, Brian Milsevic, who ultimately headed the investigation. Christensen waited. Was she done?

"What changed?" he asked, giving her another opening.

"He did."

"That happens sometimes. Not very often, though."

"I know that."

"Any idea why?"

"Guilt."

Teresa winked and smiled. The gesture startled Christensen, and he found it refreshing.

"He'd been acting like a shit. That I remember. Drinking. Other women. He's older, you know. Seventeen years' difference is a lot."

"So you just got to the point where you'd had enough?"

She nodded. "It was . . . there was just a lot of pressure at the time. Outside pressure along with everything else going on. We'd decided to split, at least for a while. It was only getting worse the longer we fought it. So it was mutual."

"And that was how long before the attack?"

"Few weeks. Then this happened, and suddenly he's married to Supervictim. I'm half-dead in the ICU. People clamoring for an arrest. Every reporter in town trying to canonize me; you know how they are."

"Black and white," Christensen said. "Victims are always one-dimensional."

"I've read the stories they wrote right after it happened. Made me sound like the Virgin Mary. Which I wasn't."

"No?"

"I was angry. I wanted to hurt him, and . . ." Teresa checked herself. "Don't ask."

"You don't trust me *that* much."

"Not a chance. You were young and stupid once too, right?"

"I'll pass on that. So, then what?"

"What was the poor guy supposed to do? He could either do the right thing, or be a heartless fuck in front of the world. 'That's the guy who walked out on Supervictim when she needed him most.' Who'd want that rap?"

Time to take a chance. "Do you think his concern and dedication to you since then is sincere?" Christensen asked.

She nodded without hesitation. "The only people who rode this out with me were the people who cared. Christ, I lost track of all the friends who stopped coming around. Family, too. Some people maybe came once or twice, early on, but months dragged into years. People found excuses to avoid us. Nobody likes to watch suffering, Jim." She paused. "You mind if I call you that?"

"Jim's fine."

"David suffered with me. I know that. You asked why he came back. What I'm telling you is that good old-fashioned guilt brought him back, plain and simple. He felt guilty as hell for not being there, for treating me the way he did."

"He's told you this?"

"He didn't have to. But he's been there ever since, eight years now. That's what matters to me. Why are you smiling?"

Christensen shook his head. "First impressions are so, I don't know. Used to think I was a pretty good judge of relationships. But once you get beyond the obvious, you realize how complicated they are, and how wrong your first take can be. People are always trying to figure out my relationship with Brenna, but not many ever get it right. I think I did the same with you and David."

"You got it wrong?"

"I think I got it wrong."

She seemed to relax. He'd found common ground, and she was starting to trust. "It's solid," she said. "Now, anyway."

"Can I go back to something you said before? About the pressure? What else was going on at the time?"

She sipped her water. "With us?"

"Whatever."

Teresa sipped again. "What wasn't going on, is more like it. Things were a mess." She kept her eyes down. "The Tidwell investigation was heating up, and David was all caught up in that. Things weren't all that swell for me at work, either. It was just, everything was piling up on itself."

Christensen scribbled a few notes and waited. Only

trust would move her from vagaries to specifics. He couldn't rush that.

"Young and stupid, like I said."

"We all were once."

Her lips stretched into a thin, difficult smile. "I'd had this, this *thing*. I won't even call it an affair. Just this angry, desperate thing with somebody at work. He was married at the time, too. I understand it now. Hell, I understood it then. It was payback for what David was putting me through. Cops are the worst gossips. I figured he'd find out. I wanted him to."

"Did he?"

She nodded. "That's when he moved out. It was what he needed to justify it to himself, but we both knew it was already over by then." She paused. "This is sort of ancient history, isn't it?"

"Maybe," Christensen said. "Some people say the past is prologue."

"Maybe," she said. "Except people can change. David did. You'd have to live through what I did to appreciate that. But he loves me. I know that now. He's shown it a million ways in the last eight years."

By elaborate arrangement, she'd come here to talk about the night she was attacked. That was the dark core of it, the memory that mattered. But for fifteen minutes now she'd been talking about her marriage. Christensen jotted a note to himself. The mind is a labyrinth, and he expected Teresa's journey back to that trauma to be long and difficult. But these were her first steps on that journey, and he wondered if maybe they were significant.

20

Christensen took a bite of his hot dog and covered the phone's mouthpiece while he chewed. His next appointment was due, and Brenna was holding on line two, but he hoped to catch Kiger while he had a moment. He glanced again at the pager number on Kiger's card, wondering if this was urgent enough to page him. No, he decided. But he did want to know why Kiger was keeping David Harnett in the dark. It obviously bothered Teresa, and the last thing she needed was another roadblock.

"Jim Christensen calling, Chief," he said into Kiger's voice mailbox. "Please call me when you get a chance. I'm at my private office for the rest of the afternoon."

He poked at line two. "Hey," he said.

"So, how'd it go?" Brenna asked.

Christensen sipped from his Coke. He needed to draw a very clear line. "Bren, don't start, OK? You know the deal. What goes on here stays between me and Teresa."

"Fine," she said. "Gotta go."

"Don't be like this, please."

"I understand."

"You're mad. I can tell. Please don't put me in that position."

"You're getting the kids?"

"Bren—"

"See you at home, then. I'll be late."

Christensen lifted the last bite of hot dog to his mouth and listened to the dial tone. Lynn's voice broke in the second he hung up.

"Jim, Mrs. Donegan's been waiting."

Colleen Donegan, blond and buff, was dressed as usual in the workout clothes of a high-maintenance trophy wife. Even that wasn't enough to keep Christensen's mind on his work. The more his interest in post-traumatic memory deepened, the more his interest waned in the lucrative part-time counseling practice he'd worked so hard to build. Compared to his research work, which allowed him to explore the maze of human memory, the idea of straight-ahead counseling was fast losing its appeal. Many of his clients were simply self-absorbed and bored, he'd decided, but the last thing they want is a psychologist who says, "Just deal with it."

So he tried to follow the ongoing saga of Donegan's life, nodding without judgment as she recounted, again, the sexual inattention of her husband, the parking-garage magnate. Christensen was briefly engaged when she announced her plan to "audition" new partners, including her regular masseur at the Fox Chapel Sporting Club and maybe the general contractor who'd been overseeing the work on her new deck. But mostly Christensen's thoughts were elsewhere, so much so that he asked her to repeat her question when she casually gauged his interest in an audition, then and there.

"Do you think any of that would make you happier?" he asked, quickly changing the subject.

"I wouldn't be half as cranky," she answered.

He didn't have a ready comeback for that, so he cut the session short and asked Donegan to think about healthier forms of affirmation. She was barely out the door when he was back on the phone to Kiger, who'd returned the call while he was in session.

"Got my reasons," the chief said. "I'm keeping this on a need-to-know basis, even with the D.A. This is a new investigation, *my* investigation, with a fresh witness. She comes up with somethin', that's when we take it to Dagnolo. 'Til then, the lid's on, understand?"

Agitated, Christensen began flipping absently through the notes he'd taken during his conversation with Teresa. "I think her husband needs to know I'm involved."

"It's my decision, sir. I assume you'll respect that."

Christensen's eyes fell to something he'd written, but he postponed the thought.

"You could've at least told me you were keeping him out of the loop. She seemed confused by it, and I looked like an ass because I didn't have an answer. We're dealing with a very strong and bright woman here, but we're also dealing with something incredibly delicate. Trust is the key. She feels there's some agenda other than helping her sort out what happened, I think she'll balk. She does that, it's over. You lose. She loses. We all lose, because then we may never know."

"It's my decision," Kiger said. "You can tell her that."

"We're in this together now, supposedly. She mistrusts you, she mistrusts me."

"I'll take that chance."

"It stinks."

"So noted. Anything else? I'm late for a meetin'."

Christensen glanced at his notes, then underlined a reference on the second page. "She mentioned something today, just in passing. We were talking about things going on in her life just before she was attacked. Pressures. She referred to something, a 'Tidwell investigation.' Know anything about that?"

The silence was long enough that Christensen sat forward. "Hello?" he said.

"I'm here."

"Something wrong?"

"Not at all. There's just no easy way to answer your question. It was a personnel matter, and you know's well as me that stuff's not public record."

"Is it relevant to any of this? That's all I'm asking."

"You tell me, sir. What was the context?"

He checked his notes. "We were talking about pressures at the time."

"On her?"

"Her. Her husband. Their relationship. She was dealing with certain things. She said the Tidwell thing was something David was dealing with at the time. But then the conversation moved on and it didn't come up again, which makes me think it wasn't all that significant. I want to follow up, but I'd rather not take that detour if—"

"This something she wanted to talk about? Or something you pulled out of her?"

Interesting reaction. Christensen sat back. "I'm not a dentist, Chief. I don't do extractions. I let people talk and try to understand what they're saying beyond their words. Sometimes the things they choose to talk about, and when they choose to talk about them, are more important than what they actually say."

"So she brought this up on her own?"

"Yes."

"Interestin'."

"So you think it's relevant?"

"Didn't say that. As y'all know, personnel matters are not—"

"Public record. Come on, help me out here. I just want to know—"

Suddenly, Christensen was on hold, listening to something Henry Mancini–ish. A full minute passed before Kiger returned. He didn't explain or apologize, just said, "I'm late for my meetin'. Anything else?"

"Forget it," Christensen said. "I'll do my own research."

Kiger sighed into the phone. "Admire your enterprise. When y'all meet next?"

"Again tomorrow. After hours this time. She has to work these sessions around her husband's work schedule, which is another reason why he should be in the loop."

The conversation ended with a definitive *click!* Christensen brought down the handset with more force than necessary.

He checked his watch: four-twenty. He had an hour before he needed to get the kids. He picked up the phone again. "Lynn?"

"Still here."

"I'm clear now, right? No one else coming in?"

"You were supposed to call the Pitt Counseling Office for a consult with Marie."

"Damn. What time?"

"Thirty minutes ago."

"Can it wait?"

"Already called her. She didn't seem upset. Just said she'd track you down tomorrow."

Christensen wrote "mea culpa!" on his Day Runner in the space under tomorrow's date, then Marie Frick's office number. "Take off, then. I'm just tinkering here for a while longer."

"You're at Harmony tomorrow?"

"Part of the day. I'll be in here around seven tomorrow evening, though. Go ahead and schedule daytime stuff as usual for the rest of the week. But I'll probably be here after hours the next few nights. No need to schedule that. I'll handle it."

"Got it. Can I ask you something?"

"You just had a raise." Christensen laughed. His secretary didn't.

"That woman in here earlier, over lunch," she said. "Was that Teresa Harnett?"

Christensen couldn't lie. "That's between us, OK?"

"I know. I've just seen so many pictures."

"This is extremely private, Lynn. No one's to know she's coming here."

"But doesn't Brenna—"

"No one, Lynn. Understand?"

She sighed. "Your life sounds complicated enough already. Mum's the word."

"Thanks. See you late tomorrow afternoon."

Christensen drained the last of his Coke and tossed the cup in the trash. The Tidwell thing might ring a bell with Brenna. He'd be surprised if it didn't. Not much going on in criminal justice in Pittsburgh escaped her notice. But he couldn't very well pick her brain at the same time he was telling her nothing about his conversations with Teresa. She'd want something in return, something he couldn't give.

Maybe he could fill in a few blanks on his own. He turned to his computer. A Web search would probably be worthless. But what about the local newspapers? Their archives were online. It was worth a shot. He moved his chair within typing distance and logged on. Ignoring the waiting E-mails, he searched for the *Pittsburgh Press* Web site. There, he clicked into the archives.

Now what? He had a name, Tidwell, but he didn't know the correct spelling. No first name, either. No context. He typed it the way it sounded and waited, expecting nothing.

"This search has found five stories matching your descriptor."

He moved his chair closer to the keyboard. Four of the stories involved a bar on the South Side called Lard's. Nothing in the headlines suggested a criminal investigation, or why a search for "Tidwell" brought them up, so Christensen called up one of those stories just in case. Lard's was owned by Reg Tidwell, who'd built his reputation around goofball publicity stunts and a menu featuring unspeakable sandwich combinations—buffalo burgers topped with celery and Tabasco, ostrich steak with purple-cabbage slaw, chipped beef and pineapple chutney. Reg Tidwell was guilty of culinary crimes, but apparently nothing more serious.

The remaining story looked more promising. Christensen called it up and watched it scroll onto his screen.

079332 EAST LIBERTY SHOOTOUT LEAVES
TWO DEAD
Date: Jan. 1, 1992
Edition: FIVE STAR
Section: METRO
Page: B-4
Word Count: 148
TEXT: Two East Liberty men died late last
night in what police say was a New Year's
Eve drug transaction gone bad.

A passing pedestrian noticed the bodies of
Alon Fitzgerald, 28, and Vulcan "Velvet" Tidwell, 31, in a secluded alley behind Ruggio's
Bakery just minutes before midnight. Coroner's investigators say the two men were both
dead at the scene, and that both had been
dead less than an hour.

Police found two guns near the bodies and
"significant" amounts of cocaine and cash. Although no witnesses have come forward, police say the evidence at the scene suggests
that Fitzgerald and Tidwell argued during a
drug deal and both drew weapons.

"They were both pretty good shots," said
East Liberty Station Watch Commander Eu-
gene Popik.

Popik said Fitzgerald was twice convicted of
narcotics trafficking in the 1980s, and that Tidwell was arrested last year on a similar
charge. He was awaiting trial.

Christensen clicked the Print button and his laser printer
whirred to life. He reread the story on paper, scanning for
any mention of David Harnett. Finding none, he tried an-

other search, this time using the full name—Vulcan Tidwell.

"This search has found one story matching your descriptor."

Christensen called up the same story he'd just read. Apparently, nothing in Tidwell's life had been as newsworthy as his death. He tried one more possibility, typing "Tidwell and Harnett" into the search box.

"No matches found."

Christensen sat for a while, staring at the computer screen, wondering whether this was a waste of time. Even if David Harnett was somehow connected to the incident, it seemed like the kind of thing cops dealt with all the time. Brenna once told him the more cavalier cops described killings involving drug dealers as "pest control." Harnett fit the mold. What kind of pressure could Harnett possibly feel from an investigation like that?

Maybe he'd ask Teresa about it tomorrow. Or not. He was walking a fine line. By focusing on specifics like that, he risked skewing their conversations, just as Teresa had done as she worried about telling her husband. That led to a long discussion about their relationship. Was it in any way relevant to the attack eight years ago? Probably not. With DellaVecchio's hearing less than a week away, there wasn't much time for detours. Besides, he was a psychologist, not an investigator.

Christensen looked at his watch. Almost five. He casually checked his Day Runner, saw a forgotten scribble, and panicked. Today was Taylor's five o'clock chess club meeting. Few things in the boy's life so delighted him, and Christensen knew nothing would disappoint him more than missing the meeting.

He ended his online connection and turned off the computer, then swept his Day Runner and the printout into his briefcase. He pulled on his overcoat, locked his office door, and headed for the stairs, hoping Fifth Avenue traffic was light.

21

Teresa arrived early for their next appointment. She was waiting in her car as Christensen wheeled into the parking spot next to her. The lot outside his Oakland office was dark because the building was deserted after five-thirty most nights. Her car's engine was running so she could stay warm, but the headlights and interior lights were off. Even as he watched from the parking spot beside her, Teresa just stared straight ahead.

"Am I late?" he asked when she finally opened her door.

Teresa didn't answer, just nodded toward the elevator. "Let's get inside."

They rode up together, but neither spoke. Christensen felt like a man on the downside of a dam ready to burst. She paced the hall while he worked the key into the lock, then pushed past him as he hung his coat on the rack near Lynn's empty desk. Teresa kept her coat on. By the time he joined her in his office's sitting area, she had a G-force grip on the arms of the wing chair.

"What happened?" Christensen said.

"He called again."

She'd been home alone the night before, drying dishes, her husband at work. Just hours before one of Kiger's investigators was supposed to run a tap on her home phone, it rang. And she knew.

"How?"

"I just did."

She'd picked it up on the third ring. Didn't even say hello; just picked it up and waited. And he'd started talking, rasping and strained. Somehow, she said, he knew she was alone. He'd stopped after a few seconds when

her best ceramic baking dish shattered on the kitchen
floor. Then he hung up.

"Like DellaVecchio's voice," she said. "Same as during
the trial."

"You're sure?"

She just glared.

"This guy, did he threaten you?"

Her whole body shuddered, and she gripped the arms
of the chair even tighter. "He said things—" Teresa
looked away, as if scanning the corners of the room. She
bit her trembling lower lip. "I'm sorry."

Christensen felt a numbing dread.

"Sexual things? Violent things?"

Teresa waved the words away. "Don't."

Christensen thought of Brenna, of the calls she'd received, and fought his impulse to push. "When you're
ready, Teresa. Just relax."

She was crying now, wiping her eyes on the sleeve of
her wool jacket. He snatched a tissue from the box on an
end table and handed it to her.

"I'm sorry," she said. She pounded her thigh with a
fist. "That piece of shit. Goddamn him."

"I know this is tough. But you're safe here."

She waited, and in the pause she seemed to regain her
balance. "You're worried about her, I know."

"Brenna? I'd be lying if I said no. But we're all in this
together now. It's us against him, whoever he is."

Christensen leaned forward. "What was different about
this call, Teresa? I've seen you handle this stuff before.
This one is different, but you're not telling me why."

"Because he *knows* things," she said.

"Personal things?"

She nodded. "That's how I know it's him. Remember
yesterday when we were talking about stuff you do when
you're young and stupid? I was younger then, maybe not
stupid, but doing things I can't believe I did. Things that

embarrass me now because they're so, I don't know, childish. Things you do when you're—" She crooked her fingers as quotation marks. "—'in love' with somebody."

"As opposed to 'loving' someone," he said.

"Exactly."

Teresa drew a deep breath and closed her eyes. Christensen could tell she was stepping away from herself, from the damaged woman she probably detested, and cloaking herself in whatever armor she'd created. The armor protected her; the distance gave her perspective.

"David's much older, you know," she said. "Seventeen years."

Back to David. Why? "What was the attraction?" he asked.

"Back then?"

She waited for the right words to come.

"He was my mentor in a lot of ways," she said. "My first partner on street patrol. That covers a lot of ground. You had crushes on high school teachers, didn't you? There's no logic to it. It's just the way we're wired. We respect the people who play that role in our lives, trust them. Sometimes those things grow into something else, or get confused with something else, and all of a sudden you're in bed and it sort of goes from there. The next thing I knew he was leaving his wife and kids for me."

Christensen nodded. "David did that? Left his first wife when you two got involved?"

"Second wife. He was married twice before me. Two kids from the second marriage."

"Ages?"

Teresa thought hard. "Lizzie's three years younger than me, so she's about 31 now. That makes Todd 28."

Christensen scribbled some notes, hoping her momentum would keep her talking. After a while, he said, "You joked about hating your father yesterday. Anything to that?"

She smiled. "No. Dad's great. But what you really want to know is if I subconsciously married my dad, right?"

"You've been reading ahead."

"You're pretty transparent sometimes."

"Sorry," Christensen said. "So?"

She let go of the chair's arms. "In some ways, maybe. Dad came up through the Clairton mill, the coke plant. He's big like David, strong as a plow horse. But Daddy always smelled like coal tar and benzene. I'd never marry somebody like that. And Daddy didn't lose interest in me when I got to be an old lady of twenty-six."

Christensen took the bait. "Let's turn it around: Do you think David married his daughter?"

She nodded as if she'd expected the question. "He married young all three times. And the women he was seeing when we split were interns, secretaries, all about his mother's age when she died if you want to get really weird about it. I think he understands it now. He's past it. But God, he was such a cliché. He was forty when we got married. Called me his sports-car substitute."

"That bother you?"

"I wasn't exactly naïve. I'd been through college. I'd been through the academy. We'd been patrol partners for over a year when we got married. It was a joke. I laughed about it, too."

"Sometimes people laugh to be part of the joke, so they won't be the object of it."

Teresa's eyes drifted around the room. Then she closed them for an uncomfortable length of time. When she opened them, Christensen sensed a resolve that wasn't there before, as if she'd been to a reservoir of it somewhere inside her body.

"I was 'in love,' " she said. "And when you're 'in love' you do things that seem pretty stupid once you're not 'in love' anymore. So back then, when David asked me to shave my pubic hair, I did it. And kept doing it. He liked it, so what the hell? It was no big deal to me."

Christensen scrambled for an appropriate response. He crooked his fingers. "You were 'in love.' "

"It's one of the memories I lost. Believe me, I could have lived a full life without it. But now I remember. Everything about it. How it excited David the first time. How it itched like hell if I didn't shave every couple days. God, it was a pain. But I still did it, and kept doing it for the first three years we were married."

Christensen felt for footing. "Do you resent that now?"

She shook her head. "Not at all. It's just, you know, one of the stupid things you do when you're young and 'in love.' "

"So you don't see it as unhealthy on David's part or anything like that?"

"No."

Christensen set down his pen and rested his notebook in his lap. "Then, I'm lost. I know you brought that up for a reason, but I'm trying to relate it to what we were—"

"He knew," she said.

Christensen felt disoriented by the sudden edge in her voice. "David knew?"

She batted his question away. Then, her lower lip trembled again. Her resolve disappeared like a wisp of smoke, and just that quick Christensen understood what she'd been trying to say.

"The caller knew," he said. "The voice on the phone."

She nodded. "After David left, I stopped shaving. I was angry. I was hurt. I was moving on. That was three weeks before—" Teresa turned her head to one side, apparently embarrassed more by her rising emotion than the subject.

"You were attacked, Teresa. There's no shame—"

She suddenly slammed her fist onto the coffee table. Christensen jumped.

"Raped!" she shouted. "He *knew*, goddamn it. This guy on the phone, talking about the stubble. 'Like sandpaper,' he said. He whispered it. 'Pussy like sandpaper.' And it seemed like he knew why I was growing it back. He knew *why*. That's when I dropped the dish. That memory, the whole history, just blinked back on, all of it. In one second. And in that second, I knew I was talking to the one who did this."

Christensen felt sick. Before, when she first came to him, Teresa was confused by a voice from her muddled past. What was she to make of the different voice she remembered whispering in her ear as she lay near death? *You never rose.* That wasn't DellaVecchio's voice. Now, a new horror. The voice on the phone, DellaVecchio's voice, whispering something about her that even she'd forgotten, something intimate and grotesque.

Christensen passed another tissue, and Teresa crumbled it into a ball.

"And he sounds like DellaVecchio?" Christensen asked.

She nodded. "But somebody could fake that over the phone. It's either him or someone trying to sound like him."

"Why aren't you sure?" Christensen leaned forward. "Something's confusing you about it."

She shrugged. "It's not like I know the guy."

"DellaVecchio? If you have a question about him I'll try to answer it."

Teresa took a deep, ragged breath. "This fetal alcohol syndrome. What's it do to the brain?"

"Depends," Christensen said. "In his case, it affected the centers that control aggression and impulse. Other than that—"

"Intelligence?"

Christensen sat back. "DellaVecchio's seems limited, but not strikingly so. He never finished high school, mostly because of behavioral problems."

"Vocabulary?"

Christensen had never had a conversation with DellaVecchio; he knew mostly what Brenna told him and what he'd seen on TV. "It's hard for me to say, Teresa. My guess, from what I know about him, is that it's limited, too. He's got processing problems. People like that tend to keep things simple. No fancy language. They just don't retain it."

Teresa leaned back in her chair and studied the ceiling. A car's headlights flashed through the office window. Christensen tried to seem nonchalant as he stood up and closed the vertical blinds.

"This guy who called, he used the word *emancipation,*" she said, pronouncing each syllable like a separate word.

"Emancipation," Christensen repeated. "As in—"

"Emancipation Proclamation. That's what he called it." She looked away. "My pubic hair. Growing it back. That's what he called it."

Christensen tried to imagine those words, that concept, coming from Carmen DellaVecchio's mouth. He couldn't. He could tell Teresa was thinking the same thing.

"If it was DellaVecchio who attacked me, he'd know that I shaved, or used to shave," she said. "He'd have seen it that night. But he wouldn't know why. The guy on the phone, he knows the story. He knows *why.*"

"But how?"

"I don't know."

"Had you told anyone?"

"I might have. I don't remember."

"Friends? Women friends? Something that might have come up in the police locker room where other women saw you?"

"Maybe. I don't know."

"David?"

"He knew I shaved."

"But not that you'd stopped?"

She shook her head. "I can't remember."

"Who else? You told me you were seeing someone, a married man. Did he know?"

She was crying as she stood up. She headed for the door, and for a moment Christensen thought she was leaving. But she came back and put her shaking hands on the back of her chair. Her face was normally hard to read, but there was no mistaking her frustration. She looked him dead in the eye, and through clenched teeth, one word at a time, she repeated her answer.

"I. Can't. Remember."

22

Limbo. The nuns talked about it as if it were a place. Not heaven. Not hell. Not even purgatory. Limbo. The place you go if nobody saves you, the place you go if God can't decide.

She'd been there. Stayed maybe two weeks before David's voice coaxed her back. It was another month before she accepted him as her husband, and only then because he'd told her so. It was a month after that before she accepted as her own the past he described. David had saved her, sprung her from limbo, gave her back her past with his photo albums and mementos and endless stories about the life she had led.

Who was she to question?

Teresa slipped from beneath the covers and steadied herself on the edge of their bed. David stirred, grabbed his pillow tighter, then fell back into a deep-breathing sleep. Her feet found her slippers, and when she had them on she stood up. Equilibrium was still a problem, so she waited until the room stopped moving before taking a step. She reached around the bathroom door to lift her robe from the hook there, hoping the door wouldn't creak. David's breathing didn't falter as she crossed the room and stepped into the hall. She felt for the stair rail in the dark.

She wanted time to think. By herself. She had her own thoughts now, her own memories. They were unexpected but undeniable, bobbing up like mines. They looked real to her. They felt real. But they didn't fit neatly into the familiar narrative of her reconstructed past. She could feel the danger, especially after her session with Christensen a few hours before.

The pieces just didn't fit.

And so she'd begun to wonder: Which did she trust? The reality presented to her by the dedicated man in her bed? Or the vivid memories that seemed to be rising, with Christensen's help, from her own black depths?

She stepped to the left side of the creaky fourth and twelfth steps. At the bottom, she angled into the kitchen. For years, she'd remembered nothing of what happened there. Nothing. She'd accepted the version she was told by David, the version supported by the evidence presented in court. But lately, memories had flickered like strobe flashes in a dark room.

She flipped on the kitchen light, squeezing her eyes shut tight until they adjusted. She scanned the room—the top-end Sub-Zero refrigerator, the polished marble countertops, the copper-faced Italian espresso machine.

The place had long ago lost its power over her. It was just her kitchen now, and the waking nightmare she'd lived there was just a story, like a horror movie described to her by friends who had seen it. That wasn't her half-dead on the floor with her torn panties around one ankle. That wasn't her gasping for breath in the widening pool of blood beneath that pulpy head, which in places looked like the lump of ground lamb that had landed in a heap where her mixing bowl fell that night. That wasn't her with the neck of a broken champagne bottle jammed far enough into her uterus that a hysterectomy was the trauma surgeon's only choice to stop the bleeding. None of that existed for her in a real way. She'd simply accepted it, never questioned it, because the retelling was all she had to go on.

Now, she felt as if she had license to test it.

From her years on the force, she remembered the concept of "leftovers," pieces that didn't fit anywhere after the puzzle seemed complete. As inconvenient as they were, she knew leftovers sometimes were the most important pieces. They were the building blocks of criminal defense; they raised reasonable doubt. They sometimes hinted at undiscovered truths, and to ignore them was a mistake. Leftovers could haunt you.

Her story, or the story she'd been told was hers, had too many leftovers, things that existed outside the strobe flashes she'd been seeing lately. Inconsistencies she'd left too long unexplored. Little leaps of logic that she'd never questioned. Actions and reactions attributed to her that just didn't seem like the way she would behave. When Brenna Kennedy brought them up during DellaVecchio's trial, she'd dismissed them as a last-ditch effort to defend the indefensible. Now she wondered.

Like the windows. They arced around the kitchen sink, offering a view of her side-yard garden. They were the reason she liked the house, the reason they bought it the year after she and David were married. Along with the atrium to the left of the big window and the glass panel in the door to the right, they offered in daylight a nearly panoramic view of that side of their property. If she was working in the kitchen after dark, like the night it happened, the yard outside would have been lit by the spotlight on that side of the house. It came on automatically for a couple hours at dusk, then any time it detected motion in the yard. It was sensitive enough that a stalking cat could set it off.

She'd been standing at the sink, making cabbage rolls. She remembered none of it, but she was sure of that much. The crime scene photographer had caught it all. The water pot was still on the stove when he arrived, although the first officer on the scene had turned off the burner. She'd separated the cabbage leaves and had them stacked beside the bubbling pot, ready to blanch them. She would have dunked them using the tongs, which were propped in the spoon holder beside the leaves. The lamb-and-rice stuffing was mixed and probably sat in one of her stainless steel bowls on the sideboard until she picked it up. She apparently had done just that when he'd swung the heavy bottle for the first time. If the metal bowl hadn't clattered to the floor, her neighbor Carol wouldn't have heard. No one would have called 911. She would be dead.

But that's how it happened. She was sure of that.

What bothered her now were the windows. Making cabbage rolls her mother's way was an intensive process of separating and washing leaves, chopping ingredients, mixing meat and cooked rice and spices. Getting to that point, where she was ready to blanch and roll the leaves, would have taken her at least an hour. At that sink. Overlooking the side-yard garden.

He'd hit her from behind with the bottle, a mighty swing that landed solid on the left side of her head. It knocked her instantly unconscious. Her blood spattered up and to the right, leaving a trail across the ceramic plate that hung there, peppering the plate's painted slogan: "Live long. Laugh often. Love much."

They said he'd somehow slipped in the side door while she wasn't looking. It was spring. If it was warm, the door would have been open wide to the evening and the garden smells outside. They said he'd eased the screen door open while she worked at the stove, slid along the row of cupboards where the wine rack sat, grabbed a bottle and silently moved up behind her. Or so the story went. All the pieces fit.

Except.

She went to the sink. Except for brief turns to get ingredients from the refrigerator at her back, that's where she would have been for at least an hour before he hit her. But as she stood there now, she wondered about the pieces that didn't fit. Straight ahead, through the banked bay windows, she had a 180-degree view of practically the whole side yard. She moved back three steps toward the refrigerator. From there, she could see farther toward the front and back of the house through the window-box atrium and the door's glass panel. True, she was working, focused on the sink and cutting boards that flanked the sink. But that time of day, the yard lights should have been on. Even if they weren't, how could someone cross that expanse without tripping the motion detector? How could he have opened the aluminum screen door without pressing the noisy release button on the handle?

"Somehow" wasn't working for her anymore.

If the investigators were wrong, that meant he either would have come in through the house's front door, or else had been hiding somewhere in the house, for at least an hour, before he struck.

She'd read the crime scene report. The front door was locked. If he'd come in that way, he'd have needed a key. If he'd left that way, hurrying and still high from the savagery, would he really have taken the time to lock it again? If he was hiding in the house, where could he have been that she wouldn't have noticed him? Upstairs, maybe, but the only way down was by taking the creaky wooden stairs that ended at the kitchen's right rear corner. They knew from the bloody print of DellaVecchio's sneaker on her kitchen floor that that's what the attacker wore. But even so, there'd have been some noise as he came down the stairs.

So how did he get in?

"Terese?"

She whirled around, suddenly off balance, a flush of adrenaline jolting her body. David was standing bare-chested, nearly filling the doorway to the stairs. As she started to fall, she grabbed for and missed the edge of the counter. Her husband crossed the kitchen floor in what seemed like a single stride and gathered her in his arms. She dug her fingernails into his rough skin, knowing she was hurting him, but battling a dizziness that left her unable to stand.

"I've got you, baby," he soothed. "I've got you."

He held her tight against him until she was steady and her breathing slowed. She felt safe in his arms. After a while, he kissed her on the top of her head.

"Didn't mean to scare you, hon."

"It's OK," she said, pushing herself away. "I just didn't hear you."

23

Chaytor Perriman's house was typical Squirrel Hill, a three-story brick-and-timber thing with gables and leaded windows and a front yard like a cliff. Three flights of concrete stairs rose like a ladder from street level, and Christensen, looking up from the Explorer parked at the curb, imagined the knotty calves that Perriman's letter carrier must have developed during the daily trek to the front porch mailbox.

Perriman's first-floor study light was still on, a good sign. Christensen needed to talk to his longtime mentor, and it couldn't wait. The kids already were asleep at home by the time Teresa Harnett left his office, so he found himself cruising Squirrel Hill after their latest private session, thinking, doubting, gravitating as he often did to this house, this man.

He felt for the cold iron railing and started up the steps, remembering the many times he'd made the same trip years ago as a graduate student under Perriman's direction. The rule then was the same as now: If the study light was on, Perriman was up and available. If not, go away. Following that rule, Christensen had come calling as late as midnight without rebuke.

He was breathing hard as he mounted the last set of stairs and stepped onto the wooden porch. How spent would he be if he didn't run three times a week? The doorbell echoed in the cavernous house, and Christensen peeked through the chintz curtains, a sad reminder of Perriman's effervescent late wife, Pearl. Since her death a decade ago, Perriman had become stooped by age and the weight of his loneliness. Still, he was a brilliant man. Perriman's lifelong study of the human mind was never swayed by academic fashion or a philosophical agenda;

common sense was never sacrificed to ego or the unreasonable demands of grant committees. What Christensen needed after his most recent sessions with Teresa Harnett was a reliable sounding board who would keep their conversation strictly private.

Perriman moved slowly toward the front door, a ghostly figure in a cardigan sweater squinting through his bifocals into the darkness outside. They talked often by phone, but it had been at least a year since Christensen saw him. He seemed smaller, more brittle. When Perriman reached for the switch for the porch light, his bony hand shook. But he recognized Christensen immediately.

"I'll be damned," he said, tugging open the door. "Just like old times."

Christensen reached across the threshold to shake his hand, startled by the coolness of the old man's touch. His circulation wasn't good. "I used to climb these steps a lot, Chaytor, but I was younger then," he said. "How the hell do you get up and down them?"

Perriman stepped aside and pulled Christensen in. The place was overheated, maybe eighty degrees, and smelled to Christensen the same as his grandmother's house did when he used to visit as a child.

"I don't go out much," Perriman said, "and I take the Checker when I do." He paused as if thinking hard. "I honestly can't remember the last time I walked up."

Perriman's phrasing gave Christensen pause. He'd spent too much time around Alzheimer's patients to ignore it. He shrugged out of his coat and laid it on a bench in the front hall. The old man's devotion to his lumbering Checker Marathon, a converted taxi, was among Christensen's fondest memories of Perriman. It was the world's ugliest car, the kind of car that looked unnatural in anything but yellow. Perriman had had his painted black when he bought it, but it was a discount job that over the years faded to the color of an eggplant.

"The Beast is still running?" he asked.

Perriman straightened up. "Two hundred thirty thousand miles and change, thank you very much. She'll outlive me."

Still sharp, Christensen thought. Still, he felt a sudden sadness. Perriman's car probably would outlive him.

He followed the old man into his study, where he'd apparently been working at his battered Royal typewriter. The academic journals that published his papers had nagged him for years to get a computer, or at least send his articles to a transcription service that could convert them into a computer-readable form. Perriman enjoyed tweaking the editors. "A Luddite's last stand," he called it.

The room hadn't changed in more than twenty years, from what Christensen could tell. It was the classic lair of a lifelong academic, a dusty, musty repository of knowledge and accumulated wisdom. Perriman never allowed his cleaning lady past the door.

"So, here you are," Perriman said, nonchalantly checking the wall clock. Was it really a quarter past eleven?

"Oh, geez, I knew it was late, but . . . I'm sorry, Chaytor. The session I had tonight went longer than I thought."

"The light was on, Jim. It's fine."

Christensen nodded his thanks. "I've got a situation. I need to kick some things around, just to make sure I'm not off base. I need somebody's viewpoint other than my own, and there's really no one I can talk to about this. You've always been my Yoda."

Blank stare.

"My teacher," Christensen said. "But this one's touchy. Has to stay between us."

The clock read eleven-forty by the time Christensen finished his update. Perriman had followed the Della-Vecchio case, and they'd conferred years ago when Christensen first questioned the apparent changes in Teresa

Harnett's memories after the attack. Perriman had been the one who encouraged Christensen to focus his research on the evolution of post-traumatic memory, and he listened with apparent pride as his student told him about Teresa's gradual recovery of contradictory memories.

"Feels good to be right, doesn't it?"

Christensen allowed himself a smile. "It's a little more complicated than that."

He explained about DellaVecchio's release and Burke Padgett's dark warning about his unpredictability; about the phone calls to Brenna and Teresa and the sniper's shot at Brenna. "All within the last two-and-a-half weeks," Christensen said. "You can guess what happened next."

"She started remembering."

"Chaytor, it's like she was a pot of hot water on a stove, and somebody suddenly turned up the gas. Everything started to boil. It's happening fast, out of control. It's scary. Then tonight—"

"Typical, in a way," Perriman said. "It's been eight years. What she described to you as 'erased' memories may not have been damage at all. Maybe it was just easier not to remember than to remember, and now all this is forcing the issue."

Christensen shook his head. "I don't think it's repression. More like regeneration. The memories were in there, but the retrieval circuits weren't working. Like Alzheimer's, but trauma-induced. Now, for whatever reason, those circuits are reconnecting."

"Because of these fresh traumas."

"Maybe."

Perriman nodded. "Interesting."

The night before, Christensen said, Teresa had been scared by the latest call, terrified by what the caller seemed to know about her.

"Then tonight, anger. The pot boiled over," he said. "She was just plain pissed. Three hours she talked. Things just poured from her. Questions. Suspicions. Accusations. This is an angry woman who wants answers I'm not sure she'll ever get."

Perriman leaned back in his ancient leather chair. Its springs creaked, the only sound in the room except for the ticking wooden wall clock.

Perriman laced his fingers across his chest. "What questions?"

"She's questioning everything now. The voice she hears that's not DellaVecchio's. How this caller knew about her pubic hair. The way the cops say it happened. How the guy got into her house that night. So much of what she remembers came from her husband, the personal memories. Now she's wondering why things don't add up, wondering about him."

Perriman drummed his fingers. "What's he like?"

"They'd split before it happened. For reasons I'm still not sure I understand, he came back," Christensen said. "And he really did help her rebuild her past, replaced the missing things from her childhood, college, their marriage."

"The tragedy brought them together again?"

"Apparently. There's a strong bond there. He gave her back something she'd lost, and she appreciates that. But there's a cop inside her, too."

"The cop wants answers."

"Exactly. Like the DellaVecchio ID. She knows something was wrong there. Hell, Chaytor, she knew Della-Vecchio's name as soon as the investigators showed her his picture. Said it right out, as a matter of fact. How? She wants to know."

"She doesn't remember?"

Christensen shook his head. "She remembers the mug shot ID process vividly. They showed her hundreds of faces, but as soon as they gave her the six-pack of shots with DellaVecchio's face in it, she blurted his name.

Doesn't know how she knew the name, but she did. And the investigators never asked her to explain it. Eight years go by, and now the cop in her wants to know why nobody questioned that. That should have been a red flag to the cops on the case. How would she know his name? Was there some sort of prior relationship there they should know about? But nobody ever asked." ·

"You think it was planted?"

"Like a seed, Chaytor. Set aside the question of why. Here was a woman with great gaps in her memory, and she was relying on people like her husband to fill those gaps. At the same time, the police were developing a case against DellaVecchio. You can bet her husband was aware of that. He wasn't directly in the loop, but his best friend oversaw the investigation. I'm sure they talked."

"So you think her husband helped skew her memories?"

"If he was convinced DellaVecchio was the guy, why wouldn't he try to goose her a little? He knows she'd be no help whatsoever during the prosecution if she couldn't remember anything from that night. So as long as he was rebuilding her memory, why not prime her so Carmen DellaVecchio's name and face were a top-of-the-mind thing for her when trial time came? These are all cops, remember? Cops with a personal grudge and what looks like a solid suspect. Can't you see it working that way? Can't you imagine them trying to push Teresa just a little so the case would gel?"

Perriman closed his eyes. He stayed that way so long Christensen wondered if maybe he'd fallen asleep. Finally, he nodded his head and said, "Layering."

"Meaning?"

"It wouldn't have to be overt. And it wouldn't have to be all at once. Maybe she had some memory of the attack, and all they did was reinforce the memories they needed, or undercut the ones that didn't fit their theory. Was there any memory of the attack?"

"Nothing significant. Not until the last couple weeks. What are you thinking?"

"Let's assume she remembered nothing," Perriman said. "Maybe her story, what became her story, was created in layers, like a painting. What if whoever, for whatever reason, started with a base coat? A description of the kitchen, maybe. Later, maybe he tells her that's where she got hurt. Suddenly she's got an image to build on, and her mind goes to work. Now she can see herself in that place, even if she doesn't know what happened there. She's in the hospital. She's in pain. Obviously, something bad happened there. Then maybe her husband tells her what it was. And that's where it really starts."

"Because he's telling her the version the police have recreated, the one with DellaVecchio already singled out."

"But at that point she's got an attacker with no face. So she starts trying to fill in those details. She wants to. She needs to. Memory abhors a vacuum, and her mind won't let it alone."

"The cops already have some details," Christensen said. "The bloody shoe print. The letter she'd received. Suddenly her attacker is a guy who wears those kind of sneakers, the kind of guy who'd stalk a woman. She's getting an image."

"DellaVecchio, if I recall, had a record."

Christensen clapped his hands together, startling the old man. "The lineup!" he said. "Brenna got the transcript of the police lineup process. Soon as DellaVecchio walked in, one of the cops said, 'Guy's got a record a mile long.' It's right there in black and white. So it's reinforced at that point, too."

Christensen stood up and put his hand to his forehead. "And the TV coverage! Another visual cue. Remember, the cops released DellaVecchio's mug shot a few weeks after it happened. They never said he was a suspect, just that they wanted to question him about the case. They do that to get the name and face out there, trying to flush out people who might know something. But God, if she'd even watched the news once—"

"His face leaves a strong impression," Perriman said. "And in that context, what else could he be but a criminal? So now she's got a face. With a police record. That's what I mean by layering. The layers build, one on top of the other—"

"Until she gets to court," Christensen said.

"And by then, she's filled in all the details. The painting is finished."

Christensen recalled the precision of Teresa's testimony, the riveting detail, her unshakable confidence when she leveled that accusing finger at DellaVecchio.

"Now," Christensen said, sitting again, "why?"

Perriman shrugged. "To make the case. Why else would they massage her like that?"

"I could believe that. Cops aren't shy about messing with evidence, physical evidence, some of them anyway. Why not tinker with a victim's memories? Teresa was an empty canvas."

"The pressure was intense," Perriman said. "That attack was so brutal, people wanted a fast arrest." The old man lifted one wavering hand and gestured across his desk. "Now, let me ask you something: Do you think you know everything the police had?"

Christensen stood up again. "I don't follow."

"I'm no lawyer, thank God almighty. Certainly not a detective. But I wonder if maybe there was evidence that never made it to court? Something damning about Della-Vecchio, but something inadmissible? Looks to me like these people were sure of who they were after, sure enough that they may have bent the rules a bit to get him off the street. What made them so sure?"

Christensen considered the question for a long time, punctuating the process by saying, "Brenna might know."

Perriman looked suddenly uncomfortable. "Can I ask you something else, Jim?" He waited for Christensen's nod. "How deeply do you trust this woman?"

"Teresa?"

"No."

Christensen wasn't prepared for that answer. "Brenna? I—"

"She's got a lot invested here, doesn't she? Professionally, I mean. She got her tail whipped the first time around, so there's a payback issue here. Don't get me wrong. I'm just worried about you."

Christensen felt suddenly defensive, remembering Burke Padgett's ham-handed implication about Brenna's tunnel vision, his suggestion that her zeal to overturn DellaVecchio's conviction had blinded her to the possibility of his guilt and the danger he posed.

"I'm a big boy now," Christensen said, more sarcastically than he intended.

"There's other evidence against DellaVecchio, some of it pretty strong," Perriman said.

"I know that," he said. "Chaytor, why are you doing this?"

His mentor studied him across the cluttered desk between them. "You've done some remarkable work here, Jim. You know how I feel about what you've accomplished. In life, not just in this case. But we're still talking about memory, and that's always uneven ground. You have to step carefully. Brenna doesn't. Her mission's entirely different."

"I know."

"Do you trust her?"

Christensen ended the discussion with a brisk wave of his hand. "Absolutely."

Perriman paused, then nodded. They both looked at the

wall clock at the same time. A few minutes later. Christensen was pulling on his coat and stepping out Perriman's front door. He trusted Perriman completely, but the old man's final question had him wondering about Brenna against his will. And what about the others in this unfolding drama? DellaVecchio, Brenna's loathsome client. Teresa and David Harnett. Dagnolo, Kiger, and Milsevic. They were working together, supposedly, but who among them did he trust?

Alone, he groped his way down the steep stairs in the dark.

24

Christensen bore down as North Highland began its slow climb toward Highland Park's Reservoir No. 1. There was almost no traffic noise this time on a Saturday, only the soft sound of his running shoes on the damp pavement, the sound of his breath in the cold midmorning air, and the occasional bellow of a hungry lion at the nearby Pittsburgh Zoo.

Annie was still asleep when he left. Taylor was up, but so focused on his new 3-D puzzle of Notre Dame cathedral that he wouldn't have noticed if the Virgin herself sat down next to him. Brenna was hunkered down, too, unapproachable behind the closed door of their home office as she reviewed her strategy for the DellaVecchio hearing on Monday morning. Because of lab delays, there'd been no test results from the possible semen stain and other evidence found on the apartment building roof, or at least no public statement from Dagnolo clearing DellaVecchio of suspicion.

He'd told Brenna nothing about Teresa's latest memory conflicts, and so she was taking nothing for granted. Without additional evidence, the hearing would proceed as originally scheduled. Brenna assumed Dagnolo would try to discredit the DNA evidence that contradicted his crime theory. To be safe, she assumed, too, that Teresa Harnett would repeat the same story and identify DellaVecchio as she always had. And if lab tests later put DellaVecchio on the roof the night those shots were fired?

"I'll deal with that then," Brenna had said.

Christensen willed himself up the hill. It wasn't steep, but it was painfully long. He shortened his stride and quickened his pace, then blew a long warm breath into a vapor trail. He checked the timer on his runner's watch.

More than a minute slower than his pace on this route just a year ago. Time was catching up to him.

As he entered the park, about to cross the road onto the serpentine path that would take him around the reservoir, he heard the low drone of a slowly approaching car. What registered when he glanced back was the three-pointed star of a Mercedes-Benz, but the car was moving so slowly he stepped without hesitation into the intersection. He was halfway across the road when he heard the car's horn, a short blast.

When he looked again, the black sport-utility was stopped at the far curb. The headlights flashed once, and as soon as he was across the street Christensen stopped and stared. The driver lowered the tinted window.

Teresa looked haggard. She waved him over, but from the apprehension on her face this was not a chance encounter.

"You really do run the same circuit every Saturday morning, like you told me," she said as he approached. "You're in a rut."

He smiled. She didn't.

"I like ruts," he said.

"Sure makes you easy to find. Mind if we talk?"

"Now?" he said.

They were scheduled to meet that afternoon at four, after David went to work. "He called in sick," she said, as if she'd read Christensen's mind. "There's no way I could get out without him wondering. But he's gone right now, off doing errands, and we live just across the ravine. Thought I'd take a chance, and here you are."

Christensen was breathing hard, starting to sweat despite the cold. "I'm not really—"

"Please, Jim. A few minutes?"

In her pleading eyes, Christensen saw no room for discussion. "Where?"

"Get in."

The reservoir loop wasn't long. Teresa drove halfway around before she spoke again, and then only to ask if he wanted the heater off.

"Unless you want me sweating right through these leather seats," he said.

Teresa obliged, then pulled the SUV into a small parking lot nearly hidden in a grove of trees. She checked to make sure that cars passing along the road couldn't see them, then cut the engine. As she sat in profile, Christensen could see the faint line of an old incision that began just under her right ear and ran along the underside of her jaw to her chin. Another one followed her scalp line from her widow's peak to eye level, then turned and disappeared into her dark hair. She'd left the house without her normally heavy mask of makeup.

"You OK?" he asked.

She faced him. "Not pretty, is it?"

"No, I mean why are you here? If it's just to tell me you couldn't make it this afternoon, calling would've been fine. You've got my home number."

"I remembered something else," she said, fixing her eyes straight ahead. Christensen looked, saw nothing but trees.

"About the attack?"

"Before that."

"Tell me."

He waited for her to blink. Finally, she said, "I got flowers. In a box, long and skinny. Tied with a green bow. No card. In my mind, the way I remember it, it was just a couple days before the attack." She blinked, finally, then turned to him again. "Roses. Two of them."

Christensen was confused. "You testified about them at the trial, Teresa. I remember that. Two red roses. You opened them because you hoped maybe they were from David, trying to make up. And when you realized they weren't you just tossed them because there was no card or anything."

Christensen closed his eyes, trying to recall Teresa's testimony about the incident. It had little impact on the trial, because no one could ever prove who had left the flowers on Teresa's doorstep or why. But that hadn't stopped Dagnolo, who let the mysterious delivery subtly reinforce his stalking theory for the jury. The flowers fit neatly into Dagnolo's fantasy that DellaVecchio had, in some perverse way, courted Harnett before he attacked her.

"They weren't red," she said. "Well, one of them was. I remember now. The other one was white."

Christensen shifted in his seat. "Do you feel that's significant?"

"I don't know. I just remember them now, lying there in the box all by themselves. No baby's breath. No tissue paper. It seems odd, doesn't it? One red, one white."

Christensen watched her, letting her talk.

"It seems like a little thing until you think about it," she said.

"What are you thinking?"

"That it's weird, is all," she said. "I mean, nobody sends two roses unless the number two has some significance, right? And different colors? Why would somebody do that?"

"So you think the colors mean something?"

"Yes."

"What?"

"Red and white," she said. "Love and death."

Christensen's body heat was fogging the car's windows. It suddenly bothered him that they couldn't see out, but Teresa made no effort to clear them. He turned her words over in his mind. Love and death.

"The D.A. always felt your attacker was courting you," he said, avoiding judgment about Dagnolo's theory. "That whoever attacked you was infatuated, maybe obsessed. 'The courtship from hell,' he called it."

Teresa watched him. "Looks that way."

"But do you buy it?"

Long pause. "Looks that way."

Christensen probed again. "You're sure David wasn't trying to make amends after you split."

"No."

"What makes you so sure?"

She shook her head. "It was over. Besides, that's not his style. Plus, I asked him. He didn't send them."

"Not even maybe?"

"No chance."

Christensen took off one of his running gloves and traced an inch-wide line across the gray windshield with his knuckle. Through it, he could see nothing but the park's bare trees. His tiny window fogged again as soon as he was done.

"Are you convinced the flowers were from the man who attacked you?"

"Yes."

"Why?"

"*You never rose*," she said. The words she remembered him whispering in her ear that night.

"But that makes no sense," Christensen said. "Two different uses of the word *rose*."

Teresa shrugged. "I don't know. I just—"

"One's a flower," Christensen said, thinking out loud. "The other's the past tense of—"

"I just know, damn it," she snapped. "They were from him. Same way I knew it was a different voice." She pointed to the center of her chest, breathing hard, as if she'd been the one running. "I feel it right here. I just know."

They sat in silence for what seemed like minutes. Finally, Teresa checked her watch. "Shit. I've gotta go."

"I can still talk," Christensen said, checking his own watch.

"I can't. David's due back. I'm out when he gets home, he'll want to know where I was. I can't keep lying to him." She waited until Christensen reached for the door handle. "I'm sorry. I have no idea what it means, but I wanted to tell you that."

"You're confident it's a real memory?"

"Red and white," she said. "Definitely."

Christensen opened the door. Cold air rushed in, chilling him inside the gray Pitt Panthers sweatshirt that was turning dark with his perspiration. He thought about the hearing, now just forty-eight hours away.

"What are you going to do, Teresa? The hearing's in two days. As of now, Dagnolo's still planning to put you on the stand."

"I know." A tear rolled onto her cheek, and she brushed it away.

"He's going to ask if DellaVecchio is the man who attacked you. He's going to ask if you're sure." Christensen let the thought sink in, then prompted her again. "Teresa, what are you going to do?"

"I don't know."

He climbed out and then leaned back into the open passenger-side door. "Does David work Sundays? I could meet you at my office if you want to talk again. Just call me at home and I'll meet you."

She nodded. The tears were coming faster now, and this time she let them flow. "Thanks."

Christensen started to close the door, but he remembered a loose end he'd meant to tie up when they talked the day before. He leaned back into the car. "Can I ask you to clarify something?"

Teresa wiped her tears on the sleeve of her jacket. "Sure."

"Earlier this week when we talked, you mentioned

something. I don't know if it's significant, but it's been bugging me."

She faced him with her sad, red eyes.

"You were talking about the things going on in your life at the time you and David split," he said. "Job pressures, that sort of stuff. You mentioned an investigation. The Tidwell investigation. Some case David was involved in."

She nodded. "I remember," she said.

"I tried to track it down, but the only thing I could find was a drug case, a double shooting. Not to be callous, but it seemed like kind of a slam dunk as far as the investigation. But you said there was a lot of pressure on David because of it. I'm not sure I—"

"Oh my God."

Teresa suddenly covered her mouth with her hands, but never took her eyes off him. Christensen whirled around, wondering if maybe someone was standing behind him, but they were alone in the trees. When he turned back, Teresa seemed disoriented, swept up in the rush of a fresh memory.

"Teresa?"

"Oh my God," she said again. "IAD."

Christensen climbed back in and slammed the door. "What is it?"

"Internal affairs," she said. "Oh God."

"I'm not following. I asked about Tidwell."

She balled her hand into a fist, then bit the knuckle on her index finger.

"Tidwell?" he prompted.

His persistence seemed to annoy her, because she turned away. "Tidwell was just street trash," she said. "Some crankhead trying to pull his nuts out of the fire. But now I remember. IAD was really going after it."

"IAD?"

"Internal Affairs Division," she said. "The cops who investigate other cops."

"They'd questioned David about the Tidwell case?"

"Twice," she said.

"And the pressure of that was complicating your marriage?"

She nodded. "It was complicated already. IAD just added another level of stress. But now I remember. We had a big fight, bigger than usual. About IAD. That's when David moved out."

The memory was abrupt and apparently disturbing, but Christensen couldn't see a direct link to the matter at hand.

"Do you think it had something to do with the attack?" he asked.

"No."

"Any idea why you reacted so strongly to it?"

She gestured again to her chest. "I felt it here."

"But you have no idea why?"

Teresa checked her watch again. "I've got to go."

Christensen opened the door again. "You're OK?" he asked before stepping out.

She nodded. "I'll call you if I can."

Christensen closed the door. Teresa started her car and backed away, spraying mud and gravel as she bumped back onto the pavement. He walked through the warm exhaust fumes and stood alone alongside the road, wondering whether she'd just led him down another dead end.

25

The old Pittsburgh Public Safety Building sat on the corner of First at the south end of Grant Street, just a block from the Allegheny County Courthouse and around the corner from the morgue. Christensen studied the structure from the sidewalk, concluding that its dull aluminum-and-colored-panel design made it the unwanted stepchild of the city's spanking new Public Safety Complex. That complex featured the modern City Courts Building and jail along the Monongahela River, which one law-and-order city councilman derided as the "Taj Mahal on the Mon."

The last time Christensen met Kiger on this turf, the circumstances were far from ideal. He had been detained for questioning just hours after the violent climax of the Primenyl investigation, in which he'd helped untangle the memories of a killer's twenty-two-year-old son. That time he'd been brought in the building's back entrance with the killer's blood still on his shoes, and Kiger had wanted answers. Fast.

This time, Christensen wandered into the lobby of the building like a lost freshman. "The chief's office is on seven, right?" he asked the sergeant at the front desk.

She looked him over. "Name?"

"Christensen," he said. "I called about two hours ago. I think he's expec—"

The sergeant tossed a visitor's badge onto the counter. "Sign the book."

Christensen signed the visitor's register, then opened his leather jacket and clipped the badge to his shirt pocket. "Top floor?"

The sergeant nodded and gestured to an elevator door to the left.

Christensen couldn't resist. "Nice talking to you," he said as he stepped to the elevator doors and pushed the up arrow.

Kiger's secretary showed him down a narrow hall and into a conference room that overlooked Station Square to the right and the Liberty Bridge to the left. Across the Mon, the city's South Side stretched along the frigid river, bracing for a lively Saturday night. In the distance, beyond a thriving row of precious restaurants and microbreweries and too-hip galleries, the dome of one of the city's dozen or so Eastern European churches rose like an upside-down onion. It lent an Old World touch to Pittsburgh's emerging new reality, a relic of the past adding dimension to the present.

Christensen sat in one of the conference room's metal-frame chairs and studied the walls. This was not some ceremonial reception area for the chief's visitors. This was a tactical operations room in Kiger's much-publicized war on drugs. Directly across from him hung a city map labeled "Locations with 10 or more drug calls, May–April, Hill District area." Each troublesome address was marked with a red pushpin. To his left, another city map was labeled "Pittsburgh Weed and Seed," the catchy name for a controversial program that increased penalties for drug violations in designated areas of the city. At the far end of the room hung a faded poster of former Steelers linebacker Greg Lloyd in full pads. Its caption read: "I would never go to work without my equipment, and neither should you. Save your life. Wear your ballistic vest today."

Christensen wiped a bead of sweat from his forehead. Was the room hot, or was it him? He waved his hand over the register, relieved to find it blasting hot air into the already stifling room. He turned around and twisted the aluminum handle on one of the windows and pushed it open. When he turned back, Kiger was standing directly across the conference table.

The chief had the look of a man who liked to startle. "Too hot for y'all?" he said.

Christensen tried to hide his surprise. "You don't see a lot of saunas with a conference table this size," he said.

Kiger reached across the table and they shook hands. The chief sat down in another of the room's dozen institutional chairs, rolled his white shirtsleeves above his leg-of-lamb forearms and leaned on the table's fake-wood top. "Never have got used to this winter weather. It'll cool down in a sec with the window open."

Christensen sat down. "I know this was short notice, so I appreciate you seeing me. You work every Saturday?"

"Most. So, you got something we need to know about?"

So much for chit-chat. "I'm not sure. Teresa and I are still talking. We talked this morning, actually. I have some questions."

"For me?"

"About a case that ended up with internal affairs, apparently." Christensen waited for a reaction. He got nothing but a blank stare. "Happened about eight years ago," he added. "Involved Teresa's husband."

Still nothing. Finally, the chief leaned forward. "Shoot," he said.

"I mentioned it before, the case involving a drug dealer named Tidwell, Vulcan Tidwell. I guess he's dead now, but he was apparently involved in something back then that triggered some sort of internal review or an investigation or something. And David Harnett may have been involved somehow. Do you remember the case?"

Kiger ignored the question. "Where y'all going with this, Dr. Christensen?"

Christensen ignored Kiger's question. "So do you know what I'm talking about or not?"

The two men stared across the table. The issue was trust, and they both knew it.

"Fine," Christensen said. "We can dance around this and play these cat-and-mouse games, or we can just be honest. That's what you promised when we started this thing. I'll start."

He paused for effect.

"Teresa's struggling. And she's struggling with things I didn't expect to be dealing with, things that on the surface don't have anything to do with what happened the night she was attacked. She's focusing on stuff that happened in the weeks before, and in the weeks after, and on the role her husband played in helping her remember."

"She's still poking holes in the story she's been telling about DellaVecchio?"

"DellaVecchio's been a non-issue so far."

Kiger waited. The man was a sphinx, his face offering no clue about his thoughts.

"All right, let's try this another way," Christensen said. "Tell me how this internal affairs division works. Generally. I know it's cops who investigate allegations against officers in the department, but beyond that I'm not sure."

"Awright. Fire away."

"How does an IAD investigation start?"

Kiger smiled. "Somebody usually gets pissed off. 'Officer so-and-so called me a faggot,' or 'Officer such-and-such threw me in the back of his car and I broke a fingernail.' Mostly that kinda boo-hoo crap. But we try to follow up."

"You don't put much stock in it?"

The chief shrugged. "It's mostly the police-brutality crowd. But when there's something to it, it's not just whining, then IAD ends up with it."

"For a full investigation?"

"IAD does fact-finding. Investigators talk to witnesses, track down everything they can. Then they talk to whoever was naughty, get his or her side of things. Then they write up a report and send it to me."

"And you decide if there's anything to it and discipline the officer?"

Kiger nodded. "If I have to, but just in administrative cases. The little stuff. It's a criminal case, we got a special-operations squad that kicks in to do the investigatin'. They go after it like any other criminal case—surveillance, wires, whatever. They find something, it goes right to the D.A., just like anybody else."

Christensen drummed his fingers on the table. "And you're comfortable having cops investigating other cops?"

Kiger's smile was patient, but his searing eyes made clear he understood Christensen's implication. "We tried havin' the dogcatcher do the investigatin', but he just didn't get it," he said. "You got a better idea?"

"Seems like a conflict, that's all."

"That's why we bust hump to make sure it's fair, sir, so nobody comes back with any conspiracy crap," Kiger said. "Way I set it up, IAD's a plum job for any officer wants to get ahead. Anybody wants a promotion has to put in two years with IAD, see what it's like on that side of things. Going in they know the deal: They cook facts to save a bad cop, it's *their* ass out the door."

Kiger jabbed a finger into the tabletop, punctuating the thought. "The system works. Ain't perfect, but it works."

Christensen saw no need to belabor the point. And yet, they were back where they'd started. The trust issue. He needed specifics.

"And you won't talk about any one case?" Christensen asked. "Because unless you do, I can't know whether these memories of Teresa's are relevant or not. But I'll be honest with you, I suspect they are. Ever since we started, she's been coming back to the same things: David. Their marriage. The tension in their lives just before all this happened. There's got to be a reason."

Kiger stood suddenly and closed the conference room door, then eased himself back into the chair. He folded his hands in front of him.

"That investigation's unresolved," he said. "I'll tell you what I can, though. So ask."

"Thank you," Christensen said. "Can you start with the background? How did it begin?"

"Started with Tidwell."

"Broken fingernail?"

Kiger shook his head. " 'Bout six months before he started talking to us, we'd popped him for dealing. Street stuff, crack, meth. He was midlevel, but he knew some of the big boys. They knew him, too. He's one of those guys we coulda nailed for a whole lot more, but we decided to work him a little, see what happened."

"Work him?"

"See if he'd flip for us, lead us to some of the folks higher up the food chain. We had a lot of ways to go with him. Coulda made it real hard on him, or real easy, depending on how we wanted to go, how cooperative he wanted to be. He didn't help us, he was looking at some serious time."

"And if he did?"

The police chief winked. "We'da worked something out. Wouldna walked, but he'da walked a lot sooner. But he knew he was facing worse than Western Pen if he snitched out the people he was dealing with. They'd have made him pay big time. So he came up with something else."

"I don't follow."

Kiger's face turned serious. "Sumbitch floated something from out in left field, something bigger'n any of us expected."

Christensen sat forward, leaning across the table. Kiger leaned forward too, close enough that Christensen could smell the sour coffee on his hot breath.

"Something you gotta understand about these people," Kiger said, dropping the volume of his voice. "They're cons, every one of 'em. Truth's something they'll tell when they run out of lies, but ain't ever seen one run outta lies yet. Blow smoke like goddamn Bessemers, most of 'em. Most of what they'll tell you is like tits on a bull, useless."

Christensen nodded. "But?"

Kiger looked around the room. " 'Tween us. You clear on that?"

"Crystal."

The look that crossed Kiger's face then was an odd mix of emotions. If Christensen read it right, he saw heavy doses of sadness and embarrassment.

"Drugs are pretty serious with me," Kiger said. "Lost a daughter to heroin, my oldest, twelve years ago this month. So it's a priority, understand?"

Christensen nodded.

"So here comes this Tidwell sayin' he knows about a protection racket being run out of the East Liberty station. Says some of my own cops are involved, says it's been goin' on for years." Kiger looked away in disgust. "That's something I'm gonna take real serious."

"And you don't think he was just blowing smoke?"

Kiger weighed his words. "Let's say he had enough information to make it credible. Credible enough for IAD to look into it."

"This special-operations unit you mentioned? Was it involved?"

Kiger nodded. "Never came up with enough for the D.A. to file, but there was sure enough to keep us asking questions."

Christensen felt a prickle of anticipation. They were moving toward the crux.

"Tidwell gave names?" he asked.

Kiger studied him. "You can assume that."

"David Harnett's?"

"He gave several," the police chief said.

"And how long after that did Tidwell end up dead?"

Kiger closed his eyes. "Coupla months, if memory serves."

Christensen leaned back. What at first seemed like an irrelevant back-alley dope deal gone bad was revealing itself in rancid layers, with Tidwell's convenient death at its core.

"You think Tidwell was murdered?" Christensen blurted.

Kiger shrugged. "Can't say. Happened on New Year's Eve. Strange things happen on New Year's Eve. Had no witnesses. What we did have was a crime scene with a lot of discrepancies. Trajectories, distance, the way the two bodies were lying. Not everything added up, but that ain't much to go on. So we just don't know."

"But I'll bet the IAD investigation ended when Tidwell died, right?"

Kiger shook his head, then checked his watch. "Just got a little more complicated. We had him on videotape. We had a bunch more questions for him we never got to ask, but we at least had the videotape. The rest was up to IAD to flush out."

The chief stood up. "I'm gonna have to get to a meetin'. Anything else?"

Christensen sifted the new information. So that was the pressure that helped tear the Harnetts' marriage apart. Teresa said her husband had been called twice to answer questions before the internal affairs panel. Even if he wasn't one of the corrupt cops that Tidwell named, the panel could have been asking him about fellow officers, pressuring him to break the police code by telling what he knew.

"Tell me something. Was that IAD investigation still

open when Teresa was attacked a few months after Tidwell died?"

"Yep," Kiger said, moving toward the door. "But it was going nowhere fast. When that happens, we mark it unresolved in the file and wait to see if anything changes. Truth is, some of the people we probably needed to pull it together turned up dead." Kiger raised one eyebrow. "Or as good as dead."

Christensen thought immediately of Teresa, not dead, but someone who by any measure should have been: a woman whose body lived on, but with her past shredded and pocked by gaping holes. As good as dead.

A few minutes later, Christensen was riding the elevator back down with that phrase and one question echoing above everything else: Were Teresa's most significant memories—the memories that might make sense of all this—lost in those holes?

26

Christensen steered off the Parkway East and onto Forbes Avenue, heading home from Kiger's office for a promised late-afternoon bowl-a-thon with the kids. He needed the break, and he was sure they were running wild while Brenna sweated Monday's hearing behind her closed office door. He felt as if he'd stumbled onto something significant. Every turn led him deeper into the labyrinth, but the trail so far was strewn with unanswered questions—maybe unanswerable ones.

The Explorer passed through the shadow of a railroad bridge and emerged into bright daylight. Straight ahead, the University of Pittsburgh's forty-two-story Cathedral of Learning loomed like a granite-gray spike in the heart of Oakland. It was one of the world's most impressive symbols of scholarship and knowledge, and he felt privileged to teach there. And yet, at times like this, he realized how little he really knew about the most confounding labyrinth of all, the human mind.

Another familiar symbol caught his eye as he navigated the heavy afternoon traffic along Oakland's hospital row. On the right, about two blocks ahead, a white three-pointed star stood in a royal-blue field atop the sign for Reed Motorcars, the city's preeminent Mercedes-Benz dealership. He changed lanes, moving from the far left to the middle lane without understanding the force that pulled him. He changed lanes again, and by the time he reached the sign he was riding along the right curb, looking for a parking spot. He'd wedged the Explorer into a too-small spot just past the dealership before he was able to focus on a question that had nagged him for a week now.

Among the many contradictions and inconsistencies he

found in Teresa Harnett, this was a minor one. But, as his late friend Grady Downing used to say, the devil's in the details. Christensen remembered his mild surprise when Teresa arrived for her first scheduled visit to his private counseling office. He was watching from the window as she wheeled into the parking lot below. He'd never considered what sort of car she might drive, but he never would have pegged her as driving a high-end Mercedes sport-utility. He had no idea what they cost, but were they affordable enough for a household supported by a police officer's income and a monthly disability paycheck?

A mild revulsion swept over Christensen as he stepped through the polished German iron on the car lot, headed for the glassy showroom. A gang of floor salesmen shuffled behind the windows, and he could almost feel their eyes lock onto him as he approached. Soon, one of them would launch himself out the door for a direct assault, trying to act less desperate than he actually was as he lurched toward his monthly quota. Christensen wasn't disappointed. The man who emerged with his hand extended had the same smarmy look as every car salesman he'd ever met, but was better dressed.

"Name's Phil," he said, enclosing Christensen's hand in a mock-sincere Two-Handed Clintonian. "Think this sun'll last?"

"Let's hope. I'm Jim."

The salesman inspected Christensen from head to toe, no doubt calculating his net worth by weighing the potential assets of his silver hair and expensive Patagonia jacket against the liabilities of blue jeans and filthy running shoes. Christensen felt as if he were being searched at an airport security station, with Phil scanning for status symbols instead of weapons.

The salesman nodded past him, toward the boxy green Explorer. "So you're thinking about moving up, eh?"

"Maybe."

"Happy to help any way I can," Phil said. He nodded back toward the Explorer. "There's a big difference, you know."

Christensen shook his head. "Between mine and yours?"

"Between any vehicle and ours." Phil flipped over a business card and held it out. Christensen wondered if he kept them spring-loaded somewhere up his sleeve. "Tell you what. I'll just let you look around a bit. See the difference between what you're driving and what we sell. No pressure. Just do me a favor. Any of the other salesmen approach you, wave this card at them. It's like a crucifix with vampires. It'll keep them away."

"Thanks."

"Just holler if you have any questions or want to take one out and see what you've been miss—"

"Actually, I do have a couple questions," Christensen said.

Phil smiled. "Which model?"

Christensen pointed to a maroon sport-utility behind the showroom glass.

"Ah, the M-class," Phil said. "So you're looking for another SUV?"

Christensen evaded the question. "I just have a couple questions, real quick ones."

Phil fixed his smile, but his eyes said "Fuck you." He turned and led Christensen into the showroom, past the other floor guys whose eyes never stopped scanning the lot's perimeter. They approached the vehicle from the back. Its badge said ML 320. Except for the color, it looked the same as Teresa's ML 430. He asked Phil about the difference.

"The engine," he said. "The 430 has the V-8. It's an animal."

"That's it?"

"More stuff, of course. Lot of real-estate people drive

that one. Maybe that's what you need in your line of work. What is it you do, anyway?"

"More stuff. You mean options?" Christensen asked.

"Your 430 has full leather, standard. Same with the heated seats, privacy glass, running boards, better stereo. You know, top-of-the-line *stuff.*"

"More expensive?"

Phil shrugged. "So price is a consideration?"

Christensen moved around to the driver's side, where the sticker was pasted to the rear window. He traced a finger down the list of standard equipment to the bottom line. MSRP on this lower-end model was $34,950 plus $595 for transportation and handling, tax not included.

"Ouch," he said.

Phil checked his watch. "Anything else?"

Christensen peered through the vehicle's window. The difference between this model and Teresa's were obvious. This one had cloth upholstery, no CD, no sunroof. The wheels were aluminum alloy. Teresa's were polished chrome.

"I saw one once, a 430, all tricked out, the whole package," Christensen said. "Leather, CD player, sunroof, custom wheels. What would something like that cost?"

"More," Phil said.

"But how much more?"

The salesman sighed. "Model like this has everything you need, just not top-end. That brings the price way down."

Christensen waited.

"So you're talking a loaded 430 out the door?" Phil asked.

Christensen nodded. "Tax, license, the whole shebang."

"Between fifty and sixty."

"Double ouch," Christensen said, looking at his wristwatch. He'd told the kids three o'clock for bowling, and he was already half an hour late. He noticed Phil calculating the value of the gold timepiece he'd put on after his morning workout.

"Nice," Phil said. "Rolex?"

Christensen shook his head. "Timex."

Phil forced another smile and backed away. "Jim, you take care now."

27

Teresa shelved her worry boxes in a spare-bedroom closet on the house's second floor, beside a pile of comforters and extra linens. She pushed the bedclothes aside and stepped back to survey the accumulated anxieties of her long-ago life.

For years without fail, at least in the years before she was attacked, she followed the same New Year's Day ritual. At the start of each calendar year, she filled a shoe-box with items that represented all of her significant worries from the year just ended. Report cards, photographs, souvenirs of good and bad dates, letters, old appointment books—reminders of events and crises that, in retrospect, seemed insignificant. That was the power of a worry box. Start each year fresh. Put old worries away. Look forward, not back.

The boxes were stacked three high on the closet's top shelf. She counted fifteen, each with a torn strip of packing tape around the outside that had kept the lid sealed, each with a year inscribed in black marker on the panel facing out. Her rule was to seal those worries away forever, but she'd broken the rule eight years before as she struggled to rebuild her past. David had brought her worry boxes to the hospital, hoping the bric-a-brac inside would help bridge the gaps between the fragments of her memory. Sometimes it did; more often she puzzled over the significance of torn movie ticket stubs, dried flowers, photographs of people she didn't recognize, and a once-worrisome collection of newspaper clippings, term papers, job evaluations, and office memos.

Quietly, so as not to wake David, she pulled a desk chair across the room and stepped up. It felt odd. Whenever she'd done so before, it had been to put another year's worries on the shelf. This time, she intended to pull a box down. She scanned the years, looking for 1991.

She moved the stacked boxes from 1988, 1989, and 1990, but found nothing behind them on the foot-deep shelf. She did the same with the others. Where was 1991? It was the year before she was attacked, and she could think of no reason why she wouldn't have put one together at the year's end. But where was it? The question was barely formed when an image flashed behind her eyes—UGG boots.

And a memory blinked back on.

She'd needed a bigger box to hold 1991's accumulated anxieties. It was the year her marriage began to unravel. No ordinary shoebox could contain her worries that year, so she'd chosen a bigger box that once contained her winter boots. Teresa stepped back and surveyed the neat rows of boxes above her. Even if she'd wanted to put 1991 with the others, the bigger box wouldn't have fit on the narrow shelf. So where had she put it?

Somewhere near, she thought. She stooped to the closet floor and dug through an assortment of plastic bags filled with old shoes and clothes bound for Goodwill and the St. Vincent de Paul Society. No luck. Where else? With some effort, she knelt beside the bed and lifted the duvet. As soon as she saw the squarish shape near the bed's headboard, she knew. She reached into the darkness, her nose tingling from the accumulated dust, and grasped a cardboard corner. Pulling it out, she was surprised by its weight. *A heavy year*, she thought. *No doubt about that.* As she tugged the box into the murky bedroom light, she noticed something else, too. Unlike the others, the packing tape was not broken.

Teresa set the box on the bed. It seemed to pulse. Had David searched for it back then? Or did he assume she'd skipped her annual ritual because of their marital chaos that year? For whatever reason, the 1991 box was un-touched.

The packing tape was brittle. It broke as she tried to slice it with her fingernail, its snap like a tiny gunshot in the late-night silence of the house. She waited to make sure the sound didn't wake her husband, then continued. The tape disintegrated as she pulled it from the box, and she collected the pieces and tucked them in the pocket of her robe. David might wonder if he found them on the floor.

Her filing system, if you could call it that, was chron-ological. She began each year with a new box, and she placed her worries inside as they occurred. The items on the bottom were worries from the beginning of the year, and they accumulated in layers right up until New Year's Day, when she would seal the box, shelve the year's trou-bles, and begin again.

Teresa lifted the lid on 1991 and came face to face with her old self, unscarred and whole, standing as one of only six women among dozens of freshly minted officers in a black-and-white police academy class photo. She checked the year on the box again. She'd graduated from the acad-emy in 1988, three years before. Why was the photo among her top worries at the close of 1991? She lifted the glossy from the box and scanned dozens of faces, so young and fresh. On the back, she found a typewritten list of her seventy-three classmates' names, ordered from the top left to the bottom right.

She looked closer at the list of names. Beside the names of Patrick Boyle and Gregory Vance, in pencil, she'd handwritten a grim notation: "KIA '91." Killed in action. She turned the picture face up and found Boyle and Vance among the rows of new officers, but recognized neither. She had no idea how they died, but their deaths had ob-viously affected her at the time. Probably the first casualties from her academy class. That's something that would have worried her.

The next item in the box was a neatly folded front page from the *Press*. She opened it and recognized the same two faces, this time in individual head shots placed side by side on the page. Beside them, the lead story's headline: "Two police officers die in Bloomfield ambush." She checked the paper's date—January 1, 1992—and started to read.

Two Pittsburgh police officers died in a hail of bullets yesterday after being lured into what a fellow officer described as a "carefully orchestrated ambush" by assailants who remain at large.

Officer Patrick Boyle, 27, and Officer Gregory Vance, 28, both assigned to the department's East Liberty station, died of multiple gunshot wounds near the entrance to an abandoned Bloomfield warehouse.

Police said the two officers apparently had gone to the isolated warehouse as part of an ongoing investigation, and that the shots were fired from a window just above the door where the two men died.

They're the first Pittsburgh police officers to die in the line of duty in more than four years.

"It was a setup from the word go," said an East Liberty officer who asked not to be identified. "This was an execution."

Official police sources issued only a brief statement late last night confirming the deaths and naming the two dead policemen. But department spokesman Lt. Michael Allman said the investigation is continuing and offered few details about the incident or evidence found at the crime scene.

Allman also refused to speculate about the motive behind the attack, saying, "The shooters are still out there, and we won't say anything that might compromise this investigation."

Teresa read on, but the rest of the story was mostly biographical information about the two dead officers. It confirmed that the men were police academy classmates the year she graduated, and noted that each had two young children. Boyle's wife was pregnant with their third. The story also quoted several of their stunned colleagues, who recounted the brief but exemplary careers of Boyle and Vance. As Teresa read, she felt a sour clench, a gut reaction to what seemed every cop's worst-case scenario. Poor bastards. Died with their guns still holstered.

Something for the worry box, indeed.

Teresa set the photo and story aside and picked up a blurry color snapshot, the next worry on the pile. That one she remembered, and she knew exactly why she'd saved it. It was taken at the Fraternal Order of Police Christmas dance that year and showed David chatting idly with one of the department's sluttiest clerks, the one she and other women in the department had assigned the brutally accurate nickname "Curb Service Carrie." Teresa felt a wave of nausea, just as she had the night she took the picture. That was the moment she finally recognized her husband as a serial adulterer. No man chatted idly with Carrie unless he had a history with her, or wanted one. Why she'd decided to preserve the moment on film, she couldn't say. A reminder, maybe? For resolve?

The erratic TV in Teresa's head suddenly blinked on again. In a split second, somewhere in her damaged brain, the memory of that moment caromed from synapse to synapse, ending finally with another memory entirely. An argument with David, bitter and accusing. Hurtful words, angry defiance.

Teresa tried to retrace the memory's path. What was the connection? She closed her eyes. Carrie? She focused on her roiling emotions, trying to snatch details from the murk. The fight. What was it about? She needed a handle, something that might help her pull the full memory from the swirling emotional fog. Christmas dance. Argument. Hostility. Carrie. David. Accusations. A slamming door.

It was coming now, taking shape in her mind. Teresa pressed her eyelids tighter together, as if light might blur the scene unspooling in her head. The argument. A slamming door. Their door. The front door. Suddenly, she saw the place. Their living room. An argument in their living room. She felt the anger all over again. Carrie. David. Accusations. She saw herself reaching, reaching. For something to throw. Now she saw it in her hand as she cocked her arm back. Small and white, the size of a baseball. But painted and irregular. Ceramic.

Then it was airborne, sailing across their living room. David ducking, an instinctive flinch. A spray of ceramic shrapnel as the thing hit their door. Then silence. She'd thrown something at David during an argument in their living room. She'd missed. Silence. Hostile stares. A slamming door.

He'd walked out.

It wasn't the only time. That was the pattern. She'd call him on some infidelity, he'd deny until proven guilty, then walk out defiantly until he crawled back a day or two later full of apologies and good intentions.

Teresa opened her eyes, her heart still racing, breathing hard with fresh anger more than eight years later. She looked around the spare bedroom and found it comforting. That was a long time ago. Things were different now. Very different. But some wounds never heal. She looked down, and something in the worry box caught her eye. A lumpy white envelope. It had slid off the worry pile and was wedged in the corner of the box, down beside the spiral-bound appointment book she'd kept that year. She lifted the envelope out and tore off one end.

A shattered piece of ceramic tumbled out, a tiny head. Hand-painted eyes and eyebrows, a bright red and beatific smile. Black plastic hair combed into a pompadour. Suddenly, she saw it whole. Round-tummied and kitschy, a pink-nippled dime-store Buddha, but one that had been customized with a jet-black pompadour for the gag-gift crowd. The Elvis Buddha. The size of a baseball.

Teresa closed her eyes again and reassembled that long-ago moment. During an argument in their living room, probably about Carrie or one of David's other casual affairs, she'd grabbed the Elvis Buddha and hurled it at her husband. It shattered against their front door, and he'd walked out. Why else would she have saved the snapshot from the Christmas dance? Why else would the Elvis Buddha's head be in her worry box? Had to be. Had to be.

She knit together what she knew. The chronology of her worry box suggested the argument must have happened between the Christmas dance and New Year's Day, when she'd clipped the news story about her classmates' deaths, made her grim amendment to the class photograph, sealed the box, and put it all away. Obviously, 1991 ended on some very low notes—friends dying in the streets, David gone, their marriage shattered like the Buddha whose head she now rolled in her hand.

How alone she must have felt at that year's end.

Another memory emerged from the fog. New Year's Eve. Serious funk. She'd locked her service piece in their fireproof safe and given the key to a neighbor for the night. She took the phone off the hook and tried to dull her aching loneliness with a fifth of Southern Comfort. She'd welcomed the dawn of 1992 alone and crusted with vomit.

But David came back, at least for a while. He must have, because she remembered their "final" break coming months later, about three weeks before she was attacked. And she remembered that vividly—how Buster hopped up into David's car; the puppy's bright brown eyes as he watched her from the car's rear window. She'd watched from their driveway until they were out of sight, then vowed to move on. No more pain. No more lies. No more . . . shaving. She let her pubic hair start growing that day. As she thought of it now, she caught herself scratching a phantom itch.

Just then, the bedroom door creaked. Teresa tensed as the door swung slowly open. There, in the dark frame, stood . . . no one. The door creaked again, opening wider. Then a sound: *Whap-whap-whap*.

Buster.

The black dog moved into the room, his roto-tail thumping the door and dresser as he passed, and found her perched on the edge of the bed. He sat at her feet, on her feet actually, and sighed, smelling like an old dog now. She scratched a muzzle that long ago had turned from black to silver, thinking of her husband sleeping down the hall, about how much had changed from those sad days to this.

Buster's ears were soft and warm, and Teresa rubbed them until her hammering heart slowed to normal.

28

Annie crossed her arms. She was pissed, and Christensen knew it. "You promised we'd go bowling yesterday and we didn't," she said. "Then you promised we'd get to the zoo early so we could be first in."

Christensen lifted his left hiking boot onto one of the stairs and pulled the laces tight. Brenna was locked in her office. Again. He was trying to keep things at home as normal as possible, but his patience was wearing just as thin as his daughter's. "It's only nine-thirty, Annie. The zoo doesn't even open until ten on Sundays."

"Shrimpo's not even ready." She shot a look at Taylor, who was pulling an oversized sweatshirt over his head. "Kelly said they were the first ones in line last Sunday, but they got there at nine."

"We'll be there when they open the gate," he said.

"But you promised—"

"Sweetheart, just stop," he said. "Please. This has been a rough week on everybody, and I'm doing the best I can."

"Why isn't Brenna going?"

"She's busy."

"As usual," Taylor said from somewhere deep in the sweatshirt. "How come she can't go?"

Christensen straightened the hood. "Your mom has a hearing tomorrow that's really, really important to her. She needs this weekend to make sure she's ready. So I told her we'd make ourselves scarce so she could concentrate."

"She doesn't want us around?" Taylor asked.

"It's not that, buddy. It's just, some days she needs time by herself to do her work. I think we should try to help her, don't you?"

Taylor shrugged. "She's always busy."

Christensen wanted to agree. It wasn't the first time he wanted to tell Brenna how badly her son needed her. Once, a few weeks back, the boy had found an old photo of himself as an infant. He was sitting in his high chair as Brenna fed him, and Brenna had been playing peek-a-boo with him from behind a Cheerios box. By his wide, toothless grin, you could tell he clearly delighted in his mother's attention. "We used to do things like that," he'd said, tracing a finger across the faces in the picture. "Now she's just all, you know, working and stuff."

Christensen hoped Taylor didn't notice him wince. Seven years ago, the boy had watched his parents' marriage collapse beneath the weight of Brenna's obsessive work habits. For the past week, he'd watched her turtling again into an intense, reclusive state in which her only words were commands and her focus entirely elsewhere. Christensen long ago had given up on changing her; the best he could do was soften the impact of her inattention on the kids. That was his role in the delicate balancing act of their relationship.

"And you sometimes feel like she's too busy for you?" Christensen asked.

Taylor looked at Annie. The boy looked as if he wanted to answer, but he hesitated. Finally, he shrugged.

"It doesn't mean she loves you any less," Annie said, spreading her arms like a pint-sized preacher, mimicking Christensen's voice, parroting the words he often used to put uncertain young minds at ease.

Christensen reproached his daughter with a look, then refocused on Taylor. "Annie's right. Your mom's a busy person, and this is just one of those times."

"I know."

"And I'm sure she's just as upset as you that she's so busy right now. You know there's nothing more important in her life than you."

The two kids exchanged a look that told Christensen they'd talked about all this before. Annie cleared her throat, apparently the designated spokesperson for the pair. She looked down the hall at Brenna's closed office door.

"We sort of think that's a load of crap," Annie said, crossing her arms again.

Christensen started to scold her for her language, but stopped himself. He looked at Taylor, who defiantly crossed his arms even as he looked away. This was serious. Annie and Taylor were united on something for the first time Christensen could remember.

"OK," he said, reeling. "I guess we all need to talk about this."

"Stop telling him that's just the way she is, and that that's OK. It's not," Annie said. "Sometimes it seems like she doesn't care, about Taylor or any of us. It's not fair."

Taylor's lower lip wavered. Christensen felt his do the same. Annie was nine years old, and in an instant she'd defined a problem that, even with his Ph.D. and years of studying human behavior, he'd managed to articulate only in his most private moments: Loving Brenna was, more often than not, a one-way street. It didn't matter how many platitudes, interpretations or rationalizations he offered. Sometimes nothing he could do or say could bridge the emotional distance Brenna put between herself and the people who loved her. He'd had to tolerate that distance in his father, who for years retreated into a quiet haze of passive alcoholism. But living with Brenna was a choice. In his darkest moments, Christensen had actually refined the problem to a nagging question: Had that choice been a good one?

He knelt down and motioned the kids forward. "I know how you feel, and I know how hard it can be," he said in a conspiratorial whisper. He put a hand on Taylor's shoulder. "There are reasons she's that way, I guess, but I know that doesn't help."

"Like what reasons?" Taylor asked, bolder now.

Christensen shook his head. "Maybe you should ask her."

"No way."

"Why not?"

Just then, the office door opened. Brenna emerged into the hallway in full stride, a piece of paper in one hand and her coffee cup in the other. If she wondered why Christensen was kneeling in the front hall in quiet conversation with the two kids, she didn't ask. She just marched up to them, thrust the paper at Christensen and said, "Try to keep the fax line clear. I've got stuff coming in all day."

Christensen looked at the unfamiliar page of type, then at Brenna. "Sure you don't want to take a break?"

She sipped her coffee, vaguely noticing their outdoor wear. "Going somewhere?"

"Jim's taking us to the zoo," Taylor said. "I told you this morning."

Brenna pretended to slap her forehead. "That's great, Tay. Just be careful."

"Yeah, Tay, be careful," Annie said. "I heard they just let the tigers run loose now."

The sarcasm was lost on Brenna, who just nodded to the paper in Christensen's hand. "You expecting anything else?"

Christensen looked again at the type on the page. His eyes fell briefly on the name Teresa, but other than that nothing looked familiar. "I wasn't expecting *this*. Sure it's not yours?"

Brenna took it back and scanned it. She saw Teresa's name, too, prompting her to read it more carefully. But in the end she just shrugged. "Nothing I need."

"No cover page?"

Brenna shook her head. Christensen examined the page's top edge, looking for the phone number of the fax from which it was sent. He found nothing, and that seemed odd. He looked up, intending to ask Brenna about it. She already was halfway down the hall.

"Thanks," he said, waving the paper. He folded it once and slid it into one of his jacket pockets.

Brenna closed the door again, and Annie rolled her eyes. "See?"

He faced the two kids. "OK. So what do we do?"

"Your call. I'm no shrink," Annie said. "Can we go?"

Christensen checked his watch. "Yep. We'll be there when they open the gate. Ready?"

"Like, duh," she said.

Christensen tied Taylor's shoes and herded him and Annie out the front door. "Be out in a sec," he called as he watched them vault down the front steps toward the Explorer at the curb.

He turned toward the office door, feeling as if he'd crossed some invisible line. For years now, he'd accepted whatever love Brenna could give him. He'd learned to live with the distance, and to play the buffer between Brenna and people—including her own son—who didn't understand. But things seemed suddenly different. If they were going to exist as a family, with or without the benefit of a marriage certificate, Brenna was going to have to deal with her problem. Otherwise—

Hell. Otherwise what?

Christensen knocked firmly and pushed through the office door. Brenna was on the phone. She shot him an irritated look, then excused herself from the conversation. She hit the Hold button harder than necessary.

"What?" she said. "Terry's helping me track something down."

Terry Flaherty, her law partner. He apparently had

given up his Sunday to help her prepare for the Della-Vecchio hearing.

"When we get back, you and I need to talk," Christensen said.

"About?"

"About everything, Bren. Just . . . everything."

"Everything," she repeated, shaking her head. "That's great, Jim. I've got all the fucking time in the world today."

"It's important, Bren. It's Taylor. He needs you. Save me some time, if not today, then after the hearing tomorrow. I'll explain what's going on, but right now I know you're busy."

"Busy?" Brenna gestured to the half-dozen cardboard file boxes on the floor, her portable DellaVecchio archive. She swept her arm over a desk littered with manila file folders, each containing some vital piece of the complex legal case she'd been assembling for eight years. Finally, with a dramatic flourish, she checked her wristwatch. "Hey, I've got twenty-three hours before I have to be in court. Maybe we could work in a vacation this afternoon, too."

"It can't wait long, Bren."

"Well, Jim, it has to." She turned her chair around so her back was facing him, and from that angle the gauzy bandage peeked through Brenna's hair. Christensen was about to ask Brenna if she minded being alone when she poked the Hold button.

"Terry? Sorry," she said. "Give me that citation again."

On his way out, Christensen made sure the house was secure. He closed the blinds at the front, set the alarm, and locked the deadbolts on the doors. The precautions gave him only the illusion of control, but sometimes that was better than nothing.

29

Christensen sat on a bench across from the lion enclosure, which unfolded behind thick viewing windows. He marveled at how the three captive African lions in the exhibit adapted to Pittsburgh's cold, damp, blustery weather. They'd adjusted their routines, their expectations, their entire metabolism to cope with the realities of life in a difficult environment. Now he wondered if perhaps he'd done that, too, and if it was still the right thing for himself and his daughters.

He'd wanted to start over after the prolonged agony of Molly's coma and death, the sooner the better, because life as a single parent frightened him beyond words. Melissa was thirteen at the time, and bitter about everything; Annie was just three. They needed a mother. He needed . . . what? Stability. A sense of family, whole and complete.

Brenna needed someone, too, but their needs were never the same. Taylor still had a father, and their relationship was sound. What had Brenna needed? A lover? A partner? A nanny? Sometimes he wondered. He understood his own feelings, looking back. She'd helped save him from criminal charges after he disconnected Molly's respirator; by the time that ordeal was over he was in love.

He pushed it; he was pushing it still. He wanted to be together. He wanted his daughters and her son to have at least a facsimile of a family, a sheltered place where love was unconditional and the relationships were reasonably healthy. But still, after six years together, Brenna, the emotional porcupine, had never really committed. A half-dozen times he'd suggested that they marry, and each time she curled inward and raised her spines. Each time she forced his retreat, he felt the distance between them grow.

Even the kids could see it now. Why hadn't he?

The lioness lay, paws up, on the other side of the window. Annie and Taylor were transfixed, chatting with a zoo volunteer. Christensen huddled on his bench, grateful for the time alone. He shoved his hands into his jacket pockets and hit paper. The strange, anonymous fax. He'd forgotten about it during that tense standoff at home. Now he pulled it out and unfolded it.

The single page had no real beginning or end. Its layout looked like a page from a transcript of some sort, with exchanges between two people represented by the initials RB and DH. The questions seemed to come from RB, the answers from DH. He spotted the reference to Teresa and thought, *DH, David Harnett.* Maybe. It began in mid-sentence:

> may have. There were so many cases like it they all run together after a while.
>
> RB: And nothing about that [unintelligible] stands out?
>
> DH: No sir.
>
> RB: Let's move on then. You said before that you were home that night.
>
> DH: Which night are you talking now?
>
> RB: New Year's Eve, 1991. You said you were home.
>
> DH: That's correct. [unintelligible] both had the night off, which is pretty rare.
>
> RB: So you weren't alone?
>
> DH: Just me and my wife.
>
> RB: Teresa.
>
> DH: Correct.
>
> RB: It was New Year's Eve. Most people go out and celebrate. But you stayed home?

DH: That's correct, sir.

RB: How come?

DH: It's amateur night, sir. All the drunks on the road. We stayed home. A lot of people do.

RB: Because of the drunks on the road?

DH: Mostly. We'd also had a disagreement [unintelligible] before, I think. Neither one of us was in the mood to go out and party.

RB: Do anything unusual? Open a bottle of champagne? Toast the New Year? Anything like that?

DH: Champagne gives my wife headaches. We may have had a beer or something. Mostly we just talked.

RB: Remember what you talked about?

DH: Nothing particular. Relationship stuff, I think.

RB: Anyone come over that night?

DH: No sir.

RB: Did either of you go out? Run to the store for anything?

DH: No sir.

RB: So you and your wife were at your house there on Morningside Avenue the whole evening of Dec. 31, 1991?

DH: Yes sir.

RB: What about during the day? Home all day?

DH: No sir. Because of the disagreement I mentioned, I'd been staying elsewhere for a few days. But I came home probably midafternoon Dec. 31.

RB: To work things out?

The page ended there, with an unanswered question. Christensen was sure the DH referred to David Harnett. Much of what DH said fit neatly with things Teresa had mentioned. He looked again at the answers, the stiff formality of his language. No sir. Yes sir. That's correct, sir. The language of a man in deference to some superior force.

Christensen flashed back to a conversation with Teresa, the one they had in her car the morning before. He remembered her astonished "Oh my God" as a memory came clear, the memory involving her husband, a drug dealer, and the police department's Internal Affairs Division. What had she said? The investigative panel had called David twice.

Christensen looked again at the paper in his hand. It had to be a transcript of one of Harnett's appearances before the IAD. But Kiger had told him those files were closed. Who would have access? And why would they fax him *this* page, which seemed inconsequential, even trivial. Odder still, why would someone fax it to his home and make sure that the fax was untraceable?

Christensen folded the paper again and put it away. He'd been so careful not to lead Teresa as she struggled into her past, but the memories she was unearthing all seemed to relate to her husband. Now this, and Christensen suddenly felt that someone was trying to lead him. But who?

"The lady over there said the one without a mane is really a boy," Annie said. "But they call him Sheeba anyway."

How long had his daughter been standing there?

Christensen stared a long time before saying, "I don't understand."

Annie rolled her eyes and pointed back through the enclosure window. "That lion. Somebody cut his nuts off."

"Annie!" Christensen said, conscious of the stares from other zoo patrons. "Watch your language." He looked at Taylor, who nodded and gestured subtly at his own crotch. "It's true," he said. "All his hair fell out when they castrated him. Sheeba's really a he, but he looks like a lioness. You can see his thing if you look close."

"Sheeba's a he," Christensen said, catching up.

"Heeba!" Annie said.

This cracked Taylor up, and off they went to tell the zoo guide.

Christensen checked his watch. Nearly noon. They'd seen everything in the zoo, some things twice, and still they'd given Brenna only half the day to herself. If they went to lunch and hit a movie, they could stay out of her hair for a couple more hours. But who was he kidding? He wasn't just trying to give Brenna time to get ready for the DellaVecchio hearing tomorrow morning. He was avoiding her. Going home meant finally dealing with what had become a corrosive problem. It meant tension and confrontation. It meant facing down the reality of a relationship in serious trouble, and Christensen wasn't at all sure he was ready for the consequences.

30

The spot along Howe Street where Brenna usually parked was empty, so Christensen paralleled into the space. Taylor was asleep in the back seat. Annie was in the front passenger seat, crunching away on the last of her movie popcorn. The realization came to him as an afterthought: Where's Brenna's car? His first thought was for her safety. His second was a wave of relief that she might not be home.

"I'll get Taylor if you get everything else," he said to Annie, cutting the engine. "Deal?"

"Deal."

He opened his door into the cold afternoon air.

"Dad?"

Christensen waited with one leg out of the car.

"I just want you to be happy."

He shut the door and turned to his younger daughter.

"Are you?" she asked.

"Mostly. Are you?

Annie shrugged. "Mostly."

"Why do you want to know?"

"I've just seen you happier, is all."

He reached across the seat and squeezed her shoulder. "Mostly's not bad, sport. It's really not. Some people never even get to mostly."

Another shrug. "Always would be better."

"Yep. Guess it would." Christensen brushed popcorn shrapnel off his daughter's face. "Know what? I miss your mom sometimes, too. It's OK to feel that way."

Annie nodded, then opened her door and climbed out. She gathered an armload of jackets and the empty popcorn bucket as she did. She shut the door with her foot and climbed the steps to the front porch. She was still waiting at the door when Christensen arrived with the dozing Taylor hoisted onto his shoulder.

"It's locked," she said.

Christensen shifted Taylor to his other arm and fished into his pants pocket for his keys, then unlocked the deadbolt and pushed into the silent house. He noticed that Brenna's office door was wide open as he keyed in the alarm code.

"Bren?"

He laid Taylor down on the living-room couch and covered the sleeping boy with a quilted comforter. Annie met him in the hall and handed him a yellow Post-it note as she rounded the corner, headed upstairs. "This was on the kitchen table," she said. "Pretty lame."

Christensen took the note. Brenna had written the time on top—3:25, just half an hour ago. The note read: "Sorry for the snit. I want to talk, too. Just not today. Better if I stay Downtown till after the hearing. Taking clothes etc. for tomorrow, overnighting at the office. Wish me luck. Tell Tay I'll call later to say good night."

An apology. An embedded acknowledgment of a problem. Christensen found those things promising. Maybe there was hope. Maybe the day's dark thoughts stemmed from his own wounded ego rather than an organic problem with their relationship. And she was right. There was no sense talking now with DellaVecchio's court appearance bearing down on her like a train.

Something unfamiliar caught his eye—a new answering machine Brenna had bought to replace the one the cops still had. Its tiny red eye winked at him from across the kitchen, and he crossed the room for a closer look. The numeral 1 was illuminated in blinking red on top. A large button in the middle said Play, so he pushed it.

"It's me."

A woman. Brenna? He leaned closer, feeling the machine's sides for a volume knob.

"Can you . . . please pick up if you're there. Hello?"

Not Brenna. Teresa.

"Shit," she said. "I'll have to call you back. It may be a while. Don't call me. Just . . . don't. But I need to talk to you, understand? I'll call when I can."

Christensen played the message again. Teresa's voice, no question, but it was warped and strained. The new answering machine, maybe? He found a Play Greeting button and pressed it. Brenna's outgoing message came through loud and clear, her voice as familiar as if she were standing beside him. So it wasn't the machine. He played Teresa's message a third time and recognized the fine thread of stress that made her voice higher and thinner than normal.

He had her home phone number, but resisted the impulse to call her there. She'd been clear on that, for reasons he could only guess. Uneasy, he went to the front door, opened it, and looked out on a quiet Sunday afternoon in Shadyside. What had he expected to see?

His next impulse was to call Brenna, and he felt a great relief when she picked up her private office line on the second ring.

"Hey," he said.

"Hey."

"You OK?"

She laughed, but it sounded forced. "Dagnolo's definitely decided to put Teresa on the stand tomorrow, which is fine because it means he hasn't come up with anything stronger. My DNA lab guy's got car trouble; we're trying to figure out how to get him to court. I need to go over some things with Carmen, and he's been out of touch since this morning. The cops all have their underwear in a bunch because his electronic bracelet's on the blink and they think he's screwing with it. Tell the truth, I'll be a lot better tomorrow afternoon."

"I'll let you go then," he said. "We still need to talk,

but it can wait. I just wanted to touch base."

"Thanks."

Christensen waited to see where she might take the conversation.

"Baby, I know I'm deep in the hole with Tay, with everybody. I'll make it up. But right now, this is where I need to be. I can't let this thing fall apart tomorrow, not after how far we've come. Eight years it took me to right this thing. But I promise, this hearing tomorrow is the goal line."

"Until the retrial," he said. "Or the next high-profile case."

"Wrong. This is once in a lifetime."

"How?"

"Jim, I'm defending an innocent man. Because I didn't do my job right the first time, he's been in prison for eight years. I can't let that happen again. I won't. Please tell me you understand."

Christensen tried. Brenna was talking about justice, but there was a difference between justice and redemption. Justice was about Carmen DellaVecchio. Redemption was about Brenna. Somewhere along the line, she'd lost sight of who she was doing this for, and who she was hurting in the process. It wasn't the first time, and that selfishness was her tragic flaw. He saw that now more clearly than ever before.

"I understand why this case is important to you." He winced at Brenna's relieved "Thank you" on the other end of the line. "But that's what we need to talk about when it's over, Bren."

There was a long pause before she said, "OK."

"So, where will you sleep?"

"I'll make up the couch in my office and use the showers downstairs at the Centre Club. I'd get home late and have to be back here first thing tomorrow, anyway. This just works out better."

"I agree. There's a twenty-four-hour security desk in the lobby, right?"

"Rent-a-cops," she said, "but they're usually awake."

"Great. Are you sure—"

"I'll be fine. You'll explain everything to the kids?"

"Yep."

"Jim?"

"Yeah, Bren."

"I love you."

The phrase was like a diamond, with countless facets, gradations in clarity, shadings of color. Christensen wished he knew what she meant. The best response that came was the one Brenna used so often: "I know."

31

Christensen woke with a start to an unfamiliar sound, like an electronic cricket. The room was dark. But which room? He rolled to his right and fell off the living-room sofa. Very dark now—the lamp was on a timer—and he was on his knees between the sofa and the coffee table. A crumpling beneath him. Paper. Now he remembered. Must have fallen asleep reading. A paper avalanche as he rolled off, showering him with the contents of Teresa Harnett's file.

Now the sound again. From the kitchen. *Chirrup-chirrup*. The new telephone?

His shin hit the coffee table and he swore as he lurched toward the kitchen. His left foot was asleep. Still holding some of the file papers, he flipped the light switch with his free hand as he hobbled past. The overheads flooded the kitchen with soft-white light, revealing a table littered with the kids' school books. His evening came rushing back at once: Brenna at her office for the night, the Sunday night homework crush, the usual bedtime battle, Brenna's nine-thirty good-night call. All followed by an unsettling fear, nagging questions, and the eerie pulse of the silent house. Something had been bugging him, and he'd decided to review the notes of his conversations with Teresa.

He found the new phone's Talk button. "Bren?" he said, and heard a ragged breath.

Finally: "No. Teresa."

Groggy, he repeated the name.

"I'm so sorry," she said.

Christensen checked the digital clock on the microwave—4:42. Pitch black outside the kitchen window. "What's wrong?"

A sob, followed by a strangled cry.

"Where are you?"

After a long, soggy moment: "Home. I'm OK."

"Can you talk?"

"David just left."

"Left? Again?"

"No, no. Not like that. He got a call maybe an hour ago, then he rummaged around in the garage for a while and left. Said it was nothing big, but he had to go. I wanted to tell you something this afternoon, but this is the first chance I've had to call you back."

"What is it?"

Teresa took her time. "I found something."

"Tell me."

She told him about her worry boxes, about the baffling collection and occasional memories she'd found as she sifted their contents. She told him how she'd found the odd-sized 1991 box under the spare bed and realized that David had overlooked it; how she'd reconciled some of the stuff from that box with what she believed were real memories. The Elvis Buddha's head and the fight with David. Saying good-bye to Buster. Suicidal thoughts. Her 1991 New Year's Eve funk. "It's weird," she says, "all this stuff coming up since we started talking. A few days ago you said something, you know, how bad memories probably wouldn't come back until I was ready? Well, maybe I'm ready. Maybe you've given me permission to remember."

"Or you finally gave yourself permission," he said.

He waited.

"I found something else," she said.

"In the box?"

"No, in a drawer, way in the back. My appointment planner from 1992. I never made a worry box for that year, because of what happened that spring, but I'd started saving 1992 stuff before the attack. I found it today, in the drawer of this old desk, and I was looking through it, and I found something and it's—" Another desperate breath. "Shit. I don't know what it is. Goddamn it. God-*damn* it."

Christensen was fully awake now. "Do you want to come over?"

"David may come back. I can't."

Christensen stopped himself from pacing back and forth in front of the kitchen sink. "Don't worry about what it means right now, Teresa. Just tell me what you found."

"It's just a note. An appointment. For the Monday after I was attacked. I don't remember it at all. But it's in my appointment book."

"Meaning?"

"I live by those things. I had it scheduled, so it's not like I'm remembering. It was scheduled."

"What was scheduled, Teresa?"

"IAD," she said. "For that Monday, it says 'IAD, 10:30 A.M. Two hours.' "

Christensen was lost. "The internal affairs investigation? The one involving David?"

"They must have called me to appear," she said. "From this, it looks like maybe I was supposed to talk to somebody from IAD that day. I'd blocked off two hours."

"Do you remember what it was about?"

"The Tidwell thing, I'm sure. That's the only reason they would have called me."

Tidwell again. David. What was the link? "Do you remember what you said?"

"That's the thing. It was scheduled for Monday. I never made it. The attack was on Saturday, remember, two days before. I was in Mount Mercy, half dead, so I never made it to the IAD appointment."

Christensen couldn't say why, but this felt like a break-through. He could feel it in the raised hair on his arms and the sudden, prickling knot at the back of his skull.

"And you think there's a connection?" he asked.

"I don't know."

"But you find it upsetting. Do you know why?"

"No."

"Teresa—" Christensen checked his frustration. For the first time, he sensed they were getting closer. When Teresa started down this path, Christensen could see no possible connection between an internal police investigation into a drug shoot-out and the vicious sexual attack on Teresa several months later. Now, at least, Teresa had found common ground. She'd been scheduled to talk with the IAD investigators about the Tidwell matter only two days after she was attacked.

"I was just thinking," he said, "that's really the first time you've put those two things together in the same time frame."

"I know."

"Any idea what it means?" He waited. Five seconds. Ten. An eternity, it seemed. He laid the file papers on the kitchen counter, determined to let Teresa lead, but the paper on top caught his eye. It was the printout of the *Press* story reporting the death of Tidwell and a rival drug dealer in an East Liberty alley. He scanned it again, focusing on the phrase "a New Year's Eve drug transaction gone bad." Both Tidwell and Fitzgerald dead at the scene, apparently for less than an hour. A pedestrian found them around midnight.

New Year's Eve? Christensen couldn't shake a feeling. The thought ricocheted from Teresa to the news story to the unfolded transcript page that lay beneath some of the other papers on the kitchen counter. Christensen tugged it out and ran his finger down the page until he found the phrase "New Year's Eve, 1991."

"Wait," he said. "You said something a minute ago about New Year's Eve. You were depressed."

"It's weird the things that come back," she said.

"Teresa, what brought it back? Do you remember?"

"The Elvis Buddha, remember. I told you. It was in the box, the broken head of this little ceramic—"

"Tell me everything you remember."

"About that New Year's Eve?"

"Is that when you had the fight with David?"

"I don't think so. It was maybe a couple days before. He left and took Buster, our puppy. I remembered all that, because I found the little head in the box and it all came back. But David came back, too. Later. Then he left again a few weeks before the attack, and that was the one I think really was the end, or at least that's how I—"

"Teresa," he said. "Focus on that night. New Year's Eve. What do you remember?"

"Just that night?"

"Exactly."

"Why?"

Christensen could see it now. He had more puzzle pieces than she did, and he pressed this latest one into place. The picture taking shape was repulsive. The urge to tell her was powerful, but he resisted.

"Don't worry about why. Just tell me what you remember. What happened that night?"

"Nothing much."

"Do better," he said. "Tell me what *did* happen."

"It sucked. I drank myself to sleep. I got sick. That's about it."

"Because you were depressed. Do you remember why?"

"David."

"Because you'd had a fight?"

"Yes. There was something else in my worry box, too. A newspaper story."

"About the Tidwell thing?"

"No. About these two cops who died in Bloomfield."

"Not the Tidwell thing?"

"Completely different. They were classmates of mine at the academy, apparently, and I saved the story in my 1991 worry box. They were ambushed."

"I remember that," Christensen said. "They never found out who did it, did they?"

"I *don't* remember," she said. "But it must have been a hell of a way to end the year. So between the thing with David, and that, it was . . . what I remember is locking my gun away and taking the key over to Carol's house. She's a neighbor."

"She knew you were depressed?"

"We talked a lot. She'd invited me to go along with her and Alec to some restaurant. But I just wasn't in the mood. We joked about it, how pathetic I was. I said, 'I think I'll just stay home and clean my gun or something.' And we laughed. But later I put the gun in our lock box and took the key over to Carol's. Didn't even tell her what the key was to, just asked her to hold it for me. I was just gonna stay home and get drunk as a skunk, and I just, you know, I didn't want to do anything stupid. I remember handing the key to her on her back porch."

"You didn't trust yourself with the gun?"

"Must not have. You think back, and you wonder how you could have got that way. But everything was just so shitty right then, and me all alone. Throw in a gun and a little booze and—"

"Wait, go back a sec," he said. "You planned to be alone that night?"

A confused pause. "That's what I said. David was gone. I was just planning to stay home and numb the pain."

"All night?"

"You mean was I alone the whole night? Yeah."

Christensen closed his eyes and braced himself on the edge of the kitchen counter. "You're sure?"

"Why?"

"Teresa, you're *sure*."

"Jesus, I'm sure. Calm down."

Christensen bit his tongue. Literally. He tasted iron, his own blood. Another puzzle piece fell into place.

"No one came to visit you that night?"

"No."

"Not David?"

"No."

"Do you know where he was that night?"

"No. He'd left a couple days before. I don't remember when he moved back in, but it was later. After the New Year. Then he moved out again a few weeks before I was attacked, but I remember that one night pretty clear."

"And you were alone the whole night?"

"Yes."

Christensen felt as if she'd handed him a ticking bomb. Whoever had faxed him that transcript page must have known that David Harnett had a serious problem. Teresa was telling him in no uncertain terms that she was alone on New Year's Eve 1991, the whole night. What stared Christensen in the face now was a clear and troubling probability: Her husband had told an IAD investigator he was with his estranged wife the night his accuser, Tidwell, was shot to death in an East Liberty alley. David had used Teresa as his alibi.

"There's no question in your mind that you were alone that whole night?" Christensen asked.

"No question at all. Why?"

Christensen's mind raced ahead. David Harnett had committed himself. He was with his wife that night, he told the investigator. They were mending wounds from their latest marital blowup. But the IAD investigation hadn't stopped there. The investigators summoned Teresa to confirm her husband's story. If she'd told them the same story she just told him, she would have completely undercut David's alibi for the night Tidwell died. Even if he had nothing to hide, they'd want to know why David lied.

Following that thread brought Christensen back to the most troubling fact of all, and it made him dizzy: Teresa was attacked two days before she was scheduled to meet with IAD investigators.

"Teresa, do you remember *why* the IAD investigators wanted to meet with you?"

"The Tidwell thing. I told you that."

"But what about it?"

"That I don't remember."

"Nothing? You don't remember the grapevine gossip about what was happening with that case?"

"Oh yeah. But it was so . . . typical. Those drug guys are vermin. First thing they do when their ship starts to go down is see who they can drag down with them."

"What had you heard? About Tidwell, I mean?"

"Rumors. The usual crap. He was talking to the D.A., trying to cut some deal. Nobody knew what it was about; they just knew IAD was looking into it. They'd talked to a bunch of people, mostly at the East Liberty station."

Time to push a little. Christensen leaned back against the kitchen counter. "Sounds to me like they were taking what Tidwell told them pretty seriously. You said they'd talked to David a couple times. They'd talked to other people. They wanted to talk to you."

"What are you getting at?" she snapped.

Christensen could feel it, something undeniable. Maybe Teresa felt it, too, but he wouldn't nudge her closer to it. If she knew what it was, the decision to confront it had to be hers alone.

"I'm just trying to make sense of what you're telling me, Teresa. The clear memories and the things you think you remember, the things David told you about your past and the things we know happened for sure. Sometimes they match up, and sometimes they don't. That's all. And

I'm trying to sort all that out, just like you asked me to. Because somewhere in that fog, I think, is the answer to the question we started with."

"About who attacked me?"

"Yes," he said.

On the other end of the line, Teresa's voice took on a sharp edge. "It wasn't David," she said. "I know that."

Christensen wanted to lay out his suspicions. He wanted to tell her what he knew about New Year's Eve and the IAD transcript and the conflict with her emerging memories. He wanted to ask Teresa why her husband would lie about his whereabouts that New Year's Eve, and if she saw any coincidence in the fact that she ended up nearly dead two days before she might have contradicted his story. What Christensen did, though, was repeat the testimony that David Harnett gave during Della-Vecchio's original trial. "David was with Brian Milsevic the night you were attacked, wasn't he?"

"Out whoring," she said.

"Whoring?"

"That much I know. I was attacked about dinnertime. At that moment, David was running a credit-card tab in some titty bar out near South Park. You think I'm stupid? You think I haven't thought the same thing you're thinking? But I had to know. I made Brian tell me the whole story. He said that's where they were when he got the page from headquarters."

"About the attack?"

"He called in, then took David outside and told him what happened. David didn't do it, Jim. I believe him, for those and a thousand other reasons."

Christensen peered into the darkness outside. In an hour the sun would be up. In five, Teresa would be in court to face down Carmen DellaVecchio.

"The hearing's today, Teresa," he said. "Dagnolo's got no choice at this point. You're all he's got. He's going to call you to the stand again and ask you the only question that matters: Who *did* do it? What then?"

Christensen felt the silence like a weight on his shoulders. Then, without another word, Teresa Harnett gently hung up the phone.

32

Christensen hit the Talk button and dialed Brenna's after-hours office line as soon as he got a dial tone. He wasn't sure exactly why. Today of all days, he couldn't tell her anything about Teresa, that her memories had jumped to an entirely different track, that Carmen DellaVecchio's name had barely even come up in all their conversations. He couldn't tell her the significance of the fax page she had handed him yesterday morning. Hell, he couldn't even tell her what he was now sure about: that David Harnett had something to hide. Without context, she couldn't possibly understand the significance of Harnett's lying about where he spent New Year's Eve 1991. If Christensen couldn't tell Brenna the whole story, or at least the story as it was developing, what could he tell her that would make any sense at all?

Nothing.

But he could at least hear her voice. He thought of the sniper shots into their bedroom, about the panic and fear and malice that drove whoever had a finger on that trigger. The threat to Brenna was real, no matter who the shooter was. Her voice. That was the reassurance he needed right now.

And wasn't getting.

Three rings. Four.

He imagined her asleep on her office couch, exhausted from a late night of work and pre-hearing anxiety. How long would it take her to hear the phone, struggle to her feet, and walk to her desk?

Five rings.

Or maybe she was ignoring it. Who'd call at such a ridiculous hour anyway? Finally, a voice. Voice mail. "You've reached the law offices of Kennedy & Flaherty.

We're not able to take your call right now, but please leave a message. Thank you."

"Bren, it's me," he said. "Just checking in. Sorry if I woke you. Just, ah, call home as soon as you get up. I know it's a busy morning, but please touch base, OK?"

The microwave clock read 5:02. On a day like today, she'd be up by six, for sure. Christensen willed himself not to worry until then, but then started to worry. He drummed his fingers on the counter. Outside, the first signs of dawn. The peaked rooftops across the alley were outlined against the charcoal sky, where only fifteen minutes before everything had been black.

The whole thing made a sickening sort of sense, but he was the only one who could see it. He alone had accumulated the troubling facts, and he alone had pieced together a terrifying theory about who attacked Teresa, or rather who had the best *motive* to attack her. At the time, her marriage to David was unraveling. He'd walked out, supposedly for the last time, three weeks before the attack. What triggered that? Teresa had been contacted by the IAD. What if her husband had asked her to flat-out lie about his whereabouts the previous New Year's Eve? What if she had refused, either on general principle or simply to protect her own job?

Maybe David *was* out on the town when it happened, but so what? Someone else could have carried out the actual attack. Besides, wouldn't that be a logical thing for a vengeful husband to do, assuming he'd be on the short list of suspects?

Christensen thought of the evidence found in Teresa's kitchen, and how limited it now seemed. A masked attacker who kept silent until he thought Teresa was safely dead. No fingerprints anywhere, just the artfully placed imprint of DellaVecchio's distinctively worn shoe stamped once like a notary seal in Teresa's blood. A savage sexual attack that was almost clinically clean, with none of the attacker's semen or blood or pubic hair left behind as evidence.

Christensen's heart was pounding as he paced the kitchen floor. He forced himself into a chair, tasting real fear in the gathering morning light. He tried Brenna's number again, and again got voice mail. He tried her car phone and let it ring until an electronic voice informed him: "The cellular customer you're trying to reach is unavailable. Please try your call again later."

On the table, face up, lay the cryptic fax that had arrived the day before. That was the wild card. Someone else suspected Harnett, too. Someone who knew that Christensen was involved. Someone who had access to internal police documents. Dagnolo? He was notorious for leaking information, but no. The man was too invested in the Scarecrow stalker fantasy he'd worked so hard to build. Milsevic? Maybe. The night Brenna was injured, he'd implied he was working a different investigative track. Or maybe . . .

Kiger.

No one else knew he and Teresa were talking. No one else had access to IAD files. Who else had clear enough vision to see the ghastly questions beneath the convenient artifice of DellaVecchio's arrest?

Kiger.

Christensen was suddenly struck by a thought so terrifying that he stood straight up out of his kitchen chair. Had anyone asked David Harnett where *he* was the night the sniper took those shots at Brenna? Then another: Where was Harnett now? Where the hell was Brenna?

The urge to talk to Kiger was overpowering. Seconds later, Christensen was on his knees in the dark living room, sifting through the spilled papers from Teresa's file. Somewhere in there was Kiger's card, the one he remembered had a pager number on it. He crawled over to the security timer for the lamp and spun it until the light clicked back on, then continued his frantic search until the chief's card finally surfaced.

He banged his shin on the coffee table again, same spot, tripping across the living room. He limped to the kitchen phone and squinted at Kiger's card. He got the pager number in focus and dialed. At the prompt, he entered their home number and pushed the # button.

Then he waited. For Brenna. For Kiger. For any reassuring words in a twilight the color of ash.

33

For the past hour, alone in his kitchen, Christensen watched the microwave clock, counting each minute that the phone didn't ring. As he waited, he turned his theory about David Harnett around and around, looking for holes. He imagined dozens of grim scenarios of revenge, cover-up, violence, all with Brenna as an unwitting victim. When the phone finally rang, Christensen jumped like a condemned man awaiting the governor's reprieve.

"Hello?" Practically shouted it, then held his breath.

"Who'm I speaking to, sir?"

Kiger. Christensen exhaled. He checked the clock—6:08. Surely Brenna was up by now. Maybe she'd gotten up already and gone downstairs to shower at the Centre Club before checking her messages.

"Got this number on my pager, but didn't recognize—"

"Jim Christensen, Chief. Sorry. I'm about half out of my mind here, and I couldn't think of anything else to do."

"It's fine," Kiger said. "There a problem?"

Where to start? Christensen tried to wring the panic from his voice. He was about to suggest, based on wisps of evidence and growing suspicion, that David Harnett may have tried to kill his wife eight years ago, and that Harnett may have done so to protect himself from Kiger's own investigators. He was about to suggest, too, that Harnett may have been responsible for murdering a mouthy drug dealer named Vulcan Tidwell.

"You still there?" Kiger asked.

"I'm just . . . this is really complicated. I'm not sure where to wade into it."

"Start with Teresa. What's going on?"

"Teresa," Christensen repeated. "OK. She's still focused on things I never expected. Her marriage, specifically."

"But what's she saying about DellaVecchio?"

Christensen shook his head. "A non-issue for her at this point."

The chief laughed, and the sarcastic edge to it was unmistakable. "She might be the only one," he said.

"What do you mean?" Christensen said.

"You watching TV? Ca-rist. *'Good Mornin', Pittsburgh!'* just led with it. You'd think this hearing was Judgment Day itself. So Teresa's not talking about DellaVecchio." He laughed again. "Well, got news for ya. Ever'body else in this damned town—"

"Chief," Christensen interrupted. "I need to tell you something, and I need to tell you now, and the first thing you need to know is that we've got two people missing that I'd like to get accounted for." Christensen knew it was spilling out, but couldn't stop it. "Brenna's one of them. Because of the hearing, she decided to stay Downtown at her office overnight. I talked to her about nine-thirty last night, but I've been calling her private line for the past hour and all I get is voice mail. She should be there, but I don't think she is. Or at least she's not answering, there or on her car phone. With everything that's happened, I'm worried."

"OK," Kiger said. "Who else?"

"David Harnett."

Christensen waited through a long pause, looking again at the clock—6:12.

"What you mean he's missing?"

"Teresa called me a little over an hour ago, very upset. Long story short, the memories she's coming up with all involve David. And now she's come up with something— something she's corroborated with an old appointment book, something she trusts—that makes me think he's involved in this a lot deeper than we ever thought. He might even have played some role in trying to kill her, and he may actually have killed someone else before that."

There. He'd said it.

"You're talking about the drug case," Kiger said.

"Right. There's a connection, I think. I got this fax—"

Christensen waited. He was sure now it came from Kiger. How would he react? When he didn't, Christensen continued.

"It's too complicated to explain right now. But basically, I think she was supposed to be David's alibi for the night Tidwell was killed."

"New Year's Eve, 1991," Kiger said.

"Exactly. When I put everything together, it looks like she wasn't even with him. She's telling me they had a big blowup a few days before. Couple months later he moved out. And not long after that she was called to talk to your IAD guys."

"That's the appointment y'all are talking about?"

"For a Monday. Somebody tried to kill her two days before. That's the sequence of events we should be looking at here. I'm thinking maybe David asked her to lie, and maybe she'd decided not to back him up. The minute she tells your investigators what she knows, David becomes a liar *and* a murder suspect. He *couldn't* let them question her."

He could hear Kiger's breathing.

"Teresa was supposed to die, Chief. She didn't, but she might as well have. Like you said before, she was as good as dead. Her memory of all that was wiped completely clean, along with her memories of a lot of other things. Who was in the best position to realize that? Who was the only person who understood she was no longer a threat? David."

"But DellaVecchio—"

"The straw man from the start, like Brenna's been saying," Christensen said. "Harnett planned for everything, because he knew Milsevic and the other investigators would be all over this one. DellaVecchio was tailor-made. He had a history, and Harnett was very familiar with it. Harnett could have hired somebody to kill Teresa, then had him plant the evidence that led straight to Della-Vecchio. He also made damned sure his alibi was solid, Chief."

"He was—"

"With Milsevic," Christensen said. "He must have known the lead homicide investigator would get the call on a high-profile case, so he made sure he was with Milsevic when it happened. It was perfect."

Kiger said nothing for an eternal moment. Then: "One problem. David's the one worked so hard to help Teresa put it all back together, right? She'd be the first one to tell you that."

"That's what I've been saying for years," Christensen said. "He was able to rebuild her past any way he wanted to, or needed to. A suggestion here. A prompt there. Then he waited for those suggestions to come back as 'memories.' He took Teresa out of the Tidwell equation at the same time he built your case against DellaVecchio. When she finally testified, she said exactly what he needed her to say. He steered her, and all of you, right to Della-Vecchio. And I think maybe he's doing it again. How hard would it be to imitate DellaVecchio's voice on the phone, or to dump one of his ashtrays on that roof?"

Kiger cleared his throat. "Lemme get this straight. Y'all are saying what she remembers is mostly what he told her? And what he told her was what he needed her to say?"

"About everything. About DellaVecchio. About the night she was attacked. About the night Tidwell died. Some memories he planted. Some he weeded out. And what she's struggling with now are conflicts between what he told her happened and the memories she's starting to recover. They don't always match up, so for her it becomes a question of trust. Should she trust David, or her own memories?"

"But if that's the case—" Kiger said, then stopped. Christensen could almost hear the inconsistencies rolling around in the chief's head. "Tell me sump'n. Why's she still with somebody she thinks mighta tried to kill her?"

"I can't answer that," Christensen said. "When I push her on it, she pushes back. She says she considered the possibility that David attacked her, even did some checking on her own. Bottom line, she just doesn't believe he could have, or would have, done it."

A skeptical silence.

"Think about it," Christensen said. "Forget the asshole who was driving her nuts with his affairs and indifference before the attack. Think about the man she knows, the one who's been with her since the attack. The husband she knows is devoted to her. He's helped give her back something she lost. He was there for her when she needed him most. How could she possibly believe he would try to kill her? It just wouldn't compute."

"Well, *somebody* attacked her. So you ain't really moved us much from where we started."

"I'd bet David hired someone. The point is, he's the one with a *reason* to kill her. That's the main thing you people look at, isn't it? Motive?"

"You're saying he carried on that devoted-husband charade? For eight years?"

"Maybe it's not a charade," Christensen said. "I'm not convinced it is." Another glance at the clock—6:15.

"Then why—"

"Could be a couple different things. Self-preservation, maybe. He needed access to her to control her memories, and the only way to maintain access was to be the devoted husband, or at least play the role. Or maybe it's just guilt.

Say all this is true, that he tried to kill her, or have her killed. The attempt failed, but in the process she lost the memories he considered a threat. There *was* a relationship there, remember, even as flawed as it was. Maybe he felt like he owed her because he'd hurt her so bad. Guilt. Or maybe it was just easier for him to love someone he knew couldn't hurt him."

Christensen's mind skipped back to an earlier conversation with Teresa, the one about her pubic hair and the reason she was growing it back. "Wait. There's something else that came up. Teresa's convinced that whoever attacked her knew her pretty well." He cleared his throat, deciding how much to say. "He knew personal things, stuff only someone who knew her intimately, and before the attack, would have known."

"David again?" Kiger said.

"Maybe. Probably. But remember, the marriage was falling apart. She told me herself she was no saint. She was seeing somebody, too. But I have no idea who—"

The possibility must have struck them both at the same time.

"Can you find out?" the chief said.

"She won't tell me until she's ready, but I can try."

"Do that."

The microwave's blue digits blinked again—6:18. "Damn," Christensen said. "I've got to try Brenna again. The more I think about this . . . You have any idea where Harnett might have gone early this morning? Teresa said he got a call and left their house a couple hours ago."

"You're thinking what?"

"I'm thinking—hell. In about three hours Brenna's going into court to prove that somebody other than Carmen DellaVecchio tried to kill Teresa. If she's good—and Brenna's very good—she'll do more than that. She'll leave so many questions hanging in that courtroom that whoever did it is going to feel the searchlight pass damned close. He's known this was coming for three weeks now. He's already tried to kill Brenna once, thinking he can shut the whole thing down if he can just shut her down. Now he's running out of time, really starting to sweat. Desperate people do desperate things. That's what I'm thinking."

Christensen closed his eyes. "I need your help," he said.

It was a reckless appeal, but straight from his heart. Kiger's reaction would say a lot, for better or worse.

"Awright," the chief said. "I'm not saying there's anything to this theory a yours, understand? But I'll send somebody over. Tell me where she's supposed to be."

34

Annie was buried in a mound of down. When Christensen peeled back the comforter he saw she had the tattered remains of Molly's old nightgown clutched to her chest. Her Silkie. It had comforted her through some rough times, and he was glad she had it now.

He shook her gently. "Wake up, sweet girl. I need to tell you something."

His daughter sat up, seemingly wide awake. She looked around her room, said something that sounded like "Where's the stool?" and lay back down, apparently still asleep.

"Annie, sweetheart, wake up. I need your help this morning. I'm putting you in charge, because I have to go."

She sat up again, looked at the dim daylight outside her bedroom window. "What time is it?"

"Early," he said, trying hard to look like he was just heading off to work a little sooner than usual. "About six-thirty. I have to go somewhere for a while, and I won't be able take you guys to school or help you get your breakfast. But I put ice packs and Pizza Lunchables in your lunchboxes. You can add anything else you want. Get Taylor up and help him get his cereal. I already put the milk on the table. Clean up when you're done, brush your teeth, and get dressed. I already called Mrs. McFalls. She'll be over as soon as she can to help you and drive you guys to school, but you have to be up when she gets here, OK?"

Annie blinked. How much of that could a sleepy nine-year-old absorb?

"I'm in charge?" she asked.

"It's a big responsibility. Can you handle all that?"

She nodded. "What's the catch?"

"No catch. I just need your help this morning because I have to go somewhere to help out on something. It's important."

Annie studied his face. "Where's Brenna?"

"She stayed down at her work, remember?"

"So where are you going?"

"Annie, I need to explain all this later, OK? Right now I just need to go. It's no big deal. Everything's fine. But I need you to make sure you guys get up and get ready for school. You'll do that for me, right? I'm counting on it."

"Taylor has to do whatever I say?"

Christensen nodded, reluctantly, knowing he was opening the door for his little dictator to abuse her power. "Don't make a big deal out of it. You know the morning routine and so does he. Just get everything done, lock up the house with your key, make good choices today, and come straight home on the bus after school. I'll try to be here when you get back."

He kissed her warm forehead and savored the sweet strawberry scent of her favorite shampoo, then got up to go.

"Dad?"

He turned, expecting she wanted some clarification about the breadth of her new power. Instead, she looked like a frightened child. He bent to her again and hugged her tight. "Everything's going to be OK," he said. "Promise."

"OK." She held up her threadbare piece of comforting silk. "Need this?"

He smiled. She was every bit as perceptive as her mother had been. "You keep it. But thanks."

The streets were quiet, the morning rush still an hour away. Christensen started the Explorer, but reached for his cell phone as he put it in gear. He punched in Kiger's pager number, then entered the number of his phone. Kiger called back within two minutes, just as Christensen was turning right onto Fifth Avenue, heading toward Oakland and the city beyond.

"Y'all're right," the chief said. "She ain't there."

Christensen felt as if he'd stepped into a hole, as if he were falling. "Where's Harnett?"

"We're tracking that," Kiger said. "No word yet."

"Tell me what you found at Brenna's office." Christensen tightened his grip on the steering wheel.

"My guy talked to the Oxford Centre security people. Looks like she signed in yesterday afternoon. She's still signed in, but she's not there. The front-desk guy never saw her leave. Coulda gone out through the parking garage. Somebody'd blocked open one of the entrances down there."

"What about her car? She's got a reserved space in the garage. The security people could—"

"Gone," Kiger said.

Gone.

"Maybe she just went out early for coffee or breakfast," Christensen said. "They check her office?"

"Slept there least part of the night. My guy says there's a sofa bed or sump'n, sheets and blankets all rumpled up. Lights were all out. Alarm set for five-thirty, and it went off like it was supposed to. Clock radio was on when they got there. No sign of a struggle or anything like that. The only thing is about the parking spot. We're checking sump'n there."

"Checking what?"

"Could be anything, but we wanna look a little closer at it, is all. Just sort of stuck out."

"What?"

"When she came in yesterday, you know if maybe she was bringing flowers or anything like that?"

Flowers? "I wasn't home when she left, so she could've been. I don't know. Why?"

"Bringing them down here to a friend or anything? Like a buncha different flowers?"

"Not that I know of."

Christensen checked his speed. He was rolling down Fifth at almost sixty miles an hour, so he lifted his foot off the accelerator.

"There was a coupla flowers down there, just lying there in the parking spot. Roses. But we don't know—"

"Wait." Christensen felt a wave of dread. "One red and one white?"

The light at Bellefield turned from green to yellow. No way Christensen could make it now that he'd lost momentum. He hit the brakes hard and the Explorer jolted to a stop. Through it all, Kiger said nothing. As Christensen sat listening to the blood pound in his ears, the chief finally said, "Wanna tell me how you knew that?"

Goddamn.

"Remember?" Christensen said. "Teresa got two roses before she was attacked. Dagnolo always claimed DellaVecchio sent them as part of that bullshit stalking—"

"Your boy could be AWOL, by the way. Or not. The damned bracelet still ain't working, and we're trying to run him down."

The comment made Christensen pause, but only for a second. "Brenna always thought the flowers were part of the setup, to make it look like DellaVecchio was obsessed with her. Either way, the red-and-white thing is the same. And it's scary, or at least Teresa thinks so. Red and white. Love and death. That's how she remembers it now, as a threat."

Christensen pounded the steering wheel. "*Shit*! Why didn't I see it?" He wanted to run the light, but there was too much cross-traffic.

"Awright," Kiger said. "I'm still home, but I'm gonna go on over—"

"Tracktron!" The thought seared Christensen like a bolt of lightning. "You guys monitor that, right?"

"The stolen car-tracking service?" Kiger asked. "What? Is her car wired?"

"That'd at least tell us something. They're pretty fast."

"Usually just a couple minutes. What's she drive?"

"An Acura Legend, about five years old. Registered in her name."

"Hang on," Kiger said, and the line went silent. The Bellefield light turned green. The Explorer lurched forward into the intersection. Christensen was doing forty before he was past Heinz Chapel, fifty as the light turned red at Bigelow Boulevard. The intersection suddenly filled with pedestrians and crossing cars, so he put the car into a sideways skid. It stopped, finally, in the crosswalk in the far right lane. A pedestrian with a familiar face stepped around his front bumper and wagged a finger at him. *Jesus.* It was Fred Rogers, probably on his way from the WQED studios on Fifth to the PAA for his regular morning swim. *My God*, Christensen thought, *I nearly mowed down Mister Rogers.* He mouthed the words "I'm sorry" through the windshield, grateful for the forgiving smile of public television's most beloved icon.

"Hang on," Kiger said. "I got Tracktron on the line with somebody Downtown. They're running it now."

The crosswalk cleared, but the light stayed red. "A silver Legend," Christensen said, feeling helpless.

"Color don't matter," Kiger said. "Sit tight."

"Easy for you—"

"Gimme that again, Jerry," Kiger said, his voice softer. Talking into another phone. "Got it. That the best you can do?" After a pause. "Will do." To Christensen, he said, "Schenley Park. Looks like down around Panther Hollow, least that's their best guess. You know any reason that car might be down there this time a day?"

Schenley Park. Maybe a mile. "I'm right there!" Christensen shouted as the light turned green. He felt his body kick into overdrive. There was no reason why Brenna's car would be in that isolated ravine in the middle of Oakland's sprawling public park, at least no reason that made sense outside this nightmare.

He looked left, hoping to make an impossible turn across six lanes. If he did, he could be at the park entrance in less than a minute. He held his ground as the other cars moved forward. Three, four, five passed. From the car directly behind, an agitated blast. Six. In his rearview mirror, empty lanes. He gunned the Explorer and lurched halfway across, nearly into incoming traffic. Tires screeched. Another blast.

"The hell you doing?" Kiger asked.

"I'm right near Schenley, on Bigelow!" Christensen shouted, edging the SUV's nose into the onrushing flow. A burst of code and descriptors from Kiger's scanner somewhere in the background. Christensen recognized only the words "silver Acura."

"Just went out on the radio," Kiger said. "We've got patrols in the area. Meet 'em, y'hear? Don't you go down in there without—"

"There's a maintenance yard or something there," Christensen said. "Off Schenley Drive, behind Phipps. Tell them to turn at the Columbus statue and just follow it back, maybe a hundred yards. A service road goes down from there, right under the bridge. I run on it in the summer."

"You wait for our car," Kiger ordered. The lazy drawl was completely gone. "They'll meet you there."

Christensen sped past the Cathedral of Learning and turned left through a red light at Forbes, sending an onrushing minivan into a panic skid. A quick right put him into the Carnegie Library parking lot, hurtling the wrong way down a one-way aisle. He forked left onto the Schenley Bridge. The car shuddered as it hit a pothole, then bounced across the center line as its speed climbed. The Columbus statue was straight ahead, and just before it he veered onto a narrow blacktop road that disappeared into the trees.

"I'm serious, goddamn it." Kiger shouting now. "You wait. You don't know what you might walk into down there."

Christensen surveyed the maintenance-yard parking lot ahead. The only car there was a dark-blue Chevy. "There's a car, looks like maybe a city car, but there's nobody in it. I don't think it's one of yours. How long's it gonna be?"

"Soon's we get a response I'll tell ya."

"Bullshit," Christensen shouted back. "How long?"

Kiger hesitated, said something to Jerry on the other line. "We're trying to divert somebody."

Christensen cut the engine and opened the door. With the phone still in his hand, he stepped onto the gravel lot outside a building labeled "Schenley Park 4th Division/Pittsburgh Department of Public Works." The road beyond the building was rutted and muddy, but as far down as he could see it was scored by a car's recent tracks. Overhead, the decrepit span of the Panther Hollow Bridge blocked the sun.

"I'm leaving my car at the maintenance building and going in on foot," he said.

"Do *not* leave your car," Kiger said.

"There's nobody here!"

"*Wait*, goddamn it!"

Christensen thought of Brenna, of the hulking Harnett, of the possibility that the two of them were somewhere down in that dim and foreboding hole. "I can't," he said.

As soon as he hung up, he hit the speed-dial combination for Brenna's car phone. Just as when he'd tried it from home, it rang and rang. He had no choice. Searching the Explorer's interior for something, anything, he could use as a weapon, he pulled the driver's seat forward and found his ancient ice scraper, with its cheery red brush bristles at one end of the long wooden handle and a molded plastic scraper at the other. It would have to do.

35

Dark. Brenna closed her eyes and opened them again. Still dark. Breathtaking pain radiated like powerful fingers from the back of her neck to the front of her skull, crushing logical thought. She thought, *Dark's good. Light might kill me.* In her haze, she imagined light like a knife, stabbing through her eyes into the pulsing pain center of her brain. In that vaporous, incoherent moment, she thought, *The dark is keeping me alive.*

She tried to move her head. Her body tensed instantly, and she drew one quick breath, sharp and desperate. Now the rest of her throbbed like a nerve rubbed raw. She heard herself moan. And something else, distant but familiar, soft but painful beyond question—the shriek of her car phone. She knew its call like the cry of her own child. Again and again, somewhere . . . else. Each ring jolted her, but she dared not move again.

She closed her eyes; the effort to keep them open was exhausting her. She imagined someone bringing a hammer down on a spot just behind each eye, crushing the stalk, reducing the optic nerve to a mushy pulp but leaving the eyeball intact. Yes. That's exactly how it felt.

The phone stopped ringing, but the earth suddenly moved. A gentle roll to one side, a jostle, followed by another sound, a muted pulse. It sounded almost like a muffled gunshot, but she knew it wasn't. The sound was too familiar—a car door's electric locks. Nothing else sounded exactly like that.

"Mmmmph," she said, and the effort to speak registered on the back of her eyelids. A thousand pinpricks of pain unfolded like a constellation, and she felt herself start to black out. Air. She needed air. She tried to open her mouth and felt the skin across her face pull tight. Something was wrong. No air came. She felt for a moment as if she were drowning, then realized she was breathing only through her nose. She probed with her tongue, but it stopped at her lips. She pressed it hard against whatever was stretched across her mouth, trying to push through, but felt it flatten against that unexpected wall. The effort pulled again at the skin on her face.

Duct tape, she thought.

For the first time, an adrenaline chill mixed with the pain. The sensation triggered something, an image that suddenly flashed in the darkness like lightning. Eyes. Vicious eyes. Staring down at her through the red-rimmed holes of a ski mask. Behind them, in the dusky moment, she recognized the track lights in her law-office ceiling. And she felt hands, powerful hands. She felt their size and strength as she surged against them, fighting, scratching, struggling against a flurry of fingers that smelled like latex and chlorine.

Then darkness. And pain. She was back in the here and now, wherever and whenever that might be.

It would be torture, but she had to explore. She curled the toes on her right foot. This time the pain reassured her; at least her primary systems were working. She tried to lift the foot, and the effort sent a searing wave up her spine and down her left arm. She braced herself for another go and tried again, extending her knee only a few inches before the foot found a wall. She pressed hard and felt pressure against the top of her head. Those were the limits of her world at the moment, a dark space maybe five feet across. She struggled against the clutching fear of confinement.

Another sound, muted again but familiar. A car door latch sprung open, maybe two in quick succession, followed by the same rocking sensation she felt before. She wondered, *the trunk of a car*? She tried to reach a finger forward, only to realize her arms were pinned behind her.

The right one was numb, asleep beneath the weight of her body. She wiggled the fingers on her left hand, felt in her grasp the deadened fingers of her right. She curled her left index finger down toward her wrist and felt duct tape again.

In the darkness, as slowly as she could, she felt behind her for other clues. Her left hand hit a rigid hump. She let her fingers explore its dimensions and play across its surface, and suddenly she knew where she was. Her hand had found the CD changer mounted in the Legend's trunk. She was curled semiconscious into the trunk of her own car, her hands bound behind her, her mouth taped shut.

This struck her, at first, as preposterous.

Then, as her mind cleared, as terrifying.

She'd gone to her law office to work, to stay overnight and work on . . . DellaVecchio. She'd crashed, late, on the fold-out couch and then . . . *Oh shit, the hearing. Jesus. What time is it? What day?*

She heard the Legend's rear door open just behind her head. The car bumped and swayed as someone crawled into and out of the passenger compartment, then stopped moving as whoever it was stepped outside again. She heard the chinking *clank* of metal on metal and the *clack-clack* of wood hitting wood, as if someone were wrestling something awkward from the backseat.

Nothing made sense. She pulled a long breath through her nose, hoping the air would clear the fog in her head.

Outside the car, she could hear footsteps, the sound of one person, maybe two, moving heavily over damp earth. Sometimes, she heard the crackle of dried leaves. Which made no sense at all. Damp ground and dry leaves? Where could that be? A forest? She was weighing that possibility when the footsteps moved away from the car, receding into some indefinable distance. When they were gone, she tuned into the other sounds coming from outside the trunk.

What she didn't hear bothered her most. Where was the traffic noise? She had no idea what time of day it was, but even if it was the middle of the night she couldn't imagine a place in the city without the hum of cars and trucks. She listened more carefully. Birds? And now something else, in the distance, from the same direction she'd heard the footsteps disappear: *Ch-shik.*

And again: *Ch-shik.*

No matter how hard she tried to make sense of what was happening, coherent thoughts wouldn't come. She was aware only of a developing rhythm.

Ch-shik.

Ch-shik.

Ch-shik.

She counted maybe four seconds between each sound, her sense of dread rising as the cadence revealed itself. Even now, disoriented by pain and darkness and claustrophobic fear, she understood one thing clearly—the sound a shovel makes as it slices into soft earth.

36

Christensen raged into the cool embrace of Panther Hollow. The trees were bare in early spring, but the branches overhead formed a thick canopy of ash, maple, and hickory. Golden shafts of morning sun showered from above, spotlighting small sections of the surrounding forest and the rutted road that was taking him down into the deep ravine.

He passed under the decrepit span of the Panther Hollow Bridge, then followed the road left, running full tilt with his ice scraper down the service road's first significant dip. Through the trees to his right, way down on the hollow's floor, he could see a fountain dancing at the center of a small pond. The branches of a weeping willow hung well out over the water. A little more than a year earlier, on a bench beneath that tree, Brenna had first suggested that they move in together. "Merge the households," she'd said, leaving him to calculate, or miscalculate, her precise levels of love and commitment.

He couldn't think about that now.

The road narrowed and got steeper. He should have shortened his stride for control, but his steps got longer as he sprinted down the damp, treacherous slope. The road leveled off, and just ahead was a small stone bridge across a rushing creek. Christensen read its chiseled cornerstone as he flashed past: "WPA 1939." Just beyond it, the road forked. One part dipped even deeper into the forest, to the right. The other narrowed further still as it rose to the left, back up to street level. Tire tracks scored the soft mud of both forks.

He stopped, panting, his breath rising in wispy vapor around his face. Damn. He crossed the bridge again, back to the last clear imprint of the tracks he'd been following from the maintenance yard. He knelt down and memorized the tread pattern, which was clearly from a snow tire. Brenna's Legend had snow tires. That much he knew.

He checked the freshest tracks on the left fork. They were wider and deeper, with knobby tread along the edges. A maintenance truck, maybe? They clearly didn't match, and none of the older, drier sets did either. He moved across the fork, knelt down, and found the snow tire tracks immediately. They bore right, deeper into the chasm.

Christensen felt as if he were running toward the dark bottom of the ocean. This far down in Panther Hollow, the shafts of sunlight became pinpoints. The gold was fading to the color of lead, and he was surrounded by the damp smell of forest decay. His ankle gave way as he stepped on a rock the size of a golf ball. Momentum carried him forward, arms tracing a desperate pattern in the air. He lurched for several strides with his chest parallel to the ground, but he didn't go down. He skipped for a few steps to test the ankle, then continued his headlong descent, the pain dulled by panic.

The road dwindled to a path. He was deep in the hollow, alone with an ice scraper, looking for a nightmare. The snow tire tracks turned left up ahead into what looked like a small clearing. The heavy chain across the clearing's entrance was down in the mud. It disappeared completely in two places where the car had driven over it. Christensen stopped to catch his breath, and that's when he heard a noise, dull and indistinct, coming from the clearing. Then he saw it. In the dim light, on the other side of a stand of maples, a swatch of silvery steel.

He stepped off the road and crouched behind a boulder, wondering whether he'd already been seen. Or heard. For the next thirty seconds, he focused on his breathing, willing it back to a resting rate. *You don't know what you might walk into down there*. Stealth couldn't hurt. Neither could self-control.

The Legend, if that's what it was, was maybe twenty-five yards away. Following the tracks would take him right to it, but he'd be completely exposed as he approached. Not an option. He might be able to make a wide circle to the right, move between trees and rocks, stay hidden until he was close enough to get a better look. The ground was a minefield of leaves, twigs and fallen branches, but it was his best shot. He moved off, stepping cautiously, keenly aware of every rustle and snap.

A minute later he was fifteen yards closer, standing behind a sturdy oak, staring at the back end of Brenna's empty car. One of the rear doors was open. The courtesy light along the door's lower panel glowed—an eerie still-life suggesting something out of order.

Then, the car moved. Or did it? Christensen blinked. A subtle shift of weight maybe, but it caused the rear shocks to sigh. He leaned around the tree, waiting to see if the car moved again, when a man stepped into full view from the woods just beyond the car.

His ski mask registered first, a black full-face cover with red trim around the holes for his eyes, nose, and mouth. Christensen thought of terrorists, of Klansmen, of cowards of all stripe who carried out their work from behind a mask. Then he noticed the shovel, spade-end up, which the man used like a walking stick as he hurried toward the car. Despite the cold, his gray sweatshirt was damp at the underarms, and there was an oval of sweat at the center of his broad chest. Fresh mud spattered the legs of his sweatpants. Christensen had no easy way to gauge scale, but the man looked well over six feet tall.

The masked man took off his leather work gloves and laid them on the car's hood, revealing hands that to Christensen seemed oversized and unnaturally white. He looked closer as the man let the shovel fall to the ground. He was wearing surgical gloves underneath the work gloves. Christensen noticed his massive forearms, and in that moment he was sure he was looking at David Harnett.

Circling to the driver's side, Harnett put his knee on the backseat and leaned into the open rear door. The Legend sagged. When he backed out again, he had a handful of black steel.

The gun was unimpressive—like the pictures in posters that urged a ban on Saturday night specials—but a gun nonetheless. Christensen tightened his grip on the long handle of his ice scraper. Where the hell was Brenna? The question consumed him right up until Harnett slid a key into the trunk lock.

Then he knew.

37

Light poured in, obliterating the darkness. Brenna felt it like an explosion as the trunk lock popped and the rear deck rose. In a sudden rush of fresh air, she recoiled deeper into the tiny space. Her body jerked and shuddered.

She'd known it was coming. The digging had stopped, and she'd heard footsteps circling the car again. As soon as the key slid into the lock, she'd braced for pain. It was worse than she'd imagined, an agony that turned her rigid, knotted her fingers and made her whimper like a child. She hated herself for that.

She bucked and turned face down into the trunk's synthetic carpet, desperately seeking relief in its dark fibers. The trunk floor smelled of ammonia and rubber and grease, and it nearly made her gag. A hulking shadow passed over her, and she welcomed it. At least it blocked the light. In that relieved instant, she turned her face and opened one seething eye toward the silhouette above her.

It was shaped like a giant beer keg with a head. She squinted, searching for detail until the silhouette had a face. She counted four red circles—two eyes, a nose and a mouth. She'd seen those red-rimmed eyes before. Then they'd seemed vicious; now they just seemed startled.

"Jesus H.," it said.

A man's voice. He bent toward her, and she felt the same hands she remembered struggling against in her darkened office. The latex smell. The stifling odor of chlorine. The power. It came rushing back to her in a sickening wave. He grabbed her upper arm, the one on top, and pulled as if it were a handle. She tried to relax, to pretend she was still unconscious, thinking, *Pick your shot, Brenna. Wait. Don't waste whatever you've got left.*

But she tensed and whimpered again as searing pain arced through her.

He rolled her forward and checked her wrists, making sure they were still secure. Then, in a single motion, he lifted her like a suitcase and set her in the wet dirt behind the car. She stared at the elastic ankle gathers of mud-spattered gray sweatpants and a familiar pair of basketball shoes. Frankensteins. Almost completely unlaced to accommodate the large feet that seemed stuffed inside. But she'd seen shoes just like them.

Last month.

In prison.

On Carmen DellaVecchio.

But it wasn't him. Too big. The voice all wrong. She looked up. The sky above was laced by branches, but that could be anywhere in forested western Pennsylvania. The man closed the trunk and bent toward her again. He hoisted her by her tethered arm, apparently without effort. Every nerve in her body came alive as she rose. He set her on uncertain feet, then leaned her back against the car trunk. She focused her strength on her neck, struggling to support her head. But it fell backward; it weighed ten thousand pounds. He grabbed the collar of her shirt, the one she'd been wearing when she fell asleep at the office, and pulled her upright again. Her head tipped forward as he held her steady with an enormous white fist that smelled like a doctor's office. She looked down at his other hand and saw the gun.

The fog cleared. *He's about to kill me*, she thought. *So that's how it ends.* Taylor's face popped into her head, first as an infant, then as a boy. She saw him with Jim, holding Jim's hand, and felt herself relax. Taylor was with Jim. He'd be fine.

Jim.

Who'd understood from the start the limits of her love.

Who'd loved her anyway.

She willed the thought away, but in its place came a cold, analytical reality. She'd known enough killers to understand what was happening. This guy knew exactly what he was doing. He'd driven her here in her own car, so there'd be no vehicular evidence to trace. Her hair, blood, any contact matter at all, would be in her own trunk. He'd waited until now to kill her; that way he could control the death scene. A smart killer would walk her to her grave, shove her in, shoot her, and bury her along with the blood and bullets and anything else that might help the cops figure out what had happened. He might get away with it, too, as long as he controlled the scene.

He leaned her forward, balancing her against the car's trunk, then eased himself around behind her. The once-numb fingers on her right hand were alive again, and she felt the smooth cotton of his sweatpants as he snaked one of his arms around her waist. He waited until her feet were under her, then said, "Walk."

She stumbled. He lifted and shoved her toward the place where she'd heard him digging. *So this is how it ends.*

She thought of Taylor.

She thought of Jim.

She grabbed his balls with both hands.

"Fuck!" he howled.

She felt him give, and saw his gun hand rising reflexively toward her head. But she was beyond pain. She squeezed through the cotton sweats with all her might. A death grip.

"Bitch!"

The gun's butt connected with the back of her head, but she held on. He turned her toward the car, shoved her forward, and pressed all his weight against her, pinning her face down against the trunk lid. She turned her head as he raised his gun hand again, saw him bring it down hard on the side of her head, peppering the car's silver paint with flecks of her blood. *Good*, she thought. *Evidence. A voice to tell my story.*

Behind her, he gasped desperately for breath. He raised the gun again, but this time he pressed its short barrel against the side of her head. *Fine, but I'm not letting go . . .*

She opened her eyes, waiting, ready. And that's when she saw Jim through a web of blood, moving like a blur from the left, a final, bizarre hallucination before the bullet. She managed one last, incoherent thought: *An ice scraper?*

38

Christensen swung hard, bristle end first. The scraper's long handle shattered with an impotent crack that left wood splinters on the dark-knit ski mask.

"The hell?" Harnett gasped, but his flinch was distraction enough. He let go of Brenna's collar and rolled to his right as the gun clattered across the trunk deck. It fell into the dirt near the Legend's back tire. Harnett tried to pull away, but—Christensen saw it now—Brenna had a vise grip on *him*. As Harnett turned, so did she.

Her eyes were empty and cold, uncomprehending. Her cheeks and the tape covering her mouth were laced by blood oozing from gashes that already had matted the hair on the back of her head and pasted several strands to her forehead.

Harnett swatted at him, but Christensen had him off balance. Still clutching the scraper's shattered handle, Christensen shoved the heel of his left hand up under the mighty chin, pushing Harnett's head back as far as he could. At the same time, he brought his right hand over the top like a sledgehammer. It came down square on the mask's nose hole, and the cartilage underneath gave way with a mushy pop. Even so, Christensen knew it wasn't over. He felt like a bull rider in the chute, straddling, for the moment, the malevolent mass beneath him. But the gate was about to open.

"Hang on, Bren!" he shouted.

With an animal cry, the bull rolled and raged left. The move broke Brenna's grip and she collapsed onto the back of the car. She was barely conscious, her fingers still clutching instinctively for soft flesh as she rolled to the ground. Christensen jumped on Harnett's broad back, riding him across the trunk as he moved toward the gun.

Christensen snaked the shattered remains of the scraper handle around his head and tried to choke him, but Harnett brushed him off like a pesky fly. He landed in the dirt maybe ten feet from the car, the remains of the sublethal scraper still in his hand.

By the time Christensen struggled to his knees, Harnett was already reaching for the gun. Christensen flung the scraper handle, hoping to distract him again, but it bounced lightly off one steely shoulder and landed on the Legend's hood. Harnett was hunched in pain, protecting his crotch with his free hand, but he calmly leveled the gun. Rushing him would be suicide.

Christensen sat back on his ankles, and Harnett shifted immediately to a wider stance. He brought his free hand up under the gun's butt and aimed the weapon in a two-handed grip, ignoring the blood streaming from his nostrils.

"Don't," Christensen said. The word emerged in a puff of his breath and he watched it disappear in the cold morning air, wondering if it was his last.

The gun was rock steady. Why Harnett hesitated, Christensen couldn't guess. But he did, and Christensen pulled the only weapon he had left.

"Kiger already knows," he said.

The broad shoulders seemed to sag, but only for a second. Christensen rose defiantly to his knees.

"*David.*" Christensen practically shouted the name. "Don't make it worse. It's over."

A contrail of breath poured from the mask, as if the man inside were deflating. Christensen waited, trying to will away a single, gripping fear: Who would raise the kids? He looked at Brenna, who lay morbidly still in the dirt behind the car. She was on her stomach, hands still bound, her face twisted toward him, her eyes open but registering nothing. Only her fingers moved, desperately clutching at the air above her back.

"You people shoulda left this alone," Harnett said.

The voice jerked Christensen back. "Too late for that. It's over."

There was a nod, followed by another stream of warm breath. Harnett moved two steps closer, so they were maybe five feet apart. Christensen stood as tall as he could while still on his knees. He saw the muscles tense in one of Harnett's mighty forearms—the one with its finger on the puny gun's trigger.

Another nod, and the barrel rose until it was pointed directly at Christensen's head. Harnett straightened his elbows and sighted him down. "It's over, all right."

Christensen closed his eyes to better see the faces that suddenly filled his head. Melissa. Annie. Taylor. *My God . . .*

A gunshot's report rang through the silent, sheltering trees, and Christensen heard himself fall. He felt nothing except the warm embrace of the people he loved, the children he'd never hold again. Then another sound, a strangled gasp. The sound of collapse, unbroken and dense, followed by ghostly silence.

Christensen opened his eyes. He'd twisted and fallen backward, so that he faced away from the car. His shoulder and one side of his head were in a puddle filled with rotting leaves. He lay still, listening, waiting for the pain. But he was conscious only of the water, of a damp, delicious chill. The pain never came.

Somewhere nearby, the crackle of underbrush. He pushed himself out of the puddle, stood, and in the same motion wheeled like a startled deer. Brenna hadn't moved. She lay maybe three yards from what looked like a stone-still block of granite. Christensen stepped forward, trying to make sense of the scene. Where was the gun? He moved closer, saw it twitching like a nerve in Harnett's pallid right hand. Without thinking, he stepped over the crumpled legs and onto that quivering wrist. Still, the gloved hand held tight.

He looked down. Harnett was on his back, his heart pumping blood through a ragged new hole in the mask where his forehead would be. He might have been staring at the branches above, but blood ran in thin streams over his unblinking eyes and from the hole around his nose. Christensen pried the gun from his fingers.

"Drop it."

The air crackled. Christensen tossed the gun away.

"Step away, goddamn it. Don't touch him again."

Christensen sensed movement in a thicket of pines to the left, but he dared not turn his head. "He's dead," Christensen said. He nodded toward Brenna. "She needs help."

"Step *away*."

Christensen took a giant step backward, then a second. A lone figure stepped cautiously into his widened field of vision. Christensen cut his eyes as far as he could toward the man, who was slowly chewing a thick wad of gum behind his outstretched hands. In those hands Christensen could see a gun maybe twice as big as the one he'd just tossed away. The gunman was long and lean in hiking boots and jeans, and the shirt beneath his stylish anorak was flannel.

Christensen thought, *Eddie Bauer.* What he said out loud, though, was "Milsevic."

39

Milsevic moved toward the fallen man without lowering his gun. When the police captain saw there was no danger, he knelt on one knee, peeled back the ski mask, and felt for the artery in Harnett's neck.

If David Harnett wasn't dead, he was dying. A ghastly hole punctuated the brow just above his right eye. Christensen moved toward Brenna, who lay dead-still in the mud. He stripped off his jacket and laid it beside her. He found the ragged edge of the duct tape that bound her wrists and began to unwind it. When he was done, he cupped one hand under her neck, rolled her onto her back, and laid her head on the jacket. She blinked as he gently peeled the tape from her mouth.

"Hang on, Bren."

She blinked again, opened her mouth and forced a breath. "H—"

"Easy."

"Hurt," she managed.

"I know."

"Dizzy."

"Relax, OK? We'll get you fixed up."

An electronic crackle. Milsevic lifted a small handheld radio to his mouth and spoke an incomprehensible stream of police radio code. The dispatcher answered back with a question. "Captain Milsevic?"

Milsevic dug the gum from his mouth and tossed it away. It landed near the front tire of Brenna's car.

"Affirmative. I was on my way in when I heard the radio call. Listen, we've got an officer down, plus one head trauma. Panther Hollow. Roll some medics for the head trauma. There's a maintenance road runs behind Phipps. My unit's parked up top, near the equipment yard, but tell them they can drive all the way down."

"The Bottoms?" she asked.

"I'll meet them there. And tell Walsh to roll someone too."

"That's one rescue and one coroner's unit?"

"Affirmative." Milsevic looked up, fixing Christensen with a stare he couldn't quite decipher. "And notify homicide. It's an officer-involved."

The two mens' eyes locked during the long pause, until the dispatcher broke in.

"Need a clarification. Previous, you said 'officer down.'"

"Affirmative. Officer down *and* officer-involved. I'm the shooter. I want this by the book."

Brenna moved, then gasped. A tear rolled from one eye, mixing with the blood and mud and damp strands of hair crisscrossing her face.

"Stay still, baby," Christensen said. "We'll get you out of here."

When he looked up, Milsevic was standing again. He'd moved away from Harnett's body and turned his back. His shoulders sagged, reminding Christensen that Milsevic and Harnett had been close friends. Christensen fought the impulse to speak, to comfort, because Milsevic was no doubt walking an emotional tightrope. There were a lot of things Christensen could say, and most of them would be wrong.

"You saved my life," he said after a while. "Our lives."

Milsevic just stared into the trees. He pulled up his anorak and tucked the gun into a holster belted into the small of his back. Finally he turned around, and Christensen saw the face of a man struggling for control.

"Thank you," Christensen said. "If you hadn't shown up when you did . . ."

Milsevic waved the words away and nodded toward Brenna. "How's she doing?"

"Maybe in shock. How long before somebody gets here?"

"Not long." He nodded toward the car. "She keep any old blankets or anything in the trunk? Something we could use to keep her warm?"

Brenna's car keys were still in the trunk lock, so Christensen reached up and turned them. The rear deck popped open, but nothing useful was inside. He noticed a damp kidney-shaped stain on the charcoal-colored carpet. She must have been bleeding before Harnett put her into the trunk.

"She was right," Milsevic said, standing over Brenna now. He looked down at Harnett's body. "He played us all for suckers."

"When did you know?"

Milsevic cleared his throat. "Been watching him since the hearing three weeks ago. Figured whoever did it would start to panic at that point. There was something about the way he reacted made me wonder. I knew he was up to something."

Christensen studied him. "That night at our house, after the shooting. You sounded like you were already looking into—"

Milsevic nodded.

"But—" Christensen looked for the least hostile way to ask an obvious question. "Aren't you the one who covered for him the night Teresa was attacked?"

Milsevic nodded again. "Like I said, he suckered us all. I'm guessing he arranged a contract hit, set up Della-Vecchio, and made sure he was with me when it happened." He pointed toward Brenna. "We knew from her DNA results someone else was involved."

"But it was a big leap to get to Harnett. When did you know?"

"Yesterday."

"Yesterday?"

The police captain turned and pointed at Harnett's feet. "See those?" Milsevic asked.

One of Harnett's sneakers had come off when he fell and lay on its side near his knee. The other shoe encased a foot that stood perfectly straight on its heel. The tread was worn deeply on one side, but was almost new on the other.

"The shoes?"

Milsevic nodded. "See how small they are? The wear pattern? DellaVecchio's shoes were missing from the jail's property room the day they released him. They sent him home in prison slippers, remember?"

"Harnett took his shoes?"

"To leave tracks. Same as he did with Teresa. He was setting DellaVecchio up again, just like last time."

Christensen wasn't following the logic. How had he known it was Harnett? Milsevic noticed his confusion.

"We still have DellaVecchio's shoes from back then," Milsevic said. "And you know what? In all those years, nobody ever dusted them for prints. So I dug them out of the evidence room yesterday afternoon." He stood up and nudged Harnett's ghostly white hand with his toe. "For whatever reason, he didn't wear gloves when he handled them. He got cocky. Who the hell would ever dust DellaVecchio's shoes for fingerprints? But that's when I knew. David's prints were all over them."

Milsevic looked down at the crumpled Harnett. He suddenly drew back his right leg as if he were going to cave in Harnett's ribs with a crushing kick of his hiking boots. His foot stopped inches short, and he raised both fists in the air, a gesture of seething frustration. "*Bastard!*" he screamed, and the word resounded through the trees.

Christensen heard the thudding approach of a helicopter. He squinted through the branches and saw it above them, holding its position, adding a low bass beat to the scene. Milsevic looked up at the familiar logo on the helicopter's door, then looked down at the radio in his hand as if it had betrayed him.

"Channel fucking 2," he said.

Christensen looked down at Brenna, who'd finally closed her eyes. Her breathing was steady.

When Milsevic turned again to Harnett's body, the rage was gone. "So many things I should have seen back then, so many things we didn't pursue, all the questions we never asked because it was so much easier to believe what Teresa was telling us. She was *telling* us it was Della-Vecchio, for Chrissakes."

Christensen felt a strange mix of loathing and vindication. He pointed at Harnett. "Because that's what *he* was telling *her*. Don't you see? Teresa wanted so badly to remember. At that point, her memory was like a petri dish. Once you contaminate it, all kinds of things grow."

In the near distance, the sound of wheels on wet dirt. Both men looked up and saw a white paramedic van moving through the trees along the service road. Behind it, a Pittsburgh PD black-and-white. Behind that, news vans from Channels 2 and 11. The police captain swore again, then bolted toward the road, waving his arms. "Back here!" he called. To the lone officer in the patrol car, Milsevic barked: "Secure the goddamned perimeter, now." Then, loud enough for the TV crews to hear: "Those sons of bitches set one foot out of their vans, shoot 'em. This is a crime scene."

Uneasy, Christensen stroked Brenna's hair. She opened her eyes just enough to see his face. "You're doing great," he said, bending down to kiss her forehead. When he sat up, her eyes were closed again and she suddenly went rigid. He felt an icy panic.

"Bren," he said, shaking her lightly. "Baby, you won."

That's when she smiled.

40

Heavenly Queen covered thirty acres of a Jefferson Boro hillside like a great green rug in the middle of a cluttered room. The cemetery was surrounded by mixed-use light-industrial, a patchwork of canvas boat-cover companies, drive-through beer distributors, and at least one professional fortune-teller, Sashay, who witnessed the future from a converted pizza place near Heavenly Queen's open iron gate. Christensen's vision was blurred by the heavy rain pounding his windshield, but he kicked the wipers up to top speed and caught Sashay's blue neon sign as he passed: YOUR FUTURE? JUST ASK.

He couldn't vouch for Sashay's abilities, but he admired her savvy. What mortal soul entering these gates wouldn't think twice about stopping? Survivors. Mourners. People looking for answers. Anyone entering a cemetery was more aware than most of the quick-ticking Big Clock that had claimed someone they knew, that someday would claim them all. Even Christensen tapped the brakes, wondering whether Sashay was open, but he steered up the hill, dodging potholes full of murky water.

He'd come to bury David Harnett. Why? The simple answer was that Teresa had asked him to come. She'd excused him from the funeral mass, where she knew he'd have to face the inevitable flock of news reporters fixated by Harnett's sensational death and Christensen's role in bringing his evil to light. But the burial was private, she'd said, invitation only. Come. Please.

"A small funeral? For a cop?" he'd said. "That's an oxymoron."

"Not this time," she'd replied.

Still, being here meant leaving the kids for two hours at the hospital with Brenna, whose eyes were still black from Harnett's pistol-whipping. It meant reliving Panther Hollow for the ten-thousandth time, wondering again how different things might have been if Milsevic hadn't arrived when he did. It meant dignifying the life of a man apparently without conscience, and trying hard not to smile as they buried the son-of-a-bitch forever.

But Christensen came. For Teresa.

He steered the Explorer around a sweeping right curve. The headstones were getting bigger the higher he climbed. In death as in life, the high-end real estate apparently went to the people whose egos matched their money. The road forked just ahead, and Christensen squinted at an indistinct figure in a yellow rain slicker standing at the Y, a cemetery security guard. The man waved him to the left, and Christensen splashed on, across the hill and then down into a valley. The headstones got smaller. Still no sign of life. He wondered how many of Pittsburgh's finest would turn out to mourn a man who had shamed them all.

The answer lay just ahead: Not many.

A dozen scattered cars were parked along the rutted road. Nearby, about twenty people stood beneath a canopy of black umbrellas, waiting in the rain as a funeral director and six saturated pallbearers lifted a gunmetal-gray coffin from the back of a hearse. One he recognized—Brian Milsevic. The rest were taller, but none of them looked like cops. Family maybe? *They had to be here*, Christensen thought. But clearly, anyone who didn't have to probably wasn't.

He parked well away from the group and pulled pliable waterproof boots over his loafers. After opening the door, he shot his retractable umbrella into the gap between the door frame and the car, then stepped out. All heads turned, and he nodded to the familiar faces—Milsevic, Teresa, Chief Kiger. It was a long walk across the slick grass, and Christensen stopped well short of the others. He stood apart, because that's where he felt most comfortable.

No one spoke as the six men set the casket on the lowering straps across the open grave. The funeral director, a thuggish man in a black London Fog, stepped forward and placed a small spray of mixed flowers atop the casket—the only color besides black, white, or gray that Christensen could see anywhere. The funeral director fussed with the blooms, a miscast rhinoceros.

When he was done, all eyes shifted to a young priest standing on the other side of the grave. His black hair was pasted to his broad Slavic forehead, and he blinked raindrops from his long eyelashes as he kissed a purple silk stole. He draped it around his neck and tucked it inside his topcoat. Then he opened his own black umbrella.

"My apologies for this weather," he said. "My influence is obviously limited."

Everyone smiled, but no one laughed.

"Thank you all for coming," he said. "We're here to return our brother, David, to God our Father in Heaven. And as I said at Mass, we do so reassured that whatever good David did in this life will be measured against the bad, and that the Lord understands that the true nature of a man is found in the balance of those two things."

The priest shifted his umbrella's position to shield his prayer book from the downpour. Christensen scanned the gathered faces and found all eyes fixed on the young cleric. No one was looking at one another. No one was looking at Harnett's casket, either.

"God is capable of astounding acts of forgiveness, and it's important to remind ourselves on this dark day that it is His judgment, not ours, that matters in the end. In that we can also find some reassurance."

The priest opened a black leather book and recited a prayer. Christensen looked at Teresa, who stood ramrod straight beside Kiger. She was slightly taller than the chief, but she had a tight grip on his arm. If her emotions were mixed, it didn't show. Her eyes were clear, her shoulders squared, her head held high. Kiger was as unreadable as ever, though Christensen was pleased by his show of support for Teresa.

The priest closed his prayer book. He picked up one side of the purple stole and held it out for everyone to see.

"In the United States, this great land of individualists, we priests are given a certain latitude in our style of dress. Within reason, of course." More weak smiles. "I chose a violet stole today, and there's a reason. Violet is a penance color, and I'd like to talk a little about penance."

An elderly man coughed, a rasping hack from somewhere in the assembly of Harnett's relatives. Not one of them looked comfortable. The priest looked at Teresa.

"I know that for many of the people here today, the pain David Harnett caused, physical and mental, will continue for many years to come. But it's important for us to remember that none of us are without sin. And whatever our brother David may have done in the past, or even in the weeks before he died, has to be weighed against how he lived his life the past few years. Whatever else he was, we know he was also a devoted caregiver who helped bring his wife back from injuries for which we now believe he was responsible. To her immense credit, Teresa even now will not deny the impact David's love and support had on her recovery."

The priest swept his arm across the people gathered at Harnett's grave. "In his efforts to help Teresa heal, David showed us all a moral side of himself. Maybe he did it out of love, or maybe as penance for what he'd done. I can't say why, and it's not my place to judge. But I know this: To truly repent, a sinner needs to fall on his knees before the Father himself, to plead for mercy, to accept as his own the pain that he has caused. That is penance. That is the way of forgiveness. That—" He paused.

"—is the *only* way. At this difficult time, in these difficult circumstances, we hope David has the courage to take that step, and we hope God will find room in His kingdom for this imperfect man."

The priest scanned the eyes of the gathered.

"Now, let us pray."

As the priest riffled the pages of his book, everyone except Teresa shuffled their feet. Christensen felt the tension ease as the priest launched into a short series of traditional prayers for the dead. When he was done, the priest reached into a silver bucket at his feet and pulled out what looked like a dripping microphone. He sprinkled the casket with holy water, muttered another quick prayer, and signaled the end of the graveside ceremony by sketching a cross in the damp air above the grave.

No one moved.

"Please go in peace," he added.

Behind them, the funeral director opened the rear passenger door of a black limousine. Teresa passed once among the gathered guests, hugging most, and then moved toward the car, the chief offering his sturdy arm to keep her from slipping on the grass. She stopped halfway and whispered something in Kiger's ear. The chief extended his hand and Teresa shook it, then offered him a hug—a gesture that seemed to fluster Kiger. He moved on down the slope to his own car, leaving his black umbrella with Teresa.

The knot of people around the grave began to loosen. The only people not moving toward the cars were the young priest and Milsevic, who were talking quietly in the rain at the grave's edge. Or rather, the priest was talking. Milsevic was watching Teresa move across the lawn toward Christensen.

"Thank you," Teresa said, reaching for Christensen's hand.

"I wanted to be here," he said. "For you."

She smiled. "You have been so far."

Her gratitude washed over him like absolution. He nodded toward the priest. "What he said about David's moral side. Did you ask him to say that?"

Teresa nodded. "But I can't forgive him. Not after everything." Her mouth began to tremble, and for the first time since he arrived Christensen saw sadness flicker across her face.

"Shit," she said, dabbing a tear from the corner of one eye. The umbrella hadn't spared her completely from the steady downpour, and in places her heavy makeup had run.

"It's OK. You're allowed to cry." Christensen looked again at the priest, who now stood alone. Milsevic was coming to join them. Christensen saw a sudden discomfort in Teresa's eyes, but by the time the police captain reached them she offered him a hug.

"Brian, thank you for coming," she said.

"The chief and I wanted to be here," Milsevic said. "David did a lot of good during his years with the department. We wanted to honor that."

"Thank you," Teresa said.

An uncomfortable silence settled over the three of them. The funeral director, still holding open the limo door, cleared his throat.

"Somebody wants to get out of the rain," Milsevic said.

"Guess so," Teresa said.

Another long pause. No one moved.

"I'd better get back, too," Milsevic said. He turned to Christensen, thrust out his hand and said, "Jim."

Christensen fumbled for something to say. "Thank you again. For Brenna, too. She wanted me to tell you that."

"How's she doing?"

Christensen shrugged. "Concussions are tricky, but I think she'll be fine. She's trying to run the hospital already, everything from the meds schedule to nursing protocols. They'll be glad to get rid of her."

"Type A all the way, huh?" Milsevic said.

"Some things never change."

Milsevic turned away and took a few steps toward his car. Then he stopped and turned back, looking like a man doing penance of his own.

"I want you to know how truly sorry I am about what happened on our end," he said. "The pressure to ice that case . . . I just didn't want to sidetrack my investigators, and I kept pushing the DellaVecchio angle. It seemed so solid. I made a bad call, and I'm paying for that now."

Milsevic now faced a departmental hearing for focusing the original investigation too narrowly. In the newspaper story Christensen had read about it, Kiger promised an impartial review of Milsevic's conduct and, if warranted, swift discipline.

"Teresa, I—"

"Brian, don't," she said. "We all—"

"As far as David shaping your testimony, I had no idea. I just knew we needed more than what we had. Something this serious, juries want to hear it from a witness, and they need to hear it loud and clear. They want somebody to point at the guy at the defense table and say, '*That's* the bastard that did this.' Anything less—that finger wavers, any hesitation at all—and you've got reasonable doubt. The game's over. Nobody wins. You know how it is."

"Brian—"

Milsevic nodded toward Harnett's coffin. "Back then, we all wanted to believe what we were hearing, never thinking he was using you the way he did. You were telling us what we wanted to hear, but we should have questioned it. We didn't, and I'm sorry."

"Thank you," she said.

Milsevic smiled weakly. He pulled a dose of nicotine

gum from his pocket, but didn't open it. He held it in his palm like a talisman. "You need anything, anything at all, you call me first. I mean that."

"I know, Brian. Thanks."

"OK, then." Milsevic looked at them both again. "I'm off. Take care."

They watched him walk to his dark department-issue Chevy, the car Christensen saw as he raced into Panther Hollow. Teresa waited until Milsevic started the engine and eased away before she looked back at Christensen. She stepped forward, close enough that their umbrellas bumped. The moment struck Christensen as almost intimate. He took a step back.

"Am I missing something here?" he asked.

"Why?"

"That just seemed awkward."

She studied him. "It was that obvious?"

"Maybe I'm misinterpreting it. I guess nobody's comfortable at a funeral."

Teresa looked away. She noticed the funeral director still waiting beside the limo's open door. "I'll be a minute," she said. "Please?" The man bowed and slammed the door, then folded himself into the dry front seat to wait with the driver. Teresa watched him, then spoke without turning back toward Christensen.

"I told you once, early on, about this thing I had with a married man at work. I didn't call it an affair, but I guess that's what it was."

Christensen understood. "Milsevic," he said. "David's best friend."

Teresa cocked her head toward the casket poised for burial. "I was so pissed at David . . . I initiated it, and I've regretted it ever since."

"You called it 'angry and desperate.' I remember that," he said. "And now it's awkward."

"What would you call it?"

He smiled. "Awkward."

Christensen felt a little awkward himself, huddled with Teresa in the gloom on a cemetery hillside. "So, what now?"

She shrugged. "Paperwork. Pension forms. Bank accounts. Life-insurance stuff—*that* should be an interesting battle. And all the accumulated crap. David has file cabinets full of stuff I still have to go through."

"That can be therapeutic."

"If you say so. I call it a pain in the ass."

"Fair enough."

She reached for his hand, but the left, not the right. She held it for a moment, then let it go. Again on the verge of tears.

"You can call me anytime, you know," he said.

"I know that."

"Emotionally, you've got a lot of unfinished business. Not just all this. I can't imagine your anger, your sense of betrayal. The next few weeks'll be the roughest. Don't hesitate. Just call or stop by. You know my schedule."

She nodded, took a long and calming breath. She glanced again at the spot where they all had gathered. "I'm staying for a few minutes. You go ahead."

"You're sure?"

"I'll be fine." She took his hand again, and he was struck by the warmth of it. "Jim, thank you."

They moved apart, him toward the Explorer, her toward her husband's grave. Christensen's mind suddenly clouded, as if he'd walked into the shadow of a raptor passing overhead. Teresa and Milsevic? What else didn't he know about her?

He climbed into the Explorer, but his hand went immediately to the crumpled sandwich bag in his raincoat pocket, to the soft lump inside that he'd plucked from the dirt that day in Panther Hollow. He'd picked it up on a hunch. Now, with Teresa's revelation, he was more curious than ever.

He started the Explorer's engine. In the streaky sweep of the wipers' first pass, he saw Teresa standing beside her husband's coffin. Then, as the windshield cleared, he saw her head pump forward. Just once. Just enough to spit.

41

The tiled corridors of Mount Mercy Hospital were as familiar to Christensen as the hallways of his own home. Even six years after Molly's accident and the months-long ordeal it began, he remembered the claustrophobic feel of the place, its antiseptic smells, the sound of nurses rolling IV trolleys back and forth. At least Brenna was out of the seventh-floor ICU, where Molly spent her last months and died in his arms. They'd moved her into the head-trauma unit on the twelfth floor two days before. No one there recognized Christensen, no one remembered how he'd barred the ICU door, unplugged Molly's respirator, and held her while she died. He walked this hallway confidently, as a stranger.

The door to room 1219 was closed, so he pushed quietly through. What he saw startled him: Annie and Taylor curled like parentheses around Brenna in the institutional bed. The bed's head was cranked to forty-five degrees, with Brenna propped on pillows in the middle. Their eyes were fixed on the overhead television, so no one saw him come in. If he'd ever witnessed so intimate a moment between Brenna and the kids, he couldn't remember it. What struck him next was what he saw sitting on Brenna's tray table, well out of reach—her cell phone.

Brenna finally noticed him.

"Hey," he said.

Annie put an index finger to her lips. "Shh."

Christensen eased himself onto the edge of the bed. On the screen, a golden retriever was narrating the conclusion of a familiar movie.

"*Homeward Bound,*" Brenna whispered. "Disney Channel. It's about these two dogs and a cat that get lost in the wilderness."

"Bren, we have the video at home. They've seen it a hundred times."

She leaned closer and spoke directly into his ear. "Does it always make Annie cry?"

"I heard that," his daughter said. "Does not."

"Does too," Taylor answered. His eyes never leaving the screen. "When Shadow comes limping over the hill, you cry. I've seen you."

Annie reached across Brenna and poked the boy, but there was no malice in it. "I should pound you, shrimpo," she said, then shrugged back under Brenna's arm. Brenna pulled her closer and looked at Christensen. He saw tears in both of her blackened eyes.

"You OK, Bren?"

She nodded her head. She pulled her right arm from around Taylor and mopped her cheek with a corner of the white bedsheet, then put her arm back. "How was the funeral?"

"Shh," Annie said.

Christensen sighed and looked at Brenna. "Feel like walking?"

He helped her up, let her get steady, then handed her a robe. The kids moved closer together, into the warm spot Brenna had left behind. Brenna took his arm as they crossed to the door of 1219.

"You got more flowers," Christensen said, pointing to a small basket of mixed blooms that had arrived while he was gone. The new delivery brought to five the number of arrangements in the room, including the ones he brought and get-well gifts from Kiger, Dagnolo, and Teresa.

"DellaVecchio finally showed some gratitude?" he asked.

Brenna shook her head, and he could see the disappointment in her eyes. "Milsevic. It was really nice of him." She took his arm as they moved toward the wide window at the end of the hall.

"He was there today, one of the pallbearers," Christensen said, and he found himself thinking again about Teresa's long-ago affair. She had told him David found out about it, and yet the friendship between the two men apparently endured. What sort of bond could survive a betrayal like that?

"The funeral was, ah, very private," Christensen said. "I'm glad I went."

"Me too." Brenna cocked her head, gingerly, back toward the room. "This was nice."

Christensen noticed that she'd left her cell phone behind. Had it ever been that far from her hand?

"What'd you think of Dagnolo's news conference?" he said. "I listened to it on the radio on the drive back."

"We were watching the movie," she said. "But he called a while ago and told me what was up. So I knew."

Christensen ran his fingers over the fading bruises at her wrist. "It's over, Bren, and it all started with your DNA results. DellaVecchio's free and clear, with an official apology."

She shrugged. "Damage control. Dagnolo knows what's next. I know for a fact that Vince Petrocelli already talked to Carmen's dad."

"The King of Compensatory Damages?"

"Can you spell *malicious prosecution*? They're gonna reach as far as they can into those deep pockets. Dagnolo's got no choice but to grovel and put up a good front about finding the guy who helped Harnett."

A familiar passion was missing from her words, as if she were talking about events she'd simply read about in the newspaper. Christensen said, "At least somebody's going to make some money off this case."

Brenna smiled. "I'm sure they'll depose you. So you need to be ready for that."

Christensen cleared his throat. "Can I ask you to help me with something?"

"Anything."

"That lab that did your DNA stuff, DigiGene. Anybody there owe you a favor?"

"I've kept them in the newspapers for three weeks now. They'd couldn't buy that kind of pub—" Brenna stepped away and stared. "Wait a minute. Why?"

"It's just . . . something bugging me. I don't know if it means anything or not, but there's something I want to get tested."

"And you can't talk about it?"

He nodded. "Sorry."

"And it's not something the police or the D.A. should handle?"

Christensen backed her off with a look. "Can you make a call? I could drop it off tomorrow morning."

"I'll make a call," she said after a long, anxious look. "Jim, if this is evidence of some sort, you should really—"

"Bren, it's probably nothing . . . I'm just curious. It might answer some questions I have. Maybe it'll raise more. I just don't know. Can we leave it at that?"

Brenna nodded. "You'd tell me if there was something I needed to know, right?"

"Trust me." Christensen kissed her forehead, then nodded back toward the room. "You know, every reporter in town is probably trying to reach you. Want me to go back and get your phone?"

"No."

At the end of the hall, she put her arms around his waist and laid her head on his chest. The concussion had affected her balance, so they swayed together in front of the window. Twelve stories below, the rain had snarled traffic on Fifth Avenue.

Brenna closed her eyes, holding him close. "This is almost like dancing," she said.

"There's no music, Bren."

"I could hum."

"OK." Christensen leaned down and kissed her again. "Anything but Springsteen."

Brenna hummed, and the tune was instantly familiar. *"The White Album,"* he said. "Nice." It took him a minute to pin it down, but the lyrics came back in a rush. He held her tight and listened, and soon Paul McCartney was singing in his head. When she reached the chorus's final verse, Brenna softly sang the words:

> *Will I wait a lonely lifetime?*
> *If you want me to—I will.*

42

"He wants to meet me."

Christensen looked up from his desk, startled by the unexpected visitor. Teresa was leaning against the frame of his office door at the Harmony Brain Research Center. He was struck immediately by the contrast between her self-confident posture at her husband's grave three days earlier and the way she looked now.

She hadn't even entered the room, but stood safely at its perimeter. Her shoulders slumped. She wasn't looking him in the eye, but at the floor. Christensen thought, *depression*.

"Hey," he said. "Come on in."

Teresa stepped forward, a small step, then another. Christensen stood and gestured to the chair across his desk.

"Sit, Teresa, sit. How's it going?"

She sat, but on the edge of the chair. "Had my regular rehab appointment upstairs. I try not to miss. It's OK I stopped by?"

He nodded. "Anytime. I told you that." Christensen sat as well. "Who wants to meet you?"

"Carmen DellaVecchio," she said. The name hung between them. "There's a story in the *Press* today. He said he wants to meet me."

Christensen thought of a dozen possible reasons why DellaVecchio would want to meet her, none of them good. Such a meeting might be marginally therapeutic for Teresa, but Christensen couldn't imagine putting the unpredictable DellaVecchio in the same room as the woman who'd sent him to prison for eight years. It would be incredibly risky on a lot of levels. Emotional. Legal. Besides, Brenna would never go for it.

"Do you want to meet him, Teresa?"

She shook her head in a way that left no doubt. "But I would like to apologize somehow. He lost eight years of his life, and I know what that's like."

"You need to stop blaming yourself for what he went through, you know. It wasn't your fault."

"It was me up there on the witness stand, Jim. I'm the one who ID'ed him. I'm the one the jury believed. And I was wrong. He knows that. Maybe Brenna could tell him how sorry I am. But face to face? I'm not ready for that. It's . . . I'm . . ."

Christensen waited while she composed herself.

"There's this dream I had for years, a nightmare. I've had it twice since David died," she said.

"The attack?"

"I'm in my kitchen. It starts all over again. I sense somebody behind me, just like always. I start to turn, just like always. And it's always DellaVecchio. Even now, even though I know it wasn't him. The thought of facing him down, looking into his ratty little eyes—"

"It's still DellaVecchio when you dream?" Christensen asked.

Teresa nodded and sat forward. "I know it wasn't him. I *know*. But in my mind, in my goddamned *mind*, it's still his face I see. I can't shake it. I just can't put another face on the freak who was standing behind me that night. I've tried, and I can't."

Or won't, Christensen thought.

"There might be reasons for that, Teresa, subconscious reasons. You *know*, and that's a rational process. But emotions aren't rational. We feel them."

Christensen tapped the side of his head. "Even if it wasn't David who actually attacked you, you know in here that he was responsible for it. But seeing him in that role is another matter. Maybe it's just easier for you to see DellaVecchio. Your subconscious might be trying to protect you that way."

Christensen studied her, then added: "Maybe you *should* meet him."

Teresa stared.

"For yourself. For closure," he said. "Maybe it'd help you put this behind you and move forward. Otherwise, that nightmare may haunt you for the rest of your life."

Teresa ran a finger along the edge of his desk. Her hand shook, and Christensen wondered what else was bothering her.

"I'm not ready," she said.

"And that's fine, Teresa. You'll know when you are."

Teresa's eyes began to drift. Christensen found it unsettling.

"Can I ask you something?" she said.

"Anything."

"What you said about the subconscious . . . you're saying there may be things too scary for me to confront, even now?"

"Sometimes denial is a good thing," he said.

She stood up and crossed to the office's tiny window, clutching her handbag to her chest. Christensen thought she might turn and leave. Instead, she looked outside at the bare birch tree that stood at the center of one of Harmony's many small courtyards.

"You learn about somebody when they die," she said. "About yourself, too. Sometimes more than you ever wanted to know."

David Harnett had murdered his accuser, Vulcan Tidwell. He'd arranged to have Teresa killed so she wouldn't blow his alibi for the night of that killing. What could she possibly have found out about her husband since his death that would be more devastating than that?

"I know what you're thinking," she said. "And I don't

know why this would get to me after everything else. But
it did."

"What did?"

She turned back, then hesitated.

"It's OK, Teresa. What is it?"

She opened the top flap of her handbag and reached
into it as she approached his desk. As she dug through
the contents, Christensen saw the gnarled, upthrust handle
of a small handgun between a compact and her car keys.
She noticed him looking and quickly closed the flap.

"Relax," she said. "I'm not going squirrelly on you.
I've always carried one."

She pulled a spiral notebook about the size of a paper-
back novel and held it out to him. It shook in her hand,
so she tried to give it a casual toss. It skidded and landed
on Christensen's lap.

He picked it up and flipped open the cardboard cover.
The opening page was filled with blocky, neatly printed
numbers in complicated combinations. A ledger of some
sort?

"David's handwriting," she said.

He'd divided the first page into five columns. The column headings, too, were numbers. Christensen read silently from right to left: 2297, 4993, 2344, 4868, 5012.
Beneath those headings, along the left margin, were what
looked like dates. Those began with 7/7/89 and proceeded
in a tidy column down the page. Each date was two weeks
apart. Christensen flipped a few pages. The chronology
continued from page to page.

Beside the dates were cryptic combinations of numbers
and letters—4K, 9K, 3K. Money amounts? Christensen
traced a finger across the page. The amounts seemed to
change with each notation, but the amounts for any given
date were equal across the five columns. He looked up at
Teresa, baffled.

"But what is it?"

"Money," she said.

"I guessed that," Christensen said. "But none of it makes any—"

"Divided five ways. It's a record of payments, and how the money was divided up."

He shrugged.

"Look at the last entry," she said.

Christensen riffled through page after page of numbers. The last page ended halfway down. The date was October 13, 1991.

"I did a little checking," Teresa said. "The last entry was about the time all the IAD stuff started. About the time Tidwell started talking."

It took Christensen a moment to catch up. "The drug dealer in East Liberty," he said at last. "Shot to death . . ." Christensen checked the last date again. ". . . about two months after this last entry."

Teresa turned away, moving back to his office window. She stared at the bare birch.

"Teresa, where'd you find this?"

"David had a safe deposit box. It was in there, along with more cash than I've ever seen in my life."

"So this Tidwell . . ." Christensen said. He flipped back through the pages, astounded by the amounts and the regularity of the transactions. "You're saying these are pay-offs? That Tidwell wasn't just talking?"

"David *was* involved," she said. "Jim, I did the math. There's almost two million dollars logged there between 1989 and 1991. Split five ways, that's four hundred thousand dollars apiece."

Christensen thought back to his conversation with Kiger. The chief had said Harnett's name was one of several Tidwell mentioned.

"And you're sure David was one of the five?" he said. She nodded. "All cops."

"Wait," Christensen said. "How do you know?"

Without turning from the window, without looking back at him, Teresa said, "Go back to the first page. The very first numbers."

Christensen did. "They're different. Four digits, not abbreviated. And there's no date next to them."

Teresa wavered in front of the glass, so much so that Christensen crossed the room to catch her in case she fell. She leaned back into him, and he smelled her hair for the first time. She used the same shampoo as Brenna.

"You OK? Maybe you should sit." Christensen cupped her elbow, and she opened her eyes. When he tried to guide her over to the chair, she resisted. She went again to the window, turned and leaned against the ledge.

"They're badge numbers," she said.

Christensen froze. He opened the notebook again and scanned the column headings. "Teresa—"

"First column, 2297," she said. "David's badge. That one I knew. Once I figured that out, I just made a couple calls to fill in the blanks."

The notebook seemed to grow heavy in Christensen's hand. He struggled for the right words. "So you know who the others are?" he managed.

"Yes."

Christensen let go of the notebook, and it thrashed to the floor like a wounded bird. If Teresa was right, he'd just dropped a handwritten record that could ruin careers, send people to prison, destroy lives. Teresa picked up the notebook and tucked it back into her handbag. A one-word question formed on his lips—Who?—but Teresa cut him off before he could speak.

"Don't," she said. "You don't need to know. You don't want to. I didn't, but now I do."

Christensen stepped toward her. "Teresa . . . that's why you're carrying a gun, isn't it? You know what it means. If David was in charge of tracking this money, that means four other people out there probably know this notebook exists. Teresa, you need to—"

She turned again toward the glass, but Christensen pulled her away, an instinct. He twisted the miniblinds shut and the office dimmed.

"Don't push this," she said, avoiding his eyes this time. "Please. I'm not ready."

"Teresa, if what you're saying is true—"

"Jim, stop," she said.

"But—"

"Two of the five died about eight years ago, all right? I knew them. Well, I don't remember them, but I must have known them."

"Why do you sound so sure?" he asked.

"We were classmates at the academy. I must have known them."

"But you know they're dead?"

She nodded. "I found a newspaper story. They were ambushed. Together. Went to a warehouse in Bloomfield for some reason, but it was a setup. They never had a chance."

A pause. "That happened the same day as Tidwell, about six hours before."

Another pause. "I'm not sure anyone else has made the connection."

Christensen felt his knees get weak. Three of the six people who knew the truth about the payoff scheme were shot to death on the same day, Tidwell and two of the cops he apparently was paying to protect his drug operation. The killings happened two months after Tidwell started cooperating with the IAD investigators, which left three survivors to share an incendiary secret.

"And now David's dead," he said. "That's four, Tidwell and three of the cops."

She nodded. The truth was unfolding, a terrifying origami.

"Who else?" he said. "Teresa, you may be in danger. Who else?"

"Please!"

"There are two others out there—"

Teresa reached into her purse and pulled out the notebook again. She flipped it open to the first page and jabbed her finger at one of the badge numbers, 4993. When she reached into her purse again, Christensen remembered the gun. He flinched, but Teresa grabbed his arm and held it tighter than he would have thought possible. Then she laid something on the desk between them. Badge 4993. She looked into his eyes.

"It's mine."

43

If she'd drawn her gun and fired those words straight into Christensen's chest, they couldn't have been more devastating. He reached across his desk and pulled Teresa's hand from his arm, then recoiled in his chair as a thousand flawed assumptions crashed around him.

"Yours?" he sputtered.

Teresa's face crumpled, and she buried it in her hands. Christensen was numb, waiting for her to look up. This couldn't be happening. He felt as if he'd stumbled into a hall of mirrors.

"I was part of it, this payoff operation," she sobbed, tucking the badge back into her purse. "I must have been. But I don't remember. Swear to God, Jim, I don't remember."

Teresa picked up the notebook and held it in her trembling hand. They both stared at the tiny, damning ledger. "I don't . . . please believe me."

Suddenly, too many things about Teresa made sense. Christensen's mind reeled with questions, but he struggled to keep his emotions in check. She'd found solid evidence of a two-year scheme to extort cash from a drug dealer, then realized she was one of five police officers who were part of it. The memory lapse was plausible, considering the level of damage to her brain. And extortion he could handle. But the other possibility . . .

"Teresa, this got way more complicated than just dirty money from a protection racket."

She nodded.

"From what you're saying, it sounds like murder. Two months after the IAD started asking questions, those cops were ambushed. The same day, Tidwell died in what looks like a setup. The timing of all that . . . they sound like cover-up killings."

"I know."

Christensen turned his desk chair around so that his back was to her. He hoped the move looked contemplative, but in truth he didn't want her to see whatever was registering on his face. Rage? Confusion? She had brought them both to a precipice, and Christensen felt every bit as exposed and vulnerable as Teresa.

"Teresa, what level of involvement . . . How much do you remember about it?"

"Nothing," she said.

"About the payoffs? The killings?"

"Nothing. Jim, it's a blank, and I swear to God nothing has ever scared me more. Nothing."

Christensen turned around. Tears had spilled from Teresa's eyes, adding desperation to her face. She held out the notebook.

"I don't know who I am, Jim. For eight years I was one person. Then I find this, and suddenly I'm not who I thought I was. Who was I? What was I capable of?"

If nothing else, Christensen understood the impact those questions might have on Teresa's fragile psyche. Psychosis was a real possibility for someone whose psychological armor lay in shards at her feet. His response would be critical, and he considered it a long time.

"I don't believe you're capable of murder," he said, even as he wondered.

Teresa's face transformed. She reached again across the desk, but this time her touch was gentler. She slipped her fingers into his hand, and he held them until the intimacy became awkward. Then Christensen let them go.

"That means a lot to me," she said, returning her hand to her lap.

Christensen took a deep breath. "What do *you* think you're capable of, Teresa? You must have been thinking about this a lot the last twenty-four hours."

Teresa brushed the tears from her cheeks. "I haven't slept. Guess you could tell."

"Tell me what you've thought about," Christensen said.

She looked away and closed her eyes. "Oh, hell. Maybe. I don't know. I was young, a year out of the academy when I married David."

"Your mentor, you said."

Teresa was avoiding his eyes. "When somebody you admire, somebody you fall in love with, tells you how things work, when they say 'This is the way it is,' you'd probably trust him, or at least I think I would have at the time," she said. "I've tried to imagine myself back then, knowing what was happening, the temptation . . . I come from a family of mill hunks. I told you that, right?"

"Clairton works, you said."

"The crash hit my family pretty hard. By the late eighties, nobody was working. That much I remember, how it affected everything." She held up the notebook. "This much easy money—"

"And David's approval . . ."

Teresa nodded. "I could see me going along. Maybe to help out. Maybe just because I was sick of it all, watching everything my father worked for go down. It bothers me now to think I'd do it, but now isn't then."

Christensen decided not to let her rationalization pass. "That car you drive is barely a year old, Teresa. And it wasn't cheap. You might have taken this money back then, but you're spending it now."

She turned and met his gaze.

"You had to wonder where it was coming from," he added.

"Yes."

"And?"

"I know it sounds lame, but David handled all that. That's the truth," she said. "From the beginning, and especially after the attack, our money was something he took care of. Do I like nice things? Yes. Could we afford them? Honestly, I wouldn't have known."

A telling answer, Christensen thought. Teresa's subconscious mind was a zealous guardian, protecting her from what she couldn't consciously face. But according to her husband's ledger, she'd been an equal partner. She was having trouble admitting that now, even to herself. For her to do so would destroy, completely and forever, the self-image she'd worked for eight years to rebuild. She was clinging to its remains like a life preserver.

"You had no idea at all about the money?" he said, testing again.

She shook her head. "I trusted David right till the end."

Christensen nodded slowly. "I understand."

He looked again at her face, where her tears had crossed the plastic surgeon's faded tracks. In a flash of grotesque logic, Christensen saw the puzzle nearly whole. The time sequence was telling. Teresa was attacked months after the two cops and Tidwell died, and just days before the internal affairs investigators planned to ask her about those things.

"Teresa, are you convinced all this is tied up somehow with the attack on you a few months after those other killings?"

"Yes."

Christensen leaned forward. "If that's the case, then, I see two possibilities. The first is what we've assumed up to this point: You were about to blow David's alibi for the night Tidwell died. Whether you knew it or not, you were about to unravel the whole thing. Or, two, you knew about everything—the payoffs, the killings, everything— and David or somebody else involved was afraid you'd tell IAD what you knew."

Teresa seemed excited by his reasoning. "I was really

pissed at David at that point," she said. "You think maybe I was trying to take him down?"

"The two of you had split three weeks before," Christensen said. "Maybe you wanted to do more than just contradict David's cover story. Maybe you wanted to tell IAD everything, as some sort of payback."

She jabbed her finger at his desk. "A kamikaze thing? That I *know* I'm capable of. I wanted to hurt David, and I didn't care how. I'd already tried. The thing with—"

Teresa gasped and raised her fist to her mouth, and their eyes locked across the desk. Christensen wondered if she was finally confronting the prospect that had occurred to him three days before, during their brief conversation after David's graveside service. One badge number was left in her husband's long-ago ledger, and Christensen was now sure whose it was. If he was right, it belonged to the man who'd been a central player in a decade-long drama of conspiracy and cover-up, and yet who from the beginning seemed to float above it all. One name fit neatly into too many possibilities.

But if they'd found the final piece to the puzzle, Christensen wanted Teresa to put it in place. The time had come to guide her back to the dark heart of it.

"Teresa," he said, "tell me about the night you were attacked."

44

Christensen pushed away from his desk and wheeled his chair around to Teresa's side. He could feel the truth like a rough beast in his tiny office, brutal, unavoidable. If Teresa sensed it, too, he wanted her to know she didn't have to face it down alone. He touched her shoulder and she flinched.

"We're just going to talk, all right?" he said. "I'm going to walk you through that night, and I want you to go with me. I'm going to ask you a lot of questions about it, and you may think some of those questions are trivial or silly. But what we're going to try to do is create a safe environment for you to remember as much as you can."

"No, I—"

"It's time, Teresa." Christensen reached for her hand and pressed it between his. "If any memories of the attack still exist, now's the time to find out. You'll be OK. I promise. This time, you're the one in control."

"Please."

"This nightmare you keep having. Where does it start?"

"My kitchen. But—"

"What time of day?"

Teresa sat back, her resistance fading. She closed her eyes. "Dinnertime. I'm cooking."

"Good. For yourself? Are you having someone over?"

She shook her head. "David was gone, but I was cooking a lot. Trying to deal with everything. Cooking took my mind off things."

"So you were just cooking to cook, making comfort food?"

"Basically."

"What do you smell?"

Teresa sniffed the air, retreating further, merging now with that distant scene. "Cinnamon."

"Good."

"And tomato sauce. I'm making cabbage rolls."

"I love those. Now, what do you hear?"

She cocked her head. "Boiling water."

"Good. Anything else?"

"No."

"Light outside, or dark?"

"Dark."

"Kitchen lights on?"

Teresa stood up suddenly and turned around, facing the small window of Christensen's office. "Yes. I'm standing at my sink, stuffing cabbage rolls."

"What's straight ahead?"

"A window. It looks into my side yard."

"What else?"

"A door. To my right. It's open, but the screen door's shut. The kitchen was getting warm, so I opened it."

"And it's dark outside?"

"Yes," she said. "Well, no. The outside lights are on. They come on automatically at dusk and stay on for a couple of hours."

"So you'd see someone coming through that yard, or someone coming through the door into your kitchen?"

"Yes."

"What's behind you?"

Teresa tensed and turned toward Christensen. Behind her eyelids, her eyes began to move, first to one side, then the other, as if searching the room. She backed away and hit the window ledge hard, but never opened her eyes.

"Teresa, what do you see?"

"Nothing. But I feel . . . something. Like I know there's someone in the house."

"Was there?"

"I don't know."

"Could there have been?"

She shook her head. "Not unless they had a key or someone let them in. I was home all day."

"Who had a key?"

"Just David. And our neighbor, Carol, the one who found me. We always kept each other's keys in case somebody got locked out."

Christensen crossed the room. He stopped maybe five feet from Teresa, who turned again and faced into the window's shuttered light.

"David had left a couple weeks before," Christensen said. "Do you think he could have come back?"

"Maybe." Teresa wrapped her arms around herself, hunching her shoulders as if preparing for a blow.

"There's somebody behind me," she said. "I know there is."

"Can you see him? Hear him?"

"I feel him. Just . . . I just know someone's there. He's there right now."

"OK, I want you to freeze that moment, Teresa," Christensen said. "Think of it like you're watching all this on a VCR. You've just hit the Pause button, and everything in that picture is stopped, except you. You can still move. Have you done that?"

"Yes."

"Are you afraid?"

"Yes."

"Don't be. He's frozen. He can't move. He can't hurt you. You're controlling everything he does. Do you believe me?"

"Yes."

"Then turn around."

Teresa turned, wary, her eyes still closed. She took one step back, pressing herself into the window blind, keeping a safe distance.

"Can you see him now?"

She nodded. Her breathing grew shallow. "He's wearing a mask."

"So you can't see his face?"

"No. The mask—"

"Is he tall or short?"

"Medium."

"Standing up straight?"

"It's not DellaVecchio," she said. "Way too tall."

"How big?"

"Average."

"So it's not David, is it?"

Teresa shook her head and swallowed hard.

"Teresa, I want you do something for me. It's going to be a little scary for you, but remember, he can't move. You're in total control. Now, I want you to reach out and take that mask off his face."

When she hesitated, Christensen asked, "Are you ready to do that, Teresa?"

She nodded. "Now?"

"Just take it off. He can't hurt you. I promise."

Her hands shook as she reached up and touched Christensen's face, peeling an imaginary ski mask from under his chin and up over his nose. He heard her gasp, a quick, pained thing, and her face reddened into rage.

She went for his eyes.

Christensen pulled her hands away, and they began to struggle. Teresa was lost in the illusion even as her eyes sprung open like window shades. Christensen saw the hatred in them, a white-hot fire. She was looking at him, but seeing the man who eight years before had crushed her skull, sexually savaged her, and left her for dead on her kitchen floor.

"You knew!" she cried. "You *bastard*."

Christensen clutched her wrists, but her rage poured out. "Knew what?"

"You *knew* I'd shaved for David. You *knew* I'd stopped. Goddamn you. Goddamn—"

Teresa's eyes suddenly cleared. Christensen eased his grip on her wrists, and slowly, gently, she reached up and touched his cheek. She bit her lower lip, hard, and collapsed into him.

"Oh my God, I'm sorry," she said, her head on his chest. "Why couldn't I see it before? I heard him, his voice, but I couldn't see him. The other badge number . . ."

Christensen put his hands on her shoulders and eased her away. He looked deep into her damp eyes, and she returned his gaze.

"Teresa, who did this to you?"

Her voice was strong as she said the name.

"Brian Milsevic."

If the revelation brought her any relief, Christensen couldn't find it in Teresa's eyes. What he saw was a woman whose mind already was two steps ahead.

"Teresa, we have to tell someone," he said.

She waited an excruciating moment. "Do whatever you want. It doesn't matter."

They both flinched as Christensen's telephone started to ring.

45

Not many people called Christensen at Harmony. Who even had the number? "I need to get that," he said, reaching for the handset. "It might be Brenna." Teresa shuddered, then nodded. "I'll wait outside."

"No, no. It's fine."

She tucked her purse under her arm. "Please. I'd rather."

Christensen watched her step through the door and into the hall, then turn right toward the vending area. At that moment, the fax machine on a nearby credenza began to ring, too. He picked up his desk phone and heard the thrum of a car engine, the hollow, boxy background noise of a car phone. "Hello?"

"Me, baby."

"You're in the car?"

"Me and the kids. Jim, there's something—"

"Bren, you're supposed to be in bed. The doctor said—"

"Jim, listen. I'm fine. But something really creepy came up about thirty minutes ago. I just feel better out of the house. I've got the kids. We're fine."

"Where are you?"

"We're fine. But I got a call from somebody Downtown, a cop friend. She told me something, and if it's true I'm a little freaked, OK? I just, hell, I just don't know what to make of it."

Christensen listened to the road drone, trying to gauge the anxiety level in Brenna's voice. He heard genuine confusion and muted panic.

"Bren, tell me what you heard. It may confirm something that just happened here."

In the background, Christensen heard Annie's voice, a

sharp rebuke, followed by Taylor's whining appeal to his mother. Brenna pleaded with them for quiet, then said, "What do you know?"

"Please, Bren, just tell me what you heard."

"The evidence on the apartment roof," she said. "They got some tests back. The DNA. It's not the answer they expected."

"The saliva on the cigarette butts?"

"Definitely DellaVecchio's," she said. "A 99.9 percent match. So that fits."

"You figured it was planted evidence all along."

"Yeah, but the thing is—"

"The semen," Christensen said. "Not DellaVecchio, right?"

"No. But it gets worse."

"Not Harnett either."

No reaction. Finally, Brenna spoke just loud enough for him to hear over the road noise: "They don't know who, baby, but it's not either of them. Somebody else was up there that night."

"Do you have a copy of the test results?" he said.

"They're preliminary, and I haven't seen them. Liisa has them at my office. I told her to fax them to me there. I'm on my way."

"Bren, wait. Don't hang up, OK? And don't come here. For now just keep driving. Understand?"

Christensen set the handset down and went to the fax machine. The cover page in the receiving tray was from Brenna's law office. He recognized the second page, half-way out, as the scattered-dot pattern of DNA test results. The letterhead was from a lab Christensen didn't recognize, Genetech, apparently the one preferred by the Pittsburgh Police Department. As soon as the fax page was finished, he took it back to his desk and opened his lap drawer. There, lying on top, was a photocopy of a similar page of results—the unidentified DNA lifted from the envelope Teresa received before she was attacked.

Christensen laid the pages side by side and saw in black-and-white what he already suspected. He picked up the phone.

"It's the same pattern as from the envelope Teresa got eight years ago, Bren. Exactly. Your friend at DigiGene said they might have some results today on the material I gave him a few days ago. What have—"

"Liisa said there's an envelope at the office. You want her to open it?"

"Tell her to fax it, Bren, fast. Just the results page. I'll hold."

The road noise disappeared, and Christensen stared at the identical genetic patterns before him. Christensen was checking for holes in the story when the fax machine's ring jolted him back.

"She says it's on its way," Brenna said.

"Be right back."

Christensen retrieved the new fax and laid the DigiGene page beside the other two. It sketched the DNA pattern lifted from the gooey wad of nicotine gum he'd plucked from the dirt that day in Panther Hollow. The identical markers might just as well have spelled the name.

"Milsevic," he said.

Brenna repeated the name as a startled question the moment Christensen lifted the phone to his ear. Had the name even blipped onto her radar screen in the past eight years?

"OK," she said finally. "Can you tell me what you know?"

"Not now, not the whole story," he said, lowering his voice to a whisper. "But Harnett, Milsevic, and Teresa were involved in something that goes way back, even before the attack on Teresa. She's got proof. She's here now. If you follow the connections between a lot of different things, you get the whole picture. Harnett and Milsevic were still part of it, working together, right up until Panther Hollow."

"But—"

Christensen saw it clearly now. Milsevic was waiting at Brenna's grave while Harnett retrieved her from the car. When he heard the commotion and saw Christensen struggling with Harnett, he seized the moment. He waited until the homicide would be justifiable, then put a kill shot in his partner's skull. With it, Milsevic severed the only solid connection between himself and the bloody clutter in their wake. With a little Milsevic spin, he became the heroic case-buster instead of the sole survivor of an obscene conspiracy.

Even then, the scene had seemed almost too contrived. It was clear as Harnett lay dying that Milsevic's analysis was too quick, too convenient. So on a hunch, Christensen had plucked Milsevic's gum from where he'd flung it, wondering even then what secrets it might reveal.

"It was perfect," Christensen blurted. "Milsevic didn't respond to the goddamned radio call about Panther Hollow. He was already down there with Harnett. *They* grabbed you from your office. *They* put you in your car. Harnett drove it, with Milsevic following. Milsevic left his car a safe distance away, then *they* drove your car into the hollow. *They* were going to kill you and pin it on DellaVecchio again. Then Milsevic—"

"But Harnett's the one who was wearing Carmen's shoes," Brenna said.

"Exactly! They were trying to place DellaVecchio at the scene, just like before. Those shoes would have fit Milsevic much better, right? He's smaller. But somehow he convinced Harnett to wear them. That way, if something went wrong—"

Brenna gasped. "The second straw man."

"Harnett was the last person alive who knew the whole story, the last person who could blow everything."

"Wait, Jim. I'm lost. You've been talking to Teresa about the night she was—"

"It's all connected!" He suddenly realized how little of the story Brenna knew. "Bren, Milsevic's the one who attacked her. Teresa remembers it now. That's why he got so worried when you found that unidentified DNA on the envelope. It's his!"

"You're sure?"

"It's right here in front of me, Bren. He knew you were getting close. That's why he wanted you dead. He wasn't sure what you had, but if anyone ever linked the envelope to him—"

"Whoa, whoa. Jim, let's go back a sec. That doesn't explain why they wanted Teresa dead."

Where to start? Down the hall, a vending machine disgorged a soft drink can.

"I'll explain later," he said. "Right now, I've got to call Kiger. This thing's not over."

"You know what you're doing?"

Good question. "I need to go. Stay mobile, OK? You and the kids just keep driving. Go somewhere, anywhere, just not home. I'll call you as soon as I know it's safe."

Christensen expected an argument, but got none. All Brenna said was, "Baby, be careful."

"Promise. I'll call as soon—"

"Jim?"

He listened, nearly choked by what he now knew. Still, he understood the significance when Brenna said she loved him.

"I love you, too," he said, and hung up.

Now what? Teresa finally understood the full horror of a conspiracy between her husband and his friend, her one-time lover. What did she plan to do with it? Christensen imagined her despair.

"Teresa!" he called.

When she didn't answer, he crossed the office floor and

leaned into the hall. An obese woman stood in the vending area, sipping a Diet Coke. She stopped drinking and said, "What?"

"I'm sorry," he said. "I was just expecting . . . Is anyone else down there?"

The woman turned around, a lumbering move, then shrugged.

"Did you see anybody else down there in the last few minutes? A woman?"

"Just got here a second ago. But the place is empty."

Christensen looked left, down the deserted Harmony corridor.

"Teresa!" he called, moving down the hall as he spoke. Each step felt more ominous. When he called her name again, all he heard was a hopeless echo.

46

Christensen sprinted back to his desk and fumbled through his briefcase for Kiger's business card. He dialed the private office line and jammed the handset between his shoulder and his ear.

"Pittsburgh Police."

"Chief Kiger, please."

"He's not available right now. May I take a—"

"It's an emergency."

"Sir, the emergency number—" the secretary said.

"No, no. I need to talk to *him*. My name's Jim Christensen. He'll understand. Is he there, or can you connect me to him somehow?"

"Please hold."

Christensen wasn't just panicked about Milsevic. He'd also made a grim, on-the-spot assessment of Teresa's fragile psychological condition. She'd arrived depressed. She'd discovered an appalling truth about herself, as well as a truth that shattered every illusion she ever had about two men with whom she'd shared everything. She probably felt more alone than she ever had in her life. Christensen tried to imagine the choices Teresa saw for herself at the moment. To confront Milsevic on her own? To take her husband's damning ledger to the police, and in doing so confess her own apparent criminal conduct? Or to self-destruct, surrendering to what surely was an overwhelming sense of isolation?

For someone in her situation, he guessed, the first impulse might be to go home to die. Christensen was thinking about the gun in Teresa's purse when Kiger drawled, "What's goin' on?"

"Teresa found something you need to know about,"

Christensen said. "And I've got some new information that's . . . Are you by yourself?"

"In a meetin', but June told me there was some kinda emerg—"

"Is Milsevic with you?"

Christensen heard a babble of voices in the background, imagined Kiger in a crowded office.

"You hang on a sec, OK?" the chief said. "I'm gonna catch this in the other room."

Christensen waited through a long pause.

"Speak," Kiger said when he picked up again.

"So Milsevic was there with you?"

"Nope. He's on administrative leave till the disciplinary hearing. Gotta coupla department heads in for a butt-chewin'."

"Chief, do you know where he is?"

"Captain Milsevic? Off. That's policy after any police-involved. Think you better tell me why you're so—"

"He's the one," Christensen blurted. "I'm sure of it. We're sure of it."

"What one?"

"Tidwell. Teresa. Brenna. We think he may have set Harnett up just like he and Harnett set up DellaVecchio. He's behind everything."

Christensen let that settle.

"What kinda new information you talkin' about?"

"A notebook," Christensen said. "Sort of a ledger. Tidwell was paying protection money to five cops, for years. What Tidwell was telling you was true, and Teresa's sure her husband and Milsevic were involved. Even she—" Christensen checked himself. Was it right for him to implicate Teresa? "She was going through her husband's things and found a notebook and a lot of cash in his safety deposit box. Thing is, Harnett kept track of how they divided up the money in this little notebook."

"It's got names?"

"It's coded, but Teresa figured it out. The money was divided five ways, and the five cops are ID'ed by their badge numbers. Three of them are dead, Harnett and . . . Remember that New Year's Eve ambush in Bloomfield, the one where two cops died?"

"Boyle and Vance," Kiger said.

"Teresa says they were involved. I have no idea about that, but we do know they died the same day Tidwell did."

"So the fourth badge number—"

"Milsevic."

"And the fifth?"

Christensen saw no way out. "Chief, she says it's hers."

Kiger cleared his throat, and started to say something. What he said, after another false start, was "Fuckaduck."

"Unbelievable, I know."

"Hell, I'd take unbelievable. This is . . . Lemme ask you sump'n. With her memory all screwed up, any chance she's—"

"That's the thing. She doesn't remember any of that. It's all from the notebook. It rattled the hell out of her, but she still brought it to me. I think we can trust it."

"Where's she now?"

"That's what worries me. She dropped all this on me in my research office in O'Hara township, at the Harmony Center, just a little while ago. But I got a phone call, and by the time I was done she was gone. Chief, I know it's easier not to believe this . . ."

Christensen looked down at the three pages of identical DNA results on his desk. "But I think I can prove it was Milsevic's saliva on the letter Teresa got back then, and his semen on the apartment roof from two weeks ago. As soon as you get a blood sample from him you'll see what I'm talking about."

A skeptical silence.

"Even if you don't buy it, we're dealing with what's real to Teresa. What I'm telling you is what really happened, I'm sure of it. But right now, that's less important than what Teresa *believes* happened. And she believes, with good reason, that Milsevic killed or helped kill Tidwell and those two cops. She believes he's the one who attacked her. She believes he shot her husband so there'd be no one left to tell the tale. Right now, both Teresa and Milsevic are out there somewhere. They're both capable of anything. First thing is to find them."

Kiger issued a disapproving grunt. "Any guesses where she's headed?"

"Home, I'd bet," Christensen said. "She was depressed. She had a gun in her purse."

"How big a lead's she got on you?"

"Maybe ten minutes. Fifteen at the outside. I'm just worried about her. Knowing what she knows, feeling what she probably feels . . . if she's self-destructive, I think she'd go there."

"Awright then—"

"But Chief," Christensen said, "she could be looking for Milsevic."

Kiger swore softly. "She ought not try sump'n like that. She's way out on a limb there, way out where I can't help her."

"I can be at Teresa's house in fifteen minutes. Can you track down Milsevic?"

"Aw, hell," Kiger said. "I ain't pulling him in, but we'll find him and keep an eye on him till we see this notebook you're talking about. Then maybe we'll start asking questions."

Christensen folded the three pages of DNA results and tucked them into his shirt pocket, then reached for his car keys. The last thing he heard Kiger say was, "Meantime, no more a that hero crap, y'hear?"

47

Christensen jammed the Explorer into reverse. It lurched out of its parking spot like a wounded animal. He raced down Harmony's serpentine drive, tires squealing, and fishtailed onto O'Hara Road, heading toward the Allegheny River and Teresa's house in Morningside, just on the other side of the Highland Park Bridge. If his hunch was right she was already there, alone with her gun and a truth that had ruined everything.

Milsevic.

Christensen saw him clearly now, the dark puppeteer behind a drama more complex and disturbing than anyone had imagined. For years people had danced and died at the end of his strings, and yet he'd risen to power on an unblemished record of honorable service. With Kiger's impending retirement he was about to seize the most powerful law-enforcement job in the city. How far would a man as ambitious as Milsevic go to protect his dark secrets?

He slowed to sixty-five as he veered right onto the Route 28 entrance ramp, then hit eighty as he merged into light traffic, announced by the engine's throaty howl. A few miles to the southwest, Christensen saw Downtown Pittsburgh's stunning skyline. Just ahead, the Highland Park Bridge crossed a muddy river that had never seemed wider.

Christensen tugged Teresa's file across the front seat and flipped open the cover. He knew her neighborhood, but needed the street address. He'd seen it once on an old police report, and he sifted the papers as he drove. At the same time, he dialed his cell phone, reciting the home phone number he'd scribbled on the outside of her file.

He hung up when her answering machine picked up. Within minutes, he was across the bridge and climbing up Baker Street, headed for Morningside Avenue. He checked the address again as he turned the corner. Her house was a block ahead on the left.

Teresa's Mercedes would have stood out like a beacon among the Dodges, Chevys, and Fords along the street, but Christensen didn't see it. He cruised past the address, trying to imagine her in the sturdy brick Victorian that stood there. The house was surrounded by a small yard, one of the few on the block with more than just a narrow concrete walkway between the lots. It was bigger than those around it, and more elaborately upgraded—the result, no doubt, of a long-ago infusion of untraceable cash.

Christensen turned left at the end of the block and left again into the narrow alley that ran between the neighborhood's main streets. The pavement passed among ramshackle garages, trash cans, and a patchwork of chain-link fencing. He recognized the Harnett house because of the yard and eased the Explorer to a stop.

The back door sat at the center of a redwood deck, not far from a covered hot tub. A backyard spa in claustrophobic Morningside? Bet that got the neighborhood grapevine buzzing. He lifted his foot from the brake and the car drifted forward, but something caught his eye. He stopped again and studied the house's rear door. Was it open?

Christensen backed up about ten feet, squinting at what looked like a small gap between the door's edge and the dark inside. He left the engine running and set the parking brake, clipped his cell phone to his belt, and opened the driver's-side door. He tested the gate at the edge of Teresa's yard, but it was held shut by a small combination lock. From there, though, he could see the back door standing open. Not much, maybe an inch, but definitely ajar.

Christensen looked both ways, up and down the alley, making sure no one was watching, then vaulted over the fence and into the yard. If Teresa was inside, where was her car? And if she wasn't, why was the back door not closed and locked? He reached for his phone to call Kiger, then reconsidered. If Teresa was inside and desperate, the last thing she needed was police intervention.

Christensen walked as softly as he could, but the deck creaked and groaned as he climbed the steps and crossed to the door. The key was in the lock. Christensen looked down. A torn white envelope lay at his feet. It was stained a deep rust color in places, and beside it stood a terra cotta planter that had recently been lifted or moved. The outline of its base was etched on the deck in the same rust color. Whoever was inside had let themselves in, apparently with a hidden key.

Christensen knocked lightly, then pushed the door open wider.

"Teresa?"

Wider still.

"It's me, Jim. You here? Teresa?"

He stepped into a utility room left toasty by the water heater on his left. A washer and dryer were on his right. Straight ahead, a wooden door led, he assumed, into the main part of the house.

"Teresa?" he called, louder this time. He rapped hard on the white door and it swung slightly open with his touch. "It's Jim. Anybody home?"

Christensen shouldered through the swinging door and stepped into Teresa's kitchen. His stomach suddenly clenched—this was where it happened. He felt a soft breeze as the door swung shut behind him, then the bite of unforgiving steel at the back of his head, the cold, insistent pressure of a gun barrel. He stood like a statue, frozen by fear as he recognized the wet smacking sound coming from just behind him.

"That's breaking and entering, sport," Milsevic said, working his gum. "Afraid you've got some explaining to do."

48

Christensen stepped fully into the kitchen, moving with the intensifying force of Milsevic's gun, clasping his hands behind his neck as he'd been told. They passed the wide kitchen windows and into a narrow hall, then left into the living room at the front of the house. The place was in order. Nothing seemed amiss.

"I'm looking for Teresa," Christensen said softly.

"I'll bet," Milsevic said. "You've got to figure a guy who vaults over a locked gate and sneaks in the back door is looking for somebody."

Gone was the contrite man Christensen had seen at Harnett's grave a few days before. The man behind him was very much in control. But why was he here? Looking for David's ledger? Come to finally kill Teresa eight years after his first attempt? As Milsevic marched him slowly into the living room, Christensen realized he had a weapon of his own: he knew the truth. But would it work on a man apparently without conscience?

"I might just as well ask what *you're* doing here," Christensen said.

Milsevic leaned in close enough that Christensen could smell the nicotine. "You might, but I don't really have to answer, do I?" He repeated the question, his voice suddenly as sharp as a blade. "*Do I?*"

"No."

"You're forgetting this is still an open investigation. So I'm the one entitled to ask the questions here, don't you think?"

Except you're on leave, Christensen thought, but he answered, "Yes."

The police captain patted Christensen down, then

pushed him toward a sofa that stretched beneath the bay window at the front of the house. "Sit."

Through the window's half-closed plantation shutters Christensen could see what he wished he'd noticed as he cruised past the house: Milsevic's dark-blue, department-issue cruiser parked across the street. He turned and confronted a large handgun much different from the service piece Milsevic had used in Panther Hollow. Kiger had probably kept that one pending a review of the shooting. This gun looked at first as if it had two barrels, top and bottom. The bottom barrel had the words SIG-Sauer on it. The top was embossed with the words "LaserShot Sighting System." Christensen knew nothing about fire-arms, but his mind flashed on a forgotten detail from the night Brenna was shot: the tiny red dot that flickered across her face just before it happened.

Even off-duty, Milsevic was dressed like a politician— dark suit, crisp white shirt, a subdued maroon rep tie. Through the shirt, Christensen could see what looked like a pair of nicotine patches affixed directly to Milsevic's chest. A wide mirror hung horizontally above an upright piano behind him, and in it Christensen could see the per-fectly tailored shoulders of his suit jacket. Not the clothes a desperate man might wear to ransack a house. What *was* he doing here?

Christensen sank deeply into the sofa's cushions. Mil-sevic lowered the gun, but didn't holster it.

"Go ahead," he said. "Talk."

"I came by to check on Teresa. She was just at my office at Harmony, maybe thirty minutes ago, pretty de-pressed. She left without saying good-bye. With every-thing that's gone on, I got worried."

"So you drove all the way over here and busted into her house just to see if she was OK?"

Christensen nodded. "I saw the back door open. I came up to check on her."

"You thought maybe she might put her head in the oven or something?"

Christensen shrugged. "I wondered. She had a gun. I saw it in her purse when she was at Harmony. I didn't know what to think. And then when she took off . . . If she was going to hurt herself, I figured she'd come here."

Milsevic crossed his arms, resting the gun against his left bicep. He was holding it by the black handle, his index finger still on the trigger.

"Funny," he said, fishing a foil packet from his shirt pocket. "Teresa didn't sound depressed when she called me."

Christensen felt disoriented. "She called you? When?"

Milsevic glanced at his wristwatch. "Twenty-five, maybe thirty minutes ago."

"From where?

Milsevic shook his head. "Pay phone somewhere. Asked me to meet her here to talk, told me to use the key out back to let myself in. Next thing I know, you're coming across the fence. Guess we'll sort this out when she gets here, but in the meantime . . ." He nodded toward his gun. "I'm sure you understand."

Christensen wished he did. Had Teresa lured Milsevic here so she could face him down in the place where, for her, this nightmare began? Or was he now snared in an even more tangled web? Christensen's stomach knotted as two images surfaced in quick succession: Milsevic and Teresa as sole survivors of the Tidwell conspiracy, and the two of them as lovers. Could they somehow be working together?

"Teresa called you here to talk?" Christensen asked.

Milsevic nodded.

"She say what about?"

"The weather." Milsevic smirked and adjusted his tie knot.

"No, really. Did she say?"

Milsevic clenched his jaw tight. "Nosy son-of-a-bitch, aren't you?"

Christensen fought panic by recreating the scene in his Harmony office less than an hour before. Teresa's emotions were real. If they weren't, she was a psychopath worse than any he'd ever encountered. No, Christensen decided, she was setting Milsevic up. He had to believe that. His only choice was to make the same leap of faith Teresa made when she first came to him.

Christensen's eyes strayed to the mirror behind Milsevic's head. No sign of life in the street outside, but he already could see the final act of this tragedy reeling toward a bloody climax. A man as calculating as Milsevic wouldn't be caught off guard. Even if Teresa succeeded, gunning Milsevic down in the same place she'd been so violated, Christensen knew she'd destroy herself at the same time.

He studied Milsevic from across the room, could almost see the man triangulating the possibilities, assessing the threat. Christensen felt the moment coming like a final judgment. If he did nothing, he'd be a mute witness to the mayhem about to unfold. Or he could try to break Milsevic first.

"So, how goes the search?" Christensen asked.

"For?"

"The other guy, the one who actually attacked Teresa—" Christensen pointed to the kitchen. "—right in there. You're still assuming David hired someone, right?"

Milsevic smiled, apparently confident they were on safe ground now. "We're working it. Put the word out at Western Pen, Lewisburg, places where the contract-hit guys usually end up. Somebody out there'll want to cut their time by telling what they know. Those guys brag. Most of them would rat-fuck their mother for a reduced sentence."

Christensen sat forward. Milsevic tightened his grip on the gun.

"You know what, though," Christensen said. "Something about that whole thing bothers me."

"That whole thing. What whole thing?"

"The David thing. I still buy the motive. He needed to stop Teresa before she talked to IAD. He was dirty, and she knew it. She knew he'd lied when he told the IAD investigators he was with her the night Vulcan Tidwell was killed. She had him, she knew she had him, and I think she was planning to take him down. The way things were between them at the time, that makes sense. So he wanted her dead. But this other thing doesn't."

Christensen stopped, waiting to see if Milsevic took the bait. When he didn't, Christensen plunged on.

"Now, I'm no cop, so maybe I'm missing something. But how could David have staged Tidwell's shooting all by himself? That's really bugging me. Think about it. There were two bodies in that alley, Tidwell and the other drug dealer. David was a big man, but pulling that off by himself . . . seems impossible, doesn't it?"

Milsevic swallowed the gum in his mouth. His face was unreadable as he popped another piece from the foil packet and started to chew.

"And then there's this other thing that happened the same day," Christensen said. "Two cops died, ambushed in Bloomfield. Boyle and Vance were their names. Some of the things Teresa's been remembering . . ."

He paused. Milsevic's stared.

"You knew I've been working with her, right?" Christensen said. "Since Dagnolo and Kiger signed off on it, I just assumed you were in the loop."

A shadow fell across Milsevic's face.

"I won't bore you with details, Captain. I'll just say she thinks David was involved in those killings as well. But again, same problem. Is that something the guy could have done by himself?"

"We already know what he was capable of," Milsevic said. "Nothing would surprise me."

"No?" Christensen looked Milsevic straight in the eye. "You know damned well David couldn't have done those things by himself. And we both know there were two people involved when Teresa was attacked a few months later. We *know* somebody other than David licked the stamp on that letter she got, and we know that letter was part of a plan to frame DellaVecchio for the attack. A complicated plan. One that needed at least two people to work."

Milsevic chewed slowly, then tucked his gum into one cheek. "You've just got it all figured, huh?"

"A hired killer wouldn't be involved on that level, would he?" Christensen slid forward to the very edge of the couch. "Those are things only a partner would do. Somebody who had just as much to lose if IAD took Tidwell seriously, or if Teresa ever told what she knew. Maybe somebody with more to lose. You following my logic here?"

Milsevic took a half step back.

Christensen nodded toward the house's front door. "My guess is David didn't have the stomach for what he wanted done here. So he gave a house key to his partner. The partner's the one who let himself in and hid somewhere in the house. He's the one who caught Teresa at the sink and crushed her skull. He's the one who dipped DellaVecchio's shoe in Teresa's blood to leave that convenient shoeprint. He's the one, Captain, who bent down and whispered in her ear."

Milsevic leveled the gun again. There was no pretense now, just the dead-eyed stare of a man without a soul. Christensen felt the danger. The clock was running, racing toward a showdown he knew no one would win. He needed to strip Milsevic of whatever defenses he had left before Teresa showed up.

"*You never rose,*" Christensen said. "She can still hear his voice, Captain. *Your* voice." He waited a beat, let that sink in. "That line from the Springsteen song: *Got to learn to live with what you can't rise above.* Teresa knew everything, not just about Tidwell, but about Boyle and Vance. That's what she couldn't live with. They were friends, academy classmates for God's sake. Husbands. Fathers. When Teresa realized you and David had cut them down to protect yourselves . . . that was the truth she couldn't rise above. That's what she was about to tell IAD."

The muscles in Milsevic's square jaw rippled. Christensen bore down.

"You weren't out bar-hopping with David the night Teresa was attacked. You were right here, making sure she'd never tell what she knew, making sure all the clues pointed in the right direction. I'm guessing you volunteered. She'd pissed you off, hadn't she? The way she used you to punish David, fucked you just to get back at him. Killing her was something that had to be done, but this was your big chance. You wanted to humiliate her the way she'd humiliated you."

Christensen pointed at the kitchen entrance just behind Milsevic. "If she'd died in there, end of story. When she didn't, well, it didn't really matter, did it? Her memories were gone, and you were in charge of the case. By the time your investigators had all the clues they needed to find DellaVecchio, David had Teresa's memories primed and ready. With you covering for David, it was perfect. Except . . ."

Milsevic's vacant eyes missed what Christensen saw in the mirror—a glint of polished black rolling past the house. Christensen couldn't be sure it was Teresa's car, but he knew it was time to go for broke.

"Thing is, now Teresa can *prove* it," he said. "David

kept a ledger. She found it yesterday, along with the cash. You were all in it together, five cops taking payoffs from Tidwell, including Teresa. The only ones left are you and her."

Christensen tried hard to look into Milsevic's eyes instead of at the barrel of the gun. "But you know what's really gonna nail your hide to the wall, Captain?"

He tugged the folded photocopies from his shirt pocket, opened them flat, and fanned them wide enough that Milsevic could see the matching sprays of DNA markers. "It's those little genetic calling cards you've been leaving behind. On the envelope you mailed to Teresa. On the apartment roof the night you took that shot at Brenna. On a wad of your gum I picked up that day in Panther Hollow."

Christensen refolded the pages.

"Like I said from the start: you can mess with memories, but you can't mess with DNA."

Milsevic's gun hand was as steady as ever. Suddenly, he smiled his winning smile. "We all make mistakes. What matters is how you recover from them."

"You didn't recover. You covered up."

"Thanks for the sermon."

"Brian, it's over."

Milsevic stepped closer. "So true, Jim. So true."

With his free hand, Milsevic grabbed Christensen's hair. He wrenched his head back and banged it on the windowsill behind the couch. Christensen felt the skin split at the same time he felt Milsevic wedge the heel of his tasseled loafer into his crotch and step down hard. The cop gently worked the wide barrel of the gun into Christensen's left nostril. Milsevic's eyes were two dark portals, empty and terrifying. Christensen knew there'd be no appeal.

Then, the moment froze. Milsevic's eyes shot open wide, an electric terror, and he eased himself back in stunned silence. Beyond the gun barrel and Milsevic's steady grip, Christensen could see Teresa looming above them both, her hand outstretched as she pressed something to the base of Milsevic's skull. She seemed calm, a vision of harnessed rage.

"My turn," she said.

49

They were all connected now in a seething triangle, a macabre three-way death circuit. Christensen's every nerve was tuned to its pulse, knowing the slightest ripple could set off a bloody chain reaction. His breaths came in short, violent bursts, but Teresa and Milsevic held their positions, breathing normally, functioning on something other than panic.

"So here we are," Milsevic said.

"The end game," Teresa replied. "I win."

Milsevic shoved his gun toward Christensen's sinuses. Christensen drew a sharp breath as cold metal hit soft cartilage. At the same time, he felt Milsevic grind his heel deeper into his testicles. He clenched his eyes shut, trying to handle the pain in his gut.

"Ever used one of these SIGs, Teresa?"

Milsevic's voice was like a specter in the room, eerily calm.

"Finest handguns in the world, but this one . . ." he said. "I don't know. It's skittish as all hell. A flinch, a reflex. Wouldn't take much."

Christensen looked up. Tiny beads of sweat had gathered on Milsevic's forehead. If he had to guess, Teresa had upped the pressure pound for pound, pushing the barrel of her gun closer to Milsevic's brain stem. Christensen adjusted his focus to Teresa's uneven eyes. They clouded with doubt, but she blinked it away.

"I still win," she said.

Milsevic smiled. "That'll be a great comfort to his family."

Teresa's resolve melted again. For the first time since the standoff began, she looked directly at Christensen. He could only return her pleading gaze. Then, suddenly, she cut her eyes toward the half-shuttered picture window behind him. In the mirror across the room, Christensen saw what she saw: a black-and-white police cruiser rolling slowly to a stop in the middle of Morningside Avenue. From Milsevic's desperate glance, Christensen knew he'd seen it, too.

A nondescript white Lincoln eased in behind the cruiser. *Kiger.* Who else could it be?

Almost at the same time, car doors slammed in the alley out back where Christensen left the Explorer. Police backup? Teresa had come in the rear door, so her car was probably there, too. Kiger would know within seconds that he and Teresa were inside. By then, the chief would have noticed Milsevic's car out front.

A single bulb of sweat trickled to the corner of Milsevic's right eyebrow. It hung there an endless moment, then fell onto Christensen's chest just as the cell phone on his belt began to vibrate. Its hum was loud enough for Teresa and Milsevic to hear. It stopped after thirty long seconds, and Milsevic flinched at the silence.

In the mirror, Christensen saw the police chief fold a phone and toss it through the Lincoln's open door, then discreetly lift the back of his sports jacket. He tugged something from the small of his back, but kept his hand there as he and the patrol officer moved together toward Teresa's front steps. To the rear, the unmistakable shuffle of heavy feet on Teresa's wooden deck.

Milsevic saw and heard it all. Another drop of sweat formed and fell.

"Payback's a bitch, Brian," Teresa said.

"Ain't it, though." His voice still strong, resolved.

"You should have killed me when you had the chance."

"I tried," Milsevic said. "Nothing personal."

Milsevic flinched at the hard rap on the front door, and again at Kiger's basso profundo voice. "Y'all open this door," he said.

The end game.

"Dead or alive, Brian," Teresa said. "What's it gonna be?"

Milsevic didn't answer, just leaned even closer to Christensen, close enough that his lips nearly touched Christensen's ear.

"Got to learn to live with what you can't rise above," he whispered. When he leaned back, he smiled his sugar-white smile. "Or not."

Christensen felt Milsevic's gun hand tense and knew he had no choice. The man was cornered, stripped of all defense, set for a final act of apocalyptic revenge. In a single, instinctive motion, Christensen grabbed Milsevic's forearm with his right hand and pushed hard to the left. At the same time, he jerked his head up and away from the gun's barrel.

A deafening flash scorched Christensen's left ear as Milsevic's body convulsed. They both rolled off the couch to the floor as jagged shards of glass rained from the wide window behind them. Christensen kept rolling, desperate for distance, aware of nothing more than the glorious sensation of being alive.

"Cover!" Kiger's voice, from somewhere just outside the shattered picture window. *"Christamighty . . .* Somebody in there better talk to me!"

Christensen crashed against a television cabinet and scrambled to his knees, pressing his throbbing ear against his shoulder. It wasn't over. Milsevic's sideways roll put him on the floor, leaning back on his elbows and staring up at Teresa. His gun lay beside him like a fallen crow, a wisp of smoke curling from its barrel. Milsevic had managed to get his hand on top of it, but the gun was pointed harmlessly toward the ancient metal radiator at his back.

Teresa stood over him like an avenging angel, sighting him down from five feet away. Slowly, using her gun's muzzle, she traced an almost sensuous path from Milsevic's forehead to his heart to his groin.

"Give me an excuse," she said.

More commotion at the back door. "*Talk* to me!" Kiger shouted from the front porch. "The hell's going on in there?"

Christensen imagined a herd of uniforms storming the scene, the utter confusion. Would any of them survive a shoot-out in such close quarters? "Wait!" Christensen shouted. "Don't come in! Please!"

A pause. "Who's that talkin'?"

"Jim."

"Who all's in there?"

"Three of us."

Milsevic seethed as Teresa traced a playful circle between his legs. He was dangling between life and death on nothing more than the thread of her self-control. Christensen had no doubt she could pull the trigger. She was waiting. The next move was Milsevic's—if he had the guts to make it.

Christensen spoke softly. "Think about this, Teresa."

"Oh, I have."

"You have options," he said.

"So does he." She nodded toward Milsevic's right hand, which still covered the gun on the floor. Still waiting. "Dead or alive, Brian?"

Milsevic's face softened. "Teresa—"

"Before you decide," she interrupted, "there's something I need to know."

Milsevic glared.

"David," she said. "He was part of it, the killings, the attack on me, everything. But then something changed. Eight years he stuck by me. I want to know why."

That was the question that still haunted her, and Christensen understood the psychological importance of her asking it now. *Eight years he stuck by me . . .* Was the love she felt real, or another cruel illusion? Even from across the room, even in so twisted a moment of power and triumph, Christensen heard in Teresa's words a sad, fragile plea.

Milsevic closed his eyes. Time slowed as he sat helpless on the floor, considering his answer. *Give her peace,* Christensen thought. *Do one decent thing* . . . Then, eyes still closed, the son-of-a-bitch sneered.

"Because David was *weak.*"

Milsevic's last conscious move was an invitation. His right hand tightened around the fallen gun. He worked a finger onto its trigger, and for a deliberate, crystalline moment he seemed to study the weapon in his hand. Then he dropped backward from his elbows, lifting the gun's black barrel toward Teresa.

She fired once.

The slug sent Milsevic's head and shoulders crashing into the radiator behind him, spattering its surface with a gory red-gray spray. The gun skittered from his hand and clanged against hollow metal. For a moment, his eyes stayed open beneath the dark pucker at the center of his forehead. Christensen braced for a second shot, but Teresa waited in tense, controlled silence. Finally, her tormentor's body slumped forward and fell to one side. Only then did she lower her gun.

"Talk to me!" Kiger shouted from outside. *"Somebody?"*

Teresa stared down at the end of a nightmare. "Nothing personal," she whispered.

"Somebody?"

When she finally answered, her voice was calm and certain.

"All clear."

50

"I'm outta here."

Carmen DellaVecchio stood up, looking frail and dangerous at the same time, like broken glass. He wore elaborate new basketball shoes, a gift from Brenna, but he was otherwise an intimidating presence in his torn jeans and filthy Steelers jacket. Christensen checked the clock on the wall of his private counseling office. They'd all been together less than five minutes—just long enough for Teresa to offer an emotional apology and DellaVecchio to deliver his opinion of it in a reckless stream of obscenities.

"Anything else, Carmen?" Brenna asked.

"Maybe it's best that he go," Christensen said. He stood up too, a protective reflex, and turned to Teresa. "Anything you want to add before he goes?"

Teresa shook her head and looked away. When her long ordeal ended six weeks before, she'd finally agreed to meet with DellaVecchio. Christensen watched her anxiety build as the date approached. Now he was worried that DellaVecchio's wrath had further knotted her tangled emotions instead of giving her the closure she needed. DellaVecchio wouldn't even shake her hand. His damaged brain left him incapable of understanding the complex conspiracy that had robbed him of eight years of freedom.

"Antonio's waiting downstairs," DellaVecchio said, reaching for the door handle.

"Your father?" Brenna said. "He didn't . . . Carmen, he could have come up."

DellaVecchio ignored the comment. "I made him drive me, 'cause I gotta see the state lady after this. But he's pretty pissed 'cause he's missing work."

Brenna nodded. To Teresa she said, "The Pennsylvania

Health Department is funding a statewide fetal-alcohol study. We arranged for Carmen to be included as a subject, in return for which he'll be eligible for state-funded treatment and therapy."

"Waste of my time," DellaVecchio said to Brenna.

Christensen agreed. There'd be no redemption. No drugs or therapy could help him, any more than glasses could help a blind man see. The damage was organic, permanent, irreversible. But when the legal ordeal was over, when DellaVecchio was free without official supervision whatsoever, Brenna had done the right thing. For so long, his freedom had been her only goal. Having claimed that moral high ground, she began looking for ways to make sure her former client didn't become the Scarecrow everyone expected him to be.

As a study subject, DellaVecchio would be obligated to report twice a month for interviews and evaluation. If he ever seemed likely to act on his violent fantasies and impulses, a therapist might be able to predict his behavior. At the very least, there'd be a written record of where they could find him.

"Carmen, you either participate, or you get a bill from me for being your lawyer for the past eight years," Brenna said. "Your choice."

DellaVecchio shifted his weight from foot to foot. "I'm going. I fuckin' told you that."

"Smart move."

Teresa watched the exchange without a word.

"Later." DellaVecchio turned and slouched toward the office door, his lagging left foot scuffing the carpet as he walked.

Teresa stood up. "Wait."

Christensen stepped in front of her as she crossed the office toward DellaVecchio, but moved aside when he saw the fresh intensity in her eyes. She approached DellaVecchio without hesitation and gently touched his forearm. A simple gesture, but one requiring raw courage on Teresa's part.

"Don't go just yet," Teresa said. She turned to Brenna. "Where's he have to go to meet the Health Department people?"

Brenna sat forward. Christensen tried to interpret the look on her face. Uncertain? Curious? "The State Office Building, down by the Point. Twice a month."

Teresa turned back to DellaVecchio, who was staring hard at the spot on his arm where Teresa's hand still rested.

"I could drive you," she said.

DellaVecchio nodded toward the door. "Antonio's here, like I said."

"Next time, then," Teresa said. "I could help you get to your appointments so your dad wouldn't have to miss work. I'd like to do that if you'll let me."

Then DellaVecchio did something Christensen found astounding. He blushed. Whatever emotion was behind it bloomed in a splash of color on DellaVecchio's pinched face. He opened his mouth, but was, for the moment, dumbstruck. And then he pulled his arm away like a man who'd been burned.

"There's buses," he said.

"I know. But I can help. I want to help."

DellaVecchio looked over at Brenna, who smiled and shrugged.

"I don't care how you get there, Carmen," Brenna said. "I know you don't want to go, but you've got to go. So the easier it is for you to get Downtown, the better off you're going to be."

Teresa touched him again, looked into the black eyes of the man who once haunted her dreams. "I won't push it. But if you get in a bind, I can help. Brenna's got my number."

Teresa's kindness seemed to panic DellaVecchio. Christensen saw in him an odd mix of emotions—confusion, embarrassment, gratitude. Teresa had reached out to him, and in that moment they all saw the impact something so simple could have on a man living life as a pariah.

DellaVecchio nodded, then backed away. "Gotta go."

Teresa didn't follow him, but stood her ground. "Just think about it, OK?"

DellaVecchio looked to Brenna for affirmation, but got only a noncommittal shrug. He turned away and twisted the handle on the office door, his eyes fixed hard on his new shoes. He left them with a single word that floated into the office like a rising balloon:

"Thanks."

51

Teresa backed her car from its parking slot and pulled away. Christensen watched from his office window as the Mercedes bumped onto Meyran Avenue, headed for the afternoon rush on Forbes. Brenna was watching too, standing beside him, and she slipped her hand into his as soon as the car was out of sight.

"You can't expect more," she said. "You did what you could."

"I know."

"We both did. For her. For Carmen. Bottom line: It was a win-win."

Christensen touched the window pane, warmed by the spring sun. "That implies it's over for them. You know it's not, especially for her."

"Kiger's already cleared her on the Milsevic shoot," she said.

"But not the Tidwell thing. I don't see him backing off just because she owned up to what she did, do you? Not with his attitude toward drugs."

Brenna wrapped him in her arms when he turned around. "She need a good defense attorney?"

Christensen shook his head. "Don't even go there."

Brenna's green eyes had regained the same shine they had before the concussion, and her hair had long since covered the scars on her scalp. Beyond the obvious, though, Christensen sensed an awareness in her that was missing before, a subtle shift in priorities. She was working less, laughing more. Appreciating the things that, to him, always gave life a precious balance. The day before, on Sunday afternoon, she'd sat cross-legged for an hour on Taylor's bedroom floor, playing Crazy Eights with her son. The day before that, she'd joined Annie on the couch to watch *Homeward Bound* again, and they both cried when Shadow came home.

"Now what?" he said.

Brenna laid her head on his chest. "We move on."

"How?"

"Together."

Christensen wanted to believe. He wanted to forget the way things were. He wanted to trust the changes he'd seen since the day he'd nearly lost her in Panther Hollow. But could he? How long would this last?

"We've got visitors." Brenna pointed through the window, at the silver Legend just then pulling into Teresa's parking slot one floor below. Christensen did a double-take. They'd driven to his office together, in the Explorer.

"Bren, who's driving your car?"

She shrugged, but with an enigmatic smile. The brake lights went off, and three doors popped open at the same time. The kids got out the near side, Annie from the front, Taylor from the back. From the driver's door stepped a striking young woman with a soft, round face. Her almond eyes were nearly hidden by a loose curtain of black hair, and a familiar camera bag was slung over one shoulder. With his first glimpse, Christensen felt an overpowering sense of *déjà vu*. Molly? He blinked. No. Not Molly.

"Melissa," he said.

"Your older daughter grew up since she was home last, didn't she?"

"It's . . . The hair, the way she walks. I can't believe how much . . . Is that Molly's old camera bag? She's . . ."

Brenna squeezed his hand. "Her mother's child."

"But it's, I don't . . . It's the middle of the term. She's supposed to be at Penn State. I talked to her yesterday."

"So did I."

Christensen watched Melissa herd the younger kids across the parking lot toward the elevator down below. It took a moment for Brenna's comment to sink in.

"You talked to her?" he said.

"I called her."

Brenna pulled away and stooped for her briefcase. She came up with a large manila envelope and handed it to him. He undid the clasp, tugged several papers halfway out, and flipped through an assortment of medical and legal documents.

"I don't understand," he said.

"Our blood tests are still good." She raised a hand to his cheek and touched it with her palm. "I don't want to postpone it again. I want to get married. It's right, Jim. I know that. I'm just sorry it took me so long to understand it."

Christensen couldn't stop his first reaction. "Today?"

Brenna nodded. "If we make the county courthouse soon. The clerk down there owes me a favor. They usually don't do marriages after four, but she said she'd wait till five as long as we brought our own witness."

Christensen pointed to the three figures below. "That's why Melissa's home?"

"I wanted all of us involved, everyone together."

"Melissa was OK with it?"

Brenna rolled her eyes. "She's jazzed. Blew off her Monday classes and took the express bus home."

Christensen pulled her to him, and they started to sway. Brenna sang softly in his ear:

And when at last I found you

If she finished the verse from the Beatles' "I Will," Christensen didn't hear. He was lost in her dizzying scent and softness, right up until the office door burst open. They turned to see three startled faces, but Christensen couldn't stop. He held Brenna tight, dancing to their private tune until Annie's, "Oh, gross," cracked them up.